Sign up for our newsletter to hear
about new and upcoming releases.

www.ylva-publishing.com

THE MUSIC & THE MIRROR

LOLA KEELEY

DEDICATION

For Kaite,

Who remains the best possible answer to the most important question I've ever asked.

ACKNOWLEDGMENTS

There are any number of people without whom I wouldn't be here, and wouldn't be doing this. First among them is my best friend, my sister, my person: Lande. The carrot to my pea, if I thanked for her all the ways she's helped me or made me a better person, I'd need a whole other book.

My bezzer, who's been there from the very start and kept me honest and whole for longer than anyone should have to. I'd be lost without her, and she'll always be in that first clutch of three to share good news with.

To the friends who talked through this book when it was a few lines in a Slack chat and a comment on who had great collarbones: Al, Luce, Sus, Marissa, Rachel, Rach, and Lil. For cheerleading and encouragement when I thought I'd give up, thank you immensely to Mayka, Ashton, Miko, Gane, and Erin.

My family, immediate and extended, for encouraging me to love books, and for supporting my enthusiasm for things that they don't entirely understand. Both my parents and my in-laws have looked after me, cheered me on, and given me homes, near and far.

I owe my Jo a debt for keeping my love of theatre and performance alive, even when it was expensive and far away. Lee, thank you for thinking this story could be a book in the first place, and whipping it into shape. Astrid, thanks for running this whole show and making all your authors proud to work with you. Thank you to everyone else at Ylva for their help in making this particular dream a reality.

And most of all to my wife, who snagged the dedication but deserves infinitely more. As the "real" writer in our house, she teaches me every day, and respects my opinions even when I don't respect them myself. She is brilliant, beautiful, and absolutely too good for me, but she made me understand love well enough to want to write thousands of words about it, so I'm happy as long as she'll have me.

Finally: to Franklin, Orlando, and Nora. Thank you for the cuddles, the purrs, and the 1am screaming fits when you thought you'd killed a mouse. It's never a mouse, you idiots, it's a catnip toy.

PROLOGUE

The audience's murmurs build to a crescendo as the last bell rings. Any moment there'll be the booming announcement, the weary words of an assistant stage manager who wishes that cell phones and anything wrapped in cellophane could be banished to another dimension. The orchestra hums in the pit, strings still reverberating with the strenuous warm-up scales, the echoes of notes—blown and plucked and struck—fading to ghosts as pages are flicked back to the overture.

Anna takes a deep breath.

She wriggles in her seat just a little, hearing the scrunch of her dress against the plush red velvet. Her feet are restlessly flexing inside her first pair of grown-up heels, a birthday present from her foster sister, Jess. The tickets themselves were a gift from Jess's mother, Marcia, for all of them. Anna hasn't asked to come to the ballet even once since she moved in with the Gales, because nights at the theater are something she's always associated with her mother.

Not even tragedy has diminished Anna's love of ballet, and when Marcia suggested it, Anna swallowed down the bitter taste of loss and gratefully accepted. Her mom would be whispering in Anna's ear right now, pointing out interesting facts in the dancers' biographies, and scouting surrounding patrons for potential troublemakers who might start snoring halfway through the first act.

Marcia pats Anna's hand instead, watching her in that quiet, careful way she has. Anna smiles, because some experiences don't have to be the same as before to be her very favorite thing.

Besides, tonight isn't some local ballet school sending sugar-plum toddlers out on stage. This is the Metropolitan Ballet, and their finest prima in two generations has been getting rave reviews season after season, every word of which Anna has meticulously collected, cut out, and pasted into her volumes of scrapbooks. She remembers so clearly how her mother did that religiously, steady hands smoothing pictures and letters into film-coated pages. When they were all lost in the fire, Anna started the tradition anew.

She's going to see Victoria Ford—the Queen of Ballet—dance, in the final preview before the biggest opening in Metropolitan history. That they even have tickets is a miracle, and Anna tries to ignore the tug of guilt somewhere around her diaphragm, because Marcia probably cannot afford this.

The music swells as the curtain rises, and Anna grips the arms of her chair as though she might float away. It's really happening. She blinks back brimming tears, determined not to miss a second as the corps begin to leap and scurry across the stage. It's magic. Everywhere she looks something beautiful is happening. These aren't just dancers; these people are Anna's heroes and they can *fly*.

The wonder she feels for the company pales in comparison as the corps parts like water cleaved by the prow of a ship. It leaves a path through their midst, revelers lining the parade route for their queen to pass. Anna feels Jess clutch her forearm, holding her in place.

With a leap that seems to hang in the air for countless seconds, Victoria Ford enters the stage. The audience goes as wild as Anna's heartbeat, decorum thrown off for the night at the arrival of a bona fide star. As Victoria crosses the stage in a series of flawless turns, leading man trailing in her wake, the applause builds and builds.

Anna's on her feet with the rest of her section, even though she can hear the grumbles about an ovation coming too soon. Jess and Marcia join her in the fervent applause, thunderclaps between their palms adding to the brewing storm in the room. Anna doesn't take her eyes from Victoria's face, grateful that she can see every flicker of emotion.

At first Victoria seems proud, perhaps even a little humbled by the adulation. Then there's a twist of irritation to her features, in the scrunch of her nose, and the faintest roll of her eyes. She looks to the conductor, who stops the score from proceeding and repeats a few bars in a vamp instead.

Anna's watched the archive footage so many times, but nothing compares to seeing this all play out right in front of her. She can almost feel the heat of the lights beating down.

Then, with a flutter of her hands, Victoria silences the audience. The clapping stumbles to a halt, and everyone takes their seat as though thrown by those very hands. A nod, and the theater full of people understands. Their appreciation is noted, but this is Victoria Ford's show now. Time to sit back and be dazzled.

The conductor builds up again as Victoria sets her feet in position. When she launches into the choreography again, the audience is held in perfect, rapt silence. Anna doesn't remember if she breathes or not for the rest of the act, but every step and turn is seared into her memory.

"The reviews will be insane," Anna predicts at the interval, grabbing for the ice cream Marcia provides. "I swear we just saw history being made, and it's going to be a smash tomorrow night."

"I'm sure we did," Jess answers, mocking only a little. "So this doesn't put you off ribbons and broken toes for the rest of your life, sis?"

"Are you kidding?" Anna says with a gasp. "How could I ever do anything else?"

CHAPTER 1

The Metropolitan Performing Arts Center, squarely in the heart of New York, is everything Anna ever dreamed it would be. She stands on the sidewalk out front, trying to take in the scale of the glass and concrete. With her dance bag on her shoulder and her hair in the neatest bun she could wrangle, she's ready to make that all-important first impression.

"Newbie!" someone says, tapping her on the shoulder. A short guy with dark eyes and a kind smile is looking at her expectantly. He has his own dance bag over his shoulder, and his cardigan looks so lived-in, so comfortable, that Anna covets it immediately. "You're gonna be late," he says.

"I've still got, like, fifteen minutes," Anna says.

"Yeah, you really want to get a head start on the warm-up here. Which means fifteen early is basically late. Ethan Vaughn, by the way."

"Pleased to meet you. I'm Anna Gale," she explains as he takes her arm and steers her around the corner of the huge building to what looks suspiciously like a fire escape. "I didn't think I'd made the company. Richard told me they almost never take anyone from regional tryouts."

"Yeah, Victoria thinks not moving to New York in advance shows a lack of dedication. But this is the first year anyone other than her had a say in who dances. I'm just glad I'm still in."

"You're in your second season?"

"Third, actually," Ethan tells her as they climb the staircase to where the fire exit is propped open with a couple of bricks. They're a few floors up and Anna knows she'll get dizzy if she looks down. "I'm really hoping to make principal this season."

"I bet you will," Anna says with gusto.

He laughs at her, but it's not completely unkind. "You haven't even seen me dance."

"I don't need to," Anna assures him. "I have a good feeling about it."

"Well, Tuesday mornings kick that out of you soon enough," he says. "Ladies' changing room in there." He gestures to a door on the right. "You want Studio C, that's four along, when you're done."

"Why are you being so nice to me?" Anna asks, remembering her foster mother's warnings about the pranks of competitive dancers that could sabotage a career in one move.

"I don't know," he says with a shrug. "I guess because nobody ever was to me."

Changing at record speed, Anna is stripped to her leotard and tights in less than a minute. She blasts her hair with one last cloud of hairspray and shoves her things in the first empty locker she comes across. Then she heads right back out to the studio, and freezes for a moment in the doorway. It's just like so many other studios she's danced in, the smell of Deep Heat and Tiger Balm mingling with stale sweat, not quite drowned out by the morning rush of fresh deodorant, perfume, or cologne. There's dust high up in the rafters, but the light is sharp and uncompromising, the ceiling of glass making the battered floor a stage with the broadest of spotlights. In here there will be nowhere to hide.

At the moveable barre in the center of the room stands Delphine Wade, the company's prima ballerina. Anna knew their paths would cross, but didn't realize they'd be taking classes together. Delphine is bending and stretching to her own routine, shorter in real life than she seems on stage. Like Anna, she's in leotard and tights, a wrap around her shoulders for warmth.

Conscious of time ebbing away, Anna finds a space at the back of the room when Ethan shimmies along to leave enough of a gap. He's firing through a series of stretches as Anna pulls out her pointe shoes, and the ribbons she at least had the foresight to cut ahead of time. She sits on the floor to make her quick stitches and, despite taking a hammer to them last night, she smacks the toes of her shoes against the floor a few more times to ready them.

She has to be perfect.

It's not hard to work out that people are talking about her. In the changing room she may have tried a sunny introduction, but this room is far too intimidating. Gabriel Bishop, probably the most exciting male principal Anna has ever seen dance, is warming up with Delphine. Tall and broad-shouldered, he shoots Anna a look and she smiles weakly. When she raises her hand in a wave, she actually gets a blinding smile in return.

Ethan interrupts then.

"I'll introduce you around once Victoria has had her way with us," he says. "We've got David afterward, much less scary."

"David Jackson?" Anna can't believe she's really here, dancing alongside these people whose names litter her programs and magazine clippings, the box left behind under her bed at Marcia's, sacrificed as a collection of childish things.

"Try not to look too star-struck," he leans in to mutter. "They really hate that."

"Good note," Anna says, working her arms up, out, and over in repetition. She's barely gotten up on her toes for the first time, her muscles slow to wake, when the door flies open with a bang. She lets herself fall into a forward *port de bras*, clearing her head and getting her blood rushing in one.

It's what distracts her from the moment she's been desperately trying not to fixate on. Victoria Ford is a legend for a reason, and Anna's been trying to concentrate on almost anything about her new job that will keep her from thinking about working with maybe the greatest ballerina in modern history.

"Good morning, *mes danseurs*," Victoria greets them, striding to the front of the room and receiving the rapt attention of every person without so much as raising her voice.

Anna is holding her breath, scared that somehow she'll shatter the moment she's given up almost every morning, evening, and weekend for over these past few years.

"Welcome to our new season."

A polite round of applause ripples through the room. Anna joins enthusiastically, clapping a second too long and blushing at her own exuberance.

"Despite certain changes to the selection of our dancers this year, I believe this will be our most dazzling season yet. I'm putting together a program that will be spellbinding, brilliant, and most importantly? *Hot.*"

Some of the more established dancers cheer. Anna doesn't dare, the sound dying in her throat. Victoria fusses with her necklace, a dark metal with a knot as its focal point. It brings her collarbones into sharp relief above the flat neckline of her Bardot-style black top.

"But for now, it's Tuesday morning and you are all at my mercy."

The laughter is a little more nervous this time. Anna's already convinced this woman means it. Rolling her ankle, which is still just a little crunchy from the past two days of travel and limited rehearsal, Anna lets her gaze flicker from person to person as they straighten up even more, clearly waiting for instruction.

"Teresa, if you please."

The dark-haired pianist Anna hadn't noticed until that moment strikes up with the theme from *Jaws*.

There's a burst of laughter, and Victoria fixes her with an indulgent glare. "Something more appropriate, perhaps?"

The music changes to something classical. Anna is too jittery to pluck out its correct name.

"Let's begin," Victoria says.

Anna follows the rest of the class and turns, placing her left hand lightly on the barre. As Victoria strolls past her, she thinks she might snap the wood with how hard she grips in panic, but the barre is still attached when Victoria finishes her circuit of the studio and calls out the first routine.

"*Pliés.* In first, *demi, demi, full, port de bras* front and back. Repeat in second, fourth, fifth. Then reverse."

Anna processes the barked command quickly—it's a fairly standard request. She touches her heels together, feet turned out, and bends her knees in first one *demi-plié* and then a second. Her knees groan a little as she deepens into the full, but it feels good. She can feel the sneaky glances coming her way, the other women scoping out the competition. It's not bitchy, per se, but Anna's felt those same searching glances every time she's started over in some new school or studio.

She keeps her neck straight and her eyes fixed on a point on the window wall, making each bend as deep as possible. This needs to be a good first impression. Victoria moves among the company, starting with Delphine and Gabriel, offering muttered criticisms to each dancer she passes. On this sweep she doesn't bother with the back row, and Ethan and Anna allow themselves a joint sigh of relief when Victoria returns to the front of the room without making a full circuit.

"Teresa!" Victoria calls, and the music changes up.

The next sequence is rattled off, but Anna grabs each detail like her life depends on it. She's never been more grateful to have an ear for detail. This time around, when Victoria passes, she offers only "lift as you descend" to Anna, but poor Ethan gets a sharp tut and "lazy, lazy." Anna thinks she would burst into tears if that happened to her.

The repetitive sets are a fantastic warm-up, and they're all sweating by the time they finish a set of *rond de jambe à terre*. The room's earlier tension seems to be settling, and Victoria actually lets a little hint of a smile play across her mouth as she watches them all in the front wall mirrors. Hard work pleases her, it would seem.

"Let's move the barres," Victoria announces, clapping her hands twice. "Then I want you all to come to center. *Allez.*"

Four of the male dancers move the barres from the center of the room in a practiced move. Anna wonders how these little duties are decided, if she'll be expected to divine what she has to help with, and what she should stay the hell away from. Being helpful is usually how she makes a good impression. Here, she doesn't have the first clue.

"*Adagio*," Victoria says to Teresa, who strikes up again.

Anna is watching the dancers around her—they make quite a crowd as she hovers at the back. She has a clear sightline on Victoria, who promptly turns her back on them once more.

Oh God. She's demonstrating. After so many years of dreaming about seeing this live once more, Anna is watching Victoria Ford dance.

"*Chassé* on one, to first *arabesque*, lift the leg, hold."

Well, it's pretty minimalist, just an indication of each move rather than anything like the fluid movements Anna has studied for hours at the Westin Center archives. She marathoned those recordings the way other people her age spent the weekend watching back-to-back episodes of *Friends*.

"*Penché* on five, six, come up seven, *pas de bourée* eight." Anna holds in a happy sigh at the grace of Victoria's movement. "*Pas de basque* on one, *attitude* two, *chassé*, *fouetté*. *Tombé*, *pas de bourée* to fourth and many, many turns."

Oh, this is a real set this time. Anna concentrates maybe as hard as she ever has in her life.

"Let's finish fourth, *tendu*, and find your fifth."

There's a murmur around the room, some feet moving as they mime the movements.

Victoria turns to face them, arms now firmly back at her sides. "Groups of five. Let's go!"

Delphine and Gabriel are the first to step forward; the other three in their group are all featured soloists. They start the routine with confidence, exchanging glances as they make those first few steps, but the focus of the room is shattered by the shrill ringing of a cell phone. In a room full of ballet dancers, anyone could have the ironic choice of *Dance of the Sugar Plum Fairy*. Judging by the groans of disgust and the way the dancing grinds to a halt, Anna knows there's only one person to blame.

She freezes.

"Am I hearing things?" Victoria spits her disapproving question at them. "Did one of you have an aneurysm on your way here and decide cell phones were suddenly allowed in my studio?"

People start to look around. Still the notes blare out. Anna can't believe someone would call her the one morning she was too distracted to flick the damn thing to Silent. When a second chorus begins, she has no choice but to scramble for her bag, muttering "sorry" as though repeating the word will somehow make her invisible.

"Sorry," she blurts again when she finally jams the damn thing to "Off". The silence is crackling, and Anna knows that what comes next won't be pretty. She turns to face her fate, ready to apologize to Victoria Ford, and all her worst fears come bubbling to life in an instant.

"The charity case," Victoria snaps. "Of course. Just another millennial who thinks the centuries-long history of ballet owes them any career they bother to pick for themselves. This is what happens when people fawn over your first tutu and tell you that you're special, Anya."

Anna opens her mouth to protest the wrong name, wounded that the only thing her hero knows about her is how she came to join the company, but not even her *name*. She feels the pity radiating from Ethan, and she's almost pathetically grateful that nobody else knows yet that she's been slighted.

"You're not," Victoria finishes with a relish that makes Anna feel bruised.

It might have hurt less to be slapped across the face. She can feel her chance to recover any ground at all slipping away by the second. "Ms. Ford—"

"Members of the company call me Victoria." She straightens even further, which Anna didn't know was possible. "But you are no longer a member of this company. Tell Rick this is the last time he'll be indulged."

That sends a gasp around the room, not to mention a few unkind giggles.

"I'm so sorry," Anna manages to say, grabbing her bag and shoving her phone into it. The stares from every corner of the room feel like lasers bearing down on her, but she'd rather endure all of them than the disgust on Victoria's face.

"Wait!" Victoria calls just as Anna reaches the door.

Great, further humiliation. Last time Anna had a dream this mortifying, she was back in high school and naked in the cafeteria. This feels a thousand times worse.

"Since your lack of consideration has knocked the sequence from everyone else's memory, why don't you take a stab at it. Show us what we should be doing now, if not for your selfish interruption."

The curl of Victoria's lip is cruel, and it's clear that Anna is already beneath her contempt. This is intended as a final embarrassment, to make sure the only memory anyone may retain of Anna Gale is of stupidity. It's every gym class that the new foster kid was laughed out of, every party she showed up to only to realize the invite had been a prank designed to make her the entertainment.

"You, you want me to—"

"Teresa!" Victoria shouts with a brisk clap of her hands. "*Adagio*, please." The music starts up. "Well?"

Anna slowly lowers her bag back to the floor. If the attention was keen before, it's blazing now, but she takes a deep breath and picks out the beats in the music. There isn't time to dwell on anything but the given routine now, and not for the first time, Anna takes position knowing she's dancing for her career, and that feels a whole lot like dancing for her life.

So she *chassés*, into that *arabesque* and the music lifts and carries her while she repeats the list in her mind. Anna has never been comfortable with an audience, able to dance for other people purely because she can shut them out with sheer force of will. These steps might not be her own creation, but she owns them from the very second she starts to move.

Her toes lift her, and her heels bring her back down. Hips tilt and shoulders twist and it's barely an effort at all to make one flow into the next, as though she's had ten secret rehearsals in her dreams. The music persists, mournful in its rippling way, and Anna lets the memory wash over her. Dancing for the first time, for her parents, seeing their smiles and their open arms at the side of the room, urging her on.

The music comes to a halt as she finishes in fifth, perfectly in sync. It's just soon enough to stop the rest of the memory coming, the fragmented, flickering flames that still dog the edges of her dreams if she doesn't tire herself out enough. The room is silent, a collective breath being held in their chests.

"Well." Victoria flicks her wrist idly in Anna's direction. "At least you *remembered* it."

"Does that mean—"

"You get to stay." Victoria claps, and the room exhales as one.

Teresa plays a jaunty imitation of Anna's ringtone and laughter erupts from every corner.

Anna doesn't dare, but she's relieved when Victoria just rolls her eyes. "If you wanted to do stand-up, Teresa, there's a club across the street. First group. Let's go!"

Anna sinks gratefully back into the crowd, and when she repeats the sequence as part of a group including Ethan, she tries to pretend like she doesn't notice how they all give her a wider berth than necessary.

The rest of the ninety minutes passes quickly enough. As the class starts to filter out, Anna feels a tap on her shoulder.

"Anya," Victoria says as Anna turns, bag already on her shoulder. "Come and see me this afternoon. See Kelly about a time."

The rest of the class moves faster on overhearing that.

Chapter 2

God.

Her fucking *kingdom* for a handful of Advil and two fingers of Scotch to chase them. Failing that, a door on her office that actually closes, because the usual day-trippers have come pouring in after class to bitch and gossip and moan. Her underlings are dedicated and brilliant, she wouldn't have hired them otherwise, but sometimes having enough staff to handle a company this size means being surrounded by far more people than Victoria would prefer.

They don't even realize that Victoria is in the grip of inspiration. Pure, undiluted genius is coursing through her veins, and not one of these sycophants can see it.

"New girl won't forget her first class," Teresa crows as she enters.

"I mean really," Derek, her head of recruitment, chimes in. "Who has their phone on anything but Vibrate these days? And by the looks of her, she could use some good vibrations."

"She can dance, though." Kelly is back at her desk, ever the competent assistant. "Can't she, Victoria?"

"What?" Victoria affects not to have been listening so keenly. A certain aloof brilliance is expected at all times, and as her idea takes shape she knows she'll need maximum theatrics to whip up their enthusiasm. "Oh, the new girl. Anya."

"I haven't seen lines like that since…well, since you."

Kelly is getting bold as she grows into the role of personal secretary and gatekeeper. The first few months were rough on her, everyone else in the building treating anyone above a size two as a curiosity, something to be stared at and whispered about. Kelly has brushed it all off magnificently, and when the younger girls in the company get out of line, she pointedly eats cupcakes in front of them until they run off in fear or disgust.

"Can you get me some time with our esteemed benefactor?" Victoria asks, tone as breezy as a spring morning.

"You actually *want* to see Rick Westin?" Derek is either stunned or scandalized. Either way the word will be around the entire company before the hour is out.

"Hmm," Victoria confirms, the very picture of nonchalance. "You see, I'm changing our program. *Giselle*? That old chestnut has been done to death. If even one of you speaks up now to suggest *Swan Lake* instead, that person is fired. I did not make my name by regurgitating clichés, and my company will not be doing that, either. That girl in there is a disruption, and by the looks of her she's some kind of corn-fed hick who thinks sophistication is a shade of eyeshadow you can buy in Sephora. But luckily for her…she just met me."

The sideways glances and murmurs come right on cue.

"That is my new star. Or I'll make her one, at least."

"But what about—"

"Derek, has asking a question that began with 'but what about' ever worked out well for you?"

He shakes his head, suitably chastised.

"Let me know when Delphine and Gabriel are done with David's class. Have them meet me in the executive dining room for an early lunch."

"What should I tell them?" Kelly asks, the frown on her face suggesting she's already dealing with someone at Rick's office about Victoria's meeting request.

"Tell them we're rethinking *Giselle*."

ᑎᓌᓂ

Gabriel holds the door open for Delphine when they enter the dining room, and Victoria allows herself a momentary smile at what a gorgeous couple they make, in publicity shots and otherwise. It certainly made for a solid, if not spectacular, season last time around.

"I won't annoy you by offering food," Victoria begins, playing the *I'm one of you* card right up front. "But there's no reason we shouldn't have a drink together."

Delphine's eyes are sharp, and there's a flicker of movement at her elbow as she nudges Gabriel. Clearly she read the room almost as well as Victoria did, while their primo remains oblivious. It's an age-old problem, but the dearth of appropriately talented male dancers makes their competition nowhere near as fierce. Women, on the other hand, conditioned by a lifetime of seeing ballerinas as the ultimate feminine grace, find a threat in every new set of pointe shoes in the chorus.

"Vodka tonic," Delphine snaps at the waiter, and Gabriel opts for mineral water.

"I know we made plans before the break," Victoria begins. "But *Giselle* is out."

"Fine by me," Delphine comes right back at her, poised as ever. "Though I think we would have killed it."

"You would," Victoria says, although the idea is so tarnished now, so yesterday that she can barely stand to think about it. "I'm going in a different direction for this season. You'll still have *La Bayadère*, of course."

"Wait..." Gabriel has spotted the blood in the water first. "That's just the fall show."

"True," Victoria says "But for spring I'll be going another way. I'll still need you, Gabriel. Delphine, you're still our prima, but I need the spring showcase for someone else."

"You're bringing Irina back up from the corps?" Delphine is gripping the edge of the table.

Victoria wants to laugh at the suggestion. They all know this is Irina's last season, as long as her prescriptions keep getting renewed. Physio, painkillers, and sheer determination are giving Irina this last hurrah. Victoria is not going to be the one to take it from her.

"No." Victoria waits for the drinks to be set down, stirring her martini with the olives on their toothpick. This is early even for her. She has choreography churning in her brain with unexpected vividness, and too long in this state of inspiration will get painful before long. A dulling of the edges, and she can do everything she intends before the day is through. "I have someone else in mind. Someone new."

"The only new person is that idiot with the phone," Delphine points out, folding her arms over her chest. "You can't possibly... Victoria?"

"I'm going to take an older, obscure ballet and give it my own spin. I know I haven't done much original work in the past few seasons, but let's just say I have something brewing and she will be the perfect fit."

"And I won't?" Delphine reaches for her glass, and for a brief, shining moment Victoria thinks she might have the balls to throw it at her. It's exactly what she would have done if someone tried to usurp her as prima.

"I know the right fit when I see it." Victoria dismisses them both as she swallows the rest of her martini, standing with minimal jolts from her knee. "You'll make this work, and we'll have a triumphant year together. Won't we?"

"Yes, Victoria," they mutter, eyes cast down.

She doesn't have time to dwell on whether they've truly accepted this. There's so much more still to be done.

The prospect of Rick is so thoroughly unpleasant that Victoria has a Xanax chased with a slug of Grey Goose from the dainty silver flask stashed in her oversized purse.

She can't even get a goddamned break from New York traffic, because she's outside his pathetic little *club* all too soon. There's no need to remove her sunglasses when the maître d' fumbles her name while frantically searching the list; she knows Rick will have left it off on purpose. At least Kelly's call has added her to the reservation.

"Mr. Westin will see you in his private room," a perky young hostess announces.

Victoria smooths down her black blazer and avoids the temptation to tousle her hair as she walks through the club behind the girl. There's something in the swing of her ponytail and farm-fresh complexion that sets Victoria's thoughts of Anna bubbling again, and she knows she has to seal this deal to get her way.

"Victoria!" He greets her with the usual smarm, standing from where he's been sprawled on a leather bunkette. "A sight for sore eyes."

"Darling." Victoria lets a little warmth into her voice. "You never come by the center."

"You have things well in hand. And I did my part by finding you some new blood. How is she?"

"Are you sleeping with her?" Victoria asks, despite her best intentions. "I can still use her, but if this is some fling, I won't disrupt the balance of my company."

"*Our* company," Rick says, exactly as expected. She can hear him gritting his teeth. "At least, I'm the one paying for it."

"And it wouldn't make a damn cent if I wasn't the one bringing it up to standard." Victoria takes a seat, leaving him standing. "I have plans for your girl. So long as she's not just for you to use once and discard."

"She's a talented ballerina, Victoria. Not a Kleenex."

"Tell me when that's ever stopped you before."

Rick shrugs, conceding her point. "I hear you're done with *Giselle*. These whims of yours, Victoria. They cost money."

"Lucky you have so much of it," Victoria fires right back. "I thought you wanted to save ballet from itself. Make it as exciting as when we danced together."

Rick wags a finger at her, in a way he no doubt finds charming. "Flattery will get you most places, you know that."

"I've never denied we were great together, Rick." Victoria accepts her drink, presumably ordered before her arrival, and the hostess scurries out. They must know it's a bad sign when Rick is forced to talk to any woman over thirty. "But I know talent. I know how to get the best out of someone's dancing."

"Nobody does it better, and that's why you're my artistic director. But if you screw this up, you're out. You know I can't carry you forever."

"Carry me?" Victoria rocks back in her chair at that. She's heard the whispers of course. But never—*never*—from Rick himself. "I thought I was the crown jewel in your dazzling assortment?"

"When I hired you, yes," Rick says. "But it's been four years and you haven't blown anyone out of the water yet. How do I know there's a truly original Victoria Ford production in you? If you couldn't do it with Delphine, one of the most technically gifted—"

"Technique doesn't count for shit on its own, and you know it." Victoria throws back the rest of her drink and stands. "But if you need me to bet the house on this idea, then consider it gambled."

"Careful, Victoria. I might think you still give a damn."

"I've always given a damn," she corrects him, turning toward the door. "But I'm not sure you do, anymore."

"Oh, I give plenty." Rick strides across the room to open the door for her.

Victoria blinks a fraction too long and twelve years evaporate. They're in the studio, he's sporting that ridiculous goatee, and she's six weeks away from the end of her career.

"Have Kelly send me the details when it's pulled together," he continues. "I'll want a preview before I sign off on this. Make time."

"It's only a week until the print run?" Victoria says before lowering her shoulders and accepting her fate. "Hard work doesn't scare me, you know that."

"Then work very hard," Rick says, the threat clear. "Goodbye, Victoria. Let's not make this the start of your farewell, hmm?"

That she makes it out of the room without flipping him off is one of the greater victories for Victoria's limited self-restraint. She knocks a vase of ugly flowers from the table in the corridor just to turn the rage back down to simmering. The ridiculous carpet denies her even the satisfaction of a good smash.

Back in the car, she summons Kelly with a press of her Bluetooth. Scanning downtown traffic through her tinted window, Victoria rubs absentmindedly at her knee. Stiff again this morning, and these heels to intimidate Rick both didn't work and have cost her at least one extra physio session. For all the good that does. Through the fabric of her pants she runs a fingertip over the valley of her scar, flicking a cursory glance to make sure the new driver isn't watching in the rearview mirror.

"I squeezed Anna in at three," Kelly greets her on the phone, not bothering with small talk. "That gives you time to stop off before coming back."

For her prescription, Victoria realizes. Kelly's been collecting them for her for so long that the doctor had the cheek to actually demand Victoria show up in person before writing another refill. The chaos of today has already blown the appointment from her mind, and she had spent most of last night working out perfectly good reasons to cancel. As though hearing her scheme, the ligament in her knee tightens enough to make her grit her teeth. She ends her call without bothering to sign off; Kelly is more than used to it by now.

"Park and Seventy-Third," Victoria barks at the driver, who's used to the brevity already. He nods in acknowledgment.

Victoria leans back against the leather of the seat and closes her eyes. As soon as she does, the first steps start to materialize, the scuff of leather against a wooden floor already forming beats only she can hear.

This girl had better show up ready to impress at three. Victoria's just bet her future on a straightforward routine and a stuttering desire to please. But there's something about this Anna, something Victoria hasn't felt stirring in her gut for well over a decade. She's immodest enough to know how exceptional she herself was, that no one since has come close to outshining her career.

But there's something in the way that girl moves that makes Victoria's own limbs stir once more, like a low voltage running just under her skin. There might never be another Victoria Ford, and she wouldn't want there to be. She just might settle for unearthing the next best thing.

CHAPTER 3

At three sharp, Anna knocks on the outer door of Victoria's office.

The redheaded woman who came to find her earlier is sitting at a desk covered in piles of paper, her head barely visible over the miniature mountains.

"I'm Anna?"

"Of course you are," the woman replies. "Did I tell you my name earlier? Well, it's Kelly."

"Got it," Anna answers with her first grin in hours, hoisting her kit bag back on her shoulder. "Do you know if Ms. Ford—"

"Victoria," Kelly corrects, pursing her lips.

"Right. Victoria." Anna stifles a sigh. She isn't going to get a single thing right today. Maybe it's not too late to catch a bus back to Dubuque, Iowa. "Do you know if this is just to yell at me for earlier? Because I am really worried I might cry if she does, and that is not the impression I was going for."

"Oh, there's no crying in ballet," Kelly scolds, but her smile is still kind. "I'd offer you one of these donuts to cheer you up, but—"

"I eat donuts!" Anna interrupts, because it's the first actual food she's seen all day. Everyone who bothered to eat between classes had some kind of smoothie or a handful of nuts. "Although maybe not right before my meeting," she says, realizing it's a terrible idea just as a door swings open.

"An-ya!" comes the yell a moment later.

Anna winces, and Kelly shoots one last sympathetic look.

"Any—"

"I'm here!" Anna says, slipping into the inner office and slamming the door behind her. "Also, and this is not a big deal or anything, but it's actually, um, Anna?"

Victoria shoots her a baleful look from where she's pacing behind the desk. "How utterly provincial. You don't think in this world a nice Russian twist might be better? It certainly sounds better than those dreadful Midwestern vowels you just assaulted me with."

"It's my *name*," Anna protests.

"How did you find the late-morning session?" Victoria changes tack. She sits in her oversized leather chair and kicks one foot up on the desk, while Anna fumbles for an answer. "Did you manage to keep your phone off for the entire session? Or should I expect David Jackson to be cursing your name?"

Anna taps the phone in the pocket of her warm-down hoodie, having checked six times on the way there that it was still both silenced and powered down.

"He was good. Great, actually. We tried some interesting exercises."

"Did you prefer it to my class?"

"W-what?" Anna is caught off guard by the bluntness. "Of course not! You're… The only reason I applied for the company was the glimmer of a chance of working with you." A hint of a smile. Finally, Anna has done something right.

Victoria gestures for her to sit in the visitor's chair in front of her desk, and Anna gets off tired her legs gratefully.

"How old are you? Older than most of my newbies, I'd bet."

"Twenty-one. But I wasn't injured or anything, I just got started late."

"Oh, I'm in very little doubt about your ability," Victoria said, her smile unmistakable this time, brief and radiant.

But there's still something about the steeliness of her gaze that has Anna on edge. Twelve years have passed since she saw Victoria dance, and it's difficult to reconcile this more severe woman with the glowing ballerina on stage. Here, Victoria wears barely a trace of makeup, and instead of the white silks and satin, she's wrapped in skintight black clothing, like bandages, only her shoulders bared.

"I can do better."

"I certainly hope so," Victoria agrees, fussing with some glossy photos stacked on her desk. "This season's program goes to print next week." She flashes a picture of Gabriel Bishop at Anna briefly. "So I have a handful of days left to make any final changes."

"Of course." Anna's heart sinks. This is just a more elaborate firing. One Victoria can really savor after giving Anna a short reprieve. "And my name won't be listed in the corps, is that it?"

"Mmm," Victoria considers the photos a moment longer before glancing toward the corner.

Anna follows her gaze and sees a shiny black cane propped against the coat rack.

"Oh, no. Not in the corps, darling. It just wasn't meant to be."

"Great," Anna says through gritted teeth, starting to rise from her chair. "Well, I won't waste any more of your day." She starts to get up.

"Principals aren't listed there, of course."

Anna sits. Heavily.

"They get their own billing."

"Who's a principal?" she whispers. This is teen-movie nonsense. It cannot be happening.

"You. Or at least you could be. Your dear benefactor Rick will want to sign off, of course. But it's my call."

"Mr. Westin was very kind to me at the auditions. I saw you dance with him, you know. The *pas de deux*—"

"Oh." Victoria sighs. "Another fangirl. How thoroughly original."

Clearly with flattery, the less-is-more approach is the way to go.

"If you're going to tell me how I changed your life, I'll need to schedule a little extra time to throw up."

Anna keeps her mouth firmly shut. She's gone from thinking she's fired to being offered the one thing she hardly dares to dream about in the space of a few minutes. It's not even entirely clear yet *what* Victoria is offering, and Anna hasn't felt this dizzy since she last went for eight pirouettes in a row.

"Anyway," Victoria continues, looking at a notepad on her desk, "raw talent is one thing. To be ready for spring, you'll have to be exceptional in every way. I'll teach you privately, on top of your usual company commitments. My time, and I hope I don't have to break this down for you, is extremely valuable."

"Private lessons?" Anna repeats. "With you."

"The demands will be considerable." This time she looks Anna square in the eye. "Assuming you have it in you."

Anna holds the stare and nods solemnly. She doesn't even know exactly what Victoria wants, but she wants to be the one to do it. "Principal" is echoing in Anna's brain like a damn Greek chorus.

"When do we start?" Anna hopes that's the right response.

"Tomorrow morning," Victoria says, standing while leaning heavily on her desk for leverage.

Anna pretends not to notice, keeping her eyes on Victoria's face the whole time.

"First session is at ten, same as today, but you'll be here for eight. I assume that won't be a problem?"

"Of course not." Anna stands and extends her hand. "I'm so grateful for the opportunity. Victoria."

Victoria stares at her hand in something between confusion and disgust, until Anna drops it back to her side.

"I don't want gratitude," Victoria says. "Just a lot of hard work."

"You got it. Should I meet you here, or...?"

"The de Valois studio. Is that the only leotard you have?"

"It's my newest." Anna looks down at her pale pink leotard, barely visible above the zip in her hoodie. "But I thought my shoes were the better investment. At least until we start getting paid."

"Leave your measurements with Kelly. If we're going to work in close quarters, I don't need my eyes assaulted. Since it's your first day, I won't get started on your hair, but you will need to discover a little something called conditioner if I'm putting you on my stage."

"Right." Anna's elation at the sudden promotion is buffeted somewhat by the fresh storm of Victoria's disapproval, but she manages to make it out of the room intact. She makes her way around Kelly's desk to mention the measurements, but Kelly looks her up and down before Anna can open her mouth.

"I know sizes at a glance, don't worry. You're broad compared to some of the girls, but still in standard range. I know what she likes, leave it with me."

"You know what—"

"Tell me your shoes are up to standard at least?"

"They are," Anna says proudly. "Although how many do you think I'll get through each week?"

"Go see the wardrobe mistress in the morning," Kelly say with a sigh. "If you have to ask, you don't have enough. And all the footwear you can trash is one of the very few side perks, Anya."

"It really is 'Anna.' Do you think you could mention that to her?"

Kelly snorts. "Good luck with that. Want that donut now?"

Anna accepts a chocolate one with sprinkles and takes off for the day.

Waiting outside the theater her sister works at, Anna ignores the glances from passing people as she drinks the last of her Frappuccino. She checks her phone with a little impatience, noting the reply of "*coming down*" landed at least eight minutes ago. Just as Anna shoves the phone back in her pocket, Jess finally barrels out of the heavy metal door, pulling her headset off and shoving it into her leather backpack.

"Well, if it isn't my sugar-plum sister," Jess teases, pulling Anna into a hug.

Anna hugs back with more enthusiasm than she meant to, genuinely relieved to see a friendly face.

"You survived the dungeons of Metropolitan, then?"

"They're not dungeons," Anna says, before realizing she's being baited. "The studios are up on a high floor and very well lit, thank you."

"So they should be, with the money Victoria Ford and Richard Westin plowed into the place. Speaking of, did you see your heroes in the flesh? Or does the company just cash in on having their names attached?"

Anna isn't sure she's ready to talk about it, not out here on the street. "I'll tell you over food," she says. "You must need some protein, surely?"

"I can finally show you the city for real," Jess says with a grin. "And look at you, out in the Theater District all by yourself. Was the couch okay last night?"

"You know me," Anna says, linking arms with Jess as they head down the street. "I can sleep on a bed of nails if I have to."

"It was secondhand, but it's not that bad. Dim sum?"

"God, yes," Anna groans.

"Okay, this place is my first gift to you in your new city, sis. You're gonna love it."

"Does that mean you're paying?" They duck inside the narrow doorway into a loud and bustling restaurant. "'Cause I don't get paid until next week."

"Fine, we'll spend my stage-managing riches," Jess says with a sigh. "Life on crew is just as glamorous as ever, by the way. Thanks for asking."

"I was going to ask over food," Anna says as a waiter waves them over to a little table in the far corner. "You know I can't concentrate when I'm hungry."

It just takes a glance at the menu for Anna to put in an order of pot stickers, and Jess orders a few more dishes for them to share, knowing her plate will be shamelessly raided whether she does or not.

Anna wields her chopsticks and smiles broadly at her sister. "It's been one heck of a day. You're not going to believe it, Jess."

A pot of green tea and small cups are set in front of them, and Anna pours for them both.

"So spill," Jess says.

"I don't even know where to start. No, wait, I totally do. Thanks *so much* for calling me before noon for the first time since I've known you. My phone wasn't on Silent. I almost got murdered on my first day."

"How would that even work?" Jess sips at her tea and waves the waiter back to order a beer along with their food. "Strung up on your own ribbons? And excuse me for checking you got there okay."

"I'm not a kid. I can read a map and get the subway just fine. And I was in plenty of time, thank you. In plenty of time for you to mortify me in front of Victoria."

"Oh, Victoria is it? How chummy."

"Everyone in the company calls her Victoria. It's, like, a rule."

"So your first class on your first day was with your own living legend?" Jess asks, reaching across the table to squeeze Anna's hand. "I'm so happy for you. That's all you've ever wanted, right?"

"That and house seats to anything that's sold out for a year."

"Yeah, don't hold your breath on that. Now stop deflecting me, and tell me how she was. I admit, I'm a little curious."

"Jess, she was… You remember when we saw her, right?"

"Hard not to, since you reenacted every scene of it for a solid year."

"Dedication," Anna says. "Anyway, it's been a decade and then some, but she's still… The whole room just hangs on her every word. She wasn't exactly thrilled about the phone, but then I did the combination and she forgave me."

"How gracious of her," Jess replies, smile tight and eyes narrowed. "I've heard some horror stories, Anna. You got off lightly."

"Did I ever!" Anna practically squeals. She can finally say it out loud to another person and make it real. "She was so impressed that she called me in this afternoon. She wants to make me a principal."

"I'm sorry, what? Anna, sweetie, I think you misunderstood."

"No, I didn't." Their food arrives, and Anna diverts her temper into popping a steaming pot sticker in her mouth. She doesn't want to fight with Jess on her first day. There's nothing that should be able to ruin this, not even the nerves in Anna's stomach, roiling at the thought of dancing just for Victoria in the morning.

"Maybe she wants you to shadow a principal? I mean, maybe soloist at a push if you have some particular look she needs," Jess suggests, picking at her own shrimp. "But I know what first days are like; it's just total information overload. You can check in the morning what she meant."

Anna sets down her chopsticks. "Jess, she called me into her office, all on my own. After letting me stay, after I did the routine perfectly. The one my phone interrupted. And she said the program isn't finalized yet, and she has an idea."

"But she wasn't firing you?"

"I thought so at first, like some kind of cruel way of dragging it out. But I swear to God, Jess, she wants me to do some secret show she hasn't told anyone about. And Rick has to sign off, but she'll get me ready, I just know it."

"Rick?" Jess mocks gently. "Wow, one day and you're in there with the name-dropping. I kinda love it. But why didn't she tell you which show it is?"

"I…don't know? She's really busy and sometimes it's like she expects me to just read her mind, but she definitely has a plan."

"This might just be a power play between her and Westin." Jess swipes at a pot sticker, but Anna defends her pile deftly. "There's always rumors that they hate each other, that they're sleeping together. That they hate each other *and* they're sleeping together. You said yourself that Rick tapped you for the last spot. Maybe this is her revenge or something."

"Wow." Anna swallows her food, tasteless in her mouth now. "I don't expect you to care about it as much as I do, Jess. But this is my dream, and it's finally coming true. Here you are, telling me I'm just some pawn in a game. Like I don't deserve any better."

"I'm trying to protect you!" Jess hisses, glancing at the people who've started looking their way. "You work so hard and you're so talented, Anna. Of course you deserve good things."

"But I shouldn't get my hopes up?" Anna wants to argue her corner, but it's not like Victoria has given her much to go on. "I mean, I was happy enough just to be in the company. Anything else is just some crazy bonus, right?"

"Just wait and see," Jess cautions.

"Right." Anna sighs. "That shrimp looks really good."

"You'll have to give up some of your horde there, keeper of the dumplings. Sharing means it goes both ways. Even if you are somehow a principal."

"If I am, I want my own bathroom." Anna sniffs. "When is my bed coming anyway?"

"Whenever you find one on Craigslist?" Jess pulls a face at her lack of organization. "Hey, I am offering up my living room to give you somewhere to live. I can't be on top of it all."

"I'll find something. Thanks, Jess. I really hope I'm not cramping your style too much."

"Just don't come in my room without knocking and we should be fine. Now eat up. I have a seven-thirty curtain and I need to stretch this off."

"If you quit stealing my food, I can stop defending it long enough to chew." Anna gets in a cheap shot of her own, but Jess shrugs it off.

CHAPTER 4

Eight was a very bad idea.

Victoria pushes her sunglasses higher on her nose and unfolds herself out of the open car door. She winces as her three-inch heel makes contact with the sidewalk, the power move seeming ridiculous now as she approaches the deserted building.

This would have been a lot easier without the hangover currently reenacting scenes from *Stomp* somewhere behind her temporal lobe, but she's yet to conjure up the ability to sleep without a few stiff drinks before bed.

Besides. The girl might not even show.

There's something in Victoria sure that she will, though, even from such a brief introduction. She's always been a quick judge of character, and an even quicker a judge of talent.

Sure enough, when she approaches the stage door there's a blond-ponytailed pile of comfortable clothing on the stone steps, clutching a Starbucks to-go cup like her life depends on it. Victoria's tempted to mug her for it.

"You can tell time," Victoria barks at her, and the pile of clothing elongates with a dancer's expected grace, revealing long, strong legs and impressive arms. "That's not a terrible start."

"I was just going in," Anna says. "Ethan said fifteen minutes to warm up, and it's only 7:40, so—"

Victoria cuts off the hangover-irritating ramble. "Not in trouble. I have to unlock the door before you can do anything. Breathe, for God's sake. Sort out your practice clothes and meet me in the studio. Start warming up while you wait."

She leaves the girl stuttering in her wake and makes the short journey up to her office. The minute the door is closed, Victoria sinks into her chair and pulls off the heels, sending them rattling toward the wall, one after the other. She retrieves a pair of flats from her closet in the corner and breathes a sigh of relief when walking is a little easier. The damn cane is illuminated by the weak morning sunlight, practically calling to her. Victoria is tempted. She can already feel the twinges on either side of her knee.

No. Not today. First impressions are everything, and this Anna might be a breath of fresh air, but that doesn't mean she gets to see even a second of weakness.

A sleepy intern appears with Victoria's morning coffee and a bottle of water that she takes without a snippy comment for once. She makes her way through the complex to de Valois, named as a nod to the founder of the school where Victoria completed most of her training. She's pleased to see Anna is already working steadily, at the barre. From the glass panel in the door, Victoria watches with rapt attention as the clean lines develop with each repetition, joints and muscles working in a fluid rhythm that pleases her. Yesterday's decision begins to feel validated by this alone.

It's not easy to sneak up on someone alone in a studio full of mirrors with no music playing, but Victoria manages to startle Anna all the same. It's a good sign for the girl's focus.

Retreating to the piano stool, Victoria flips through the folder she'd wedged under her arm and sips at the coffee. After a moment of expectant silence, Anna goes back to her warm-up. When sufficiently heated, the pale gray hoodie hits the floor and the intensity of the movement starts to build.

"Most days," Victoria begins to speak, and Anna's motion barely stutters, "you'll do your usual warm-up class before coming to me, depending on your personal schedule. Check for changes daily."

Anna nods vigorously, apparently desperate to get something right. That eagerness will have to be worked out of her a little.

"The first week is a lie. Don't get fooled into thinking it's anything like this easy. You'll still be in the corps for *La Bayadère*, since you need the practice. I'll spare you *Coppélia*, though it's not a favor, simply a matter of time."

"Okay?" Anna hasn't stopped, but now she's turned into a new exercise, watching Victoria in the mirrors. "Are these clothes…?"

The tights are light, the leotard a faded navy. Kelly will come through with something more suitable, but the legwarmers are a little garish. In her flat shoes, Anna isn't quite as commanding as she could be.

"Fine, fine." Victoria sighs. "Work on keeping your hair fully out of your face. No partner wants to get whipped in the eyes with sweaty strands that got loose."

"Partner," Anna repeats. "Right." She pauses to reknot her hair in a tighter bun on top of her head. The fingers move quickly enough, but she fumbles a little under Victoria's close attention.

"Today I'm going to run you through everything and anything that comes to mind." Victoria stands and moves closer, pleased when Anna only falters on one step.

Their eyes meet in the mirror, and Victoria supposes her own reflection doesn't look too bad for this early and hungover. The Chanel sweater she picked out as a nod to autumn fits perfectly, and the cropped pants make her legs look as straight and whole as they ever did. "I need a feel for your technical ability and your fluency in terminology. Should I expect problems?"

"No." Anna's breathing just a little harder than before. Erratic drops of sweat appear along her hairline. "Has anyone ever told you that you kind of drown people in information?"

Victoria balks at the bluntness. Nobody's spoken to her like that—outside of an argument—in years.

"Because I expect you to *keep up*," she practically growls, and that briefest display of spunk retreats behind a sudden cloud. "Whoever taught you that routine has you doing everything in the wrong order."

"I am?"

"Our classes will fix that," Victoria barrels on. "Get your pointe shoes on, we have work to do."

Anna scrambles for her bag and makes the change.

The shoes seem to be good quality stock shoes, though nothing like Victoria's preferred Freed of London. Clearly, nobody has taken Anna to see the shoe room yet. Rick probably won't have bothered to point out to her the few company perks, like the customized pairs Anna can now have made for her.

A moment later, Anna is up on her toes and taking the first few tentative steps. The boxes in her shoes don't make much noise, so at least she smacked them or took a hammer to them appropriately in preparation.

"Well, let's see your *grand jeté*," Victoria demands, getting a disbelieving stare in response. "Before hell freezes over, preferably."

"But…"

"But what?" she snaps. Almost everyone fails this test.

"With all due respect, you just said my warm-up was crappy," Anna talks down to the floor, cheeks flushing furiously. "And even if it wasn't, I'm nowhere near warm enough for the big jumps yet."

Victoria lets her twist in the wind. A whole minute elapses, and she never takes the glare from Anna's bowed head.

"Well done," Victoria says with the briefest of nods. "I can't tell you how many experienced dancers would have carried on. While I want you to do everything I ask of you, and I expect you to push beyond any previous limits you may have, that can never come at the expense of doing something your body can't handle. Are we clear?"

"Crystal clear." Anna looks up again at last, her color calming and relief apparent on her face. "So what should I really start with, Ms. For...Victoria?" she corrects herself in time.

"Let's see those *tendus* again." Victoria directs her back toward the barre. "I want to find out where all your flaws are."

∞∞∞

"Well," Victoria announces after a full hour has passed, *grand jetés* and all. "That wasn't completely hopeless."

"Thanks," Anna gasps, bending double and clutching her hips. "I swear, I've kept fit all summer. That was just…"

"It was supposed to leave you like this." Victoria crinkles her nose at the dishevelment. "The first few weeks in the corps will leave you wishing you were dead. Otherwise you're not working hard enough."

"Good note." Anna sits heavily and grabs a bottle from her bag. "You know, it's funny."

"Funny?" Victoria repeats the word with appropriate disgust.

"Yesterday, when you called me into your office. I thought you were promoting me to principal. But I get it now."

"You do?" Victoria takes a seat by the piano again.

"Because of my phone screwup, you just had to make sure I had what it takes. But don't get me wrong, I am thrilled to be in the corps for *La Bayadère*."

Victoria frowns at the slightly uncouth pronunciation.

"And if I can prove myself, I'll gladly do *Coppélia* or anything else you want. Rick did tell us to expect two shows a night sometimes, and I'll be ready."

"You didn't misunderstand," Victoria corrects.

"No, my sister explained—she's a stage manager on Broadway—that maybe you were talking about a solo or something. That would be amazing enough."

"Do you think, Anya, that I offer private coaching to everyone? That I have the time or inclination to usher every corps dancer through their paces in person?"

"Well, I was kind of surprised," Anna admits. "And it did sound like you meant it. Only this morning we've been talking about how inexperienced I am, so I figured I must have been wrong."

"Your sister is not the director of this company," Victoria snaps. "And the day we take advice from the performing monkeys down on Forty-Second is the day I quit this sorry business for good."

"O…kay?"

"You'll be my spring principal. If you're being coy because of money or contracts or…something." Victoria twists her fingers in disgust at the banal administration of it all. She is trying to be an artist here, for Christ's sake. "Then I'm sure we can arrange something."

"I get it. I'm sorry." Anna holds her hands up in apology.

"Apologizing every five seconds is wearing, and not becoming in a principal," Victoria warns.

"Wait, won't the other principals hate me?" Anna asks, much too late.

It's so comical, the widening of the eyes and the quivering lip, that Victoria almost laughs at the sight. She hasn't seen this level of naiveté in years.

"Oh, not just the principals. The rest of the corps and all the soloists you're leapfrogging too."

"People will hate me." Anna looks sick. "That's not…"

"Are you backing out? Because I already deposed my prima for you. Do you think I want to go crawling back?"

"You already told Delphine Wade?" Anna gasps. "Oh, this is so bad. I have to explain to everyone that—"

"No one cares. Least of all me. Learn to handle it, because it's part of the job. Not one of these people would get out of the way for you. If you want to be everything I can make you, you won't get out of the way for them. Understood?"

Anna considers for a long moment. "Yes. Yes, it is."

"Let's not turn this into an after-school special." Victoria almost groans at the solemnity. "I'll put the rest of your time with me on your calendar. Pay attention because it will change every day. Kelly has your number?"

"She does."

"Then go. Inflict yourself on whatever's next on your schedule."

"I did okay?" Anna asks.

It would be so heartbreakingly easy to shoot her down. A pointed silence would be enough, Victoria knows. She's the master of them. Something in her allows a terse nod, one she regrets the second Anna all but skips out of the room.

Too soft. How will she ever learn if Victoria lets her off so lightly from day one?

Kelly is the next interruption, arriving with shopping bags that are no doubt intended for Anna.

"I can take them to David's class for her," Kelly says.

"Let me," Victoria commands. "Speaking of which, when Rick signs off next week, we'll have to look at Anna's contract status. And the insurance."

"That's, wow…okay. She's good, Victoria. I saw that much. Is this really the play you want to make?"

Victoria, after considering for just a moment, pushes off her stool and walks down the corridor to disrupt David in Studio C. He doesn't like interruptions one bit, running his classes like a military boot camp. Victoria can respect that, but David, in turn, respects her too much not to let her get away with the occasional moment of bad behavior. He's always had a soft spot for a diva. That's why she picked him as her second-in-command.

The door is ajar, probably wise given the terrible ventilation in C and the warmth of early fall already building for the day. Victoria pushes the door enough to slip through, dragging the bags behind her. It's Gabriel who notices her first, and Delphine isn't far behind. In fact, Anna, deep in conversation with that cardigan boy at the back of the room, is among the very last to notice Victoria's presence in the room.

"Victoria!" David strides across it to greet her, kissing each cheek with customary smoothness. "To what do we owe the honor? You have these lazy kids later, don't you?"

"Mmm, I suppose I do." Victoria can hear the whispers, low enough to not miss a word she says. "I have a little something for Anya. Can I borrow her a moment?"

"Anya?" David looks around until Anna reacts, stepping forward like she's facing the firing squad. "Oh, is that the new girl's name? Let's move, then. Nobody keeps Victoria waiting."

Anna shuffles forward, looking at David as though he can somehow save her from this.

"Kelly was going to bring these, but I thought I'd drop them off myself," Victoria explains, thrusting the bundle of bags toward Anna. "Can't have my newest principal underdressed. It's mostly practice clothes, tights, leotards. But, knowing Kelly, there'll be a few fun things in there too."

"New principal?" David mutters.

"Anyway, I'll see you later," Victoria says, letting the wave of murmurs carry her from the room like an outgoing tide. She hasn't lost her flair for captivating the room.

In the meantime, Anna might be starting to discover just what it's like to be hated. And that, as much as anything else Victoria can teach her, is going to make her exceptional.

CHAPTER 5

Anna takes her time packing up after class.

She's not exactly in a hurry to join the rest of the female company members in the changing room, not when they've done nothing but stare daggers at her every time they've made eye contact.

Ethan, to his credit, lingers over throwing his sweats and hoodie back on, waiting until the room is clear to whistle long and low over her haul. "Got yourself a sugar mama already?"

"No," Anna snaps back at him.

He shrugs, not committing further. He does, however, root around in her new bag nearest to him. "Carolina Herrera." He pulls out something black and gauzy. "This is McQueen, I'm pretty sure."

"I thought they were just leotards," Anna grumbles, rooting through the bags herself. "See? Just regular Elevé ones. But damn, there's a lot of them."

"Did I overhear right? What Victoria said about principal?" Ethan gathers some of the bags and hands them over. "'Cause I mean, you sort of made out like you're this newbie from the sticks, and I've been feeling sorry for you…"

"I am! She's got some idea that I can do something in the spring, I guess? She doesn't really give much in the way of detail."

"Whoa." Ethan stops her before they can finish walking out of the studio. "Anna, that's a freaking huge deal. Congratulations."

"You don't hate me?"

"Oh, I totally hate you. But I'll get over it. Just like most other people will, when you get to know them. You okay hitting the lockers by yourself?"

"I'll be fine," Anna says, marching off down the corridor. "I have the first studio rehearsal for *Bayadére* after lunch, so it's not like I have a choice."

"See you there!" Ethan calls after her.

Anna barrels on, trying not to wince at how exhausted she already feels.

Her delaying tactics at least have been mostly successful. When Anna enters the changing room she's relieved to see the rest of the company has filed out again, off to smoke or make calls, maybe gulp down an espresso and call it lunch.

She wrestles with the oversized bags from designer stores, shoving them into her locker to take home later. That's when she hears another locker slam.

Normally Anna knows better than to turn around and involve herself with someone else's bad day. Maybe she's just too desperate to get someone in this strange place to like her.

Only, when she turns to see who's slamming doors, Anna suddenly can't breathe.

"Yes?" The woman snaps eventually, pulling wild curls into a slick bun that puts Anna's own attempts to shame. "Take a picture, hmm? It lasts longer."

"You're…"

"Ir-ina," she answers, as though speaking to a particularly stupid child. "You, I don't recognize."

"I haven't seen you in classes—" Anna interrupts, her heart racing.

For a moment, a world-tilting moment, she had thought her mother was in the room with her. Anna never saw the resemblance from clippings. Her mother laughed it off the few times it was ever mentioned, and Irina had still been dancing with the Bolshoi in the years when Anna attended the ballet with her mother. But the slender profile, the pale eyes, and those wild curls all seem torn from Anna's memories, and she isn't quite sure how to get her breathing back under control.

"I was detained in Kiev." Irina sighs. "Are you the attendance monitor?"

"No, I'm Anna," she says, crossing the space and realizing this is one person who hasn't seen the display of favoritism. She offers a hand. "I'm new this season."

"Anya?" Irina repeats back, shaking Anna's hand for the briefest possible second, barely touching her. "It doesn't matter, I won't remember. Names are not so important."

"Right." Anna tries not to frown. "I'm really thrilled to be working with you. And Victoria, obviously. I mean, it's a great company. My mother was a huge fan of yours," she exaggerates, because something in her just needs to put the two women in the same sentence.

"Was?" Irina looks amused as she hangs her leather jacket in her locker.

Anna pretends not to see when a plastic baggie is pulled from Irina's pocket and palmed away.

"Did she stop liking me?"

"She died," Anna blurts out. "But before that, she saw you dance in Moscow. She told me all about it. I wish she had been around to see you join Metropolitan. We would have been at every performance."

Irina looks at her for a long moment. "I'm sorry for your loss," she adds. "But I've been here for almost twelve years. That sort of devotion would be expensive."

Anna nods, fighting back unexpected tears even as she laughs at Irina's dry humor. "I was going to eat before rehearsal. Did you want to grab something, maybe?"

"You 'are sweet." Irina sits on the bench and pulls her boots off, wriggling out of tight indigo jeans. "But for me, it's physio first. What kind of mood is Vicki in today?"

"Your guess is as good as mine," Anna answers honestly. "It doesn't seem like the worst mood, though."

"Good. She promised me a full season, and it might just be to piss off Westin, but I plan to dance as much of it as possible."

A pang of guilt hits Anna. Is this someone else she's stealing an opportunity from?

"Well, I'm sure you'll be great," Anna says, which earns her another wry smile. "I'd better go get that lunch, huh?" She closes her locker and departs with an awkward wave. Irina doesn't return it.

When Anna steps outside, she runs into Ethan, who thrusts a brown paper bag at her.

"Quinoa bowl and some fruit," he says. "When I saw you hadn't made it to the café yet, I thought I'd be your knight in shining armor."

"Thank you," Anna says with real enthusiasm, because the way to her heart is most definitely through her stomach. She grabs a banana from the bag and peels it quickly as they walk. "Did you eat?" she asks around a mouthful.

Ethan shows her his own bag and pulls a wrap from it. "We could head up to the roof terrace and make a lunch date of it, if you like."

"Oh." Anna feels her stomach sink as she swallows. "That's so nice. But I'm really not dating right now. I swore I wouldn't even look the entire first season, because—"

"Whoa, Anna!" Ethan waves in front of her face. "Not that way inclined. I was just being cute about the date."

"I wondered where I'd got a straight dancer from. Is Gabriel Bishop the only one around here?"

"Well, he's straight for Delphine." Ethan sounds disgruntled now. "But far be it from me to gossip."

They sit on the roof, wolfing down their respective lunches.

"Did Delphine and her coven give you shit back there?" Ethan asks as the sun warms them a little.

"They were all gone. Just Irina. She's really something up close."

"She's old school." Ethan starts flicking through his phone. "Her ankle's pretty shot last I heard. Can't kill the bionic woman, I guess."

"She seemed fine," Anna lies, closing her eyes and trying not to think about the drugs she saw that were definitely not prescription vitamins. "I totally fangirled and made an ass of myself, though. My mom saw her, with the Bolshoi? I babbled the whole story like a stage-door groupie."

"Your mom's a bunhead, too? That must be wild. I haven't seen mine in twenty years, and my dad tells his friends I work construction."

Anna blinks at him.

"Sorry, I have this overshare thing."

"That's okay." Anna holds his shifting gaze to make sure he knows she's being sincere. "My mom didn't have the dancing gene herself; she just loved to watch. It's how I got into it, I guess. Oldest story in the book, right?"

"Did she take you to see Irina?"

"No, she passed away even before Victoria came to Metropolitan, so she missed Irina coming here to replace her." Anna is showing off a little, but she can't help it. She's studied the history of this company the way other people know baseball stats and stock prices. The changing headshots each season are a Rolodex in her head, some fleshed out by the few times she could afford to see the shows in person.

"You must have been young then. I mean, it's eleven years since Victoria retired."

"Twelve. Yeah, it was before that. I did see Victoria, just not with my mom."

"Lucky you." Ethan's getting restless and throwing his phone back in his backpack. "I mean, I've seen the videos. It's something, working for a living legend. People still rave about her, even now that the memories are getting kinda dusty."

"Does she ever talk about it? Why she stopped, I mean? Because I followed her career… But there was never a clear answer. Just rumors, a lot of speculation. Does she ever tell you guys about it?"

"About why she stopped dancing?" Ethan drains the rest of his juice. "Oh, sure. Was it my first month? No, my second. Victoria comes in, hugs each of us individually, and invites us into this circle of trust, sitting on the studio floor. Told us the whole story, start to finish."

"Really?" Anna gasps.

"No!" Ethan bursts out laughing. "Anna, she wouldn't waste her breath telling us the choreography if she didn't have to. We're all just so many dancing puppets to her, until we do something special or useful. Like you must have."

"I don't know about that. I need to walk this off. You up for taking the long way back down?"

"Sure, shall I lead the way? Or are the corridors starting to make sense?"

"You lead. But I'll pick it up quickly enough, just you wait."

"Of that, Anna Gale, I have no doubt."

Anna hopes Victoria's next grand entrance will keep attention far from her, but the room divides into those who watch their leader, and those who turn or bend to shoot glares at Anna. She stays stretching on the floor, looking only at Ethan until she catches Gabriel smiling at her in the mirror behind Ethan's head. Without much confidence, Anna smiles back.

"I'm not here to babysit you," Victoria announces, nodding to Teresa at the piano and David, who's curled neatly on a windowsill, his impressive arms still bulging the tight black material of his shirt.

The day has grown progressively gray outside, the lunchtime sun all but faded now. The studio, all stripped white wood and mirrors, reflects as brightly as any stage lighting might. Anna can't help feeling better for being bathed in the brightness.

Her shoes are holding; she hasn't felt the shank give any under her sole yet, so Anna slips them back on and ties the ribbon securely. The company settles, a restless murmur fading out as Victoria flips through some papers on top of the piano.

"Principals, you only have to endure today before your private studio time. Soloists, you need to see out this week and next before your schedules let you work on your pieces. Corps? Well, this is as good as it gets, *mes enfants*."

The groan that goes up is good-natured. Anna knows she's in a room with about sixty people who all want this as badly as she does, or they simply wouldn't have made it this far.

"Now get used to hearing the word *arabesque*," Victoria continues. "Ladies of the corps, you had better be especially attentive to this, because by the time we get this show up, you'll be doing thirty-nine in a row. The first one to break the sequence— that's twenty-four of you doing this in perfect unison—will be fired. Not one wobble. Not one failed elevation. Do I make myself clear?"

"What Victoria means," David continues, unfolding himself, "is if any of you do that after being appropriately rehearsed, you're in trouble. This week you should relax, learn—"

"And devote your entire pathetic existence to mastering it," Victoria finishes.

David rolls his eyes behind Victoria's back, and the assembled company has the sense to smother their laughter.

"Teresa, they'll be doing nothing but *Kingdom of the Shades* until it's perfect, so you can put the rest of your sheets away for now. David? I'll leave you to it. Make my *chaine d'ombres*."

The line of shadows. It's one of the classical ballet sequences she's most wanted to perform, but this is her first real chance.

"All right, company, on your feet!" David urges them.

Victoria makes her way back to the door. She veers toward Anna at the last moment, bending to offer her a quiet instruction.

"Wait for me here after rehearsal," she says, and Anna feels the dull ache in her hamstrings increase at just the thought. "I need to see more of what we ran through this morning, to make sure you're ready."

Anna takes her seemingly natural spot next to Ethan, her one friendly face. This part she's ready for. She's going to be one of the twenty-four tutus that she's dreamed of being a hundred times or more.

She's really, truly going to be in the ballet.

Chapter 6

She doesn't like the new physical therapy suite any more than the one she was treated in, but Victoria has been alerted to Irina's return and knows better than to let her evaporate into the hollows of the building without speaking to her first.

"Vicki," Irina calls mockingly, head hanging upside down off a massage table. "Anyone would think you were waiting for me."

"I have spies everywhere. You're two days late, Irina."

"Will I lose any ability for doing thirty-two fewer *fouetté*?" Irina asks. "No, silly me. You'd have me dance on my hands before you'd stage *Swan Lake*."

"Both can be arranged." Victoria nods at Kim, their in-house orthopedist, who also runs the physical therapy team. "I'm changing the program, so your solos aren't settled yet, before you ask."

"A change in program this late?" Irina sits up sharply, spine curving as she wraps her arms around her knees.

Defensive, great.

"If you want to kick me out, you could have saved me the plane fare."

"I know how much you like flying," Victoria says. "Not to mention we paid for the ticket. Dr. Sawyer, could you give us a minute?"

"Kim," she insists. "I'll be back with ice packs in a little while, then."

"How bad?" Victoria asks when they're alone. "Don't bullshit me."

Irina clambers down from the table and walks across to stare Victoria down at close range. Her slight height advantage seems more prominent while Victoria is in flats.

"Name it. I can do it," Irina says through teeth that are only slightly gritted. "Come on, one prima to another. I have taken your demotion with grace, but you know I still belong at the top."

"Delphine is my prima," Victoria corrects, and she hates to have to do it. "Not to mention I've uncovered something new. Someone who, with a little coaching, might end up on our level."

"You mean…" Irina calculates. "The new girl? I believe we just met. She must be something exceptional in the studio, because I saw only another star-struck child."

"That's the one. Is that really all you think of her?"

Irina sighs and gets back on the examination table. She glances to the office to see if Kim has reappeared with the ice that is apparently growing more necessary by the second.

"Perhaps there is more to her," Irina says, relenting. "Until I see her dance…"

"She'll need an ally," Victoria says, finally giving voice to the half-baked idea she'd had when coming to find her erstwhile ballerina. "To get the best out of her, I'll have to be tough. I also need her competitive fire stoked, so I've set her at odds with most of the company. That said, I don't want her isolated. I need to know that she's coping, whatever I throw at her."

"You're giving me your ugly duckling?" Irina looks disgusted. She considers Victoria for a long moment. "Not so ugly though, hmm?" If Victoria's steady expression flickers at all, Irina seems to catch it. "Such a cliché, thinking with your…well, I would usually say *dick*. I would expect this from Richard, but you were supposed to be above all that."

"I am. Will you keep an eye on the girl or not?" Victoria feels snappish, uncomfortable that anyone would even speculate on an attraction to Anna. The girl is nothing but a malleable piece of clay to be choreographed, and to turn that into anything else is just tawdry. "Let me remind you that this *job* would keep you on contract even if another injury should flare up. You'd be certain to see out the season on full salary."

"Very well," Irina agrees with bad grace.

Kim reappears with gel packs, looking to Victoria for permission. It's granted with a wave of her fingers.

"Did you see that Liza Wade has announced her final season?" Irina says. "My phone has beeped too many times already to tell me."

"No?" Victoria reaches for her own phone, shoved in the pocket of her pants. "Though it's about time. San Francisco must be as bored of her headlining as we are."

"I wonder where she'll go next?" Irina muses. "Something contemporary?"

Victoria shudders. "Even I don't think that badly of her, Irina. Get on with your physio, and I'll see you for *Coppélia*."

"That fossil," Irina groans. "You are a sadist."

"Remember to keep an eye on Anna," Victoria warns, taking her leave.

"As if she were my own duckling," Irina calls after her, snorting with laughter.

Victoria supposes whatever she's taking this month is finally kicking in. Which means the pain is back to tolerable at least. For right now, that's going to have to be good enough.

ᏫᏬ

Victoria takes the scenic route back to her office, via the auditorium.

The house lights are dimmed, but not to performance levels. It gives the auditorium a warm glow despite nothing on stage being illuminated. Victoria hesitates in the wings before she allows herself to step out on the battered boards.

She's been in here a thousand times for stage rehearsals, for performances, and sometimes just to scream at incompetent stagehands, but so rarely does Victoria get the space to herself. As she breathes out, it barely seems to disturb the dust around her. She feels at home again, for the first time in too long.

The ornate gold of the balconies reflects the yellow warmth of the lights, and while Victoria's own preference is for sleek, modern lines, in this cavernous space she can feel the connection right back to dancers in petticoats dancing under gas lighting. Rows of red velvet stretch out to either side, and at this distance they seem uniform and plush.

In a few strong strides, she's downstage center. If she closes her eyes, she can almost feel the hum of it, a barely contained audience glued to their seats. The collective intake of breath at the start of a leap. The ragged, spontaneous applause when something that looks dangerous lands successfully. Flowers arcing up and onto the floor at her feet, lilies clashing with freesias and overwhelmed by orchids, a migraine disguised as a carpet of blooms. The shouts of *brava*, the whistling, baying, stamping power of the crowd that always wants more. It should be the eerie whispering of ghosts, but in Victoria's head it drowns out everything but her own thundering heartbeat.

Twelve years and it hasn't lost an ounce of its power.

Victoria hears a door creak at the back of the orchestra section and turns her back to pretend to be inspecting something on the rigging. How mortifying it would be to be caught in such a sentimental moment. She gathers herself, and exits through the wings.

There's work to be done.

◠◯◯◯

Fielding a few calls makes Victoria a pleasing ten minutes late for the end of the *arabesque*-fest Anna has just been subjected to.

Sure enough, the girl is sitting on the floor with tired legs extended like two sides of a triangle, the faint jump of muscles visible beneath her white tights. David has worked them hard.

Anna scrambles to her feet on seeing Victoria.

"I'm ready!" she swears, throwing her phone back into her hold-all where it rests against the wall. Anna should have pulled her hoodie back on; she rubs her arms briskly to ward off the chill.

Victoria looks down at Anna's feet, seeing one shoe already removed. "Done?" She nods to it.

"Shank went," Anna sighs. "I felt it on my last repetition."

"You didn't go over on the ankle?"

"No!" Anna says. "Felt it on the way up, so I stopped in time."

Victoria nods. It's the moment to get Anna up to speed on her new reality in yet another way.

"Well, don't pluck another pair of sad little stock shoes from your bag. It's time for you to meet Susan."

"Susan?" Anna says. "Who's Susan?"

"Well, you should probably call her Ms. Ramos. But Susan is going to change your life."

"More than it already has been?" Anna slaps a hand over her mouth. "Sorry," she says, compounding the list of habits she'll have to break before long.

"Come along." Victoria sighs. "I really shouldn't be pandering to you like this, but I don't have time for you to get lost in some woodland glade along the way."

"To where?"

"The shoe room, Anya. You're really going to have to learn to keep up. Things go at a different pace around here."

"Okay," Anna agrees, grabbing her things and switching out her remaining pointe shoe for flats. "Whatever you want."

"That's right." Victoria smirks at the ease with which she controls the girl. She had planned on another tough session for Anna, but how can Victoria be expected to work with someone whose materials are simply not up to scratch? It would be like instructing someone to paint the Sistine Chapel when they've only brought finger paints.

She heads to the door and waits pointedly until Anna catches up and opens it for her with suitably flustered deference. Victoria leads the way to the elevator and nods for Anna to call the damn thing. She does, pressing the button a few too many times.

CHAPTER 7

"Susan?" Victoria tries to follow a pattern in the rustling somewhere in the rows upon rows of costumes. "Ramos! Get your ass out here. I have a newbie."

There's a thump and muted curse of acknowledgment.

Victoria hangs back, satisfied she has been obeyed. It gives her a chance to watch Anna, face lit up like one of those excruciating moppets in a tacky Christmas commercial. The wide eyes, the lips parted in genuine amazement, the sweeping motion of her arms as she twirls on the spot and takes it all in. Even though the most impressive items are in climate-controlled storage farther back, the sea of satin and tulle and leather and lace, tinged by the dust and mothballs and dry-cleaning fluids, is almost enough to make even Victoria giddy.

She rarely comes down here. Summoning Susan to her office usually suffices, and costume designs for each production are decided in the airy meeting rooms upstairs.

"Newbie?" Susan asks, bursting forth from the middle of a row of velvet and brocade jackets. "Not possible. Every year the newbies are in here trying to steal half of my stock and call it company perks."

"Hi?" Anna actually does that awkward half wave like she's just wandered out of a Disney Channel sitcom.

Victoria pinches her nose and breathes through a spike of irritation. Then her phone starts ringing.

"Take her through the best options," Victoria instructs, pulling it out and frowning at it. Rick. Perfect. "And whatever customization, get it over to them today. Give her the closest possible to what she likes for now, to cover until the first order arrives.""

"I have done this before," Susan says. "Ma'am," she appends, after Victoria's glare. "Come along, newbie," she barks at Anna, who falls in step right away, following the path that leads to the rabbit warren of shelves that hold the company's shoes.

Having let Rick roll to voicemail, she hesitates for a moment. If he's changed his mind already, or worse, come up with some uninspired change of his own as some demented tit-for-tat… She returns his call.

"Victoria!" He sounds breathless when he picks up, and she doesn't dare speculate why as she heads back into the corridor. "I want to come see our new girl like we agreed. And I need to bring a date and a couple of new investors, so make it a little showcase, would you? An hour on Saturday should do it."

"That's before—"

"They want to see some ballet. Gimme a break here. This way I'm out of your hair by nine. She's ready, right? This discovery of ours? If not, I want an impressive plan B ready."

"She will be," Victoria says through gritted teeth, not correcting "ours" to *mine*. "I could bring in a couple of other principals, if you really need a show."

"There's the visionary I hired." Rick chuckles around the words. "Give it the Victoria Ford effect, and one of these checks will cover all your chopping and changing for the rest of the season."

"Fine. I'm about to lose you," she says as the elevator pings its arrival. "Call Kelly if there are specifics."

Victoria ends the call. She has too much work to do for Richard Westin to be in her head. She considers going back to start Anna right away, but the girl will need rest. Not to mention that pulling together an impressive enough scene for the showcase will require some serious planning and choreographing. For that, she works alone.

The hum of anticipation settles in her stomach, and Victoria suppresses the start of a smile.

It's a challenge, that's all. And overcoming those has always been what she does best.

"Wow," Anna says for the fifteenth time. "No, seriously. Wow."

"You can stop clutching and start trying them on anytime you like." Susan pulls another pair of shoes down from a high shelf. Anna offered to help with the reaching, but she'd been glared at, then a small stepladder was produced.

This room is Anna's Ollivander's wand shop. It's a lamppost and a sprinkling of snow away from being Narnia. If she were to win a golden ticket, it would be for this gigantic space, not some chocolate factory. Okay, maybe a detour to the chocolate factory too. At every turn there are beautiful, untouchable things.

She takes a seat on the bench and pulls on the first pair of shoes. They're far better quality than anything she's ever danced in before, the corset satin like a kiss sliding against her skin. Something about the arch of the sole isn't right, though; it feels intrusive in a way she isn't used to.

"Not the Capezios, then," Susan surmises, bringing another pair down and watching Anna's expression.

"Oh! They might be fine," Anna insists. "Just different. I just need to get used to, you know, how it feels."

"Listen, this isn't an outlet mall. You don't have to compromise for *kind of good enough*. And Victoria wasn't kidding. She doesn't let you use anything as an excuse, especially not something that can be avoided. Putting that shoe on should make you feel like you can—"

"Leap buildings in a single bound?" Anna teases, pleased when she gets a brief smile in return. "I just don't want to cause any trouble, you know? It's a miracle I'm even here, so I'm trying to keep my head down."

"You sure have a funny way of showing it." Delphine Wade steps into view, in yoga pants that have to be designer and the softest gray hoodie Anna has ever seen. It takes a ridiculous amount of self-control not to reach out and touch it. "I don't believe we've officially met. Anya, wasn't it?"

"Um, sure?" Anna responds, standing up like she's a soldier on parade. "I mean, actually it's Anna. I think you're amazing. But I guess you get that a lot."

"You'd be surprised by how it doesn't get old." Delphine extends her hand.

Anna shakes it, faintly stunned.

"I suppose you think I'm here to claw your eyes out and tell you to get the hell out of my company, don't you?"

Susan moves her head back and forth between them.

"That would…not totally shock me?" Anna shrugs. "But I swear what I just said is true. I didn't go looking for any of this. I just wanted to be normal, like any other dancer."

"Clearly you're not. Victoria is a lot of things, but she's not a bad judge of talent. I assume she wants me to hate you, because it'll make you better or some kind of mind game. Which is exactly why I'm not going to. Unless you give me a reason."

"I will really try not to do that." Anna is so relieved that her grin is wide enough to hurt her cheeks. "And if you need to jump the line here, let me get out of your way."

"You're getting your shoes?" Delphine nods to Susan, who pulls a bundle of pointe shoes from a cube in the shelves marked with Delphine's name. "Who are you going with?"

"Well, she's not a Gaynor Minden girl like you," Susan announces. "I've got those piled up in her size, but you don't suppose…"

"Oh, that would be fun. I always wanted to wear Maltese Cross, but they just don't work with my toes. He's so in demand, though…"

"Who is?" Anna asks, losing the thread of the conversation.

"The Maltese Cross maker at Freed." Susan climbs back up her ladder, yanking things from higher shelves.

Anna has read a million *Tribune* and *Times* articles on ballet. She can't believe the details she used to obsess over in her favorite dancers are now the details of her own life.

"A nine, wasn't it?"

"Freed of London?" Anna tries to clarify. "Oh wow, that would be insane, but they don't just have them lying around in the store. Not these handmade ones, anyway."

"Each maker has their own stamp," Susan says, and Anna lets her explain, like she hasn't been obsessing over the Freed shoes and their makers for years. "We have a few Bell girls, and I know the San Francisco girls are crazy for Castle and Butterfly."

She hands over a pair and Anna turns them over, running her hands over the soles, where, sure enough, the little fish symbol rests to signify the person who handmade these shoes with such impeccable attention to detail.

Anna knows, honestly, before she slips the first one on.

These are her shoes.

Oh, the cutdown needs to be a little lower to stop it rubbing, and she needs to stitch in her elastic the way she likes it, but the moment they slip over her heel it's Cinderella and the Prince: a mortal lock.

"Huh," Susan remarks as Anna stands again and goes up on her toes. "Well, it'll be nice to finally put these back on the order; it's been weird not to add it all this time. Irina was the last one, and she hasn't worn them since…well, it's been a while."

"You have everything you need?" Delphine interrupts. "I'm taking Anna here for a green tea and a real initiation."

"I'll put a rush on it. Come back in the morning, newbie. I'll tweak enough of these to get you through until the first delivery."

"Thank you," Anna says, sincerely.

"Let's go," Delphine says. "I'm about to show you the Metropolitan Center's best-kept secret."

"Tea?" Anna confirms, because she's still not entirely convinced Delphine doesn't want to lure her to the huge atrium and toss her over the railing. "I could drink tea."

Victoria's office is no sanctuary this week, not in the chaos of a new season. Kelly is an effective gatekeeper, but the sheer hubbub outside makes it impossible to concentrate. She gathers her things and sneaks out via the fire escape, in no mood to be accosted by everyone with a problem or a half-baked observation.

First, there's the delicate matter of wrangling her principals into an unplanned showcase. Irina will be easy enough—the prospect of antagonizing Rick is all the incentive she needs. Victoria plucks her phone from her purse as she slips into the backseat of her waiting Mercedes, the driver already summoned with a text.

"Delphine?" she asks when the phone is answered. It doesn't sound like Delphine Wade's usually snippy greeting. The fact it was answered the first time with Victoria being the one to call is unusual enough.

"No, she's uh, well, she had to go complain about her tea," comes a familiar, bumbling response.

"Well, well." Victoria smirks into the phone. "You've got considerably more game than I gave you credit for, Anya."

"Game?"

"Going out of your way to court the very people you're alienating." Victoria rolls her eyes. The traffic around her is familiar, almost soothing. She watches the glide of irresponsible but well-executed undertaking from the next lane over and files the motion away for later. The weave of cyclists and irresponsible pedestrians darting out in her peripheral vision keep the choreographing part of her brain ticking over. "I doubt even I would have been so bold."

"She was there when I got my shoes. And she invited me to tea. I don't want to have enemies. I'd much rather make friends."

"Do Hallmark know about you?" Victoria can't contain her sarcasm. "If you could relay a message to your new best friend, tell her we have a schmooze session on Saturday. You, too, for that matter. When you all get in tomorrow, check the updated schedule. And tell Gabriel to pick another boy who can keep up with him. I want the best."

"What about Ethan?" Anna asks. "He works so hard."

"Promoted to principal and already you're calling the shots?" Victoria can't resist. "You think you can work with cardigan boy?"

"I can work with anyone." There it is again. Under that corny-as-Kansas exterior, that glint of steel. Victoria feels her heartbeat spike in anticipation. This is the one, all right.

"Then bring the Will to your Grace along tomorrow. He might not thank you for all the extra work, you know."

"He wants his break, just like everyone else. And he's really good."

"Of course he is," Victoria drawls. "This is my company. Really good is actually below our minimum standard."

"Can I ask what a schmooze session is?"

"You should ask your new buddy Delphine," Victoria says, before thinking better of it, with a hearty sigh. "Though, since it's important, I should point out this is the test for Rick that you're working toward. The one you cannot blow, if you want a future with this ballet company."

Anna gulps at the news.

Good. Nervous is something Victoria can work with.

"I'll work hard," Anna promises. "I can come back today if you need—"

"I have planning to do," Victoria interrupts. "The muse is a fickle thing, and I've already had to flee the building. Once I have a suitable environment to create the necessary art, I can finish choreographing the dazzling sequences I'm going to give you."

"Great!" Anna sounds excited, so that part of the plan has worked at least. "Have I mentioned that I really appreciate this chance to—"

Victoria hangs up.

She has her limits.

The car rolls uptown toward her apartment, and she drums an *adagio* beat on the inside of the door. She closes her eyes to envisage the positioning, and tells herself that it isn't the new girl she's picturing in each pose.

CHAPTER 8

"If you're a pickpocket, you're doing kind of a lousy job," Delphine announces, setting the corrected pale green teas on the table before plucking her phone from Anna's hand. "You look a little shell-shocked."

"Victoria called," Anna manages to say, before taking a hearty slurp of the tea and hissing at the temperature against her tongue. "She, uh, told me to tell you there's a schmooze session on Saturday."

"God, just when I thought I might actually enjoy one of the last free weekends. Out of season gets shorter every year, and we spent most of this one in Europe. You don't have to play secretary for me, you know," Delphine changes tack. "I already decided not to hate you, remember?"

"Right." Anna takes a steadying breath. "She wants Gabriel as well. And Irina."

Delphine frowns.

"I volunteered Ethan too. Oh God, what am I doing?"

"Hell if I know." Delphine sighs, sipping her tea and watching Anna over the rim of her cup. "You're really not some Machiavellian schemer, are you? This farm-girl naiveté isn't even an act. Where are you from, Kansas?"

"Dubuque." Anna sticks with the easiest version. She doesn't know whether she can trust Delphine the way she instantly trusted Ethan. "I moved a lot as a kid, but Dubuque is home."

"Well, I'm from Kansas," Delphine replies. "But I have the feeling you already knew that. You might not be scheming, but you must know ballet for Victoria to be interested in you."

"I actually met your sister a couple of times," Anna admits, and instantly regrets it when Delphine's expression hardens and she sets down her tea a little too carefully. "In San Francisco. I have this friend… He introduced us when I was looking at schools."

"And she just fell over herself to help you pursue your dreams?" Delphine's voice is tight. "Guess that applies to everyone who isn't her sister."

"Oh, no!" Anna rushes to correct her. "She actually sort of put me off. Well, she tried to. Told me every little girl wants to be a ballerina but that almost no one has what it takes."

Delphine relaxes a little at that. "That does sound more like Liza. We're not close."

"This is her last season," Anna can't help but blurt out. "So it's just you, you know, in the spotlight after this."

"Well, apparently that's not true, either," Delphine snaps.

For a moment, Anna thinks she might really have blown it this time.

"No. I'm not blaming you for whatever crazy idea Victoria got in her head," Delphine says. "She's brilliant, but God, don't try to keep up with her. Still, I'd rather dance for her than some old white man."

"Like Kevin Winters?" Anna is fascinated by and terrified of the man in equal measure. She knows he discovered Liza, and brought Victoria home from London, but only Liza stayed at the San Francisco Ballet. She gives him credit for her career. No biography of Victoria Ford gives Kevin any prominence at all. "Did he—"

"I'm Victoria's discovery," Delphine says. "She picked me out of the corps in Toronto, and she enticed Gabe over when he felt restricted in San Francisco. So yeah, we all bitch. But we owe her a lot. And you know she's still the only female artistic director of any of the major companies, right?"

Anna nods at her Feminism 101 reminder.

"Now, please tell me you're not another dreamy-eyed chorus girl with her eyes on my man?" Delphine asks, the threat beneath the words evident. "Because that is honestly the last point of friction, and I'll be so disappointed if we have to be enemies over that."

"I don't!" Anna protests. "I mean, he seems great, don't get me wrong. But I'm not doing that whole thing. I never really have."

"Oh." Delphine winks across the table. "Batting for the other team. I get it."

"More of a…" Anna blushes furiously and wonders why she ever let Delphine kidnap her from all those simple, beautiful shoes. "Switch…hitter?"

"Hey, I asked, but you don't have to tell," Delphine reminds her, and it's honestly the kindest thing anyone has said to Anna since she arrived in New York. "Do you have someone?"

"Nah." Anna sips her tea. It tastes like perfume, diluted. "It's just me, this job, and I'm crashing with my sister for now. Until the company housing comes up. Kelly's email said next week, maybe the week after."

"You have a sister?"

"Yeah." Anna doesn't elaborate on that, either. Her defenses have been down too much already, first around Ethan and then around Irina. Just because she was already thirteen when Anna met her doesn't make Jess any less her sister. Besides, Liza and

Delphine grew up in the same house, and it seems they can barely stand one another. "She's not in this, though. Broadway."

Delphine smiles, the first one not to crinkle her nose. "Chorus girl?"

"Stage manager. She's at the Booth. I'm going to meet her when I'm done."

"Invite her up here someday, if she doesn't have a tedious little matinée or something. You've just made friends with the prima; you should take shameless advantage of that."

"We're friends? I mean, of course we're friends. You'll love Jess, she is so much cooler than me, and no way would she ramble like this and…"

"Finish your tea." Delphine pats Anna on the forearm. "And then you can tell me everything you know about Saturday."

∞∞∞

Anna skips dinner out in favor of having the small apartment to herself with enough cheap takeout for at least two people, her body crying out for protein by the time she actually sits down to eat.

A handful of Advil and the requisite rattle of vitamin bottles to top up on B, C, and B12 punctuate some half-hearted sorting through the clothes Victoria brought. She texts Ethan to warn him that he's going to be in a showcase Saturday, but when he replies Anna simply cuts him off with *details tomorrow*.

Losing herself in a few old episodes of *Gilmore Girls*, Anna spends most of the evening dozing or getting up to swap out her ice packs. It's only when she hears the key in the door around eleven that she realizes she should have tidied up her clothes haul. The things from her own luggage are hung everywhere Anna could find for them, and everything else is still in flashy designer bags that are strewn across the floor.

"What the hell?" Jess demands. "Where did you get the money to go *Pretty Woman* yourself?"

"I didn't spend a penny. It's part of my company wardrobe."

Jess raises an eyebrow. "Really?"

"Yes, really!" Anna makes a point of picking up a couple of leotards, clearly standard ballet-school wear. "And I get custom-made shoes, too, did you know that?"

"Well, you have to figure," Jess says, relaxing a little. "The way they work you there, it'll be a new pair twice a day."

"At least." Anna gathers her clothes into a pile, already distracted at what to pick for the next day. "You know the Freed shoes I used to always obsess about? Well, I get those."

"Sounds great." Jess pours herself a large glass of white wine from the fridge. "You having some?"

"Not worth it. I sorted everything out with Victoria, though."

"Oh, the principal mix-up?" Jess looks exhausted. "I hate to say I told you so, Anna."

"No, no…" Anna is going to enjoy this just a little bit. "I was right. They're sorting out a new contract, and I'll be, like, some big deal in the spring program. Victoria's going to direct me herself. Well, if we pass this test on Saturday anyway. Pretty much dancing for the money to be allowed to do it, I think."

"Anna!" Jess sets her wine down and drags her sister into a hug. "That's awesome! I am so proud of you."

"You are?" Anna mumbles into the hug.

"Of course I am!"

"You're the best sister, Jess." Anna wriggles free and collapses back on the sofa that's also her bed. "I was talking to Delphine Wade about you today."

"*The* Delphine Wade?" Even Jess is impressed. "You're getting fancier by the day, Anna. Don't forget me in that rarefied air up at the Metropolitan Center."

"She said I should bring you to lunch," Anna says. "We're *friends*, can you believe it?"

"Of course I can," Jess teases. "Who wouldn't want to be friends with a big dancing dork?"

"Hey!" Anna whines, but she laughs right through it. "I met Irina today too."

"The Madonna of ballet. Because she only uses her first name. Let me guess: she wants to adopt you?"

"No," Anna huffs, thinking of her mother with a fresh pang. "But we had a very cool conversation. I told her my mom saw her dance in Moscow, so I guess that's like bonding, right?"

"I wish making friends was the biggest problem in my job." Jess groans as she sinks down onto the other sofa cushion. "Have I mentioned lately that I want to kill all my actors?"

"Once or twice." Anna gets up to refill Jess's glass and hand it to her. "I have private rehearsals tomorrow. Dancing with Delphine and Irina, and some of the boys… It's all happening so fast."

Jess sympathizes, patting Anna's hand. "This is what you always wanted, Anna. I know plenty of people tried to talk you out of it—no one more than me. Don't start listening now, or you'll regret it."

"I already got your wine, you don't have to butter me up. You want to see my new clothes?"

"Tomorrow. If you're home before I head out, you can do a whole fashion show, I promise. I can't believe I'm going to bed before midnight," Jess says, but she doesn't protest when Anna pushes the bedroom door open. "Dance pretty, little sis."

"I'll try."

⟳⟲⟳

Victoria doesn't bother announcing herself; she simply appears in the doorway and waits for the exiting crowd of dancers to part before her like the Red Sea. They dutifully comply, and Victoria enters the studio to find Anna and Delphine deep in conversation, Irina draped over the portable barre like she's been shot, and the Vaughn boy staring at Gabriel in unabashed adoration. That adoration certainly seems to be putting an extra flex into his preliminary stretches.

"Morning," she grunts in their direction, directing Teresa back to the piano with a click of her fingers.

The pianist scrambles to comply, accepting the sheet music Victoria hands.

"As Anya here probably informed you," Victoria says to her remaining five, "our lord and master has requested a command performance Saturday evening. Since we all like being gainfully employed, I assume there'll be no complaints?"

"Why me?" Irina asks. "At this point, surely it will just antagonize him."

"You're walking proof that my gambles pay off. You're going to dance this season to the end, Irina. Starting here."

"Uh, Victoria?" Ethan raises his hand like a kindergarten student in need of a bathroom break. "I just wanted to check that you meant me? Anna's new, so she might have been confused…"

"She picked you," Victoria says with a snap in her voice. "Unless you're saying you're not up to the job?"

Ethan shakes his head and steps back toward the mirrors, out of her firing line. It explains how he's survived this long.

"Delphine and Gabriel, you'll reprise your *pas de deux* from *Rubies*."

They exchange a glance Victoria doesn't care to decipher.

"Irina?" Victoria receives a sullen glare. "Your *Bluebird* can be dusted off, yes?"

"A *Sleeping Beauty* to put the audience to sleep?" Irina sasses, but the relief is evident on her face. It's by far one of the least strenuous options Victoria could have put on her shoulders. "Fine."

"Tell me, Cardigan Boy," Victoria says, "you understudied Gabriel as Romeo last season, yes? And you went on in Berlin?"

"Yes, ma'am," Ethan confirms.

"I seem to recall your balcony scene wasn't a total disaster, so you've got yourself a Juliet here in Anya. I'm giddy with the romance of it all."

"Right." He shoots Anna a grateful look.

"As for you, Anya." Victoria rounds on her then, advancing across the room. "Juliet is obvious, but when dealing with the less artistic, a sledgehammer is sometimes necessary."

Anna swallows hard and nods like a marionette with a loose string.

"I think I'll teach you my Kitri variation," Victoria says, deciding in the moment. "It's short, but it should put some of that athleticism on display. Have you danced it?"

"You mean, um, *Don Quixote*? Not really. I've seen it, though."

Victoria rolls her eyes. "George Bush saw my production of *Don Quixote*. It doesn't mean he can dance it."

"I don't know," Gabriel interjects. "I think he has the hips for it."

The nervous laughter relaxes them. Victoria allows it, stalking back toward the piano.

"You all know Rick, you know what he expects. We do the mini-show, and we let them pour champagne down their throats until a check is cut or I dismiss you. Any questions?"

Anna looks like she might ask, but she doesn't raise her hand.

"Delphine, Gabriel, Irina, we'll make time Friday to check you've refreshed. See Susan about costumes. She'll have everything from the tour filed away."

They murmur in vague agreement.

"Ethan, you refresh with Gabriel on Romeo, then we'll spend some time tomorrow and Friday getting you and Anya confident around each other. Drop her once and you're back to the corps for life."

He nods and grabs his bag.

Anna waits, patient to a fault.

"I hope you had a good warm-up, because you're not going home today until you get this variation within touching distance of where I want it," Victoria says.

Her threat gets only a beaming smile in response.

"You can go." She dismisses Ethan with a wave of her hand. "Teresa, a recording will be fine. I'm sure you can find some other ivories to tinkle."

Teresa fiddles with the sound system and scurries out after handing a remote to Victoria on the way past.

Alone at last. To get the best out of Anna, distractions will have to be kept to a minimum. Despite her talent, there's a flighty quality.

"I'm ready when you are." Anna fiddles with the heel of her right shoe.

Victoria only glances at it, sure Susan will have done the right thing as always, when the snap of recognition hits her.

"You went with Freed," she says, and Anna smiles even wider. It's maddening. "Someone thinks highly of her feet."

"Maltese Cross." Anna's smug for the first time.

Victoria loses her train of thought for a second, because that she didn't expect. The steel is there beneath the puppy eyes and boundless enthusiasm.

"Susan made them fit so well, and she already placed the full order."

"You have decent taste in one area of your life, then." Victoria clicks the remote and music blasts for a second. She lowers the volume with fast, irritated jabs at the button.

"I know Irina used to wear them," Anna offers, shy again.

"She did. In fact, those have been the prima's choice for most of the past two decades in this company. Well, until Delphine and her fondness for space polymers or whatever sales pitch she fell for."

Anna's smile falters, and she pales despite the earlier flush to her complexion.

"They didn't tell you?" Victoria tuts. "Yes, Anya. I'd say you're wearing my shoes. How literal of you, when trying to follow in my footsteps. It's not exactly subtle."

"I didn't know. But I just knew they were for me the moment I pulled one on. I can go ask Susan to recommend something else if you want, I just—"

"Don't be ridiculous. It's not as though I'm using them, is it? Besides, you've found your shoe. I would be a terrible ballet mistress to interfere with that. Now, get rid of that top layer and we'll start in second."

Anna throws off her sweater, exposing a sunny yellow leotard. It's a vast improvement on her earlier attempts. "Yes, Victoria."

That kind of compliance is something Victoria could get very used to.

CHAPTER 9

"Again!" Victoria snaps, and Anna bends double, trying to pull in a deep enough breath. She holds up a hand in something like surrender.

"Drink," she gasps, stumbling toward her bag. It's been well over an hour, and Victoria has been relentless. Anna plucks a vitamin water from among her tape and spare shoes, twisting the cap off before Victoria can complain. Most of the bottle is downed in one long swallow, and Anna pulls a towel out to mop some of the sweat from her face.

"I'm waiting." Victoria taps her foot, her impatience perfectly in sync with the beat.

"How…am I doing? I thought I nailed the *pas de cheval* that time."

"You know there are mirrors on every wall to avoid that kind of delusion." Victoria gestures toward them. "I'll tell you if you ever *nail* something. And learn to stop mangling the French language, or keep your mouth shut on Saturday."

Anna nods. Apparently a positive attitude is going to get her precisely nowhere. She tosses the towel and the bottle back down and stands straight again in first position, arms tensed and ready for Victoria's barked command.

"Remember, *developpé devant croisé, glissade, cabriole derrière.*"

"It's so cool, because this isn't the version I saw," Anna starts to explain. It's not that she doesn't understand; she can already see the steps in her head. Dragging her foot up to the knee of her standing leg, making a triangle before fully extending. A display of control. After that a simple side step-and-jump, followed by her favorite: the bold leap of the cabriole where her legs press together in midair, fully off the ground. It's as close as she's come to flying.

Victoria's stare is frosty. "I forgot to ask the Mariinsky choreography to accommodate your limited exposure. I'm trying to play to your strengths, Anya. Or is that not obvious?"

"These are my strengths?" Anna gets an eyebrow raise in return. "Right, got it."

"Now try to summon something less bland, less American. You're young, you're Spanish." Victoria reels off the details of Kitri like a shopping list before pausing, her voice dropping low and sultry. "You're *caliente.*"

Hot.

Anna chokes for a second, even though her drink is long since swallowed.

It doesn't deter Victoria from continuing her lecture. "You got your man, you've got the ring on your finger, and you're showing off. The triumph of true love, all bound up in how you dance."

"It's a little strange to be starting at the end," Anna says in her own defense. "I mean, I bet a lot of people would feel that way. If you want, I could learn—"

"No time. You want to wallow in deep background, be my guest. But you'll have to give up sleep to do it. Focus!"

Anna jumps at the force of Victoria's command.

"Focusing on the correct details is enough to master any variation. Context be damned."

"Right." Anna accepts her fate. "Sure. Okay, I'm ready."

"We'll see," Victoria says, cueing up the music. "Now, start by learning how to count."

♋♋♋

"I came to check for bloodshed," David announces from the doorway before striding across the studio to where Victoria has settled on the low windowsill. "Where's your new pet project?"

"She said something about eating before she passed out."

"And you're going with Kitri? I hear Rick is looking for a command performance."

"You haven't been roped into it, Mr. Jackson," Victoria reassures him, smiling back when that easy grin of his breaks out. "You still have your Saturday night free to work on your frown lines."

"As opposed to getting drunk and misbehaving with the support staff?" David leans on the unused piano.

They're both dressed in black—though not so matching that it looks like a uniform.

Victoria slips gingerly from her seat and approaches him.

"Speaking of gossip about you… The new girl's really up to it?"

"Her Kitri is already… God, David. I haven't even started on the fan work, but I can see an audience in raptures over it. The best part is that she has no idea. That lack of awareness of how they'll see her will be stunning to the audience. If I can preserve it."

"Well, yours was one hell of a star turn," David reminds her. "Think she can live up to Victoria Ford hype without an explosion of ego?"

"Hard work doesn't seem to be an issue, but her focus is shot," Victoria says, worrying out loud. "It can be trained into her, but whatever else I think of Rick, he knows talent when he sees it."

"Well, it's that or she's a mole sent to sabotage you."

"Don't even joke. I'm more than aware that I'm on thin ice with him."

David's stoic silence is all the confirmation Victoria needs of how far the rumor has spread.

"It's okay. I have a plan. You think I don't know how much more vulnerable I am with Liza Wade looking for her next big challenge?"

"You think he'd call on Liza?" David folds his arms across his chest. "That would be low, even for Rick."

"She's taken everything else I want," Victoria reminds him, only to be startled by the sudden reappearance of Anna in the studio doorway, with a brown bag of something clutched in her hand. "Don't just stand there, Anya."

"I can wait if you're in a meeting."

Victoria jerks her head to indicate the girl should come in.

"I wasn't sure what you liked, so I asked the cafeteria guy and he said coffee," Anna continues, removing a tray with two steaming to-go cups from inside the crumpled paper. "I hope that's right." She hands one over to Victoria.

David gives the girl one of his trademark stares, clearly fascinated.

"I'm sorry, Mr. Jackson," Anna plows on, fussing with the plastic top on her coffee cup. "I didn't know you'd be here. But you can have my latte if you like? I haven't touched it yet, I swear. Pumpkin spice?"

"That won't be necessary." A smile twitches at David's lips for just a second. He reaches in his pocket and pulls out a folded wooden fan, handing that to Anna instead.

When he places it in her upturned palm, she almost drops it.

"Victoria's going to show you the fan work at some point today, and I think you deserve a head start. Don't let her work you too hard, Ms. Gale."

Victoria takes a sip of her latte. It's her exact order, down to the extra shot and soy. Anna must have sought out the building's one competent barista.

"Well?" Victoria demands as Anna looks on expectantly.

David departs with a wave over his shoulder, and Anna looks down at the fan she's clutching.

"I suggest you finish your drink before we get that fan involved."

"Of course," Anna slurps a mouthful from her cup, the bright smile restored by sugar and caffeine. "Almost done."

"That…" Anna pants. "That was it this time. Right?"

"Your arms are a mess." Victoria enjoys how that last hopeful smile falls. "I told you to move with Spanish flair. Instead you're giving me the chicken dance."

"My hands are on my hips," Anna protests, taking up the stance again, back ramrod straight at least. "Where else can my arms go? They're still connected to my shoulders." She hesitates, as though Victoria might suggest Anna dislocate them next. It wouldn't be Victoria's most unreasonable demand of a dancer.

"Perhaps if you stopped grabbing on to your hips like they're the last chopper out of Saigon…" Victoria sighs when Anna's change in grip is barely perceptible.

Catching sight of the rack of costumes in the corner, Victoria seizes on her solution. She strides across and rifles through the rustling fabrics until she finds a suitable handful of black tulle. Crossing the room to where Anna is choking down more water, Victoria tosses the tutu at the girl's head.

Anna looks up and catches it in the nick of time.

"Well, put it on already."

Anna is on her feet in an instant, yanking the material up over her knees and hips. Only when it's in place does she run her fingers reverently over the satin trim.

"Now place your palms flat—lightly—on top of the tutu. Classical form, Anya. Wrists down, not jutting out like you're hailing a cab."

"But—"

"No," Victoria says with a huff, because they're so close to something that even Rick can't pick apart with his mansplaining. Without thinking, she steps in and wraps her fingers around both wrists, pushing them into position with no small amount of force. "Here."

The girl goes rigid under her touch. Victoria can almost feel Anna vibrating with new tension. When she's sure the position will hold, Victoria steps back with a reluctance she didn't expect. She touches her dancers daily, wrenching legs higher and arms lower, aligning hips and tilting chins. This is no different.

"Better," Victoria says.

Anna sucks in a relieved breath.

"Now, once more without a mistake, and we'll get that boy up here to start wooing you. Don't let all of this fall out of your head to make room for Juliet."

"Do you think we'll be ready for Saturday?"

"You say that like you have a choice." Victoria pauses, hands on her own hips now, and stares Anna down. "Again!"

ⵔⵔ

"Is she gone?" Ethan whispers from where he's facedown on the studio floor, two long hours later.

"Yeah." Anna grunts, letting her arms take the strain as they're draped across the barre, holding her up. "You were so good!"

"Me?" Ethan pushes himself up to sitting. "She yelled at me, start to finish. You, on the other hand... You've been holding out on me."

"I'm nothing special."

"I've danced with a lot of girls. You're the first one that made it genuinely effortless to lift. Seriously, I feel like some kind of circus strongman over here."

"You smell like one too," Anna teases. "Or at least like you've been hanging out with circus animals. I don't think I'm much better. Tell me there are showers somewhere nearby?"

"Changing room is nearest. You ready for Gabriel and Delphine tomorrow? That's before I even get into the whole Irina deal. I'm not too proud to admit that lady terrifies me."

"I don't have a choice," Anna replies, and it's not as mournful as it might be. Something in the way Victoria's never happy and never quite lets up makes Anna feel like she can dance right through the floorboards if she has to. "If I'm going to do...all that stuff, I have to be perfect."

"Well, you're already my favorite Juliet. Although I'm more of a Mercutio man myself."

"Of course you are. Let's get out of here before she changes her mind and makes you pick me up again."

ⵔⵔ

Victoria pauses just inside the studio door, surveying the condition of her dancers.

Irina is tucked into a corner, legs extended and an ice pack on her ankle as she prepares a new pair of shoes with the usual brisk determination. She scores the sole and trims the leather with a box cutter, strokes firm and decisive. Now and then, the former prima glances toward the center of the room where Delphine and Gabriel are still stretching at the portable barre, their movements slower and deliberate now, more maintenance than working up a sweat.

Which leaves Teresa hesitating at the piano, watching Ethan and Anna with a frown. Not that either of them is aware of being watched. The boy is sneaking glances at Gabriel, which Victoria can hardly blame him for. It would be like walking past Michelangelo's David every day and not turning his head. It seems Mr. Bishop is aware of the attention, as he hikes his shirt for a moment, flapping the cotton to get some cool air against his rippling abs. That's enough to make Ethan falter in the hamstring stretch he's been pretending to do.

The intrinsic drama of the familiar company members makes Victoria forget Anna for a moment, so it's a jolt when Victoria's gaze finally settles on her. Flushed in the cheeks, Anna is grinning to herself about something as she tightens the knot in her hair and pulls a pale peach cardigan on over cooling deltoids and biceps. Victoria frowns at how it matches the leg warmers today—too cutesy by far. The leotard and tights are a shade of brown Kelly would know better than to provide, so Anna is persisting with her own wardrobe.

Victoria claps her hands, making everyone but Irina jump.

"Teresa, you'll stay for this," Victoria says. "There's too much to get through, and I need a musician, not a jukebox."

"I already cleared my day," Teresa says with a happy sigh, throwing herself back down on the piano stool and leafing through her folder. "Anything you need, Victoria."

The ass-kissing is barely worth an eye roll by now, but Victoria musters a valiant effort all the same.

Anna has snapped to attention, beaming at Victoria like she's glad to see her. It's surely a sign that she wasn't worked hard enough yesterday.

"Irina, you'll start us off." Victoria gestures to the center of the room for Irina to take position.

Gabriel rolls the barre away. He and Delphine take up spots by Ethan and Anna to watch.

"Delphine, Gabriel, I'm assuming I don't have to reinvent the wheel here?"

They nod in unison, confident in their own prowess. Victoria can take at least some of the credit for that.

"Then Anya. Solo first, then we'll take another pass at the kids from Verona. You'll try very hard not to ruin my entire season. Won't you?"

Every head in the room turns to Anna. This time she doesn't wilt. She looks like she might, her gaze darting toward her feet, but she holds her head up and squares her shoulders. With a subtle splash of showmanship Victoria wasn't expecting, Anna places her hands perfectly as they rehearsed yesterday, her wrists positioned as though Victoria's hands were still holding them in place.

"Yes, Victoria," she answers, solemn in her sincerity.

"Fine." Victoria dismisses the earnestness. "Irina, I don't recall the *Bluebird* taking place horizontal on the floor. It might be *Sleeping Beauty*, but Florine is awake at least."

The Russian curse that comes Victoria's way is as familiar as it is impenetrable.

"You really want to throw me in Rick's face first?" Irina demands, standing straight and still in closed fourth.

"All the better to forget how you piss him off by the end. Investors expect my biggest names, darling. They don't care what an ass Rick was to you when you first took over from me. Whenever you remember how to hit the keys and make noise, Teresa…"

The twittering, trilled notes begin, and Irina moves as though compelled by some unseen magnet. Her timing has always been uncanny, and she hums the notes under her breath, hiding the startling soprano only a select few ever get to hear. Not many know that before the Bolshoi pulled Irina into their ranks, Mariinsky courted her for both ballet and opera alike. Victoria can't help wondering what it might have been like to have the choice, to have a path available without the pain Irina has to shoulder now.

Delphine and Gabriel pay polite attention, but Anna and Ethan are rapt as Irina moves her arms with trademark grace and rattles through the *piqués* on the downbeat, turning what could be the steps of a flamingo into art with scarcely any effort. The *échappés* and *passés* are as effortless as breathing, and Victoria remembers why she could almost have danced this one in her sleep.

"Less fluttering!" Victoria snaps as Irina comes out of the pirouette with her hand motions loose. "You're in love with the bird, but still human."

"Yes, tell me the story some more," Irina says with a snort as she comes to the end. "You're always trying to find yourselves in the narrative. The dance tells the story for you, if you let it."

Anna snorts, and Victoria shoots a glare over her shoulder to silence it.

"From the beginning," she announces, turning to warn Delphine and Gabriel. "Your *Rubies* had better not be this rusty."

It's not as though Anna is stupid. She knows dancing third after Irina's variation and then the well-oiled smoothness of Delphine and Gabriel is supposed to make her nervous. If she can't handle it here, in a quiet studio with a handful of the people supposed to be her peers, then how can she cope with a paying audience? So it isn't allowed to matter that she feels queasy, and the floor beneath her feet no longer feels quite solid enough. She is *not* messing this up on her first real shot.

Ethan smiles at her, probably relieved his head isn't on the chopping block yet. The notes for Kitri's big moment start to play, and Anna gives one more nervous glance at her colleagues. Nobody is feigning disinterest this time; they're watching her like hawks.

But the music does everything Anna needs. Her cue comes toward her, a gust of wind at her back that pushes her into motion exactly as directed. Every lift onto her toes is aided by the lilt and sway of the melody, and if it's just a fraction faster than it ought to be, well, Anna can handle that, too.

She steps, she spins, she defies gravity at certain moments. It's like one of those fairy tales she loved as a child—a lucky princess with enchanted feet, or magical slippers. There's no need to count, or chant anything like a mantra. Victoria catches her eye as Anna moves toward her, and that might even be the hint of a smile on her face.

That's all it takes to make her stumble. The easiest of distractions, not fixing her spot on the wall before a fast turn, and Anna lands too heavy, missing a handful of steps while she rights herself. There's no chance to pick back up. A clap of Victoria's hands and the music comes to a halt.

"Again!" she shouts across the studio at Anna. The music picks up from the start, and Anna takes up her position. She'll get it this time. She just has to.

♾

"You." Irina grabs Anna when they're in the hallway, and for a moment Anna is absolutely terrified. Irina's curly hair has come loose from her bun, and with the exertion and the glassy sheen to her eyes, it's a lot like being grabbed by a madwoman.

"Yeah?"

"You can dance," Irina proclaims. "Vicki, maybe she's not so wrong about you."

"Thank you." Anna heaves in a sigh of relief. "Oh God, really? I have no idea how I'm actually doing, but it has to be perfect tomorrow and—"

"Apparently you can also talk." Irina sniffs, then raises a hand to her nose where a trickle of blood is starting to escape.

"Irina!" Victoria calls out as she approaches them. It's enough to make Irina look trapped, and Anna reacts before she can think, pulling off her favorite cardigan and pressing it to Irina's face as a makeshift compress.

"Oh my gosh, I'm so sorry!" Anna wails, summoning every bit of amateur dramatics she's ever participated in. "Irina, I just didn't see you and I was swinging my arm like an idiot."

"Yes," Irina agrees after a stunned moment. "Like an idiot."

"I hope it doesn't bruise," Anna pleads.

Victoria doesn't seem fooled, judging by the shrewd crinkling of her eyes, one that shifts when Irina turns to her with a questioning look.

"I have some great concealer if it does. I can get you some…"

"Have Kim ice it," Victoria says. "You probably need a shot of something anyway. And Anya? Be more careful. This is a ballet company, not a playground."

"Of course."

They both stand still until Victoria is down the hall and out of sight, whatever she wanted from Irina apparently forgotten.

"Thank you," Irina grunts, pulling the soft wool away from her nose. "I suppose now I owe you one, hmm?"

"No! That's not why…I just thought you needed some first aid. No biggie."

"Sure," Irina says with a slow grin. "Hidden depths, *malenkaya*. You want to come meet the famous Kim? You'll be bringing an ache or a pain to her soon enough."

"I could meet Kim," Anna agrees, nodding even though she wants nothing more than to crawl home and sleep. "What's a…malinky?"

"Little one," Irina explains. "Not in height, perhaps. But in status. Here." She hands back the cardigan, blood soaked into one sleeve. "Tomorrow, you'll come to my place, pick out something to replace it."

"Oh, that's not necessary. Victoria gave me a bunch of things and I—"

"I'll get you ready. You have to look the part too."

"Then…okay. If you think that will help?"

"Yes," Irina replies, leading the way down to the physical therapy department.

CHAPTER 10

She has a bag in her locker with the silver leotard and most expensive-looking matching tights from Kelly's selection. There's the basic hair-and-makeup stuff she's been doing since she got past glitter spray, but Anna knows she doesn't know how to do anything special with that by herself. Passable is the best she can hope for. Part of her still can't believe Irina offered help so freely yesterday, even though they'd also had a perfectly nice late afternoon talking about stretches and injury prevention with Kim in the PT suite.

There's a part of Anna that's still waiting for the pranks and backstabbing. Every other company seems rife with it, and Metropolitan has its own urban legends of dropped scenery and *accidental* shoves down staircases, predating Victoria and Irina.

Can Anna really trust that because a few people have been nice in her first week that they won't turn on her? That every step she takes out in front, into the warm glow of attention, doesn't make her a target for jealousy and bitterness?

She rests her forehead against her locker door, skin damp and hair still wet from the brisk, cool shower. Something gnaws at her, something like a gut feeling telling her Victoria wouldn't stand for that crap. Not just because Delphine threw around some grudging credit, but because Victoria demands the same excellence in behavior that she does at the barre. It's not a feeling of safety, exactly, but Anna thinks it might be something like trust.

"*Malenkaya!*" Irina strides into the room. "Unless you wish to dance in your towel, you should get moving."

"So we're still on?" Anna grabs for her clean pair of jeans and a sweater to guard against the chill that's creeping into the New York air today. "I just wanted to check—"

"Still on," Irina confirms. "You have a hat? You can dry your hair at my place."

"Sure." Anna pulls her favorite beanie from her bag and throws it on the pile. "I brought some options for tonight too. I'll be dressed in two minutes, I swear."

"Meet me in the lobby. It's not so far."

Anna yanks clean underwear up her legs and hurries to put on the rest of her clothes.

∽◌◌◌∾

"You're late," Victoria says with a huff, opening the door to Kim and her giant bag of torture devices. "Does that mean I get out of the physically impossible parts this week?"

"I'm late because you don't want anyone knowing I come here on a Saturday," Kim reminds her. "I had to hide out in that overpriced bakery while three people who know us both stopped hanging around in the street."

"And they say nobody knows anyone in New York," Victoria mocks, pulling the arms of her gray sweater down over her hands. She leads her way to the home studio, where the mat is out and the rollers are lined up.

Kim tenses some bands around her wrists that are clearly going to mean lots of stretching in Victoria's near future.

"I saw you in heels twice this week," Kim says. "And you're out of alignment again. Did you go and get your refill?"

"Of course I did," Victoria snaps. "Or did you think I switched to meditation?"

Kim holds her hands up in surrender. "I was just asking."

"I know." Victoria sighs. "How's the rest of the company? Anything else I need to be aware of?"

"They won't trust me if I tattle on every ache and pain. You probably get more honesty out of Irina than I do. Morgan's hip is about back to full strength, so I'll speak to David about her program. Otherwise they just want painkillers and plenty of massages. It's early in the season."

Unable to divert Kim any further, Victoria starts her stretches, muscles flexing beneath the running tights and sports bra.

"Nervous?" Kim grabs Victoria's heel, making her stretch farther.

The pain spikes, and Victoria hisses through her teeth. Kim waits. With a grunt, Victoria continues the exercises.

"I haven't been nervous in about thirty years," Victoria scoffs. "My dancers don't let me down. The new girl will be no exception."

"For all your bitching, this is looking pretty good," Kim informs her, nonchalant as ever. "Better than it's been in a while, despite your suicidal attachment to four-inch heels."

"Yes, I'm just one good stretch away from reviving *Swan Lake*." Victoria sighs

Kim starts up with her alternatives-to-ballet diatribe again, and that's the point Victoria decides she's had enough.

"I'll finish the repetitions," she says, as terse as she's ever been. "You can go."

Kim doesn't move, more than accustomed to this little routine. Like a knotted muscle she can't resist dragging her knuckles over, Kim can't help pushing at Victoria's carried damage. The slightest hint of weakness or uncertainty tonight, and Rick will steamroll her in front of their exclusive audience.

"D'you need me in tonight?" Kim asks from the doorway, packed up again in a minute flat. Victoria ignores her, stretching her arms and completing the rest of her workout in sullen silence. Eventually Kim takes the hint and lets herself out of the apartment, leaving Victoria to continue to push herself far past the point of her current tolerance.

She's in frustrated tears when she hits the shower, the icy blast a necessary shock to the system. She fights the impulse to step away from the chilled torrent that rains down on her, passing through the shivers into a kind of shock. Victoria takes gasping breaths until finally the pain starts to be drowned out. The elusive numbness turns the sound down on everything but her own heartbeat and the spray of the water.

The apartment is quiet when she steps out of the bathroom, wrapped in a towel and still shivering. The sky is starting to darken, fall evenings closing in by the day. She makes her way to the dressing room off her bedroom. Tonight, she has to be the not-so-faded jewel, dazzling, and appropriately severe. Aside from Rick, she can handle these clowns. Charming investors was as much a part of her education and career as the pirouettes.

Hesitating over the familiar rows of black, Victoria sighs and reaches instead for the splashes of color at the end of the rail. Getting her way will be worth making the exception.

♈

"Jesus!" Anna gasps when Irina opens the door. The building is some kind of converted warehouse, and the ceilings put to shame some of the theaters she's danced in. "If you tell me this is rent-controlled, I might hate you."

"It's mine," Irina says with pride. "Bought to celebrate the end of my first season in New York. Who could afford it now? It's not so perfect: the pipes, the crazy neighbors. But it's home."

"I'm moving into the company accommodation soon. This light is amazing. How do you ever leave the house?"

"Masochism? And because I don't want Victoria to come here and hunt me down."

"She does that?"

"Would you be surprised?"

Anna shakes her head and steps farther into the huge living room at Irina's gesture. The brick walls are a dark gray that somehow doesn't absorb the light. Stripped pale floors and lots of glass make it feel like a shabby-chic extension of the Metropolitan Center, and Anna can't help wondering if that's what made Irina love it: a home away from home, but a space still worthy of the spotlight.

"You came from Russia?" Anna asks, uneasy in silence. "The Bolshoi must have been something else. I saw the tour, a few years back, but—"

"These things are more romantic from a few thousand miles away." Irina crosses to the open-plan kitchen, bereft of any sign of food save for a lopsided bowl of oranges, and retrieves a bottle of vodka from the freezer. "Dutch courage," she tells Anna, pouring the cold liquid into heavy tumblers and not the shot glasses Anna would have expected. "Or Ukrainian, to be more accurate. Just like me."

Anna takes the glass and bites back a surprised remark at the shared heritage with her mother. "All your biographies say Russian. I didn't know."

"It was all confusing for a while. I was lazy about correcting people. At first I didn't speak enough of the language, then later I didn't care what they knew about me or not. It's much easier that way. You," she adds, downing her drink, "will have to learn to be good with the press and the critics. The Russian ballerina can be an ice queen. The girl who looks like the sun has to be nice."

"No one will want to talk to me." Anna scrunches up her face. She sips the vodka and lets it burn her throat. It's not unpleasant. The thought of a defensive drink or two is more appealing as the minutes march toward her moment of truth. "I'm sure they'll still only care about Delphine, or try to get Victoria to give an interview. Or you, of course."

Irina refills her glass and splashes more into Anna's as they stand at the kitchen counter.

"Come," she announces. "Nobody ever had a good makeover in a kitchen. And remember to pick something you'll keep. I owe you for your ugly little woolen thing."

"Hey!" Anna makes a weak protest. She's had that cardigan since middle school. "At least it was absorbent. We can't all look like models."

"You should try it some time." Irina leads the way toward a bedroom that's a bit less dramatic in scale but fastidiously tidied. The dressing table is arranged at perfect angles, and every splash of color is coordinated. The bed is made up like a hotel, just asking to be bounced on.

"I'm kind of scared to touch anything," Anna admits, taking in the huge canvas that hangs above the bed. Something abstract, but Anna can pick out the lines of *port de bras*, or at least she thinks she can. It's possible that half a lifetime of obsessing just makes her find it everywhere.

"Touch, touch," Irina commands, rifling through a stack of sweaters folded so neatly that even the fussiest employee at the Gap couldn't find a fault. "I don't have many pale colors, though. Since I'm not twelve."

"Point taken." Anna takes a sweater Irina tosses on the bed. In charcoal gray, it's the softest thing Anna has ever touched. She presses it to her face and sighs contentedly.

"That was easy." Irina's tinkling little laugh takes them both by surprise. "Now what did you bring to dance in? Lay out options, I'll find you something better, and then I'm going to introduce you to eyeliner."

"I wear eyeliner!" Anna tips out her leotards and folds the sweater back into a sloppy square. "Sometimes. Liquid is hard, okay?"

Irina reappears with what looks like a suitcase. It opens to reveal stacks of cosmetics and hair clips. Anna can't even name half of the brushes or colors.

"So how is it?" Irina asks, musing over Anna's clothing choices.

"How's what?" Anna replies.

"Being ridden by Victoria," Irina answers, impatience at the edge of her tone. "She's always given me a certain…respect in the past few years. I think she must be a good teacher when you're still new."

"Well, she demands the best." Anna's happy to be on safe ground again. Victoria has been the whirlwind that swallowed her week, filling even the minutes when Anna's free of the studio, dominating every conversation and almost every thought. "Clearly I have a lot to learn, but this is why I'm here. To work with her."

"*For* her," Irina corrects, but she's teasing. "Wear the black," she decides. "Add red for Kitri, and something silver for Juliet. Your shoes are up to it?"

"Maltese Cross," Anna answers, feeling like she finally gets to whisper the shibboleth, to be granted access to this secret society of every woman she's worshipped or admired. "I heard you used to like them."

Irina shrugs, returning to her wardrobe to select something for herself. "Royal blue." She plucks the leotard from a large selection. "If I must be Florine, I'll look the part."

"What about this?" Anna picks out a thin gold belt from beside the leotards, pushing into the space next to Irina. "You know, for the suggestion of royalty? You know what? Never mind, that's a dumb idea and…"

Snatching it from her hand, Irina considers it. "Good."

"You don't have to—"

"Have you developed the little crush yet?" Irina changes tack at a dizzying rate, and yet again Anna feels like she's barely keeping up. "It's funny to watch the new ones every year."

"A crush? Who even has time for that? I barely remember how to get to bed every night."

"Gabriel?" Irina tries. "I suppose you know you're not the type for Ethan?"

"I should get dressed." Anna scoops up the black leotard. "Is there a bathroom, maybe?" Changing in the locker rooms is one thing, but in Irina's home she feels self-conscious.

"You're not one of my groupies." Irina considers the idea, as though Anna hadn't spoken. "And Victoria wouldn't work with you if you were stupid enough to get involved with Westin. That leaves Delphine of course, but somehow I think you might be more interested in the Queen herself, hmm?"

"That's…ridiculous!"

"Happens every year." Irina gestures to the door in the corner. "Why do you think her ego is the size of Russia? Bathroom is here, for your sudden shyness."

"Okay, but can we just be clear that I'm not—"

"She would chew you up and spit you out anyway. Not that Victoria is likely to be interested. Still, you never know with that one. Unpredictable."

Anna sighs in exasperation. It's not like Irina is even listening to her anyway.

CXOO

Anna has to admit Irina knows what she's doing. Glancing in the studio mirror in what now counts as "backstage," Anna concedes she looks more glamorous than she ever has. Her hair is perfectly tamed, and the shading of her face is a careful mask of precision that looks as natural as her own skin. Even the blood red tutu Irina found in Wardrobe is sitting perfectly, as though tailored just for Anna's waist.

They're early, and Anna still has her shoes to put on, but she can't sit for long enough. Left alone behind the black curtains, she paces, unsure of whether she deserves to be here, wondering if tonight is when this bubble of a dream finally bursts.

Her interruption comes from Victoria herself.

It may be the way the light hits, or seeing Victoria in anything other than black for the first time, but Anna is struck dumb at first sight.

The jade green dress is sculpted to Victoria's body, a tailor's dream in sharp lines and gentle folds of fabric at every strategic hint of a curve. The split on one side is daring, enough to make Anna's breath hitch. The low neckline, the absence of straps, and the gentle brush of Victoria's hair at her shoulders completes the vision.

"There you are," Victoria mutters, fussing with the gold necklace that rests at the base of her throat. "What? Why are you staring?"

"Your…hair," Anna settles on. "I haven't seen your hair down before." It has the benefit of being true, save for a few photoshoots lost in a scrapbook, years before.

Victoria rolls her eyes. Apparently something that inane isn't worth one of her pointed remarks.

"Rick wants to see you beforehand." She gestures for Anna to follow. "Try not to talk too much."

"Um, sure? Now?"

"Only if you want to dance with this company. Yes, now." Victoria actually snaps her fingers in front of Anna's face to get her moving quicker.

Just as Anna gets one foot in front of the other, Victoria treats her to another one of those scouring looks that makes every skin cell feel exposed. Anna hesitates, awaiting the inevitable judgment.

"I'll say this for you: you scrub up well."

"I do?" Anna seizes on the compliment, and her cheeks warm under the makeup.

"Yes, but this is ballet, not a beauty pageant. So get the introductions over with and get back to warming up. Do *not* embarrass me."

"Victoria?" Anna has to say it now. "You look, um, amazing. I mean, you probably know. But I wanted to say it."

For a shimmering second, Anna thinks that might be a smile about to break out, but Victoria purses her lips instead.

"If you're quite finished…"

"Right." Anna sighs. "Go be charming. Got it."

CHAPTER 11

"Well, well." Rick greets them with his Hollywood smile, flute of champagne already in hand, and a blonde younger than Anna hanging off his other arm. "If it isn't my newest discovery."

"Hello again, Mr. Westin."

Anna doesn't blush when the attention of everyone in the small throng turns to her. She's been on stage and been stared at like a curiosity before. What does startle her, and make her cheeks turn pink beneath the flawless base Irina applied for her, is how Rick's proprietorial greeting provokes a reaction in Victoria.

One moment Anna is simply standing beside her new mentor; the next Victoria has a death grip on Anna's elbow, steering her a full step closer to her.

"Well, you did send her to me." Victoria's voice is breezy in a way Anna doesn't recognize. "But you sent me a member of the corps, Richard. I'm going to show you a star."

Anna's stomach sinks at the new ratchet of pressure added to the evening.

"Big talk, Victoria," Rick starts to fire back, when he's interrupted by an older gentleman who can apparently not contain his enthusiasm a moment longer.

"My late wife and I saw you at your debut in London," he gushes.

He grasps Victoria's offered hand in both of his, but shakes it delicately, as though she might be made of china. This does nothing to loosen the grip of Victoria's other hand; in fact she curls a third finger around the base of Anna's bicep, reminding her not to stray even an inch.

"Iris always told anyone who would listen that you changed her life that night, Ms. Ford," he continues.

"Please," Victoria says kindly, "we're all friends here tonight. You call me Victoria. Did you visit the ballet together often, Mr. Jebsen?"

"Now Victoria, that also means you call me Paul. And yes, every show of the season, at least once. And the pilgrimages to London and Paris twice a year. It was a great honor to give her that happiness, but her true highlight was always seeing you. You were always her favorite. We were there, in fact, on your—"

Rick is the one to interrupt that departure into dangerous waters, and Anna didn't expect that much empathy from him. As he diverts Mr. Jebsen, scandalized that he hasn't been given a drink yet, all Anna can focus on is the dissipating tension from Victoria at her side. Her grip had tightened almost enough to bruise, but even when she relaxes, Victoria doesn't let go.

There's a moment, maybe half a moment, where Anna has the kamikaze impulse to open her mouth and try to say something comforting. Her self-preservation kicks in not a moment too soon, and she smiles brightly at the other guests instead.

Victoria collects herself quickly and steers them back behind the curtains. When Victoria relinquishes her grip, Anna tries not to mourn the loss of contact.

"Not terrible," she proclaims, casting her eye over the now-arrived Delphine and Gabriel.

Victoria immediately turns her attention to Gabriel, directing him out to greet the patrons, holding Delphine back a moment with some further instruction before sending her to do the same.

"Oh my God," Anna sighs, hiding behind the clothes rack with Ethan. "Is it always like this?"

"How would I know?"

Victoria peers over the rehearsal piano at them. "Where is my pianist, Ethan?"

"I'm here," Teresa announces, appearing from behind the black curtain. "I was trying to warm up my baby out there when they all came waltzing in."

Anna assumes Teresa means the stunning grand piano out in the studio, wheeled in from somewhere to set the tone for the evening. No rehearsal uprights for the chosen guests.

"I was waiting in your office before that?"

Something in the questioning tilt of Teresa's voice makes Victoria flinch, and Anna catches it. There's certainly something being implied there, some kind of standing arrangement. Anna looks at Victoria, stunning in green and gold, short blonde curls catching the light, and there's definitely a pang of something like...*no*.

Not happening. Irina isn't right about everything just because she says it with an accent and a wry expression. Anna excuses herself to check her phone, just in time to see Jess's text.

I'm here.

Anna darts right out the back of the studio, opening the fire escape door and calling down to her sister. Jess takes the steps two at a time, even in heels. It's kind of an honor that she's fished out one of her two dresses for the occasion, coupling the black cocktail dress with a blazer stolen from Anna's piles of clothes.

"I'm so glad you came." Anna greets her with a hug, ushering her back toward the studio. "You don't have to kiss up to anyone for me, though. I already did the rounds with Victoria. I can introduce you to Rick, if you want—"

"It's a wonder I don't trip with how you just love dropping those names," Jess says, teasing. "Just point me to the bar and a canapé, and I'll do the rest. You want to go for drinks after?"

"Sure. I mean, if I don't have to do anything here."

"Knock 'em dead," Jess says, with a soft punch to Anna's arm before they reach the doors of the studio. "I'll try not to embarrass you."

"You could never embarrass me." Anna wants to steal one last steadying hug, but Victoria is on the prowl again, heading Anna's way from backstage. She nudges Jess toward the drinks and seats, and ducks back within the curtains where Victoria catches up to her.

"Kelly would have handled guests for you," Victoria says, looking past Anna to see what Jess is doing. "The infamous sister who said you were wrong?"

"That's not… I mean, she wasn't trying to ruin it for me." Anna frowns as Richard Westin approaches her sister. "She supports me. It's okay that she came tonight? I just realized nobody else invited anyone. Oh God, was that wrong?"

"It's fine." Victoria is dismissive again, distracted. "Are you sure you're warmed up enough?"

"I'll do a few more stretches while Irina goes on. You know, I haven't seen her since we got here."

If she's not mistaken, there's a flash of panic on the face of the unflappable Victoria Ford.

"Leave her to me. Go see if your Romeo is ready."

"Okay."

The soft sound of piano music begins beyond the drapes. Teresa is in place, and the night is officially beginning. The surge of nerves, that sick feeling in her stomach, is offset by knowing Jess is out there watching. Anna has never had a disaster in all the times she's danced for her family, and tonight cannot be an exception.

✲✲✲

Victoria sends Kelly and a server off in search of Irina, but just as Rick calls the small audience to some kind of order, Irina appears. At least she looks the part in blue and gold, her hair tamed and her makeup less dramatic than usual, even if she looks a little clammy under it.

"Ready?" Victoria asks. She's always been decent at public speaking, but small talk and chatter just seem like so much noise when a dancer's body can tell a much more compelling story.

Irina snorts, her derision plain.

Victoria eyes her for a moment, wary of the shift in mood. God knows what it's taking to get Irina through this, and it's affecting her demeanor more sharply by the week.

"Some of us push through the pain, hmm?"

It's nowhere near the worst that Irina has leveled at Victoria, but in that moment her wounded rage ignites in her chest. Her hand actually twitches with the impulse to strike, like she's back in school and only a swift yank of someone else's bun will serve as an outlet for her anger.

"Make sure you do," Victoria spits back at her, and steps out to officially begin the evening.

Rick shuts up at last, and Victoria seizes on her cue. "Ladies and gentlemen," she begins, mentally biting back *children* when her gaze lands on Rick's date. It's barely an audience at all, but she feels their attention wash over her like a wave.

Victoria stares them down with a fake smile, not missing how Anna's sister is assessing her. "Ahead of a very exciting season at Metropolitan Ballet, Richard and I wanted to treat you to a special preview. A world exclusive, in fact."

A murmur goes through the room, and Rick preens.

"We begin tonight with a reminder of Metropolitan's greatest strengths. We may not be an old company, comparatively, but our pedigree has always been spectacular. When I retired, we were fortunate to recruit one of Russia's most exciting performers, and though you won't be able to tell…" Victoria can't resist one cheap shot. "Irina has now been dancing for us longer than she was with the Bolshoi."

Polite applause rings out.

"So please, sit back and enjoy something of a retrospective." Victoria winces inwardly at how corporate it all sounds. "You'll get to see Delphine Wade and Gabriel Bishop, of course. Our brightest stars insisted on dancing for you tonight. But most importantly, tonight we look to the future. Pay close attention, because tonight is an *I was there when…* moment you'll all be dining out on for years to come."

Victoria retreats to more enthusiastic applause, cuing Teresa with a nod.

The silence is momentary at best, but Victoria swears her heart doesn't beat until the notes of Irina's entrance fill the air. The music is loud enough to cover the noise of pointe shoes for the audience, but Victoria retreats into in the black drapes and hears every tap and scrape of satin against the floor.

It's less than two minutes, as most of the great solos are, but Victoria has gathered her outer steel by the time Irina makes it back from the thunder of applause that belies how fewer than twenty people populate the audience. The minute Irina passes out of public sight, she's limping.

Anna is distracted from where she stands, ready with Ethan, pulling away from him to ask after Irina, but Anna is waved away by Irina who sinks onto a waiting chair.

"Are you okay?" Anna asks, but Victoria pulls her away with a hiss.

"You're on," Victoria reminds Anna. "Or did you expect Teresa to vamp with the entire score until you're done playing nurse?"

"But—"

"Go!" Victoria snaps, and Ethan has the sense to lead her away. With one last glance back at Irina, Anna disappears beyond the curtains. Victoria could swear the girl actually looks angry.

"What do you need?" Victoria demands.

"My bag." Irina nods toward it. "But go watch. You're useless until you do."

"Nonsense." Victoria tries to dismiss her words, but she's still nursing a grudge and it really is too tempting to see Anna dance for an audience.

Ethan's introductory solo is almost over, and Victoria skirts back toward the doors where she can watch from the side. In the wings, technically. It's where a good teacher should be when a star pupil is performing. There's a momentary doubt before Anna comes into Victoria's line of vision. What if Anna is no better than every other girl in the company? What if she wilts under the attention that comes too soon?

The timing turns out to be perfect, because Victoria is in position the very moment Anna starts to move. It's not a complex *pas de deux*, but it looks impressive to the uninitiated. As Victoria holds her breath, Anna becomes Juliet in the first graceful throes.

Oh, the concentration on her face is a bit too pronounced, and her hair is already coming loose, but she's exactly what Victoria prepared her to be. Not bad for barely a week's work. The hushed awe from the crowd—even Rick is paying attention for once—suggests they're already starting to see it too.

Victoria was right.

Victoria *is* right.

All too soon Anna is taking her bow, Ethan having the good sense to take a step back and let her pull focus entirely. Victoria runs the tip of her tongue between her teeth in anticipation. This is what she's been waiting for, in four long years of running this company. This is the difference between a good season and a great one.

Anna's rushing her way back to the anonymity behind the curtain, and Victoria makes her way back to deliver the first verdict. She glances at Rick to see if the impact has been felt. Judging by his furrowed brow and the way he's tapping frantically at his phone, he finally sees what Victoria identified in one morning.

There's an intermission of sorts, despite the short length of the program. An excuse for Rick to ply the donors with more drink and gauge their interest level. Victoria sees her chance to retreat and regroup.

She might even spare a compliment for Anna.

Irina is flopped over the back of her chair when Anna skips backstage again, Ethan trailing behind her. She's high on the exuberant clapping, the satisfaction of every step landed, and every turn and lift finished securely. The last thing Anna saw before retreating was a double thumbs-up from Jess, the highest, nerdiest praise her sister can offer.

"You really okay?" Anna asks, but Irina waves her away.

Delphine shoots Irina an irritated look from where she's stretching with Gabriel. They'll be on just as soon as Richard Westin lets the investors sit down again.

"Did you get some—"

"It's fine, fine," Irina dismisses, groaning softly to herself. "Look out for Vicki."

"What?"

"She means I'm right behind you," Victoria supplies, clicking her tongue in impatience. "It wasn't exactly complicated."

"Victoria." Anna waits. She can't ask. She won't embarrass herself by asking.

"You managed not to fall on your face," Victoria bestows the faint praise as though it physically pains her.

She's rocking back on her heels as though she's been handed something heavy and breakable, bracing for whatever might come next. Honestly, Anna thinks she might float from how a handful of words has made her feel. "Though your acknowledgment of the audience is awkward to the point of rudeness."

"Not everybody takes fifteen curtain calls," Delphine interjects, because there might be a lot of things in this company, but privacy doesn't appear to be one of them. "If that's all she can find to criticize, Anna, then you must have danced it flawlessly."

Anna deflects. "You're on now?"

"As soon as Rick stops begging for cash," Gabriel answers, giving Anna one of his dazzling smiles. "So hopefully before midnight. You ready to Kitri out there?"

"We'll see," Victoria answers for her.

"Fuck this," Irina decides, pushing herself out of her seat and staggering back toward the stage. "I want a drink."

No one reacts at first, frozen by the suddenness of Irina's outburst. She's clearly taken something, as she's walking more steadily, but slurring slightly. Anna realizes she can't be unleashed on the investors in this state and steps between Irina and the curtain just in time, wrapping an arm around her waist and diverting her back to the chair.

"We'll get you a drink," she promises. "Better than the flat champagne out there, right?"

Anna knows fine well it isn't flat and if she had to pay for a bottle she'd be struggling to make rent that month, but it seems to appease Irina for a second. The crisis is almost averted until Irina tries to turn away from Anna, lashing out and accidentally backhanding her across the cheek. The crack of hand against skin is loud enough to make Delphine and Ethan gasp. Anna opens her mouth but no sound comes out, her intake of breath disrupted by the sudden sting of pain.

"Sorry," Irina mutters, snatching up her bag and departing for the locker room with an uneven gait. She doesn't look back, and everybody else waits for Anna's reaction.

"I'm fine!" She tentatively touches her cheek. It's hot already, and she has to click her teeth together to avoid an audible hiss of pain as she prods.

Rick's introduction of Gabriel and Delphine disrupts at the perfect moment, Teresa's keys ringing out their entrance music and sending them out on stage. Ethan takes the temperature of the room and heads out after Irina.

"Crisis averted," she tries, but it falls flat under Victoria's stony glare. "Sorry if I was manhandling her. I just didn't think when I got between her and the room full of important people."

"No," Victoria agrees, her voice tinged with acid. "You didn't think. That much is painfully clear."

"I was just trying—"

"I warned you about focus. Here we are trying to launch your damn career, and you're running around looking for wounded birds to keep in your shoebox and nurse back to health."

"Victoria, I'm sorry but—"

"Not another word," Victoria commands through gritted teeth. "Get some ice from the caterer in case that comes up bruised. I don't want Kitri looking like she just got out of the drunk tank."

With that, Victoria takes her leave, and Anna has little left to do except switch out Juliet's silver accessories for Kitri's blood red ones. "I'm fine by the way," Anna mutters to herself as she wriggles out of one tutu and into the other. "Thanks for asking."

She takes up position at the gap in the curtains, pressing her face close to see the athleticism and grace of Delphine and Gabriel in action. They dance together perfectly, and Anna feels a pang that she doesn't have such a great, unspoken trust with Ethan or anyone else yet. It hasn't been very long, she reminds herself. Still plenty of time to make new friends and develop the ones she already has.

The end of their *Rubies* segment is fast approaching, so Anna retrieves her water and takes a sip. Any minute now she'll hear her name. She'll have to dance her solo without Ethan or anyone else to deflect some of the spotlight. This is usually where Anna would want to throw up from sheer nerves, but with the first performance under her belt, there's a steely kind of calm.

Right now, she's going out there to dance for her promotion, and hopefully to impress her sister along the way. She blocks out concern about Irina and focuses on dragging her toe boxes back and forth across the well-scraped floor.

Anna Gale is ready. She just has to hope the audience is too.

CHAPTER 12

Victoria is watching this one from the audience. She's already assured of her choice, but it won't do to undermine Anna by ignoring her big moment. Irina's drama can wait.

Delphine and Gabriel bring the house down—predictably—and Rick is on his feet yet again to show off. He jokes about how he was Delphine's first leading man and she was his last leading lady, and Delphine manages to keep a rictus grin on her face throughout the whole speech.

Victoria reaches past the champagne at the improvised bar and pours herself a stiff double vodka with an extra slug for good measure. She brushes away the nagging second of guilt at having forgotten she'd set a *date*, as Teresa insists on calling it. The occasional stress release barely warrants that kind of label.

As Victoria sips at her drink, the sister ghosts from her seat in the back row of chairs and nods toward Victoria's glass.

"Jess Gale," she introduces herself. "No one said there would be a real drink available."

"Help yourself, Jessica." Victoria steps aside and waves to indicate the bottle.

Jess pours some into her empty champagne flute, unapologetic.

If she were the gambling type, Victoria would make a bet with herself on which tack the other woman will take. She suspects the word "*blunt*" will be a fair description.

"Anna's good," the other Gale begins—a respectable gambit. "She's always been good."

"Then I would think you'd be glad someone finally noticed." Victoria feels the defensive hackles rise. She doesn't insulate herself from questioning, but even at their most fractious, the divas of her company know that Victoria holds their livelihoods in her hands. "Instead of trying to tell her she's delusional."

"She told you I said that?" Jess raises her eyebrows before settling for another swig of her drink. "I don't mean to be rude—"

"And yet I suspect you'll manage it." Victoria rolls her eyes as Rick invites more applause. Jess doesn't join in. "Your sister will be given the chance her talent deserves. Enjoy your evening, Miss Gale."

"Wait!" Jess finishes her drink and sets it down. "I just look out for her. I always have. I've lived through her ballet obsession half my life, Ms. Ford. This is her dream, and it shouldn't be messed with because of some internal politics. Pick someone else for that."

"Oh, for God's…" Victoria sees that Rick has finally taken his seat again, clearing the stage area. "I'm not in the habit of promising anyone anything. But if it keeps Anna free of distraction, can I give you my word that she isn't in any kind of crossfire?"

"That depends." Jess doesn't relent, and Anna will be on in a moment, no doubt seeking out her sister in the audience. "What's your word worth?"

"Let me put it this way," Victoria says, running out of time and patience, "if Anna's out, then so am I. Enough?"

Jess nods, seeming not to recognize the value of the promise she's just been given.

The music strikes up, and Teresa's fingers make light work of the Spanish-infused trills. Victoria doesn't cede ground, but right before Anna appears, her sister slinks back to her seat, ready and waiting with a beaming smile.

There's barely time to heave a sigh of relief, let alone wonder why Victoria made that concession for basically *a nobody*.

Anna's on, and the season starts here.

ꝏꝏ

The minute Anna touches her toe to the floor, the decision is made: no holding back.

If she's going to dance this, right from the very depths of her soul as Victoria seems to demand, then she can't hide from anyone. That includes the ghost of her parents, of the flames that took them from her. Aside from her dreams, when she isn't too exhausted to dream, while she's dancing is when Anna's heart is most vulnerable.

And Kitri, with her flame red costume and music that seems to contain the crackle of a modest home burning to the ground, leaves Anna exposed. She heard everything Victoria said about joy, about overcoming in the end, but that isn't who Kitri is to Anna. She's the woman trapped by convention, almost married off to a man she doesn't love, and chased by a knight who mistakes her for someone else. Only by risking everything does Kitri get what she wants in the end. It's joy, but it's a form of vengeance, too, and Anna feels that energy thrumming in her.

Life isn't fair, she chants in her head as she launches into the first, feted Kitri jump, bending her back leg as high as she can when the first leap comes, almost brushing the back of her head. It draws gasps from the room. *But no one can make me live a life I don't want*, Anna continues, her footwork tight, controlled. She flicks her fan open with the lightest twist of her wrist and sweeps low, drawing early applause.

If this is the zone, she's in it.

The scant minutes pass in a blur, the faces watching her faded out. Anna steps and jumps and turns and it happens exactly as it should. Her sequence of pirouettes—she can almost see the toreadors who should flank her as she moves across the space— falters only for a split second on the second to last. She finishes *en pointe* and the applause seems shockingly loud from so few people.

Jess, of course, is the most effusive. Climbing on her chair, she whistles and leads shouts of "bravo" that the rest take up right away.

Anna beams, clasping her hands and trying to curtsy better than she did after her dance with Ethan, not sure what she was doing wrong. Only coming up from that does she see Victoria, unmoving. Her hands aren't raised in applause and she isn't making any noise at all. Instead she sips at a glass of clear liquid and sets it down, never taking her eyes off Anna.

It's impossible to tell what she's thinking, so Anna nods one more time and bolts.

Victoria watches the cluster form around Rick, and if this was ten years ago they'd be reaching for their checkbooks. Instead, it's become a contest of who can pledge the biggest wire transfer on Monday. He's in his element, and for a moment Victoria feels the old fondness for the boy who danced with her, who became the one partner in her life who's ever lasted. Even if it is more like guerrilla warfare these days, and they were a disaster in the brief romantic experiment offstage, he's still there.

He meets her eye over the crowd and gives a less-than-subtle "okay" sign.

Victoria nods toward the curtains, silently asking if she should bring Anna out for a round of handshakes and blushing at compliments, but Rick dismisses with the slightest frown. Of course. *Preserve the mystery.* If Rick understands anything, it's the mentality of rich jerks. He summons Victoria over instead, and she grits her teeth for the requisite schmoozing.

"Now, ladies and gents…" Rick has to make it splashy. "Let's have a round of applause for the woman responsible for tonight. I send her hamburger and she somehow gives me prime rib." Sharing the credit. He must be in a good mood.

Victoria holds her hands up against their adulation, but a little part of her starts to crave the clapping in the very second that it trickles to a halt.

"A word?" she asks, the better to get it over with.

Rick deflects an investor and steps aside with her.

"Now, Victoria, a little patience," he cautions, but she lacks the patience for kissing up tonight.

"You saw it." Victoria stands with her hands on her hips, defying him to argue with her on this. "That's in a week, Rick. Imagine what I can do with a full season."

"She's good, but we can't bet a season on someone so raw." He stays just north of scolding her. "I'm not saying she can't feature—pick a solo or two in something splashy—but you're putting the cart before the horse on this one. Scale it back."

Victoria's grin is fixed. She's used to having to compromise, to cajole others into seeing it her way. Rick isn't usually one of those others.

"She's ready," Victoria says.

Rick bares his teeth in response, just quickly enough that others might mistake it for a smile.

"Have the program back in order for the print run," he warns. "And next time someone brings up your retirement, how about you give a straight answer instead of letting me save your pride, hmm?"

"Rick—"

"Whatever, it doesn't matter. What does is that I can't protect you from a flop, Victoria. No matter how talented you used to be."

With that gut punch, he turns her with a practiced touch at her hip and unleashes his charm on the wealthy men trying to buy a little culture.

If Victoria keeps smiling, she can almost convince herself she doesn't feel sick.

By the time she escapes, Victoria is exhausted. She slips backstage and listens to Rick lead his group out—only the biggest donors are invited to drinks at his godforsaken club.

Delphine and Gabriel are long gone, experienced enough to know when they're not needed. Victoria knows how precious free time is, and she lets her dancers have what little there is. Just because she has no use for downtime doesn't mean everyone else is similarly addicted.

Irina hasn't returned, but Anna has changed, her hair in a loose ponytail. Her sister is nowhere in sight, and Victoria can't say that disappoints her.

"You waited." Victoria doesn't like stating the obvious, but she's a little off her game. "The sixth pirouette—"

"I know," Anna deflates, hanging her head in shame. "At the time it didn't feel like much, but then I replayed it over and over in my head. If you want me to go again now, I can tell Jess to go home without me."

"You…" Victoria shakes her head, as though she might have water in her ears. "You're saying you'll rehearse with me now, just to get it perfect?"

"Sure." Anna drops her bag. "I mean… Oh! You probably have plans."

"Your face," Victoria says, deflecting. "It's not bruising too badly." When did Anna get so close? The girl hasn't moved, Victoria realizes as she reaches out to touch the faint pink mark over Anna's cheekbone.

Anna tenses, so Victoria doesn't press down. She withdraws her hand more slowly than she should.

"It's fine," Anna insists.

"Well, you'd know by now if it was broken. And Anya?"

"Yes?"

"I'm not going to make you rehearse again now. Go, have a life while you still have an hour to spare."

"You're sure?"

"Am I ever anything but?"

"I've only known you a week…" Anna's grin is slow, impressed at her own daring.

Victoria shouldn't indulge it, but a hint of a smile won't kill her.

"So I didn't screw it up completely?"

"Predictably the men in suits are falling over themselves to throw money at my little experiment. I assured Rick I could polish you up even more. People like shiny." It's a sin of omission, at worst.

"Right. I should go check on Irina. She didn't look so good."

"What did I *just* tell you about other people's problems?"

"There's a way to be a person. You said I had free time, so it's up to me how I use it, right?"

"Fine," Victoria snaps. "Don't say you weren't warned."

Victoria waits for the quiet to settle again. The building exhales quietly, dispersing bodies into the neon and first cold snap of a New York fall. Victoria sits on an abandoned chair, knee twinging at a night spent on the forbidden high heels, and lets herself breathe all the way out.

∞∞∞

"Jess?" Anna gave only vague directions to the locker room, so she isn't sure her sister will have ended up in the right place. Victoria Ford can take her precious freaking ballet and shove it up her—

"There you are." Anna greets Jess from the door of the room, a little stunned that Jess is currently propping up five feet eight inches of floppy ballerina.

"I heard her lashing out, so I came in to calm her down," Jess says. "There was some crying and now I think she's sort of asleep...*on me*?"

Anna rushes across to help. "I know where she lives, it's not far."

"Is this what the new intake have to do? Usher the old-timers through their crises?" Jess asks. "Because babysitting actors is my job, but this shouldn't be yours."

"It's been intense" is all Anna will confess. "Let's just put her safely indoors and go get a drink, okay?"

"Victoria happy?" Jess asks, and it's just too nonchalant.

Anna can't even bring herself to ask. She gives a nod.

"You kicked so much ass tonight, little sis."

"I screwed up a pirouette." Anna groans as they leverage Irina through the doorway between them and start shuffling down the hall to the elevator. "Which at this stage in my career is like forgetting how to walk. I should kill myself, basically."

"And yet here you are, all limbs intact. So you can't have really screwed it up."

"I think it's officially on," Anna admits, pulling Irina's arm tighter over Anna's shoulder. The last thing anyone needs right now is Irina hitting the floor. "Do you think that means I'll really have to do...I don't know...press? Photos in the program, all that jazz?"

"Not jazz," Jess answers in her best *Anna, you idiot* voice. "Ball-et. Remember?"

"You're hilarious," Anna deadpans. "She's kinda heavy for someone so skinny."

"Sssh!" Irina half grunts from where she has her head on Jess's shoulder. "Calling me heavy, *malenkaya*."

"Well, I guess she knows who I am? Irina? If you're conscious, could you maybe help with the walking?"

She tries at least, as they exit out the side of the lobby and toward the impressive building that houses Irina's killer apartment.

Jess raises an eyebrow when she sees where they're heading.

"S'ry hit you," Irina mumbles.

Anna hopes her sister doesn't hear. Judging by the way Jess almost drops Irina right there, no such luck.

"Dancing accident!" Anna soothes her protective sibling. "I got too close at a dumb moment."

"Sure?" Jess asks.

Anna nods, and they continue steering Irina across the darkest side of the plaza, sticking to the shadows as much as possible.

⌒◌◌

Sundays have become Victoria's favorite day somewhere in the mix. Maybe it's the high of coming off a Saturday night performance that lingers in her bones, or maybe it's just the thrill of having gotten exactly what she wanted, again. Either way, she's in a far better mood.

It's a full class schedule today, but nothing that's on Anna's roster. The new photoshoot is arranged, subject to Anna agreeing to come in on her dark day, but working a Monday once in a blue moon isn't the last sacrifice Victoria will ask of her. Better that Anna get used to it now.

"Kelly?"

"Yes, all-knowing ruler?" Oh good, wiseass Kelly showed up to work today, in a cat sweater and ripped jeans no less.

"Did you get the company housing arranged for Anya yet? I have to drag her in tomorrow for a photoshoot, so something new and shiny to distract her would be great."

"I freed up that one-bed you used to—"

"Fine, fine," Victoria interrupts. "Keys?"

"Wait, you're going to take her?" Kelly can't hide her amazement.

"I'm cultivating a working relationship," Victoria explains, completely truthful in every word. "Don't act like I never do anything for my dancers."

"By all means, if you want to revisit old stomping grounds then…catch!" Kelly pulls a set of keys from one of her pockets and tosses them toward Victoria, where they almost fall short but skid across the desk in loud, faltering bounces.

"What time is she done with David?"

"Around two," Kelly answers, the human encyclopedia of the entire company's schedule. "Should I call your car for then?"

"Mmm." Victoria picks up the keys and shoves them in her purse. "Do that." She waves Kelly away.

CHAPTER 13

Anna takes her time in the shower. On the way in she'd dropped into a drugstore and picked up the most expensive conditioner they had. Probably not up to Victoria's standards, but a start at least.

She's humming their last bout of rehearsal music as she comes back into to the locker room. Distracted, it isn't until Anna reaches for her locker that she realizes she has company.

"Jesus!"

"The comparison has been made," Victoria drawls. "But he only walked on water, not *en pointe*. You take your time, don't you?"

"It's nicer than my sister's shower," Anna says, her heart pounding. "And well, conditioner takes longer than normal." She tugs at the loose tuck of her towel over her chest, willing it not to suddenly spring apart on her.

"Speaking of your living arrangements," Victoria says, from where she's sitting on the long bench that bisects the changing area, "when you're dressed, meet me out front. We have an appointment."

"But isn't Kelly—"

"Out front, Anya." Victoria stands in that fluid way that makes Anna think of black satin ribbons. "Unless you want to dance your debut season with backache from sleeping on a lumpy couch."

"Sure." The flush of a good session after Saturday's relative success is deserting her in favor of a wave of nerves. "Out front. I'll just get some clothes."

"Well, I'm not staying for the floor show," Victoria calls back as she heads for the door, but at least she sounds amused. "You know that I don't like to be kept waiting."

Anna grabs her jeans from her open locker and waves them at Victoria in acknowledgment. It's dorky, but Victoria leaves with a short, satisfied nod.

"What now?" Anna groans. She can't believe she thought that the actual dancing might be the most terrifying part of her new job.

Rushing as fast as she can, she towel-dries and braids her hair down her back before pulling dry clothes over slightly damp skin. It's not the most put together she's ever looked, but it looks way better than her usual efforts from her old wardrobe. The gray

T-shirt is almost a little too revealing with its dipping neckline, but Anna hopes her mother's necklace will divert some attention. Black jeans and her favorite sneakers are dressed up with a cute jacket from Victoria's haul. A bit of lip gloss and mascara, and Anna is as close as she'll get to ready.

∞∞

She's prompt, at least. Victoria barely has time to check her watch a second time before Anna comes barreling across the foyer, skipping down the broad steps with a gambol that would put mountain goats to shame.

Victoria nods toward the car, sunglasses firmly in place. Her driver is distracted, so Anna opens the door for her. That expectant grin should be irksome, but Victoria's never been one to look a gift horse with good manners in the mouth.

Anna slides in on the other side, having taken her time to walk around the car.

Perhaps the nerves set in at the thought of confined spaces; Victoria knows she has that effect on the hardiest souls.

"So when you said this was about my living arrangements…" Anna trails off, fixing her seat belt and scanning the traffic as the car pulls out.

"I have time, for once. And if I see the place for myself when you move in, it preempts any whining in two months because you don't like the drapes."

"If I don't like the drapes I'll just change them," Anna says. She's just that little bit more sure of herself.

Victoria pulls Anna's sunglasses off when Anna turns to look at her, a chance to inspect the aftermath of Irina's damage last night.

"You did bruise."

"Hardly at all," Anna lies, hand rising to cover the mark automatically. "I iced it as soon as we got home from Irina's, and again this morning."

"From Irina's?"

"Someone had to get her home."

A touch of reproach; that's daring.

"So where are we going?"

"Not far," is all Victoria feels like divulging. They could have walked, but the power balance feels more intact in a chauffeured car. "Why? Somewhere else to be?"

"I was just going to run through Kitri again." Anna settles back against the leather, shrugging. "That wobble on the second-to-last pirouette is still bugging me."

Victoria smirks. "You know you're not actually dancing *Don Quixote* this season, right?"

"Still," Anna sighs, leaning back against the headrest, almost relaxed.

Victoria studies her a moment in peripheral vision. There's a stillness, a solidity there. In a life punctuated by fragility and chaos, that slow-blinking, easy-smiling kindness isn't entirely unpleasant to be around. God, her shrink will have a field day if she starts talking like this out loud.

"How attached are you to your day off?" Victoria makes the effort to say it almost sweetly. "I know being dark on Monday is sacrosanct, but I have a photographer who owes me a favor and we need to shoot immediately if we're going to revamp the brochure."

"Like new headshots?" Anna asks, still looking out of the window. "I just got them done before the auditions, I'm good."

"Headshots?" Victoria scoffs. "Well, God knows we could do better than the Shirley Temple knockoffs with your résumé. No, the shoot is for the season program."

"But you're just putting my name in it!" Anna laughs around the words, seemingly more nervous than when called out in front of the entire company. "The program is for… It has… People will be so pissed!"

"How am I supposed to launch you as my principal if no one knows what you look like?" Victoria makes the reasonable point, but Anna is practically scrabbling at the leather seat, as though she can back away from the very idea and escape into the trunk of the car. "Being a principal is not just about dancing. There's a certain media presence, although we'll preserve the air of mystery around you for as long as possible. The visuals? Nonnegotiable."

"But I'm just… I mean, I saw Delphine's photos from spring and that was like *Vogue* or something. I…don't look like that, Victoria."

"Which is why Susan and her best people—who, despite constantly wearing cargo pants, know *everything* about fashion—will be on the case. It takes a village, Anya. When are you going to start trusting that I know what I'm doing here?"

"It's a lot of change," Anna says, finally settling down again just as the car rolls to a stop. The doorman is scurrying across to open the door.

"One thing at a time," Victoria tells her, and the way she says it might even be approaching kind. "Let's go see where you'll be sleeping off all my rehearsals."

⟅♡⟆

When Anna sees the doorman building that's her new home, she's expecting a tiny studio stashed away on a middle floor. If she's lucky, there'll be a closet and a microwave. It's not like she's ever needed much more.

Victoria falls into conversation with their doorman—Julio, Anna manages to catch—and instead of heading for the building's slightly ancient-looking elevator, they stay on the first floor and head to the back of the building.

Anna follows Victoria through the door that leads into a courtyard. Julio leaves them there, smiling at Victoria as he goes. It's not enough to distract Anna from taking in her surroundings. There's a tree in the center, a bench in front of it that she can already see herself tucked up on, flipping through a book with a steaming mug of coffee.

"Here." Victoria shoves a keychain toward her.

Anna puts her hand out to accept it. Silver ballet slippers, of course. There must be a whole batch of them. On it are three keys.

Victoria nods toward a door in the far corner of the courtyard.

"This is my apartment?" Anna strides over, caught up in the excitement now. There's a little panicked voice still drumming a beat about photoshoots and glossy programs, but that will have to wait. She fumbles with the keys, but recovers before Victoria's huff of impatience gets all the way out. One, two, three, and the heavy door, painted with more than one coat of black paint, swings inward.

The hallway is short and nondescript, but Anna is already in motion. It opens up into a living area that, even with sofas and bookcases, leaves enough space for stretches and yoga on the floor. The kitchen Anna barely glances at, but she does register the appliances and huge fridge/freezer. She'll be able to keep herself in smoothies and freeze her shoes to toughen them up too.

The bathroom is at least twice the size of the one in Jess's apartment, with a claw-foot tub that makes Anna's tight muscles practically sing. The shower in the corner has glass walls, and before Anna can form a protest, she realizes that for the first time in her life she won't be sharing the bathroom with anyone.

Victoria follows, uncharacteristically silent. It's only when Anna bounds over to the bedroom, coming to an abrupt halt in the doorway, that she even remembers Victoria is there.

Anna still manages to bump into her arm and Victoria grumbles, "A little warning."

"This is really for me?" Anna can't help asking. "I thought company housing meant roommates, or some kind of dorm."

"Would you like me to go and round up some corps members to sleep on the floor?" Victoria sounds almost puzzled. "If this is too lonely for you, I assume you have some ridiculous stuffed bear you've had since kindergarten or something."

Anna isn't expecting the twist in her chest. She's gotten so used to people knowing and stepping around the subject that it's hard to face it head-on.

"I don't, actually." If she sounds upset, so be it. She is. "Turns out teddies are just as flammable as everything else in my childhood home."

"Your home—"

"Burned down, yeah." Anna walks over to the sliding closet door, barely seeing the empty rack and shelves when she opens it. She blinks furiously, determined not to embarrass herself with tears now. "Don't worry, it was a long time ago. It doesn't affect how I dance."

She doesn't hear Victoria move.

"I disagree," Victoria murmurs, much closer than just a moment before. "But I don't disapprove. Whatever it is, it works for you."

"Great," Anna can't help but snap. Victoria doesn't know, Anna tells herself. She isn't being intentionally mean. "I guess it was all worth it, then."

"There's a lot I don't know about you." Victoria steps between Anna and the open closet door. "And I can't promise that will change. But I'd be a terrible boss if I didn't point out that this story of yours could lead to better press. Everyone loves a sob story."

Victoria has the decency to look disgusted even as she says it.

"I won't do it." Anna closes her eyes, gathering her resolve. A breath. A beat. She opens them again. "And I am so grateful for this opportunity, but I swear, Ms. Ford. If one word of it goes to some…reporter, then I'll be on the first flight back to Dubuque. I'll never dance again before I'll use their memory for some puff piece."

"You really think you mean that."

God, that's patronizing, but Anna stares Victoria down, tears pricking. If she holds Victoria's attention, maybe she won't notice the slip.

"You said 'their.'"

Of course she didn't miss it. Anna braces herself for something unkind about pulling herself together. Instead there's just the gentle touch of Victoria's hand on her forearm.

"Your parents?"

Anna nods, and the urge to bolt grows stronger by the second. There's a reason she doesn't tell people. At least Victoria looks uncomfortable for the first time since Anna met her; she might just be human after all.

"I thought we were just talking property damage. I didn't… No reporter will hear about it from me, okay? Now, will this little shack do?" Victoria waves at the space around them, offering the change of subject like a lifeline.

"Hardly a shack." Anna steps away and makes a show of sitting on the end of the bed. "I don't think I have enough stuff to fill it."

"You'll build it up," Victoria says, but she still looks squeamish discussing such personal things. "You're still young. This place doesn't need much. Some fresh flowers once a week, so it feels like you actually live here. That's how I did it."

"You lived here?"

"Briefly." Victoria's frown slips back into place, the momentary softening over Anna's tragic past erased as though by the flick of a wand. "There was a time when a place without stairs was a blessing. The elevator in my building is unreliable."

"When you were injured," Anna surmises. She holds her breath after putting it out there.

Victoria flinches.

Anna would feel guilty, but why the hell should she after *everyone loves a sob story*? "Julio remembers you from that long ago?"

"He was in the corps before that," Victoria says, putting her hands in the pockets of her fitted black pants. She misdirects Anna's clumsy jab with ease. "Blew out his Achilles after six months, never came back. We always try to keep people in-house. If they can face it. Are we done with all things domestic? I have a center to run."

"You didn't have to," Anna begins, but she's too tired to be petulant. "So…what time do I need to be in tomorrow?"

"Ten." Victoria walks slowly back out of the bedroom, with one last glance at the stripped bed and the empty nightstands. The hallway is well lit, and for a moment she looks like she's caught in a spotlight. "We'll meet in de Valois and see where they want to set up."

"I'll see if I can hit the salon on the way there."

"Susan will handle it," Victoria reminds her. "You have the keys."

"Victoria?" Anna doesn't know what comes over her. "I don't have anything in— obviously—but did you want to grab a coffee? I saw a place two doors down…"

"Like I said." Victoria draws herself back to her full height, remote again. "I have a center to run. Ten sharp, Anya."

As abruptly as she does everything else, Victoria takes off. Her footsteps barely echo despite the emptiness of the apartment. Anna almost wants to call after her, though she has no idea what to say.

Anna prods the mattress with the flat of her hand and considers her new bedroom. A place of her own. One so empty that she can't stand it a moment longer. She's going to grab some things to start making it home, and maybe Jess will come over for pizza later. Anna grabs her keys and follows Victoria's path back to the outside world.

◯◯◯

"Kelly said you were out earlier." Teresa slips through the door of Victoria's office in that way she has, furtive but drawing attention to the sheer discretion of it. It sets Victoria's teeth on edge, even as she wades through a stack of documents awaiting her signature. "Anything fun?"

"Not particularly," Victoria says, fighting back a sigh. "Did you need something?"

"I just wanted to check on your stress levels. Big night last night, and usually—"

"It's a new season. Things are going to be different. I need to focus."

"On her?"

Oh, the jealousy is uglier than Victoria expected. The briefest jolt to her ego isn't worth this contortion of Teresa's otherwise pretty face.

"People are already talking, you know. Think you're throwing it all away on some rube with a ponytail."

"People?" Victoria repeats. "Or person? Because I'm sure you remember my ground rules. I couldn't have been clearer."

"Oh, you're clear all right," Teresa says with a sneer. She fishes some music from the stack in her arms and slaps it down on Victoria's desk. "You wanted these. Or last week you did. You've probably changed your mind."

"At least be subtle." Victoria ignores the sheets even though she does still need them. "I can assume this won't affect our work together? This little tantrum?"

"Why would it?" Teresa retreats, casting a longing look back over her shoulder like she really believes she's Deborah Kerr in some doomed romance. "We're all professionals, right?"

"Right." Victoria pulls off her glasses. "It really is nothing personal."

"Huh." Teresa hesitates with her hand on the door. "See, right up until then it wasn't actually hurtful. Fuck you, Victoria."

"Out of your system?" Victoria asks when Teresa lingers.

The girl nods.

"Good. Go, scream into a pillow if you think it might help. We'll start fresh on Tuesday."

"Okay." With that, Teresa is gone.

Victoria sighs and leans back in her chair, the leather creaking under her shoulder blades. She can't afford these distractions. A reminder pings on her calendar, and Victoria puts her glasses back on just to glare at it. Therapy on Monday at nine thirty. Well, that one can go at least. Victoria fires off a message to Kelly to cancel it.

There's a night worth of work in front of her, but still she hesitates to dive in. She shakes her head to dislodge the image of Anna, forlorn in front of empty closets. The clumsiness of unearthing her parents' death still rankles. Even if it does explain Anna's air of quiet mystery. Well, it's something to channel into choreography. No reason Victoria should give it a second thought.

Which is exactly what she tells herself when it becomes a second thought, and a third and fourth. She should be sketching out sequences in Benesh notation, but much like a frustrated composer, the bars on her page remain frustratingly blank when they should be full of the symbols that denote the steps and direction.

For distraction, she flicks through Teresa's music. The tune comes to Victoria unbidden, the rich humming her father would soothe her to sleep with as a child. The words replay in Victoria's head: *their memory.*

Usually she can spot the tragic ones from a mile away. Anna is deceptive, not a word Victoria would have picked out for her at first. Those bright, sunny smiles don't give away anything of the pain she must be carrying. How heavy is the loss if the girl can still barely speak about it, other than in such an oblique way?

One perk of being the boss means Victoria rarely has to moderate what she says. She can claim that every mean comment is intended to be character building, something to motivate the right kinds of people. Even so, Victoria wishes she could take back calling it a sob story. If ever there had been a time to wait for all the facts, it was then. So maybe Anna will hate her a little, temper the hero worship. It can only help in making her great.

CHAPTER 14

Anna arrives a little after nine, practically sneaking along the corridor to the studio. Inside there's already contained chaos—sheets draped on the few surfaces and various bits of rigging being moved in front of the mirrors, only to be covered with even more white sheets.

It's Susan who spots her first.

"Come on, kid. Let's turn you into a glamazon."

"Is Victoria—"

"Still in her office, so enjoy the peace while it lasts. She's on a tear this morning, and there aren't enough bodies in today for us to use as a shield."

"This isn't a big deal, right?" Anna can't help the nervous giggle. "I mean, it looks like a big deal, but it's just a couple of shots to put in with a bunch of other ones, that's all."

"I sure as shit hope not," says a deeper voice from behind them. "Christ, Ramos. I hope you've got something planned for this one. I don't do 'wallflower' as a concept."

"Leave her alone, Michelle," Susan warns. "You're here on promise of good behavior, remember? And Anna is gorgeous, so don't start. She'll just be dramatically gorgeous when I'm done."

"Michelle Willis." Towering over Anna and Susan, she's clutching one camera, with another slung around her neck. With shocking white-blonde hair and an outfit that's more rips than it is denim and leather, she looks more suited for a punk band than a photo call. She sticks a hand out to Anna, who shakes it gingerly.

Some flashes go off as guys in tight jeans test the equipment; it's blinding for a few seconds.

"I'm your artist for the day. Or the poor schmuck who owes her career to some action shots of Victoria, whatever you prefer."

"From the *Times*?" Anna can't quite place her.

"I'm freelance," Michelle says with a grimace. "Everyone is these days. But it's funny you should mention my one-time employer..."

"Leave her alone, Willis." Victoria approaches, her words echoing Susan's earlier warning. "I told you, this exclusive is visual only. And we're paying you to do our brochures, not pad your portfolio."

"But isn't that just confirming that ballerinas have nothing to say?" Michelle says, tone teasing. "I could do your lame-ass brochures in my sleep, but I could do something way edgier for the *Weekend* supplements. You can even do all the talking if you want. It's been a while since the press got anything out of you but a prewritten release."

"That's still more than the vultures deserve."

Michelle and Victoria stare it out for a moment, before Michelle breaks the tension with a shrug. Her heavy leather jacket creaks as she moves off to join her crew.

"So…I should get changed?" Anna ventures, hoping Victoria's glare doesn't turn on her next. "What do I get to dress up in?"

"Right this way." Susan steers Anna toward the racks that dominate the corner of the studio where the piano sits. "You're gonna love my makeup guy."

∽◌◌◌∾

Victoria can't help prowling the floor of de Valois, kicking at trip hazards and rearranging badly hung sheets as she goes. She shouldn't have renamed this room for her favorite space in Covent Garden. The two studios have little in common beyond mirrors on the walls.

She rarely gets nostalgic for London, but the start of the season always reminds her of that formative spell at the Royal Ballet—the outsider American soloist who leveraged her years in London into being crowned principal before returning in triumph to San Francisco, then New York.

Of course all the initial art was shot before the end of last season, since the company wasn't expected to change significantly. Trust Rick to throw this talented new wrench in the works.

Just as she's about to bark at Ramos to move things along, the flurry of activity in the corner finally ceases and Anna is yanked out of the director's chair they've been surrounding like vultures. She's there in the black leotard and tutu that mark the settled aesthetic for the company's publicity this year. It's a significant upgrade from last year's virginal white that didn't catch the eye at all.

It shouldn't be impactful but, as Anna strides across the floor—still barefoot and in search of her pointe shoes—Victoria feels the difference on a gut level.

No bun in Anna's hair at Victoria's instruction, but the way it's been pulled back suggests someone's fingers have been raked through it, and it works in contrast to the innocence of Anna's expression. The black eyeliner might be too heavy on a less open face, but it draws attention to those sparkling blue eyes, so much so that even Victoria can't deny staring for a moment. A hint of gold at Anna's ears, a ring on her middle finger, and lips barely a shade or two above nude. She's a photographer's dream; even Michelle won't be able to find much to bitch about.

"Shoes," Victoria snaps as Anna looks up, ribbons dangling from her fingers. "We don't have all day."

Anna hurries, sitting heavily on the floor to tape her toes and pull on the customized pair, hands deft as usual.

Susan comes over, mumbling something Victoria can't overhear, and Anna lights up again with one of those beaming smiles. Victoria turns away, irritated.

"Seriously." Michelle comes up, trusty Nikon around her neck and a light meter in hand. "This is a waste of a day just to get you a couple of profiles for the season spread. I've seen it—it's not bad this time around—but you're just making a last-minute tweak. Why not make a splash and look like you had this planned all along?"

"Even if I changed my mind, it's weeks before a feature will run." Victoria crosses her arms over her chest. Her sweater is black, a little lower cut than normal. Paired with her favorite black jeans, comfortable at every seam, she still feels Michelle's gaze lingering. "No, wait…don't tell me."

"My editor had to pull something for next weekend, so if I give her the nod this morning, four pages are yours. I haven't written in a while, but you've got red-pen rights if you don't like it."

"Giving me editorial approval?" Victoria's hackles raise in suspicion. She shouldn't antagonize Rick this soon, not when she hasn't worked much more with Anna, but putting her plans in print makes them almost impossible to undo. "The last thing you wrote about me was that I was washed up and Metropolitan should have taken Liza Wade instead of me."

"I owed Liza a favor, okay?" Michelle shrinks a little under the scrutiny. "I know I owe you bigger, but you dropped me a long time ago for your flavors of the month."

Anna is back on her feet and stretching out her legs in a gentle warm-up that shouldn't dislodge hair or makeup.

"Fine," Victoria says. "I admit I could do with the publicity. The brochure alone doesn't make a loud enough statement. This all comes through me, nothing to Rick, understood?"

"Atta girl," Michelle teases. "Man, you still can't stand anyone else being the boss, huh?"

"He's not my boss," Victoria says. "He just writes the checks."

"Whatever you say. You might want to get your flunkies working on your look now," Michelle suggests, setting the light meter down and pulling out her phone to tap at. "Because I just told my editor the feature has you too."

"Michelle—"

"Done deal," Michelle cuts her off. "I'll be gentle."

"First time for everything." Victoria considers her options. She doesn't miss the rigors of full dress and makeup for every performance, that's for damn sure. That said, it wasn't entirely awful to dress up on Saturday night to woo the crowd a little. It only takes a moment to catch Susan's eye, and with a jerk of her head, Victoria is on her way to be plastered with products and have her hair tugged at.

"Well," Susan can't help commenting as she rifles through the rack, plucking from the selection a sheer black blouse that Victoria recognizes as Givenchy. Of course it's exactly in Victoria's size, and Susan doesn't even need to double-check herself. That precision is still a pleasure to watch in action. "I never thought I'd see the day."

"Well, it's not like I'm shy," Victoria says. "I just haven't felt like making myself the story. What do you have for Anna if we want to go splashy? Not for the official materials. The *Times*."

"Of course," Susan says. "Have you broken the news to Anna yet?"

"After her promo shots. Why should she care if it's a few more flashes?"

"She won't." Susan is working through the racks again, holding up something red that Victoria almost wishes she were tall enough to pull off without heels.

"Though I suspect we might need a fistful of valium for the interview part," Victoria says.

"Interview with the *Times*?" Susan throws a judgmental look before an eyeshadow brush causes Victoria to close her eyes. "Well, that's going to upset some people who've been more than accommodating so far."

"Not my problem." Victoria ignores the faint pang of guilt for Delphine. It is something of a coup, and Liza will no doubt be on the phone to snipe at her sister the minute the spread hits a newsstand. Still, bulletproofing her plan is the most important thing here, and Victoria is a master of contingencies. Anna is going to be the star of the season, and that's not a reflection on Delphine. If she takes it that way? Well, Victoria will tell Delphine to adjust.

"Sounds like asking for trouble to me," Susan says as Victoria takes the blouse from her, hair still being teased and coaxed into curls. She gestures at Victoria's half-finished look. "But damn, I'd forgotten you could still turn all this on when you feel like it."

Victoria rolls her eyes.

♪♪♪

Anna's cheeks are starting to hurt from smiling, so it's a relief when Michelle barks at her to "get serious." They run through a variety of poses, Anna spending most of it *en pointe* until she's instructed to turn or bend to catch certain lighting angles. She can't wait for this weirdness to be over, especially when Michelle switches to handheld and gets right up in Anna's face. Isn't that what zoom lenses are for?

"Thanks for that," Michelle says as she walks past them. "I was talking to Ramos about some aerial shots with flowing fabrics. The crew here can rig up a swing and I'll edit it out in post. We'll start with some basics in black, though. I'll need at least three or four looks."

"Why?" Anna blurts.

"Options." Michelle shrugs. "You okay with getting hoisted up in the air?"

Anna nods. It's just a jump where someone holds her in place.

"Dare I ask about an actual concept?" Victoria turns her focus on their photographer.

"You can ask while I'm getting some practice shots." Michelle points toward the area in front of the cameras. "Let me get my lights balanced for you."

"And me?" Anna chimes in. "Do I change, or…?"

"Side by side," Michelle decides. "I'm thinking, Victoria, you want to go with possessive, if this is about staking a claim so Rick can't take the credit by spring."

"You want possessive?" Victoria repeats, a displeased curl to her lips. "If this is another pitch for your BDSM ballet series…"

Anna almost falls over at that. Thank God she has decent balance.

"Whatever," Michelle says with a groan. "You're good to go, so let's get the Chosen One in shot with you."

"Come along, Anya," Victoria says. "The sooner we do this, the sooner everyone gets to go home."

Anna complies, one foot in front of the other. Somehow it feels like the longest walk of her life.

♪♪♪

It doesn't seem foolish until Anna is standing barely a foot away from Victoria, awkward and unsure all over again. Only then does Victoria realize how she's framing herself: the aging artist and her bright young muse.

At least Anna scrubs up well, so there's no mortification on that front. She seems very focused on the translucent material of Victoria's shirt, and in that moment she's grateful Kim's been so insistent on keeping her in shape. A lifetime of strenuous exercise and limiting diet laid the groundwork, and God knows this place keeps her active.

"You could both start by acting like you've met before," Michelle says.

Victoria rolls her eyes. Laying a firm hand on Anna's shoulder, she steps in closer. Both of them stand, facing the camera, the only contact palm against half-bared shoulder; it's nothing spectacular. It's enough to let Anna accept the new normal, though, and she finally relaxes under Victoria's light grip.

"So when you two get done saying Mass…," Michelle snorts, but she's up in their faces a moment later, catching them close and off guard.

Victoria wants to recoil, but there's an example to be set. She's been on display since she was five years old. This isn't any different. When Michelle steps back to frame them some other way, Victoria lets her hand trail down Anna's practically naked back, the touch barely a suggestion. At her waist, Victoria grips again, pulling Anna closer in a one-armed embrace of sorts. It's a lazy power move, but Anna leans into it without hesitation this time.

Good. Better. It even shuts Michelle up.

"It needs…something," Victoria mutters as they mix up the complementary poses. "Right now we could be anyone, anything. It has to scream *ballet*."

"I'm wearing a tutu." Anna points out the black mesh, and it's not an unreasonable point.

"Yes, and next round you should try one of those adjustable skirts everyone's so crazy about. Brings attention back to your legs. Can we get a little spray over here? She's starting to dry out."

A junior styling minion is sent over with a bottle of hydrating mist, and Anna is sprayed with very little ceremony. It brings out the light tan on her legs, and the sheen is almost tempting to run fingers over.

"I don't think I can do a real magazine spread," Anna says, sudden and urgent. "It's too much. Nobody else—"

"Stop that," Victoria says. "Stop worrying about everyone else and putting them in front of your own success. If I teach you nothing else, Anya, at least let me teach you that. Nobility is severely overrated."

"But—"

"Wait here." Victoria holds up a finger to halt Michelle in her tracks. It gives her an excuse for a lens and filter change, anyway. It only takes a moment to retrieve her purse and the copy of *Vogue* she shoved into it this morning. "Look," she commands Anna, handing it over.

Victoria hasn't looked at the black-and-white spread in years, but she remembers the chill in the air with perfect clarity, the way the rough cement of the balcony felt under her arms, against the backs of her thighs. Bare legs, a slip of a black dress, all attitude and boundless ambition. She can't give those things to Anna, but she can help her recognize them.

"Wow, this is your first *Vogue*," Anna breathes.

For a moment, Victoria can see her as an adolescent at the stage door, voice awed and eyes wide. Did Anna ever stay after a show? Victoria can't pretend she ever paid much attention; most nights she'd slip out through a side door and into the anonymity of a New York evening.

"I had this, but then I lost it."

It would be so easy to make a cutting joke. Chastened by the previous day, Victoria chooses her words more carefully, in case Anna means lost in the fire.

"You can have that one, then. I hope your shrine to me is appropriately unsettling, Anya. I don't believe in half measures."

"Oh, I've got the votive candles and surveillance shots, sure," Anna teases right back, the shadow that passed over her chased by another brilliant smile. "Do I need a lock of your hair too?"

"Not bad," Victoria says. "Susan has some dresses, but I don't think we've quite set the world alight with this duet, do you?"

"No," Anna admits. "What would make it more? It should be striking, like your choreography."

"You already got the gig. But as ass-kissing goes, points for effort. You have more ribbon in that sack you lug around?"

"Of course I do," Anna answers with a faint eye roll of her own. "What are you thinking?"

"Gimme," Victoria says.

Anna does as she's told. A moment later Victoria takes Anna's hand, and slips the pale peach ribbon around her wrist, starting with one firm knot. "Willis, get over here."

"Oh," Michelle announces on seeing Victoria's intention. Leaving the camera dangling around her neck, she steps right in and ties the other end of the ribbon tight around Victoria's own wrist. "This might work. Tug of war?"

"Something like that," Victoria half agrees. "Start with that, and then maybe wrapping around our arms, almost binding us together?"

"Definitely." Michelle positions them.

Anna is utterly compliant as long as she's tethered to Victoria.

The flashes start to fire again in earnest.

"Okay?" Victoria asks, when they turn from staring down the camera to focusing on each other.

"Fine," Anna says. "Dresses after this?"

"Start with the red." Victoria reaches for more ribbon, wrapping it around their touching forearms. "And don't spend too long on that swing. You'll need all your ribs working this week."

"Of course." Anna squeezes Victoria's hand where their fingers are intertwined, her palm as warm as the ribbon is cool. "You don't think this might look...you know?"

"Let them speculate." Victoria shrugs off the question. "Speculation sells tickets."

"That's kind of cynical," Anna argues.

"Business always is." Victoria gives Michelle and her camera a downright seductive glance. Anna watches before following suit. Judging by the increased flurry of shutter clicks, they're on to something.

❧

Still on a high, Anna clutches the magazine all the way downtown on the subway. Only when she emerges in Tribeca does she think to preserve her precious gift by easing it into the protected section inside her bag that usually holds a laptop or her jewelry. For some reason the score from *La Traviata* is in her head, and so she hums it on the short walk of a few blocks to Jess's apartment building. Maybe Anna will indulge herself—one trip with all her things in a cab would be preferable to hauling it over two or three by subway. She's trying to guess at cab fare when she opens the door with Jess's spare key.

Perhaps that's why it takes a moment to register.

There's the sofa, same as always. Only instead of Anna's clothes, or her folded bedsheets and pillows from the night before, there's Jess. At least Anna's pretty sure it's Jess, because the leggy ballerina on top of her—one with very long legs and curly hair, is blocking most of Anna's view.

"Oh my *God*!" Anna yelps, almost concussing herself on the open door as she tries to turn around. "What the...? Oh my *God*!"

"Hey, calm down." Jess starts to soothe her, but it sounds honest-to-god muffled and Anna doesn't want to think about what might be pressed against Jess's face and *oh this day just got weird.* Weirder than Victoria Ford-tying-her-up-in-ribbons weird, and nowhere near as pleasant.

"Did you at least move my clothes before you...you..." Anna covers her eyes with one hand and picks her way to her pile of bags, grabbing as best she can with only one hand free. The room smells like, well, sex, and neither Jess nor Irina seems to have their breathing back under control yet.

"Don't be a prude, *malenkaya*," Irina says, tone teasing, and she sounds a little toasted for this time on a Monday afternoon.

"Don't," Anna warns, looking up long enough to make eye contact and see Irina's sly grin. "I have to go settle into my new place. Just...whatever."

"Anna, wait!" Jess calls after her, but Anna has momentum and she won't be stopped. She rushes out of the apartment with all the bags she can carry, grateful she repacks most things before leaving each morning. Trying to stop Jess stealing her T-shirts has finally paid off. Her sister's current lack of any clothing is not something Anna wants to dwell on. How the hell did they get from Saturday night to that? No, no. She doesn't want to know.

She's going home, or to what has to pass for it now. Stumbling over the last few steps, Anna makes up her mind about that cab. She hails the first one she sees, and it miraculously stops for her. She hurls her bags into the backseat. There are only a few hours of her day off left, so she may as well enjoy them.

CHAPTER 15

Days blow past surprisingly fast, not least because Victoria works Anna harder than she's ever worked before. They barely talk beyond barked instructions and the occasional hesitant question from Anna. Their individual rehearsals are curtailed by the demands of the corps for the coming shows, as Anna picks up *The Nutcracker* as well as *La Bayadère*.

There are grumblings from everyone after a few days. Where Anna hoped David would be a kinder prospect, his rehearsals are still the ballet equivalent of boot camp. The competing sets of choreography are like overlapping drumbeats in her head, but she smiles and raises her arms and does it all over again.

She dances, she eats, she sleeps.

She rubs arnica into everything that aches and ices her feet with as much care as she can muster. Aside from the chatter during classes and the occasional lunch with Ethan, Anna doesn't speak much with anyone. Jess texts and calls in decreasing frequency, finally accepting Anna's silence.

Avoiding Irina is easy enough at first when Anna's face still flushes at the sight of her, but the warm-up classes are only so crowded and avoiding eye contact is tricky with mirrors on every wall. In the hurry to escape one morning after a week has passed, Anna bumps into her on the way out of the room and gets only a knowing smile in response.

The brochures have been printed but not delivered. Anna can't wait to see them, but she's far more nervous about Michelle's article and photos due to run in the Sunday *New York Times*. When the day finally rolls around, Anna leaves for the Metropolitan Center just a little giddy at the thought of stopping by the newsstand at the end of her block. She could have looked online of course, but that just doesn't feel right. She doesn't make it out of the building before she's accosted by her sister, who smacks her on the arm with a rolled-up copy of the *Times*.

"Enough!" Jess barks at her. "You've had your sulking time, Anna."

"Don't even talk to me," Anna says, hoping the doorman on duty today doesn't overhear.

"Oh, quit the puritan-in-a-tutu routine. We talked about this before you moved here. We're grown-ups now, and I'm not going to act like we're in high school just to give you a comfort zone."

"You could avoid banging my colleagues." Anna's huffy and not caring if she sounds it. "I mean, how did you go from helping her home to that, anyway?"

"Anna Gale, if that is your way of saying you want the juicy details—"

"Fine!" Anna yanks the newspaper off her sister. "You're buying the coffee. And don't crease me!"

"Anna, it's really… I mean, you might wanna take a moment."

"It's bad? Oh God, I knew Michelle hated me on sight. I haven't seen the brochures yet, but—"

"No, no." Jess grabs her by the shoulders. Weekend brunchers and joggers pound past on the New York sidewalk, barely batting an eyelid at the emotional scene playing out between sisters. "I mean, it's gonna blow your mind. You might want to sit down before you look at it. That…that is the real deal."

"You're not messing with me?"

"Would I risk that right now?"

"Oh God." Anna groans. "It's like I can't breathe right. I want to see, but I don't know if I can look."

"There's a coffee shop around the corner." Jess steers Anna and her newspaper in the right direction. "Let's do this."

∽∞∾

"Victoria?"

She hears it, but there's a more pressing matter of reallocating the second bar of—

"Victoriaaaa?"

It's gone. She'll have to start the sequence again. Victoria tosses the pen she's been idly twirling at the open door.

"What?" she barks.

Kelly appears with a stack of magazines in her arms. "I knew you wouldn't want the rest of the paper, but I picked up a few extra along with the office subscription."

"Give." Victoria bends her fingers impatiently, beckoning Kelly forward.

Instead of handing them over, Kelly spreads the semi-glossy magazines across Victoria's otherwise tidy desk, only the pad she was taking notes on disturbed by the display. "Michelle *was* supposed to send these for approval on Monday."

"Did you really think she would?" Kelly asks. "I don't think Anna will be here for warm-up yet, but should I send someone for her?"

"I'll ask for Anya when I need her. Don't you have work to do?"

"Fine," Kelly mutters. "It's pages twenty-two through twenty-five, by the way."

Victoria's fingers twitch toward the nearest copy. She trusts Michelle, after a fashion. The new season brochures delivered earlier are seamless, drawing attention in all the right ways. Anna will stand out but not overwhelm. It's honestly not Victoria's most interesting concept, but that's just something to keep people happy when they're shelling out for overpriced champagne before taking their seats.

This is the real campaign now, no matter how Victoria had to be coaxed into it. Adaptability has been her greatest asset in the past twenty years, and there's no reason for that to stop now. Seizing the opportunity presented, even if it means putting herself back in a spotlight she's been deliberately shunning. Not to mention how Rick will blow a fuse on seeing it.

She grabs. She flips. Page twenty-two.

Well. Michelle certainly hasn't lost her touch. The shots are just as striking as Victoria expected.

She lays the magazine down but lets her right hand linger over the page. She must be imagining it when her index finger trembles for a fragment of a second; the bump from where she broke it after a failed lift is more pronounced now, as she grows older and the skin thins slightly. The reminder of fragility is blown away as she traces the peach satin wrapped around her own photographed arm, and over Anna's in turn. Only when every inch is mapped does Victoria let her gaze flick to the head of the page where their profiles face off against each other.

Oh. That will do. That will do very nicely indeed.

♋♌♋

"If you make me wait for the coffee to be made, I swear…" Anna trails off as Jess unfolds the paper and its insert magazine on the table between them.

"Get ready." Jess flicks through the pages and smooths out the stunning first shot.

The white background, their profiled faces. Anna doesn't see herself at first, drawn instantly to Victoria. It's the angle captured countless times in publicity shots and freeze frames, because a dancer with that natural poise knows how to hold herself at all times. Whatever Michelle has done after the makeup artist worked her magic has erased at least a decade, and for a moment Anna sees them both as peers.

This is her life now. Photoshoots with her idol and showing up in the Sunday *New York Times*.

Anna looks up at Jess. "Wow?"

"Wow is right. There's more."

"I know, I was there." Anna lingers for a moment longer, tracing the binding ribbon around their forearms, remembering how it felt to have part of her pressed against Victoria for long minutes, and the way Victoria had so nonchalantly entwined their fingers, the skin of her palm cool and dry against Anna's faintly damp and nervous one.

"So turn the page. Come on!"

"I'll turn if you tell me how you got Irina into bed…or, well, sofa."

"What makes you think I made the first move?" Jess hedges, smiling a little too eagerly when the waiter brings their coffees and Danishes. It's a delay that doesn't deter Anna one bit. "She must have remembered where I worked and came over after the Sunday matinee to apologize."

"Uh-huh."

"I was going out anyway with the crew, so she tagged along. A few glasses of wine later, we went back to my place. When you got home Monday afternoon, well, that was the encore."

"Of the encore?"

"Something like that." Jess flushes, staring at the table.

"Are you still seeing her?" Anna has to know. It determines whether she's getting over this or holding a petty grudge a little longer. She feels proprietorial over Irina in a way she doesn't entirely understand. It's nothing she could confidently explain if pressed on it, so she's going to have to find a way to deal if Jess is pursuing this.

"Couple of times," Jess admits. "You know, with these hours—"

"Well, don't tell her embarrassing stories about me," Anna pleads. "I don't want the whole company knowing my high school disasters."

"Seriously, look at the rest of the magazine. This is your big break. It's really happening." Jess pats Anna's hand.

"It is?"

"Do you get to keep the dress?" Jess asks. "Even I would borrow that one."

"It's at work. I guess I could ask Susan if you need it for something."

"Don't go to any trouble for me." Jess sips her coffee. "So come on, tell me how they rigged the flying shots."

⟳∂∂

Victoria arrives at the studio just in time to overhear the last of Delphine's rant. Most of the room has cleared, but Morgan and Teresa are taking their sweet time to maximize what they overhear.

"—trusted you! Which, by the way, is a big deal for me. For weeks you've been acting like my friend, and I've kept cool about you coming for my job. Enjoy the *Times*, Gale. Because it's the last press you'll be doing this season."

"Delphine!" Gabriel is physically holding her back at this point, and Anna is ashen. There's sweat beading on her forehead and she's gripping the barre with both hands. "Come on, you know it wasn't her call."

"That's right," Victoria says, and the focus of the room rolls to her as surely as a riptide changes a swimmer's direction. "When I want your approval on the marketing strategies of this company, Delphine, I'll ask for them."

"Go fuck yourself." Delphine breaks free of Gabriel's grip and barrels past Victoria, out the room.

Gabriel picks up their things and gives an apologetic shrug that could be for Anna or for Victoria. "She'll calm down," he says. "She always does."

Victoria clicks her fingers and the stragglers hurry out.

"Victoria, I'm sorry," Anna begins. "Please don't do anything to Delphine for cursing at you. It's me she's mad at."

"Anya, if I took action every time a Wade called me something unpleasant, I'd never do anything else. Artists need to express themselves, and that's all Delphine was doing."

"But—"

"You've seen it?"

Well, that stops the girl mid-babble. She blushes, of course, and looks to her feet as though she'll find answers in her shoes.

"Yes."

"And?" Victoria keeps the click of impatience from her tongue. It's suddenly desperately important that Anna liked the shots. For morale, of course. It wouldn't do to have her self-conscious or embarrassed by them, to have that lingering over their rehearsals in the coming weeks. But how could she be? Even Victoria, perfectionist to the last, has almost no bone to pick with the image choices or the composition.

"They're amazing." Anna looks up, takes a deep breath, and makes eye contact. "I looked at them and I felt...you know."

"Beautiful," Victoria supplies. Why in the hell did she just say that?

"I'm sure anyone would look good if Michelle—"

"Not true." Victoria waves a finger. She steps a little closer and Anna snatches up her bag from the floor. "It would be just as easy to make someone look tired, even ghoulish. Michelle's skill is in bringing what's already there to the surface."

"Well, it made me feel pretty good. Until now."

"How many times am I going to have to tell you to own it? You have an astonishing talent, and this kind of exposure comes with it. Delphine will be over it in a week, when *Vogue* wants her to model some capri pants or something."

"Astonishing?" Anna repeats, and God she's instantly glowing at the praise. "Is that really what you think?"

"Would I be staking my reputation on it otherwise?" Victoria snaps, but she feels exposed under Anna's wondrous gaze. "I expect this is the last time I'll have to reassure you on this. It's about the work, Anya."

"*Anna*," she pushes back, softly spoken but with just a hint of steel. "If I'm so important to your plan, then I think it's time you got my name right."

"That's your big demand?" Victoria tries to downplay it, but she knows a test when she sees one. With a firm hand, she reaches out to push Anna's bag down and out of the way, though she never lets go of it. "Fine. Anna."

Victoria thinks she's prepared for the smile, but it's so quick to blossom that she smiles back on sheer reflex, almost ruining her carefully maintained *froideur*.

"Here," Victoria adds, thrusting a brochure toward Anna. "Toward the back."

The rifling sound of crisp pages fills the air between them, and the vellum smell of freshly printed materials competes with the other sundry scents of the previously crowded studio. Victoria can pick out the warmed notes of Anna's perfume through it all, something light and clean and probably by Clinique.

"Oh my God," Anna whispers. Her hands are shaking.

Victoria considers a steadying touch, and opts to lightly grip the fold of the booklet instead. It works, and Anna gathers herself.

"I had every one," Anna starts to explain. "Every season since I was born, even before I started to come and see the performances. And my mother's too. London, Paris, Moscow. If she could see this…"

"If you need copies, Kelly will arrange that. I'm sure your mother would be proud, but remember this is just the beginning. There's a lot of work before you come close to realizing this potential."

"I know. I'm not so sure she'd be proud of how I've upset Delphine."

"Toughen up." Victoria lets go of the pages she's been holding in place. "I'm not going to listen to this hand-wringing for months." With that, order is restored. "I'm canceling our session this afternoon."

"Wait, why?"

"You've been working hard this week. And out of sight, out of mind might not be the worst idea while Delphine cools down. Go, be young in New York. You must have a million things you want to do."

"Not really," Anna admits. "Everyone I know is here, or keeps theater hours. But that's not your problem, of course! I just... I can get laundry done. And catch a movie, maybe."

Victoria groans under her breath. "Do you know anything about art?"

"I almost went to art school."

That derails Victoria for a moment. She tries to picture all this perfect movement wasted in a painter's smock or godawful dungarees.

"But I couldn't give up on this to do it. Maybe if I hadn't got in this year..."

"There's an art fair, a friend is running it. I said I'd put in an appearance, but I only know what I like. If you might actually be useful, in terms of knowing whether something is worth investing in—"

"I can be useful." Anna jumps right in. So eager, as always. "Should I dress up?"

"No more than usual. My car will be out front at three."

"Thank you." Anna gives another one of those easy smiles, and for a horrifying moment Victoria truly believes she may be subjected to a hug. "I guess it's a date!"

It's endlessly entertaining, how the color drains from her face the second she finishes saying it. There's the world's longest mortified silence before the stammering begins in earnest, and Victoria just rolls her eyes.

"Don't embarrass me in front of actual people."

Victoria strides out, her pain level low and her mood something approaching pleased for a change. She notices Teresa lurking in the hallway, and the wounded pout on her face suggests she overheard every word. Well, that should finish the job of setting Anna apart from the company. It also has Victoria conveniently out of range whenever Rick's hangover clears and he happens to flick through the paper.

Coffee, Victoria decides. Then she'd better get Kelly to find her a non-dismal art fair to trail around for an hour later today.

CHAPTER 16

Anna gets done with David's session earlier than expected, so she's out front and waiting by Victoria's car just before three. Knocking on the window, she waves at the driver to let him know she's there, and gets a slight smile in response. There's no indication the doors have been unlocked, so Anna fiddles with her purse and tries not to look too awkward.

She looks toward the grand building in anticipation, but it isn't Victoria who she sees coming down the steps of the Metropolitan Center—it's Teresa. A stack of manuscripts gripped like a shield as always, she looks harried in a way she hadn't during the rehearsal. Just when Anna is deciding whether to wave or not—it's not like they've ever really spoken—Teresa changes course and strides right over.

"Listen," Teresa says, sounding quite friendly, "I was going to let you just make a fool of yourself, but some of us care too much about Victoria's reputation for that."

"Uh, a fool of my what now?" Anna asks.

"You can't be expected to understand how genius works, so let me put you straight. So to speak." Teresa tucks the bundle of sheet music under her arm.

"You know, I'm not really looking for advice, thanks." She and Victoria are both adults and have real, professional reasons to get to know each other a little better and build some trust. Plus, something about Teresa's haughty attitude slams shut Anna's generally accommodating nature.

"Fine. Let her chew you up and spit you out." The anger is real, and it sounds so spiteful. "Don't say I didn't warn you. It takes a certain kind of person—"

"Uh, Teresa—"

"Don't interrupt me!" She's doing that scary intense whisper-yelling now, but Anna has to shut her up. "You think you're hot shit because you get up on your toes ten times an hour?"

"Teresa—"

"I could be playing on my own concert tour, but instead I'm here. Playing *twinkle, twinkle little moron* for all of you."

"If the job's so beneath you," Victoria all but purrs from where she's now standing behind Teresa, "you should feel free to explore other career opportunities. There's no shortage of people who can count to four and move both hands at the same time."

"Victoria! I—"

"Don't make it worse by fumbling for an explanation. Go home, Teresa. When I see you in the studio Tuesday, you'll be back to normal. Or not. But this is your last warning."

Teresa fumes and looks like she might actually stamp her foot in frustration.

For a fleeting second, Anna feels the urge to speak up, to shoulder some of the blame. She hates to see anyone implode like that. Then she remembers she didn't do anything wrong, and in the face of affecting her own career and relationship with Victoria, she stays quiet. For good measure, she pulls a face at Teresa while Victoria isn't looking Anna's way. What it lacks in maturity, it makes up for in satisfaction.

"Anna, darling," Victoria says next, and she lays her hand heavily on Anna's forearm like she does it all the time. "We're going to be late, and my friends are waiting to meet my new star."

"Right. Let me get the door for you," she says, bright and breezy for Teresa's benefit.

Victoria nods in approval as Anna opens the back door of the car, slinking past her in a wave of delicate perfume and a tailored black-and-white dress that hugs every line of her figure.

Anna jogs around to the other side, feeling Teresa's glare on her the whole way. Only behind tinted windows and closed doors does Anna relax. Her conscience prickles as they pull away from the curb.

"You know, she—"

"Don't you dare." Victoria is fussing with her phone, but she pauses long enough to shoot a sideways glare at Anna. "If you try to take one scrap of the blame, Anna…"

"Fine," Anna huffs, talked out of it in an instant. "I didn't know you two were dating, although I don't know what that has to do with my dancing."

"We're not. And it has nothing to do with anything other than petty jealousy, which I have about as much tolerance for as I do lazy *tendus*. Are you only here to gossip? Because I can let you get back to that laundry anytime you like."

"No! No. I'm really looking forward to seeing some art. I've only been to one gallery since I moved here, can you believe that? Some of the greatest art in the world right on my doorstep, but I just don't find the time."

"Well, if launching your ballet career is getting in the way of staring dreamily at walls." Victoria seems ready to launch into one of her peevish rants but pulls herself up short. "I know it's demanding. You just have to trust it will be worth it. The paintings will be there when the dancing is done."

"You see a lot of art, then?" Anna asks, and it isn't meant to be a dig, but she realizes how it could sound like one.

Victoria blinks at her in surprise.

"Oh no, I just meant—"

"That I should have the free time now I can't dance," Victoria finishes, far crueler than Anna would ever be. "Thank God your feet aren't as clumsy as that mouth of yours. And I did, for a while. I had time off before I came back to the company as director."

Anna considers asking then. It almost seems like an opening for the right kind of delicate question. Just forming the words send her into a spiral, though, and Victoria's phone rings before Anna can ask anything more.

The fondness in Victoria's voice for whomever she's talking to startles Anna, and she tries to feign an expression of not listening at all, tapping at her own phone like there are messages to answer or emails to read.

"Bye, darling," Victoria finishes, shoving her phone in her bag. She watches Anna out of the corner of her eye, as though anticipating some nosy question or other.

Anna holds her tongue. The road is busy with weekend traffic, and they slow to a crawl making their way downtown.

"Which school?"

"What?" Anna isn't expecting the question and honestly Victoria sounds a little bored about asking.

"Which school did you *almost* study art at?"

"Oh. The New School. I had an offer from Chicago, too, but I don't really like the winters."

Victoria looks impressed at the caliber of school. "You turned them both down to keep dancing?"

"Yeah. I mean, it's not like being an artist is any more secure as a profession. And I love it, I do. Painting is peaceful, but I can go for a long time without it if I have to. That's...not true about ballet."

"You don't have to try and impress me," Victoria says. "You're off the clock, so you can care about things outside of the Metropolitan Center."

"I know," Anna says, although a little part of her is still straining for that elusive approval. The few grudging compliments she's had so far, even the fact of her promotion itself, have only left her hungry for more. "But I'm not going to lie about it, either. It is that important to me. I didn't always care, when I was younger. For a while I wanted to ignore it altogether, but not now."

"Because it reminds you of your mother." Victoria doesn't ask; she simply states it as a fact. "Mine always insisted I should write, pursue something more academic. But my father...he saw the dancer in me."

"And a lot of people thank God that he did," Anna says, perhaps as sincere as she has ever been. "Is he gone?"

"When I was seventeen. He was unhappy for a long time, but he saw my first season. And with all the dramatic flair the Fords are renowned for, he must have decided he could leave. I'd found my place in the world."

"I'm so sorry," Anna says, but she knows how inadequate the gesture is. "You have to figure he'd be proud though, right? I'm sorry, is this weird? I never usually talk about this stuff, because people who haven't lost... Well, they never get it, do they?"

"Platitudes and patronizing smiles," Victoria agrees as the car comes to a halt outside what looks like a burned-out warehouse. "Well, we're here. Let's put that New School-worthy art brain of yours to work, shall we?"

"Is there anything I need to know about your friend?" Anna asks as they step out onto the sidewalk.

Victoria shakes her head, dismissive again. That moment in the car is over. Sunglasses on even though they're heading indoors, and Anna doesn't know what else to do but follow along. She measures her long strides a little, matching Victoria's less even pace.

⟳♂♂⟲

Still shaking off her oversharing in the car, Victoria is barely prepared for the shriek that comes from the gaggle in the corner. It's one of Kelly's little miracles that she unearthed an invitation from an old friend Victoria could actually tolerate. The flurry of air kisses and half-exchanged life updates is almost pleasant.

The reception is warm and everyone acts as though they expected Victoria all along, which at least avoids scrutiny from Anna, whose blue eyes never stop roaming the converted industrial space. The girl misses nothing, which bodes well for following the choreography at least. Only when Victoria maxes out on small talk does she draw Anna away from where she's fallen into conversation with one of the artists.

Frankly that chat had been a little involved for someone who's supposed to be focusing on her unexpected new career at the forefront of American ballet. Anna shouldn't be letting underdressed hipsters who lean in too close monopolize that much of her time.

"What do you think?" Victoria gestures to the array of canvases. "Any hidden gems? Or should I leave all these to decorate uninspired apartments all over Brooklyn?"

"There are some great pieces," Anna starts to gush, her face lit up like a crew with rigging is following her around. "But it all depends on what you like. Now, Irina has this amazing canvas—"

"You've seen Irina's art?" Victoria is a little impressed. "Oh yes, your chivalry in taking her home."

Anna casts about for a new subject, uncomfortable with the topic of Irina. "My apartment is great. I really wanted to thank you. I spoke to some people and I know I could have had a way less cool one, in the dorms or whatever."

"Your due as a principal." Victoria is rarely secretive about the strings she can pull, but hides behind the perks of the position this time. "I can't work you until you drop and send you back to a single bed and ramen."

"I make pretty good ramen," Anna teases, and it really shouldn't be charming. "Good preparation for life as a starving artist. I don't think any of this stuff feels very 'you,' Victoria. I mean, from what I know about you."

"Which isn't very much," Victoria points out, and a little part of her almost buys the first thing she can touch, just to prove Anna wrong. Then she sees the conversation buddy approaching, now having acquired an actual fedora from somewhere, and Victoria decides this art really is quite overrated. "I should let you get back to your afternoon. This was clearly a waste of time."

She shouldn't bring Anna out of the safe confines of the Metropolitan Center. She shouldn't blur these lines between directing and socializing. A rookie mistake.

"Oh, well I was having a nice time," Anna offers. "But I'm sure you have a million more interesting things to do than kill time with the new girl. I'll make more friends eventually; you don't have to feel sorry for me. And hey, amazing dances don't choreograph themselves, right?"

"Oh, they do," Victoria corrects, steering Anna toward the back of the room, where the original contents of the space are stacked in piles and badly covered with tarps. The presentation is appalling, and Victoria groans inwardly at the amateurism. "Well, in my case David and the resident choreos do most of the work. Artistic directors are big picture, conceptual. I just happen to be great at the micromanaging, too, because I've danced the steps in most cases."

Anna nods, wise enough not to disrupt a Victoria Ford story.

It's easy to forget how people lap up the mythology, as though Victoria has some special insight into the human condition just because she's had exceptional control of her limbs for most of her life.

"The trick," Victoria says, and she can't stop, because it feels good to unleash all these words on someone, to express something other than disdain or frustration for a job poorly done, "is to take the artifice out of it."

She doesn't expect Anna to understand, waits instead for an inane question.

"You mean don't think of it as making a dance," Anna says. "But more like… God, I bet you can say this so much better, but just make it how people move. That's what it should look like."

"Who taught you that?"

Anna shrugs, maddening again. "It's just…it's what it feels like when you teach me. Sure, it's all technical terms and pushing that one degree straighter, one inch lower, but…you're not training me to do a perfect Italian *fouetté*. You're training me to show how a street dancer would move if she woke up one day as a queen. Maybe I'm way off, sorry…"

Victoria makes sure she doesn't betray the wonder of being understood with her expression, but it takes all her years of training not to give herself away.

"No, that's close," she admits. Even she isn't so cruel as to leave Anna dangling like that, not when she's done so well. "Although I haven't taught you Mercedes's dance at all, so don't start Queen of the Dryads with me when I made you Kitri."

"Right." Anna laughs, looking delighted not to have been shot down.

Making her happy shouldn't be this easy. It's not a skill Victoria has ever possessed, for all her abilities.

"Anyway, it was nice of you to invite me, but I can get the subway home," Anna says. "Clearly this place is a bust."

"Nonsense." Victoria grabs her last chance to salvage the afternoon. She needs to get Anna back into a suitable mindset for when they pick up on Tuesday, not least for dealing with Delphine's still-simmering rage. "It's a waste of time, but there's no need to expose yourself to bubonic plague on the subway. We live on the same street, Anna. If you want to head home, that's where we'll go."

"If you're sure?" Anna nods back to the artists in the corner. "What about your friends?"

"I'm sure they're still stunned that I showed up at all," Victoria admits. Today she's just giving far too much away. "I'll call the car." A quick summoning text barely takes a second to send.

"Whatever you want." Anna falls into step as they move off. "I'm really honored you invited me, Victoria. Even if it did piss off Teresa."

"Call that a bonus," Victoria says as the car approaches. "Although it could be less convenient than the other dancers being mad at you. Just keep the beat in your head and don't rely on her too much until she gets over it."

The drive uptown is uneventful, and although they don't talk any further, Victoria finds herself surprisingly reluctant to part when the car rolls to a stop outside her building.

"I'll need you right after warm-up on Tuesday," she says instead.

Anna turns, seat belt still on. "I'll see you then," she says in a breathless rush. Anna lets herself out of the car on her side the same time as Victoria does. Their gazes meet for a moment over the roof. "Have a really great Sunday."

With that, she's jogging through stopped traffic to her side of the street, not so much as glancing back.

Victoria slams the car door a little too hard, and retreats toward the sanctuary of her apartment.

CHAPTER 17

"*Malenkaya*," Irina pounces at last on Tuesday morning, when Anna has a mouthful of banana and nowhere in particular to be. "I thought I might find you here, on the roof."

"It'll be too cold soon," Anna says after swallowing. She deliberately doesn't look at Irina, keeping her gaze on the New York skyline instead. "So I'm enjoying it while I can."

"You people have an embarrassing idea of cold." Irina sniffs.

Anna can't help noticing that while she's in UGGs and a hoodie, Irina is already in a polar fleece coat over her dance clothes.

"Speaking of cold, are you done freezing me?" Irina asks.

"Freezing you out," Anna corrects without thinking. She jerks her head to the empty space beside her on the bench. "I don't want to talk about you and Jess. It's weird for me."

"You're dancing well," Irina says. "I hear good things, and every warm-up you're bursting with energy. And you should not worry about Jess. She's an incredible woman."

"Don't be gross. I feel like this is going somewhere that will make me cover my ears."

"Then tell me about Vicki instead," Irina drawls. "And all your talking. Do you stay late after rehearsal, braid each other's hair?"

"No, but she's a great teacher." Anna draws her knees up to her chest. She's wary of saying more after Delphine and Teresa's outbursts. She doesn't want anyone else to hate her, and if she can forgive Jess for intruding on Anna's world, she should stop shutting Irina out too. "And I think I'm getting it. Enough to stop some of the yelling, anyway. I think it helps that we talked."

"You talked?" Irina snorts, pulling painkillers from her purse and dry-swallowing. "Victoria doesn't talk."

Anna turns to her, on the defensive. "When we went out on Sunday, we talked about art, and choreography. I feel like I impressed her, maybe a little. That *is* actually possible, right?"

"Out?" Irina seems confused for some reason.

"Yeah, Victoria took me to this art show, and honestly, it was like she didn't even want to be there at first? But we had this cool conversation about movement, and I think it was progress. Or something."

"Well." Irina stands again, then stretches and drops to touch her toes "You truly are the Chosen one," she says when she's upright again. "I've been here every one of Victoria's years in charge, and even before when she was just consulting. Not one time did she ever take me to see the art. Not Delphine or any of the handsome boys, either. Work events only."

"I'm sure she must have done it with other people." Anna tries for nonchalance, but something deep in her chest tightens and burns for a moment. "It wasn't a big deal."

Irina nods toward the door leading back to the staircase. "I wouldn't be so sure about that."

"You know what my dream answer is here," Victoria tells David, easing herself into the director's chair he set up for her without needing to be asked. "You get that ass out of retirement and back on my stage. Everyone knows men get those extra years."

"My ass is willing, but my shoulders disagree." David is a little gruff as always, but less rigid when it's just the two of them in the studio. "Though I could still throw you around if I had to. You were never a strain."

Victoria basks in the compliment for a moment. "And you were always a more charming leading man than Rick. Since you won't slap on some Deep Heat and help me, I need a partner for Anna."

"I'd stay away from Gabe," David cautions. "Delphine's particular boat has been rocked enough for one season. Now, don't get that glint in your eye, Victoria. This isn't the Wade you want to mess with, remember?"

"How limiting, to only irritate one of them at a time."

"You heard she's in town?"

Victoria balks at that. "Liza is in New York?"

"You know there isn't a ballet dancer in this country who sneezes and I don't hear about it," David reminds her. "Through me all things flow."

"Sometimes I forget what a gossip you are. What do we know about the lesser Wade's reasons for being here, then? If she's planning to upstage me somehow, I want to be prepared."

"How could she?"

David's loyalty is faultless as always.

"But the reason I brought it up is that she's meeting with Rick tomorrow," he continues. "Dinner somewhere public. Paparazzi-in-the-parking-lot public."

"Oh, *fuck* him." Victoria drums her fingers on the wooden arm of the chair, considering her play. "As pushbacks go, it's lacking in subtlety. I guess that means he did see the interview."

"I'd imagine so. Plus, he has his spies," David reminds her. "Any reports going back to him won't be all that positive about the new kid yet."

"She's doing fine." Victoria stops drumming and massages her temple. She's going to have to commit now, not just to Anna's starring role but what it will actually *be*. "There's nothing anyone can say to Rick that will change that fact."

"Not even your piano girl?"

"What?"

David hesitates. Clearly this is uncomfortable territory for him. "I've never been especially interested in how you let off steam. But Teresa strikes me as someone who doesn't take rejection well, and she's privy to a lot of your work here."

Victoria shrugs.

"There's nothing secret there. Rick just doesn't want me having my way without a fight. Now, do we have a suitable male soloist in this company?"

David lays a reassuring hand on her shoulder. "One way to find out."

∽∂∂∽

Anna is expecting an empty studio when she arrives for her time with Victoria, but instead Gabriel and Delphine are lingering, Delphine on the floor and yanking off her shoes.

"I can wait out—"

"Stay," Gabriel insists. "Delphine was just saying she wants a word with you. I'll go," he adds, smiling at Anna on the way past.

"How was rehearsal?" Delphine asks. She's been down here working on her solos and *pas de deux* with Gabriel while Anna ran through *La Bayadère* with the rest of the corps.

Anna's a little overheated still and hesitates answering by taking a long swig from her water bottle. "Exhausting. We're adding in *The Nutcracker* rotation now. I'm hearing the drums in my sleep. Yours was good?"

"Look at us, so civil." Delphine laughs as she stands, shoes in hand, ready to toss. "You wouldn't know you were trying to dethrone me, would you?"

"Delphine, I—"

"Relax, Anna. I know Victoria's handiwork when I see it. I admit the high-profile photos stung, but I'm getting over it. Giving you a rough time was how I deal. You're okay though, right?"

"I guess." Anna is aware that Victoria will be there any moment, so she drops her bag and fishes around for a pair of shoes. That's weird; she could have sworn she had two or three pairs right on top, freshly collected from Susan. A bit more rummaging through her possessions unearths a decent pair at last. "So we're cool?"

"Well, I have to go have dinner with my sister tonight," Delphine begins to explain, zipping up her hoodie. "It's making me realize something."

"It is?"

"That I'm going for Liza's job." Delphine gives Anna a testing look. "Maybe you're a sign from the stars or something, but I've done about all I can here at Metropolitan. If I ever want to put all this crap with Liza to bed, I've got to at least try to make it in San Francisco. To finally impress Kevin Winters."

"Wow," Anna exhales the word in relief. "That's amazing. You should absolutely do that."

"Because it leaves the path clear here for you? I can see why you'd agree."

"No! I mean because it's what you want. And if we both have a good season that helps, right? It only lifts us both up, rather than fighting and letting the company suffer."

"My company is suffering?" Victoria asks, lurking in the doorway again. She is way too good at sneaking up. "Well, I suppose I should thank you for bothering to come dance with us, then, Anya."

Anna winces at the return to the wrong name, but she doesn't dare correct Victoria in front of Delphine.

"I didn't mean it like that. Delphine and I were just talking about how we can have the best possible season. For everyone."

"I hear we've been graced by a state visit." Victoria directs that at Delphine. "Anything you want to share, Little Wade?"

"Your guess is as good as mine." Delphine shrugs.

Victoria considers that for a moment, then seems to accept it.

"I'll report back after I have dinner with her tonight, if you'd like?" Delphine says.

"I would like." Victoria looks impressed by the loyalty. "Do you want to stick around and show your colleague how to do a *sissone fermé* that doesn't make her look like she needs a bathroom break?"

"Just show her tape of yours, Victoria," Delphine suggests. "You know nobody else is ever going to be good enough."

"That's sadly true." Victoria sighs.

Delphine leaves with a small nod, and Victoria turns to Anna. "I had requested Teresa, but she's gone home with one of her migraines. So we'll work with just some backing tracks today."

"You're still choosing dances? I guess I just assumed…"

"Dangerous thing, assumptions." Victoria overenunciates the *p*" and it only draws Anna's focus to her mouth.

How unfair that someone who could dance so well also communicates so clearly with words. Victoria's cutting sentences and witty rants so often make Anna feel fumbling and stupid by comparison. No matter how much enthusiasm she has for her subject, she never expresses it well.

"Well, I don't mind what you want me to dance."

"Oh, I'm so pleased to hear that," Victoria says with mock relief at Anna's approval. "You'd get a lot more done if you got those shoes out of your hand and onto your feet, though."

"I know," Anna grumbles, pulling up her legwarmers and stomping over to the rosin box in the corner. "What are we starting with?"

⟳⟳⟳

It should be infuriating how unbreakable Anna's spirit is, but there she goes again with bouncing right back. Victoria wonders now and then just how far she can push her, whether it would be satisfying to reach the point where Anna actually loses her temper.

"We can start with those *sissones* I mentioned," Victoria calls out, poking at the sound system that's wired into every corner of the studio. A few experimental prods later and sweet strings fill the air. Almost soothing, compared to the noise that populates the rest of Victoria's days.

"I was surprised we're doing *The Nutcracker*," Anna pipes up from the floor.

Today she's opted for a leotard that's more athletic, something they'd wear in gymnastics, with a racer back. Coupled with running tights, she looks ready for the track, in teal and blue. Victoria's surprised that she doesn't entirely hate it. At least the legwarmers and footwear are appropriate.

"You know, since you hate being traditional and all," Anna adds.

"I don't hate tradition. I simply live to shake it up. You haven't seen all of my upcoming productions for this season, remember. The fresh take on *Don Quixote*, *Jewels*, whatever else. I can't burn you out in your first year. But economics dictate *Nutcracker* at Christmas. If we want to stay in business, anyway."

"I love it. Maybe I never outgrew it, but it's the first ballet I ever saw."

"Okay, enough with the biopic." Victoria knows it's a little harsh, but she's distracted and needs to get Anna through her paces. That will push the world back into perspective and allow Victoria some time to think. She finds herself resenting that she knows yet another fact about Anna. "Ready?"

Anna scuffs her feet through the rosin one at a time. "Yeah. I'll start with the jumps."

"Good girl," Victoria answers, absentminded as she tries to picture any of the men of the company at Anna's side. Victoria doesn't mean to say it at all, but Anna lights up like Times Square at the accidental praise. Of course, it spurs her on to complete a series of perfect short jumps as though she'd never been sloppy with them last time out. Victoria stabs at the tiny remote in her hand and skips to a faster piece.

"Fine, so you've practiced." She counts the beats for Anna. "Let's see if you can fix your wobbly pirouette from the showcase."

"Oh!" Anna's elation is wiped from her face at the reminder. "Of course. I know I can do better, I've done that many before without—"

"Dance!" Victoria snaps at her. This talking really has to be stopped.

And Anna, always ready to obey and execute orders flawlessly, is up on her toes without another moment of urging. She's looking to Victoria for approval as she does it, leaning into the turn to weight it correctly.

Only as she completes the first rotation, Anna cries out in pain.

"Son of a—"

Victoria is by her side in an instant, helping Anna down onto the floor. "Ankle?" she gasps, the panic rising in her throat.

"No," Anna grunts, bending forward and yanking at the ribbons binding her feet. "My toes, they…Jesus!"

Victoria looks down in time to see the blood trickling down Anna's foot. No breaks, fortunately, the toes just seem to be the regular level of battered and taped. But there's a sparkle that catches the light, and Victoria snatches up the discarded shoe to confirm it.

Broken glass. It must have been stitched behind the satin, right on top of the box where it wouldn't be felt until the worst possible time: with Anna's full weight on top of it.

"Kelly!" Victoria calls out, knowing her assistant is around somewhere handing out new insurance cards.

Anna is fussing with the cuts, and Victoria gently guides her hand away. It's only then she sees her own hands are trembling, with Anna's steady one held between them.

"Surface cuts," Victoria assures her, and she gives in to the urge to smooth Anna's loose strands of hair from her face.

Anna leans into the gentle touch, eyes closing for just a second. "On purpose?" she whispers, opening those blue eyes again, her expression so wounded.

"We have to assume." Victoria pulls the Hermès scarf from around her neck and wraps it carefully around Anna's foot. Giving attention to the wounds lets her stop staring into those blue eyes. "Whoever did this will be punished. I promise you that."

They wait for Kelly, the only sound passing between them coming from the gentle sobs Anna can no longer hold back.

CHAPTER 18

When Kelly takes too long to show up, Victoria pulls out her phone and summons Kim herself.

As they wait for the physical therapist to arrive, a nosy little crowd forms outside the door, but no one is brazen enough to actually enter while Victoria is crouched between Anna and the onlookers. Focusing on these details helps Anna not wilt under their curious gazes; her tears dry quickly.

The injury doesn't even seem so bad as adrenaline courses through her system. Shock, probably. Should she ask Victoria if this is shock? Would Victoria even know? Anna wriggles her toes experimentally beneath the expensive-looking scarf. It isn't remotely absorbent.

It can't be that bad. Anna has the same bruised toes and bumps as every other professional dancer; she can't think of a time she hasn't had some kind of pain in her feet. She's danced through twists and sprains, flu and fever, and she has rarely fallen other than a slow slide of exhaustion to the floor. Sometimes there's stumbling in a bad landing, but the reason she's made it this far is that she does have good balance, and the ability to use her body well.

"What have we got?" Kim pushes through the crowd, muttering something to them that makes most of them scatter.

Anna was sort of hoping for more than just the resident PT. Kim is a fully qualified doctor, and the rational part of Anna knows that, but in the pain and confusion of it all, she just wants to be as well looked after as possible.

The question jars Victoria from her silent fuming. Anna swears her nostrils actually flared at one point. "Fucking *glass*," she spits.

"Well, no blood spray," Kim observes, crouching.

Victoria stands. She looks a little unsteady on her feet and, despite sitting on the floor, Anna leans to offer a steadying hand.

Victoria doesn't seem to notice.

"So not the worst it could have been," Kim continues. "All toes accounted for. Not nice, but not the worst. I'll clean it up."

"Here?" Victoria demands. "I want her treated somewhere sterile. Get some of these spying vultures to carry her down."

"I mean, if you want to just wait for a paramedic," Anna begins, but she's interrupted by her own hiss of pain as Kim tweezes out some glass. When did she put gloves on? She's fast.

"Ice and painkillers coming up as soon as I'm done," Kim promises. "I don't need to move her, Victoria. I have everything here in my kit. If it looks like any went deep or broke off, I'll take her for an X-ray, but that shouldn't be necessary. Best to do it by feel."

"Oh, then I'm fine here," Anna says.

Victoria gives her a long, steady look and seems to breathe out fully for the first time in ten minutes.

"It wasn't nice, but it's not much worse than losing a nail," Anna says.

"Don't play this down," Victoria warns, and she looks as tense as piano wire again.

Anna would have shrunk back from that just a few weeks ago. Now she folds her arms over her chest and lets Kim work on the cuts, wincing as the antiseptic goes on next.

"You could get an infection," Victoria says, "cellulitis probably, and then you risk losing—"

"Calm down," Kim warns, and there's a look between them that Anna can't interpret. "If she did get a *mild* infection, I can handle that too. You might not be familiar with anything outside of the benzo class, but antibiotics do exist, Victoria."

They're interrupted by one of the younger male soloists pushing through the bodies at the door.

"Hey, David sent me up to see if you still need a leading man?" He draws himself up, trying to look impressive. "Just have someone mop up the blood, I guess."

"Mickey, isn't it?" Victoria sounds sugar-sweet, and the murmurs from the hall pick up. They know what comes next.

"It's Mike, actually."

God, he probably thinks that's a winning smile. Anna wonders if that hair product will smear when Victoria wipes the floor with him.

"Oh." Victoria does that fake-fascinated thing she does, like she's really filing away his name as something important. "Thanks for putting me right, *Mike*."

"Hey, no biggie."

Oh God. He actually reaches out to pat her on the arm. Victoria looks at the offending limb as though he just slapped toxic waste directly onto her skin.

"Get. Out."

"You know what? Let me show I'm a team player and help her down to physical therapy." Mike heads over to Anna, completely ignoring Kim. He reaches for Anna's arm and tries to pull her up, as though she's just resting after a series of lifts. She resists, a dead weight to him, but he still jerks her arm enough to make her yelp at the additional pain.

Kim is the one to shove him aside, but she only just beats Victoria to it.

"Kelly!" Victoria calls out.

"Yes?"

"Security, now. His things will be left by the trash once you have an intern clear out his locker. Tell David we now need a new male soloist as well."

"Wait, you can't—"

Victoria turns on him.

"This is my company. *She* is my principal. And you just jeopardized her recovery from a deliberate injury that, I assure you, more heads will roll over. So consider yourself lucky, *Mickey*, that you're just the first to make my list today. Because it will be much, much worse as I work my way down."

"Whatever," he says, practically spitting in her face. "With my ass there isn't a ballet master who won't find a place for me. Enjoy tanking your season, bitch."

"By the time you hit the street you'll be blacklisted with every company in the country, so keep talking and I'll rack up some international minutes too." Victoria nods to Kelly, who gives a quiet but long-suffering sigh.

The security guards meet him at the door.

"What happened?" Irina asks as she arrives, munching on an apple and taking in the scene with her usual detachment. "Kick a mirror on your turns?"

"It's nothing," Anna mutters.

"I'll call your sister." Irina pulls her phone from her bag.

"Enough!" Anna is sick of being babied. She doesn't need family summoned like she's been sent to the school nurse. She's a grown woman and she isn't made of sugar glass.

The moment Kim finishes taping the gauze in place, Anna is on her feet. Okay, that stings. A lot. "If we're all done treating me like a toddler who scraped her knee, I'm going to take my stuff and go home."

Even Victoria is startled, and maybe faintly impressed.

Anna roots through her bag for slip-on shoes that just about fit, even with her toes wrapped. Thank God she always buys a little bigger to allow for the days when her feet swell. With as much dignity as she can muster, she marches out of the studio with fresh tears in her eyes.

She makes it down the corridor and around the corner, out of sight. For all her toughing it out, Anna still feels like her chest might cave in. She just has to make it to the locker room, where she can lose it in private.

Someone did this *to her*. Her bag had been messed with; those shoes had been planted. Victoria didn't even blink when considering that the sabotage might be deliberate. Someone hates Anna enough to try to really hurt her, to cause a fall that could have had her out for months. Or the glass could have been driven in deep enough to risk her toes staying attached, maybe even an arterial bleed.

She knows in her gut it was probably Teresa, but due to the nature of a competitive environment like this, she can't be sure. Anna doesn't want people to lose their jobs and careers over it, but there's a heated little knot in the pit of her stomach that wants much, much worse for Teresa if she's responsible. The mental image of slapping her sycophantic little face comes to Anna just as a hand is laid on her shoulder.

"Irina, please—"

᙮

Of course she assumes it's Irina; after all, Victoria has tried to cultivate that very relationship. Despite whatever millennial drama is going on with the sister, the two seem to be getting closer. None of which matters, because Victoria is the one reaching out to touch Anna.

"Guess again," Victoria rasps, her throat tight and a little sore from her firing outburst. She's going to hear about that from Rick as well as the legal team. Her body is still trembling from the adrenaline of the first fight, and she has plenty more in reserve. "Are you sure you should be up and walking?"

When Anna turns, sitting on the locker room bench, she has tears in her eyes. Despite the bravado, she's wounded far more deeply on an emotional level. The movement has knocked Victoria's hand away from her, and it's startling how much Victoria wants to reach out again. She resists, both hands back by her sides with perfect poise.

"Will you find out who did it?"

"Absolutely," Victoria promises. "There's nowhere to hide in this building, not from me."

Anna considers that, blue eyes downcast for a moment before fixing Victoria with a steady gaze. "I want them to be as scared as I just was. I want them to have that moment of thinking, 'Here goes everything I've worked for.'"

"Does that mean you want to watch?" Victoria has never seen this side of Anna before, and it's as dazzling as it is terrifying. So calm, so controlled, so utterly sure of her vengeance.

"No." Anna shakes her head. "But tell me when it's done. It's okay that I'm going home?" She's back to her usual mild-mannered self, pulling her hoodie tighter around her shoulders and then zipping it higher. Protective clothing that can't protect much.

"My driver is out front. I know it's not far, but trust me it's going to feel like a marathon with your toes like that. Let him drive you the few blocks, and he'll help you inside if you need it."

"Why are you being so nice to me?"

"Because someone stuck enough glass in your shoes to land you in the hospital, or out of the season. But I've always believed that if at least one person hates you, you must be doing something right."

"You got pretty mad at Mike."

No question, not explicitly. Is Anna intrigued by the ways in which Victoria will lash out, so long as it's not directed at her? It's impossible to tell, but there's something beckoning in that wounded expression that makes Victoria want to end the day with heads on spikes, just to cheer Anna up a little.

"That was nothing," Victoria says. "Let Kelly know if you're okay to dance tomorrow. No, wait." She snatches Anna's phone from her hand. It unlocks without a code, not exactly shocking for Little Miss Sunshine.

"What are you—"

"My cell number," Victoria explains, adding herself to Contacts with only a slight fumbling to find the right app. "You'll be one of the precious few who doesn't come through the office. Do not abuse the privilege, understood?"

"Understood." There's a hint of that smile, at last.

Now it's just a question of those cuts healing, hopefully overnight, and getting back to the studio if they lay off *pointe* work for a session or two. Victoria leads them out into the hallway, toward the elevator. She even presses the button.

"Go. Heal."

This time Victoria sees it coming, and there's nothing she can do about it. Anna throws herself into the hug like she's being caught in the middle of a *pas de deux*. Anna has absolute faith that strong arms will be waiting for her, and Victoria is not about to start letting her down on a day like this.

∞∞∞

Oh God. Of all the idiotic things to do, but…Victoria is hugging back. Like "she forgot her parachute but they both jumped out of a plane" levels of hugging and holding on.

It's unexpected that Victoria would be the one to hug tighter, but Anna revels in the squeezed closeness of their bodies. This is the kind of comfort she's been silently crying out for, and now she's getting it from the unlikeliest source.

They're interrupted by Irina and Kim on their way back to the physical therapy suite in tandem. Victoria springs back as though caught kicking puppies, shamefaced for a split second until the usual superior expression slips back into place.

"I'll see you tomorrow," Anna promises, slinging her bag over her shoulder. Her toes sting in an agonizing little cacophony of aches and pains, and she's glad for Victoria's offer of the car. Every part of her wants to look back, especially when Kim keeps walking and Irina stops to talk with Victoria, but a moment later the doors are sliding shut.

∞∞∞

"I'm feeling homesick," Irina says. "What next? A push down the stairs? Or more classic, perhaps? The fly crew just forgot to tie that rope, or the batten came loose… Squash the poor little ballerina for a moment?"

"You're being melodramatic." Victoria tries to wave off her concern "This isn't the Bolshoi, Irina. These girls don't take it that seriously."

"Not like you and me." Irina winces as she pulls away from the wall she's leaning on. She nods back to the now-closed elevator and the departed Anna. "That's why you'd have been a hit in Paris, Vicki. The obsessives make the mark. Now you're chasing after the boo-boos of the new kid? You didn't put your coffee down when Morgan dislocated her hip, and that was some screaming."

"She's back dancing."

"Barely. And we both know that once it goes…it goes again. Until it doesn't set back quite right, and then it's off to unemployment."

"What's happening with you and Anna anyway?" Victoria asks, looking around for eavesdroppers. "You're supposed to be befriending her, but I hear things—"

"I can't have a little friend of my own?" Irina says with a sneer. "Jess is none of your business, and none of Anna's, either. You're not in charge of me outside of these walls, and barely within them."

"Defensive?" Victoria smirks. "Oh Irina, you've got it bad. When you don't care, you brag about your little conquests as though they're part of your treatment. You must like this other Gale."

"Don't speak of me liking a Gale after I catch you holding one in your arms," Irina warns her. "I hear things too. Like why brokenhearted girls might be lashing out at your new pet of the month."

"You've got proof it was her?"

"I wouldn't tell you if I did." Irina leans in, and Victoria sees the dilation in her pupils. Overmedicated again. High, to be accurate. "Snitches get stitches, isn't that your lovely phrase for it? Not that I'm the only one who might know."

"I'm going to enjoy firing her." Victoria smooths out her black pants and shirt, crumpled from all the kneeling and hugging. Her neck feels bare without its scarf, and she scratches absently at the tendon on the left side. "It would save me a lot of maneuvering with Rick if I had proof. Or a witness."

"You won't get either. Unless you dangle a promotion that one of the kids jumps for."

"Go see Kim." Victoria feels the fire roaring in her veins again. Teresa won't have gone home with any kind of ailment. She'll be somewhere nearby to bask in her seeming victory. "Clearly you were on your way down before you stopped to mess with me."

Irina gives one of her joking salutes, but she lets it fall quickly, face suddenly serious again as Victoria walks away. "Hey, she's okay? Anna?" she calls after Victoria.

"She will be."

♋

"Jess, it's not that bad." Anna eases herself onto the sofa, kicking her taped-up feet on top of the pillow that's been with her since she first moved in with Jess and Marcia. She brought it to the sleepover the night her parents died, and it's been with her ever since. "I'm sure you get the same crap with all your divas."

Jess pulls a beer from the fridge, bringing one for Anna, who ignores it when she puts it on the table. "Bitching is one thing. Sabotage is completely different. Now, I know you think it's this Teresa girl, but sometimes the people who make their beef obvious aren't the problem."

"Oh, you think Delphine Wade made peace with me just so she could crack a martini glass or two into some satin? I'm not that important."

"Don't rule anything out. Did Victoria call the cops?"

"No, it'll be handled internally. I'm not rocking the boat, not this soon." Anna changes her mind and twists the top off the beer. Time to change the subject. "How's it all going…with Irina?"

Jess takes her time about her next mouthful of beer. She doesn't usually drink before a show. There's only an hour before she'll have to be back at the theater and yelling at the crew.

"Good, Anna. Like…way better than I expected. She has some stuff she's working on. You know this is her last season, but she wants to try for one more. We talk about stuff that I don't get to talk about, with anyone. And my Russian is rusty, but I get to use it with her."

"You can talk to me about anything. Well, not in Russian."

"No, I mean…she doesn't know me already. She just wants to find out, you know? And she is so gorgeous."

"And yet she seems to like a total dork who did her junior year abroad to study Chekov."

"Hey! Not that weird in a theater degree."

"It's a little weird," Anna argues. "And there's nothing to worry about? You know how some dancers, with the pain and all—"

"Totally under control." Jess shuts it down fast, draining the rest of her beer. "You know, if you're really okay, I need to get my ass into work early today. Anything else I can get you?"

Anna raises her beer to show she's okay, reaching for her laptop to cue up something to watch. "Thanks for checking on me. You're not bad, as big sisters go."

"Wow, such praise. You'll call me when Victoria asks you to help hide the bodies, right? I know this guy with a van."

"I'm very pleased everyone wants to go avenge my injured feet," Anna says with fake solemnity. "I'm sure she's being very professional about it."

"Nowhere?" Victoria hisses.

Kelly puts the clipboard to her head in exasperation.

"She's not anywhere in the building. And we've tried calling her at home. Even sent an intern over with some migraine medication as a courtesy. No answer."

"This is not acceptable. Surely the fact that she's going into hiding proves—"

"There's always the cops. Behavior like this is a crime, Victoria, and it could escalate. Do you want to explain to Rick why we're suddenly uninsurable?"

"And the police crawling over the building for a catfight won't make an even worse impression? Be serious, Kelly. Something about you should be." She gestures to Kelly's brightly colored dress.

"My money's on Teresa comes in tomorrow like nothing happened." Kelly straightens up and adjusts her cardigan over the dress. "You have the rest of the night to come up with a legal, professional solution."

"Do you need me to help?"

"You've been quite unhelpful enough for one day," Victoria says with a sigh.

"You know I live for your performance reviews." Kelly returns to her desk, flipping through stacks of paper for whatever is next on her never-ending list.

The evening is ticking by, and Victoria loses herself in paperwork before the restlessness of a grudge unsettled has her in motion again. After grabbing her purse and jacket, she hesitates over the cane. It has been a particularly long day, and her knee hasn't forgiven her for all the fussing over Anna.

As her driver approaches Victoria's building, he makes the signal to pull up in front while they're sitting in slow traffic. "Actually." She taps him on the shoulder. "Can you leave me across the street?"

She's going to check on Anna. Isn't that what any responsible boss would do?

Chapter 19

Anna seems genuinely stunned as she opens the door, opening and closing her mouth while the words refuse to come. Taking pity on both of them, Victoria motions to be let in.

As Anna stands aside, Victoria takes in the view of what was once briefly her home. Personal touches everywhere already. Tendrils of kindness and a fondness for twee decorating items are evident on every wall and surface, down to the warm blankets that drape the sofas.

"How are they healing?" Victoria asks. She should have brought something—a bottle of wine perhaps. Except that would confuse a perfectly valid check on an injured employee with something social.

"Fine, I guess." Anna hobbles a little on her way back to the sofa.

She moves the blanket and pillow she's clearly been using for comfort, and Victoria sits on the space she freed, propping her cane on the arm of the couch. Anna looks unsure for a moment, before sitting next to Victoria.

"You haven't changed the dressings yet," Victoria points out with a tut of displeasure. Didn't she give the lecture about infection? She must have saved too much of her temper for that idiot boy. "How's the arm?"

"My arm?"

"From Prince Smarmy trying to yank you off the floor."

"Fine," Anna says. "One good thing about these shoulders is that I'm practically a guy on upper-body stuff. Did you—"

"Nothing yet." Victoria turns away so Anna won't see the disappointment on her face. "But tomorrow is another day. I've been told my temper is like wine, all the more potent for having some time to breathe first."

"I can believe it. Can I get you a drink? And then I'll change the tape and gauze," she adds when Victoria attempts to interrupt. "I'm lucky—a few Band-Aids will probably do it."

"Do you have vodka?"

"For my toes? I was going to just use some antiseptic."

"To drink, Anna."

She nods in understanding and hobbles into the open-plan kitchen to retrieve two glasses.

Expecting a barely touched bottle to be unearthed, Victoria's a little impressed when a half-full one is yanked out of the freezer. "Should I be asking you for ID before you pour that?"

"I'm not that young," Anna calls back. "And you can talk. You probably still get carded at bars."

"Only from men trying to hit on me. I'm pushing forty. But that was a decent attempt at kissing ass."

"It wasn't. You really don't look it." Anna's half-smile over her shoulder is a little daring, so she can't be feeling entirely sorry for herself. "Ice? It's pretty cold already."

"Contrary to popular opinion, that's not actually what I'm made of. Neat is fine."

Anna passes her the drink, settles back on the sofa, sitting stiffly to make sure only her heels make contact with the floor.

Victoria sits primly, knees pressed together, nursing the tumbler on her lap. She takes a testing sip, and the warmth in her throat is welcome.

"What you said, earlier," Victoria begins, and then stops. She sees the tightrope stretch out in front of her, knowing what she's exposing herself to by starting this line of discussion. "That feeling might not go away for a while. That you could have lost everything, I mean."

Anna's brow is furrowed, but it relaxes as she apparently begins to comprehend.

"That it was the moment your career ended," Victoria finishes.

"But it didn't."

"No," Victoria says. "It didn't, this time. I'm not trying to scare you."

"You usually are."

"Being okay helps chase the feeling away, but just don't expect it to be instant. That's all I wanted to say."

"What about when you're not okay?" Anna takes a sip, as though rewarding herself for being brave enough to ask. "What about when it really is over in that moment? I mean, I guess you don't know until afterward; when you see the doctor, when they've tried everything."

Victoria shakes her head. "You know. Right then and there." She taps short nails on the side of the glass. "It's different."

"My teachers always told me to prepare for it. Once they realized I wanted to go pro, anyway. Even Marcia—my foster mother—did the math for me one time, when I had to choose between college or training."

"The math?"

"I can't explain it as well as she did, but… The more years you dance, every year that passes you're much closer to the end of it all, even without the freak injuries or accidents. That, at best, with luck and conditioning and good genes, no ballet dancer gets further than about fifty percent of their life before they have to give up. That's locked in from the start."

"Our careers aren't just short." Victoria drains her drink, wishing Anna had brought the bottle. "They're brutal too. There's no compassion in how it ends. If you're lucky, like that handful, you'll quit while still dancing your best. Or in that first slight decline, before it's too late. That's the best any of us can hope for."

"That's not what you got." Anna sets her glass aside and reaches carefully to put Victoria's beside hers on the table. "You should have had another ten years, maybe more."

"And end up like Irina?"

"She's happy." Anna can't help defending her, loyal to a fault. "Or happier than she would be without it."

"That really depends on how you define happy." Victoria shouldn't be here. Anna's seen the opening now and is going to keep pressing. And there's a genuine concern Victoria won't hold out against those startling blue eyes, clear and filled with compassion. She stands, and the pain is down to a dull ache once more. "Don't forget to do those dressings."

"Wait! Um, please?"

"I have things to do." Victoria pulls back from the hand Anna extends, allowing it to brush the cuff of Anna's jacket and no more. "I'll see you tomorrow. We'll keep you off your toes for a day or two, but there's plenty of work we can do."

"Victoria—"

"Good night. I'll see myself out." Victoria moves quicker than she expected, buoyed by the painkillers and the vodka. She's outside before Anna can catch up to her.

"Nope," David says the minute he sees Anna enter warm-up. "You're on the injured list, Gale."

"Only for pointe work," she argues, grasping the strap of her bag. "I'm not going to just sit on my butt all day."

"Round here we call it an ass," Delphine mocks gently, patting Anna on exactly that as she strides past. "How are those feet, newbie?"

"Well, they're still in working order," Anna says. "I'll be careful, I promise," she adds for David's benefit. "I won't even put my pointe shoes on, but I'll keep up with the class."

"I suppose it stops you adding a muscle twang to the list." David sighs. "But if I get grief for this from Victoria…"

"You won't."

idk if I want them to get together or not

Anna scurries to take her regular spot next to Ethan. He's smiling over at Gabriel but snaps back to pay attention when he sees her.

"You okay?"

"Not you too," she groans. "What's the rumor mill saying?"

"That you lost three toes." Ethan grins wide, enjoying the drama. "That the blood sprayed up the entire eight-foot mirror. That you collapsed on top of Victoria, pinning her to the ground."

"I did not!" Anna protests, loud enough to draw attention from half the room. She gives a nervous wave until they all look away again, before turning back to Ethan with a hiss. "Who told you that last one?"

"Actually, I made that one up. Did you really get in a fight with Mike?"

"He got in one with Victoria."

"And now he's toast." Ethan begins his stretches, and Anna follows suit. "It's never dull around you, I'll give you that."

"Sometimes I really wish it was."

I need more than Ethan scenes

A stack of tedious paperwork keeps Victoria behind her desk, but it means she's exactly where she wants to be when Teresa makes her move.

"Knock, knock?" she says, although the door is wide open. It's one of Teresa's more irritating attributes—her need to always play for cute when it doesn't suit her.

"Oh, there you are." Victoria puts her phone down on the desk. "You know, I felt bad about the other day. Did you get the painkillers and water I sent over last night?"

"I…I crashed with a friend." Clearly Teresa isn't expecting to be accepted back into the fold that easily. Whatever little performance she's been working on won't be necessary. "My place is all the way in—"

"Brooklyn," Victoria finishes, her smile fake and tight. "I remember."

It's enough for Teresa to blossom under the attention.

"What's all this I hear about someone blowing out yesterday? I miss all the good drama."

"Well." Victoria gestures with a tip of her head, as if Teresa should come closer and hear the real story. "You know Mike, don't you?"

Teresa doesn't commit to more than a nod. "He hits on everyone, yeah."

"Well, apparently he's quite the prankster. Thought he'd welcome the new girl to the company with a bit of broken glass."

"He…he did what?"

"Oh, I know it was him." Victoria sighs like she should have seen it coming. "Although honestly? She won't be out for long, but I think he did me a favor."

"A favor?" Teresa grips the edge of Victoria's desk.

"Anna isn't up to it." Victoria clenches her fist, overselling it a little. She doesn't want to tip over into mime. "He denied it of course, but I think he just saved my season. If not my career. I could have lost it all on that mediocrity."

"But I heard you fired him." Teresa makes her first slip. Clearly she's more than aware of what went on yesterday. Or thinks she is. "I mean, you did fire him?"

"Well, I had to for show," Victoria continues, forcing herself to lay a hand on Teresa's forearm, as though they're partners in crime. "But let's just say that Mike will find himself getting a very impressive offer from San Francisco by this time tomorrow. Kevin owes me a favor or two."

"No!" Teresa can't hold it in. "Victoria, are you saying you're happy someone hurt your little pet?"

"I'm not *unhappy*. And anyone who spared my considerable blushes deserves to be rewarded."

"It wasn't Mike! Why would you think that walking STD has the brains? He's barely even spoken to her. I knew, Victoria. I'm the one who saw she was a waste of your time."

"You, Teresa?" Victoria is careful not to bite too quickly. "Don't be silly, you don't have that kind of boldness in you. In your playing, yes. But you're no secret agent. Why would you in the first place? Surely not because of us."

"I'm not that crazy about you," Teresa says, though they both know different. "But I'm not the only one who has your back."

"You're not?"

"Richard came to me," she continues. "He's worried you've lost your edge. He simply suggested that if you can't be talked out of Anna, maybe someone should help you by taking her out of the equation. I don't think the *Times* coverage helped."

"Of course not." Victoria makes it sound so understanding. "But you'd have been here for me now, when I have to put it right for the rest of the season. Wouldn't you?"

"That's all I want," Teresa reassures her, and she actually leans in to kiss Victoria.

She ducks away just in time, swiping her cell phone from the desk and pressing Pause on the voice recorder. Victoria holds up the phone and lets realization sink in, as surely as heels returning to the floor after a perfect *grand-plié*.

"Well, it wasn't quite busting Lance Armstrong, but I suppose I should be glad you didn't take up my whole morning with your sniveling."

"Victoria—"

"Shut your damn mouth." She thinks of Anna, of that gleam in her eyes yesterday. *I want them to be just as scared as I was.* "It goes without saying that you're fired, but I'm going to enjoy marching you out of here myself. Now, should I have Kelly post it to social media before I hand it over to the police? Or should we wait for the coverage of the trial?"

"I was just trying to show you that I care!"

"No, you weren't." Victoria wags a finger at the excuse. "But if you want to work anywhere but a dive bar for the rest of your life, you'll make yourself available to me if and when I decide to take a little revenge on Rick. And you will apologize to Anna."

"Like hell." Teresa finally finds a little spine at that, straightening and pulling away from Victoria's desk altogether.

Sad, how small and pathetic Teresa looks in her fussy dress, the patterns too bold and the cut unflattering, that bland brown bob hanging across her face. Victoria wonders how she'd ever been interested.

"You might not like it, but you're still making an ass of yourself to the whole world," Teresa says. "She isn't good enough, and you'll be a laughingstock."

"You're just making me wish I could fire you again, with feeling. You mess with my season again, and you'll wish you were dead. Understood?"

Victoria calls for Kelly—time to get a witness in after all. She takes Teresa gingerly by the arm, expecting resistance, but the girl is as easily led as ever.

"Yes?" Kelly asks when she meets them at the outer office door. "Oh. Did you need me to call an exterminator?"

It's almost enough to make Victoria laugh, given the circumstances. But that would undo a career's worth of severity. "Really, Kelly. You'll come with us while Teresa apologizes to Anna, before I hand her over to security."

"That didn't take long," Kelly says, almost conversational. "Cracked like a soft-boiled egg, did she?"

"I'm right here, you know," Teresa says with a scowl.

"Sure you are, hon," Kelly says. "But you keep announcing that to people, that's my advice. You don't exactly make much of an impression." She turns to Victoria. "Anna's in with the warm-up class."

This year, Kelly is definitely getting another raise.

♈♈

Anna's almost starting to hope that every interruption to a class or rehearsal won't be her fault when the studio door opens with a bang. There stands a furious Victoria, grasping Teresa like an escaped prisoner. Teresa for her part has her shoulders rolled, staring at the floor and trying to make herself invisible.

Victoria nods to David to turn off the recorded music. "As some of you may know, there was an incident yesterday in studio," she says. "Anna, our newest principal, was deliberately injured by someone who works closely with us all." She pushes Teresa forward. "Or should I say, *worked*."

The dancers exchange glances.

"This matter has been handled internally, and if I hear a whisper of it outside this building—including Twitter, Instagram, or the Polly Pocket journals you keep under your pillows at night—then you'll be fired with immediate effect. As the final word on this matter, Teresa has something she'd like to say."

She, of course, says nothing. Victoria actually prods Teresa in the back. She mumbles, just about.

A little part of Anna wants to die at the attention. She knows half of the room is staring at her as intently as they are at Teresa. Before, she would have tried to melt into the wall, or at least crouch down under the barre. She sees the protective rage in Victoria, though, and does what a principal should. Anna steps forward, free of the crowd of bodies.

"I didn't catch that," Anna says when there's no second attempt. "Did you want to see the cuts on my feet first?"

"I'm sorry, okay?" Teresa practically spits it, dragging an unkind look up and down Anna's bright red T-shirt and black leggings. "You clearly didn't die from it."

"Well, that was gracious," Kelly says with a snort, tucking her bright red hair behind her ear. "Security are here, Victoria."

"Then let's take the trash out, since I think that's as good as we're going to get." Victoria turns Teresa away from Anna.

It seems the moment is over, but Anna is relieved to get the tiniest quirk of her lips from Victoria before she practically drags Teresa back into the corridor.

"If we're all quite done with *Masterpiece Theater*," David bellows, turning the music back on. "Nobody leaves here until you've worked up a sweat. Even you, Gale."

"Yes, sir," Anna answers, almost skipping back to her spot.

She feels ten pounds lighter and the cuts on her toes are barely stinging at all. There's a dot or two of blood on her slippers, but nothing major. She catches Irina's eye in the mirror, busy with her own work on the other side of the room. A nod, one professional to another. Maybe they can grab lunch together later. It's not like Anna's going to get to do her corps rehearsal anyway.

Or maybe, just maybe, Anna can shake off the awkwardness of this morning and take some lunch to Victoria instead. It would be the best way to say thank you, after all.

There's a flutter in her stomach as she stretches along with David's barked instructions. Which is definitely just about the culprit being caught. Nothing at all to do with the thought of Victoria maybe agreeing to another private little chat, this time over salads and bottled water.

No. That's not something Anna feels excited about at all. And she's getting better at lying to herself about it.

CHAPTER 20

Anna doesn't need to go all the way to the office, catching Victoria on her way out of the shoe store instead.

"Thank you," Anna says, with what she hopes is her most winning smile. "I feel much better knowing she's being punished for what she did. And I kind of overstepped yesterday, so either way I figure I owe you lunch at least."

"Coffee, lunch… I'm all for buying people's affection, Anna, but it's not exactly a winning strategy with ballerinas, is it? Even former ones."

"Right, but you still *eat*," Anna says. She shouldn't be entirely surprised that twelve years out and Victoria is still strict with her diet. "I mean, I eat more than the others with this crazy metabolism, but tell me you're not still living on nuts and salad like most of the dancers? And…" She wilts under Victoria's disbelieving look, hand on her hip in that coquettish way she has. "There I go again with the overstepping. I swear I can stop it."

"I'm not sure you can." Victoria snatches the paper bag from Anna's hand and peers inside. "Lots of protein, anyway. Why don't you just take this home, treat your *crazy metabolism* to a midnight snack later?"

"Oh, sure. I didn't mean to assume or anything. I should go eat before rehearsal."

"Take that home," Victoria continues, as though Anna hadn't interrupted at all. "And come have lunch with me in the executive suite. We might even have it to ourselves, this early in the season."

"Really? I mean, I don't have rehearsal for an hour." Anna didn't expect to be forgiven so easily. There's something about Victoria this afternoon. She seems lighter. Realization dawns that it's the sheer pleasure of catching and firing Teresa. That should make Anna shudder, and when it does, it's not exactly in an unpleasant way.

"Let's go, before you talk yourself out of it. I had an idea last night, and it's time we talked it through."

"What kind of idea?" Anna follows Victoria down the hallway toward the public part of the Metropolitan Center, with its triple-height atrium and breathtaking artwork. Most days she finds an excuse to come through this part of the building, just to prove to herself she really works here.

"How are the toes?" Victoria changes the subject as they enter the public café that leads into the more exclusive restaurant.

"Healing." Anna remembers coming here for the first time with her mother, the way the lights sparkled so much she didn't realize there was a roof.

"You're up in the stars, Anna," her mother whispered, and even in daylight, Anna can still feel that hitch of excitement in her breath every time she steps into the space.

One of the catering staff scurries to open the private dining room, and by the time they're seated, an actual waitress comes to take their orders. Quite a step up from the grab-your-own-salad arrangement Anna is used to, when she isn't bringing food from home. She blindly orders the first thing with chicken and a sparkling water, oddly pleased when Victoria does the same.

"Okay," Victoria says, rearranging her cutlery. "So we have a small problem."

∽∞∾

Honestly, she never intended to tell Anna about the Rick revelation. It's one thing to ask the girl to take on a challenge beyond anything she's prepared for, but quite another to have her go against the man who effectively gave her the job. But Victoria's anger is still roiling in the pit of her stomach, sloshing waves of it that threaten to race up her throat.

"What kind of problem?" Anna asks.

"Teresa's spiteful little move wasn't entirely her own doing." Victoria drops the bombshell. She's impressed that Anna barely flinches. "I'm sure if you think for a moment you'll work out the one person over my head that she might answer to."

"Richard Westin." Anna glances around the private dining room as if saying his name will conjure him up. "But he's the one who brought me in."

"I've been summoned to dinner with him tomorrow night, in fact. I assume he means to spring Liza on me as an unpleasant surprise," Victoria continues. "Since she's retiring, that makes her a firm favorite to replace me."

"Why would he do that? If you... I mean, not hate, but everyone knows about your rivalry. Why would he force you out for her, of all people?"

"It's possible he told me to go slower on your promotion," Victoria says. "So the *Times* piece might have pissed him off. But I won't give her the satisfaction of thinking I can't handle a simple meal just because of her presence."

"Maybe Delphine could go?" Anna says. "As a buffer, I mean. I'd go if you like, but I can't keep inviting myself to meals. You're going to get sick of me pretty soon if I do."

"You would do that?" Victoria can't help but be suspicious. Is the girl really so selfless? Or does she want to get close enough to confront Rick herself? "Because Delphine and Liza squabbling is just as tiresome, believe me. Having you there might…well, it might annoy Liza for a start."

"Then count me in. I guess that makes it good timing to know how you're going to use me? I mean, for the season."

Blushing. Again. It shouldn't be so appealing, and yet Victoria finds a smirk twisting across her lips.

"It's a doubleheader, of sorts," Victoria says, interrupted by the sparkling water being set on the table. They've remembered to put lime in hers instead of lemon without instruction. Could the catering staff finally be reaching competence? "It's something I've been wanting to do for years, but most of my girls don't have the physicality for it."

"What is it?" Anna's practically bouncing in her chair.

"Well, the first part is flipping the script on gender roles. You mentioned those shoulders of yours, and I think you have a point. I've seen your arm work, and I would have let you throw me around back in the day."

The mouthful of water Anna's in the middle of taking almost ends up sprayed across the table.

Victoria braces herself out of instinct.

"You'd probably be more careful than a lot of the men I worked with," Victoria continues. "We'll need approval from Delphine of course, but Gabriel and that boy you're friends with can give you some coaching. And there's always David. Safest pair of hands I ever worked with."

"You want me to…be the boy?" Anna asks, uncertain. She sets her glass back down, considering. "Everyone always talks about gender stuff, but that usually just means letting the guys do a pirouette."

"Yes, yes. Like we haven't been doing seven in one since we were fourteen, I know. Maddening. Rick was always fond of that gimmick. I'm talking a whole other level. A prince, whoever. The romantic lead."

"Won't that have all the old people having heart attacks in the balcony?"

"For a start, the really rich conservative ones sit in the orchestra seats. Stairs are a liberal conspiracy. Maybe they can't drag that much jewelry up one floor."

Their food comes out, neatly plated and with dressing on the side. Victoria pauses until they're alone again.

"That would be one facet, but what will launch you…is a traditional ballerina part."

"But not classical?"

"No." Victoria's impressed Anna caught the distinction right away. Dealing with someone on her level at last, or someone who will be, with the requisite training. "A revival that's long overdue. *Gala Performance*."

"You want to do a gala?" Anna's face scrunches in confusion. "Of what?"

Perhaps that decision about her level had been premature.

"The ballet called *Gala Performance*," Victoria says with a snap, spearing a piece of chicken with her fork. "Surely you've heard of it. The Russian, the Italian, the French ballerina?"

"Oh!" Anna looks giddy again. "So I'd do that as well as playing the boy in something?"

"Done right, you'll make headlines like no one has since…well." Victoria indicates herself with a flick of the wrist. It isn't lost on her that there hasn't been a star ballerina in the twelve years since she last danced. Good reviews, sparkling notices, sure. Not the *dancer of a generation* and *Queen of Ballet* monikers that were slapped on Victoria as soon as she broke out. The ballerina whose name is recognized even by non-ballet people.

"How?"

"Well, Irina will make a splendid Russian, and she deserves one more principal role. Delphine's the heartbreaker, but a comedienne with it. That makes her a perfect *Française*. As for you…"

"The Italian?" Anna scrunches her nose. "I don't exactly… Plus she wins! She outdances the other two. I can't dance better than Delphine and Irina. Are you kidding?"

"Anna." Victoria sets her cutlery down, closing her eyes for just a moment. When they open again, she looks around, making sure they're completely alone. "I don't say this lightly, and it will take a shitload of work to make me right. But you have to start believing me when I say this: *Yes. You. Can.*"

Instead of responding, Anna flushes dark pink again and shoves some rocket in her mouth, presumably as a way to close it.

Victoria waits her out, picking at her lunch.

Only when Anna has drained her glass does she finally respond. "Okay."

"Okay?"

"I'll believe you," Anna says. "So where do we start?"

"Do not summon me at ungodly hours," Irina barks at Victoria as they enter. "I have agreed my schedule."

Delphine is lying on the floor, legs up and extended as she works through some stretches. Irina is in no hurry to join her, standing at the barre with the perfect posture that's been commented on in almost every review in her career. "A military bearing," *The Washington Post* called it. They weren't wrong. Her black leotard and track pants are a stark contrast to the pastel-toned soft lines of Delphine's leggings and shrug. Anna compares her own gray running tights and tank top, feeling like she might have something approaching her own style at last.

"Well, you never *check* your schedule," Victoria fires right back at her on her way to take up her chair in front of the piano.

"What else do I get?" Irina has a glint in her eyes at Victoria's veiled promise.

"A principal role." Victoria wriggles into her director's chair, nodding at the prone Delphine, who gets slowly to her feet. "A cross-generational celebration of the uniquely talented primas at Metropolitan Ballet. Tudor's *Gala Performance*, modernized by yours truly."

"Well, hell," Delphine pipes up at last. "Victoria Ford had an interesting idea. What took you so long?"

"We can go back to *Giselle* if you want to run your mouth and spend two weeks sobbing all night."

"Hey, it was a compliment, I swear," Delphine says. "I guess we all know who the Russian is going to be. And I have the Italian coloring—"

"We have makeup," Irina cautions. "And wigs. Or is the passport all that matters?"

"There will be no Italian," Victoria says.

Anna frowns at her. What the hell? She's supposed to be the Italian.

"Delphine, you'll be our French ballerina. Nobody else will get the laughs from it that you can."

"And I assume Girl Wonder is here for moral support?" Delphine shoots an apologetic glance Anna's way; it isn't personal.

"Instead of the Italian, the American," Victoria says. "As corny as Kansas in August, but ultimately the powerhouse of modern ballet. And I have another show in mind for you, too, Delphine, but we'll talk that through tomorrow."

"Are you changing the outcome?" Delphine has her hands on her hips now, realization dawning on her. "Or are we 'beaten' by the American, as we would have been by the Italian?"

"What do you think?" Irina butts in. "You think we go on in New York without saying American ballet lights the world? This production can be as wrong as the original. We all know the Russian should win both."

"It's a celebration of all three schools," Victoria says. "There will be a victor, as such, but I like to think of it more as passing the baton, sharing the spotlight, all that nonsense. I assume it won't be a problem?"

"I'll let you know" is all Delphine will commit to. "You know I'm skipping dinner with Liza tomorrow though, right?"

"Yes, but I'll be taking *Bayadère*'s first stage rehearsal, so I will see you there," Victoria says. "I have company for dinner, thank you. Bitch at Liza on your own time. In the meantime I expect you both to show the leadership of a prima and former prima and make this the success it deserves to be."

"And Richard?" Irina asks. "You think he'll like this when we could be packing them in at *Giselle*?"

"He'll like it well enough." Victoria shuts them down. "Especially when he finds out who's playing the role of Stage Manager."

Delphine works it out first. "You're kidding me."

Anna is suddenly screaming inside her head, not daring to hope this means what she thinks it means.

"We're finally going to share a stage?" Delphine asks.

"It's a gimmick." Irina hurls the word like an insult, hands on hips. "But damn, Vicki. It's a good one."

"You're going to do the show?" Anna thinks there has to be misunderstanding. "With us?"

"Oh, keep up!" Victoria's compliments from yesterday are washed away by the iciness of her response. "Of course that's what I'm doing. It wasn't exactly subtle, Anna."

"Right."

"Ladies, I'll have to do some work with this one." Victoria tilts her head in Anna's direction. "Not least on her ability to derive things from context." She turns to Delphine and Irina again. "When I bring this into your schedules next week, I want nothing but teamwork. Do I make myself clear?"

"Crystal," Delphine says with a nod. "Good luck, Anna. You're going to need it."

"Thanks," Anna says weakly.

"We'll work with you," Irina offers. "But that means you come up to our level, *malenkaya*. We don't come down to yours."

"Exactly," Victoria agrees. "Now you all have other work to do today, so get the hell out of my studio."

◯◯◯

"Again!" Victoria snaps, clicking the music back to the start. They've been at it for two hours already. "No, wait."

Anna responds to the command without conscious thought, her feet only just back in fifth.

"Your extension is the laziest I have seen in years. It's as though you've had that leg amputated at the knee."

Anna knows that isn't true. Her extension would be just fine by anyone else's standards, but Victoria is never happy unless every muscle in Anna's body is vibrating at the barely concealed tension of a tripwire. She holds her hands out in surrender, palms upturned. If Victoria wants something different—something better—she's damn well going to have to explain what she wants in detail, for once.

"Tell me," Anna pleads. "I can get it if you just tell me."

"Sit." Victoria clicks her fingers from sheer impatience. She started out dressed for the dinner Anna knows they're going to be late for, a dinner that's probably just three martinis and pushing a salad around their plates at some overpriced French place.

Anna sits heavily on the floor, each leg feeling like it's been caked in cement, muscles jumping beneath the skin. Her toes are stinging, some of the healing cuts newly irritated by the amount of time spent on them.

"Watch," Victoria commands, and before Anna can fully appreciate what's happening barely a foot in front of her face, Victoria takes position in fifth and runs through most of the sequence as if it's her hundredth repetition of the day. It helps that she barely has to use her bad leg, but even so it's a revelation.

"Oh my God," Anna gasps. She can't help it. Victoria Ford is dancing in front of her. Not minimalist instructions where she barely has to lift her feet, but the true flowing moves a generation of little girls grew up wanting to emulate. It's Christmas Morning and a surprise trip to Paris, only it's over too fast. Victoria is standing over her, hands on hips, glaring at Anna's openmouthed admiration.

"Were you paying attention?"

Anna shakes her head. She knows better than to lie by now. "Sorry. I'm watching now, I promise. Show me, please?"

Victoria looks for all the world like she may refuse. She's been more severe than usual. Chasing Anna around the floor tonight seems to have heated her up, though, and she shed the creamy silk blouse twenty minutes in.

"As you lean in," Victoria is saying, clutching the remote as the music starts again, "you have to give full extension on the trailing leg, otherwise you ruin the lines entirely. Can't you see that?"

Anna can see that. She can see Victoria's leg, extended with textbook perfection, close enough to reach out and touch. The movement of her leg has caused her skirt to ride up over that pale shin, and for the first time Anna sees it: the faded but still vicious white scar. It's just the cracked end where skin had obviously split, but she's never had a chance to really look at Victoria this closely before. It's clear this has been kept covered.

Self-preservation has never been Anna's strong suit. From where she's kneeling on the battered wooden floor, she reaches out and touches the very edge of the scar. Victoria manhandles Anna most rehearsals, pushing her lower or grabbing her to steady wobbling turns. They touch frequently, without preamble, but Anna realizes just a fraction too late that the common thread is in who initiates the contact.

"How dare you." The words are a growl as Victoria returns to standing, a little too roughly.

Anna is brushed aside by the force of it. It's the same mistake she made in her apartment, of crossing one line too far.

"Is that what you've been waiting for?" Victoria demands.

"I—"

"There's a reason I've never spoken to the press about this injury," Victoria continues, barreling over Anna's attempt to speak. "I warned you off the other night. I forgave you and then you throw it back in my face…for what, Anna? A little gossip to share? Was it really worth it?"

"I didn't mean to pry! I wasn't thinking!"

"If you think you can fondle my legs and get the untold story, you have another think coming. Get out of my sight. Go find Wade and Bishop, tell them we're going back to *Giselle*."

"What? You can't do that!"

"I can do anything I want. This is my company." Victoria's expression is livid, and Anna knows if she gives up now, if she accepts this mistake and walks out, she is done with the Metropolitan Ballet. She's probably done with ballet forever.

"Listen!" Anna snaps, and the force of it actually startles Victoria into silence. They're both breathing a little heavier than they should be, Anna still frozen in place on the wooden floor, Victoria staring down at her in quiet fury. "That wasn't why I touched you. Of course I'm curious about…that. I'm not a monster. Everyone wants to know, and I think that's how you like it."

"Oh, don't you dare—"

"I touched you because I wanted to," Anna admits, to herself as much as to Victoria. "Because I keep wanting to. It's stupid, and I'm sorry, and I won't *ever* do it again. But you can't blame me for motives I didn't have."

"So now you're just another horny ballerina?" Victoria scoffs. "How predictable."

"And for the record? If you ever needed someone to talk to? I would be here for you. Because it's the least I can do, with the opportunity you're giving me." Anna hesitates, because that really is too far. "In the meantime, I'm here to learn. So do you want to see my damn extension or not?"

She holds her breath. Victoria scowls at her, arms crossed. The wait stretches on until Anna starts to regret not exhaling.

"Fine. But you'd better have been paying attention."

"I was," Anna insists, and she bends into it as though she'd never done it anything other than perfectly. "See?" she demands, looking up at Victoria from waist height. "Is that better?"

"You'll do," Victoria says with a huff. "Now we have to address your awful turn three bars later."

"Fine."

"Fine."

Anna stands again, waiting for Victoria to reset the music and instruct. It's hard for Anna to believe she's getting away with it, even though her cheeks are burning and she feels light-headed. Her blurted revelation is hanging in the air around them like residue from a smoke machine, but Victoria doesn't seem to notice.

"Victoria? We have dinner with Rick in less than an hour. If you want me to get ready…"

"Hit the showers, then," Victoria says without turning around.

Is Anna imagining it, or does Victoria's voice strangle just a little over the word *showers*?

"And don't wear anything too ridiculous."

"I'll see you out front?"

"Well, that's where the car will be."

"Okay." Anna gathers her bag, scrubbing a towel over her face. She forces herself to stride straight to the door. Hesitating as she passes Victoria would be certain death at this point. "Thank you," she whispers instead.

Victoria doesn't so much as twitch in acknowledgment.

CHAPTER 21

"Jess, you don't understand—"

"What, she's got some force field you're not allowed to penetrate?" Jess scoffs down the phone. "Come on, Anna. She's not that special. Even if you did get all gropey."

"Aren't you supposed to be on my side?"

Jess's smothered chuckle is all the confirmation Anna needs.

"If you're still going to dinner it can't be that bad," Jess makes up for it a moment later. "What did she say after you copped a feel, anyway?"

"I wasn't! I didn't… Jess!"

"Sorry, 'accidentally made contact.'" There's no hiding the laughter this time. This story had better not be shared with her girlfriend, either.

"You don't understand—the dream I've had since I could walk, basically, is to see Victoria Ford dance right in front of my face. It actually happens and I ruin the whole thing by turning into a grabby hands. What is wrong with me?"

"Science may never find the answer to that question," her sister teases. "But seriously. Hair down, hemline up, and put on shoes that are harder to walk in than being up on your toes. Go out looking your best, you'll be too busy getting hit on to worry about what she's thinking. Might make this whole dinner from hell go better too."

"You're no help," Anna says, but she picks out the strappy heels and a black cocktail dress all the same. "If you don't hear from me by breakfast, have them drag the river for my body, okay?"

"Yeah, I'll get right on that. Try sitting on your hands if the urge strikes again."

"Bite me." Anna sighs, but there's no denying she feels a bit better as she ends the call. She pulls the dress on over clean lingerie and checks herself out in the mirror. Not bad, admittedly. With a few swipes on her phone, she finds a reliable makeup tutorial that doesn't look like she just escaped a horror movie, and gets to work. Whatever damage she's done, she has to make up for it by the end of the night. And while Victoria couldn't be less interested in the so-called *horny* ballerina she's trying to make into a star, there's no harm in trying to look like something of a catch.

∽◯◯◯∽

Victoria has the snarky comments about timekeeping, and the fact that restaurants do actually close, on the tip of her tongue. Only, when her eyes lift from her phone, she's momentarily struck dumb by the sight striding toward her down the steps of the Metropolitan Center.

Long legs are hardly a rarity in the ballet world; toned ones even less so. Still, there's something in the way the Jimmy Choos make Anna swagger that has Victoria completely enraptured. It's fortunate it takes Anna so long to saunter over, otherwise she'd find her boss and mentor almost entirely speechless. Thankfully she doesn't seem to expect much beyond the head-to-toe raking of Victoria's gaze and a jerk of her head to say "get in the car." Only when inside, trapped by their seat belts and moving, does Anna pipe up.

"I hope this looks okay," she begins. "I didn't even realize I had these shoes in among the new things. You did mean these for me, right?"

"Well, you don't look *ridiculous*, at least. I could almost mistake you for an adult woman with her life together."

"Listen, about before—"

"Don't ruin fighting your own corner with a groveling apology." Victoria raises a finger to warn Anna off. "I'm irresistible. You have the whole heroine crush. It spilled over, you made your case for staying… Really, the matter's resolved as far as I'm concerned. If I'm not offended by it, you certainly don't get to be."

"I…uh…irresistible?" Anna half snorts the word.

Victoria glares at her, just a little. "Like I said before, do you really think you're the first?"

Something in Anna deflates at that, perhaps realizing her own lack of originality. The Midtown traffic is snarling, the usual on a Friday evening, and not for the first time Victoria misses the option of being able to walk long stretches in heels, hopping on the subway to save time when the roads are gridlocked. Still, it will serve Rick and Liza right to be kept waiting.

"I'll fix that turn, you know," Anna mutters a minute later. "We didn't get time today, but I'll show you tomorrow."

"We'll see."

Anna leans in, her perfume delicate and teasing even through the haze of Victoria's own spicier choice. "I mean it. I know how to get it now I have the extension right. I'll do better tomorrow. No distraction. No accidental…whatever."

Somewhere in the pit of Victoria's stomach, something twists in disappointment. Despite the flare of temper before, Anna's touch had been thoughtful, almost gentle.

Far removed from the doctors and physiotherapists who'd treated with deft hands and occasional necessary roughness. Not that Victoria had lacked for physical contact in the more obvious ways. Teresa was hardly the first to keep her company, but none of those encounters and flings had invited casual exploration.

Just another reason to keep this woman at a professional distance. And yes, very much a woman. To see her in such a stylish dress and killer heels made the very idea of dismissing Anna as a *girl* impossible.

"Fine." Victoria sighs. "Just save that perky angelic routine for Liza. Be sure to remind her at every opportunity how young and vital you are, for my amusement if nothing else."

"If you say so. What about Mr. Westin?"

"Leave Rick to me."

The car starts making progress at last, the congestion easing as they make it past the bottleneck caused by tourists and tour buses. They're traveling against the exodus from the Financial District, meaning the journey is over in just a few minutes. Anna taps the driver on the shoulder and mutters something in his ear that makes him stay put. When Victoria's door is opened for her, she knows it's Anna, having scurried around in heels.

"And they say chivalry is dead," Victoria drawls.

"Just to check," Anna says, "am I here as your bright new prospect, or as…"

"My date?" Victoria can't help teasing. Of course the subject hasn't been entirely dropped. "Well, Anna. I think that's up to you. Come on, there's a dirty martini screaming my name."

Victoria begins the march from the sidewalk to the restaurant entrance, startled only three steps in by Anna's arm casually slipping through hers. They present to the maître d' as a united front, and it's more than a little welcome.

♾

Anna knows her grip on Victoria's wrist is too tight, but she can't bring herself to relinquish it until forced to by the fact their waiter seems insistent on them occupying two separate seats. Richard looks as scruffy-rich as ever, no tie of course, but his blazer is perfectly tailored despite the faded T-shirt beneath.

It's safer to focus on the appearance of the man who stands to greet her with two kisses to the cheeks that press a little too hard and a little too long, because next to him, still seated, is possibly the foremost dancer in America. Liza Wade, apparently human and ordinary, running a finger around the rim of her glass.

Meanwhile, Victoria, the Queen of Ballet, is unimpressed with being greeted second, and she grumbles to Rick about his choice of "fast-food joint" without ever acknowledging that Liza is there.

How can she ignore that glossy brown hair that falls in the perfect chin-length bob? Those dark eyes that don't seem to miss a single thing happening at their table, even though Anna barely dares to glance in that direction for a second at a time. The dress is blood red, seemingly a perfect fit. To anyone ignoring the taut definition of the muscles, Liza might seem almost fragile; she certainly makes Anna feel like a Clydesdale in comparison. But she's all barely contained power, and her bicep twitches as she pushes her drink aside and waves the waiter over for some muttered conversation about the specials.

"Sit, sit," Rick urges. "We're all friends here. Or we will be. Anna, it's a delight to see you again. I hear this one"—he nods toward Victoria—"has been working you hard."

"You could say that," Anna answers with a gracious smile. "But I'm just happy to be learning."

Liza sends the waiter scurrying off as though he just heard the kitchen is on fire and turns her attention back to the table.

"You must be the famous Anya," she announces, giving the kind of appraising look that makes Anna cave in on herself under the pressure of it.

"I've already tried that game," Victoria interrupts, an unlikely savior. "Her name is Anna. But don't worry if you can't keep up on the spelling. Everyone will know her name soon enough."

"Will it be in *Le Monde*?" Liza asks, settling back in her chair like she's holding court. "You know, I've been back from Paris for a while now, but I still reach for that news first."

Victoria mutters something that sounds a lot like *pretentious* under her breath. Anna doesn't want to speculate on which word follows it.

"How long did you dance with Paris Opéra?" Anna asks, trying to be the polite one. "Was it three years?"

"Just two and a half," Liza corrects, lighting up briefly as though Anna has asked the perfect question. "Though it felt like a decade. But San Francisco is home. And when home has the greatest ballet company in the world, it's hard not to go back."

Victoria snorts audibly at the notion of San Francisco being the greatest anything, and Anna resists the urge to nudge with her elbow.

"Now speaking of the greatest, I understand more changes are afoot in our humble company." Rick isn't able to finish pouncing as the waiter returns to take their orders.

Anna hasn't even looked at the menu, but everything sounds as if someone on heavy-duty medication picked four random ingredients and threw them together. She settles for the safest option—some kind of salad with pomegranate and a bunch of things she can't pronounce.

She's expecting Victoria to order three martinis as an entrée, but she's querying the waiter on a variety of things before settling on something that involves pea panna cotta, the wobbly thought of which leaves Anna feeling slightly nauseated. Thank God there's wine, and she knocks back most of her glass the moment it's poured.

"I've made some changes, yes." Victoria picks up the thread again. "Though I can't see why you'd want to discuss them in front of someone who's technically the competition. After all, if San Francisco suddenly throws Liza over for someone young and fresh, well, that impacts on our PR splash just a little, wouldn't you think?"

Victoria doesn't sound like herself. Gone are the abrupt punches on her consonants, the clipped tones that have everyone scurrying at her command. She brushes at the cuff of her silk blouse as she talks, drawling and almost wheedling. Like she's daring Rick to deny her anything. He seems charmed by it, worst of all, as though this is the version of Victoria he's been waiting for.

"But"—he wags his finger in cartoonish style, flashing his oversized watch—"what did I tell you back at our showcase?"

"To give this season the Victoria Ford treatment," she says sweetly. "And others must feel suitably threatened, to do the old glass-in-the-shoe trick."

His concerned expression is transparently fake. He's all but grinning. In that moment, Anna's allegiances are no longer even fractionally divided. She's on Victoria's team, and every step she dances will be about getting one over on this smug creep.

"Really, must we talk shop?" Liza interrupts their power plays, tucking a strand of hair behind her ear. Her earrings are delicate strands of gold that catch the light. "If we must, can we at least talk about something new? What *do* you have planned for this magnificent creature, Vicki?"

"A darling little revival, that's all," Victoria says through teeth that sound suspiciously close to gritted. "I think we've all seen *Giselle* and *Swan Lake* often enough to make our heads spin, don't you? About time I launched a star in something less conventional."

"Less to compare her to, of course," Liza counters. "Less need to be exceptional if she's following in fewer footsteps, is that the logic?"

"No." Victoria drains her martini. "It's called originality. Didn't they ever mention it when you took my place in Paris?"

The energy shifts then, from polite indifference to something far more tense. There had been rumors Victoria was destined to be the first American prima in Paris, only for Liza to take that honor the season after Victoria's retirement. Many had joined the company over the years since Maria Tallchief, but none had been given the spotlight until then. Having danced in London and San Francisco and New York, it should have been a crowning glory for Victoria. To miss out on it must have only added to the heartbreak and frustration of retiring the way she did.

Rick takes over. "Whatever you're doing, Victoria, we need to talk about expectations. We're what, three, four years in? You've set the course now, using the press. So that makes it win or bust, is that fair to say?"

Victoria is rigid beside her, and with anyone else Anna might risk a reassuring pat. With Victoria, she fears it will send her ricocheting toward the ceiling.

"You made yourself clear. We don't discuss employment matters in front of the company though, you know this."

"Well, you're the one who brought her."

It's an accusation, and Anna doesn't like it one bit.

"Anyway, since I've had a chance to see Liza this week, I thought I'd clue you in on her plans."

"I didn't care about those plans when we all danced together; I'm mystified as to why you think I would be now."

"You have a habit, Victoria," he says, with another round of the finger-wagging, and Anna wants to break it off at the knuckle, "of considering my threats to be empty. The way you carry on doing whatever you want is proof of that. But if we're not the toast of the town by season's end? Liza has very graciously agreed to come in postretirement as artistic director."

Liza preens a little, and Victoria flinches ever so slightly as she absorbs the blow.

Anna reaches for her wine again. This is bad. Terrible. The no-good dinner to end all dinners, and she's endured her own attempts at cooking.

"Why?" Anna can't stop herself asking. "If you're rooting for Victoria to succeed—for both of us to have a good season—why would you have a replacement lined up?"

"Because, little lady"—Rick turns to her, the excess of hair product glinting in the soft light of the restaurant—"I believe in investing in the future. Now if that's you"— he holds up his hands as though accepting the blame—"I'll be glad to say I picked you out. But with or without you two, this company will prevail."

Anna opens her mouth to reply, but then Victoria's hand is on her thigh, pressing hard enough that even her short nails feel like they might pierce the skin. It's enough to shut Anna up.

"Well, if that's all you came to say I won't bother choking down this bland excuse for a meal," Victoria says, gathering herself as she stands.

She moves a little too fast, stumbling just for a fraction of a second on her bad knee, and Anna is ready to spring to the rescue. Thankfully she isn't needed, but she makes to get up and run after Victoria anyway. It's Rick who sits her back down with a hand on her shoulder.

"She won't flee, that's not her style. Let me talk to her, kid. I know her a hell of a lot better than you do. You stay here and look after Liza, okay?"

With that, he takes off in the same direction as Victoria, leaving Anna speechless in her chair.

"So," Liza picks up as though they were barely interrupted, "what's the gossip with my baby sister? Delphine never tells me anything, not even about her and Gabriel. You and I could be very good friends, Anna… Means you're safe next season either way, if you want a little insurance."

With considerable effort, Anna conjures a fake and friendly grin. "I like the way you think, Liza. Did I mention it's an honor just to be here tonight? Because I meant to."

Liza takes the bait, laughing that fake little laugh of hers and motioning for another bottle of wine. As she berates the waiter for taking a second too long, Anna's mind is made up. She isn't doing one damn thing to help this woman, and she's going to make Victoria's season a splash if it breaks every bone in her body.

Nodding, she laughs at whatever tedious joke Liza is telling. The sooner they get this over with, the sooner she can go check on Victoria, who must be seething wherever she's run to. The thought of that alone makes Anna hurt in sympathy, which is another problem she is not dealing with right now. At least the overpriced wine goes down easily.

CHAPTER 22

Of course he follows her, and righteous though her anger is, Victoria doesn't make much effort to evade him. Richard catches up to her eventually outside the bodega where she's just charmed a Marlboro from a teenager, who's lingering in case she asks for more than a smoke.

"Those things will kill you," Rick warns, and he has the decency to look at least slightly shamefaced about it as he pulls out his own pack. "Don't make me chase you all over the city, Victoria. Neither one of us is fit for that these days."

"When did you start hating me?" she asks. "A bit of light backstabbing I expect; it comes with the territory. But that was a real betrayal, and I didn't see it coming."

"Liza offered." Rick joins her at the corner with a shrug. "And I've spent twelve years taking the blame for the biggest loss in ballet. Even now you still won't tell the real story, won't clear my name."

"You really think people blame you for my injury?" She's been putting the pieces together, too slowly. "Just because I didn't go on daytime television and sob about it for sixty minutes?"

"I thought hiring you four years ago would stop it." His sigh is long and weary. "Why would you work for me if I was to blame? But people are idiots and they stick with that story."

"Was that reason enough to risk injuring an innocent girl?" Victoria won't feel sorry for him. He got to dance on for years after her. "Did you really think Teresa wouldn't crack the minute I pressed her? She's besotted with me."

"I was trying to show you how it upsets the balance of the company." He turns, ready to walk away. "What?"

"You *hurt* her. Do you have any idea the damage that could have been done? She could press charges, Rick. I'd support her all the way."

"Oh, aren't you the devoted director?" He snorts. "Careful, Vicki. I might think you're the one blurring the personal and professional here. Mind you, Liza might have already turned her head."

"I have no worries when it comes to Anna, whether it's Liza or the program I've picked. You're the one who declared war, Rick. Don't blame me when I win."

He shrugs, turning and making his way back down the block to the restaurant. Victoria shivers slightly, the evening having cooled enough that her silk blouse isn't enough protection for someone with her body mass. It can't be long before Anna comes looking for her, surely? She's a little surprised her phone isn't blowing up like she's a high school senior who missed curfew. Taking her time about it, she walks the short distance back to the restaurant, grinding the butt of the cigarette under her Louboutin when she's had enough.

The restaurant is a fishbowl because Rick and Liza are about tied in who most likes to see and be seen. It means Victoria has a decent view without getting too close, and it takes only a glimpse to confirm Anna is still firmly in place at their prime table, sipping from her glass before laughing at something Liza says. Given that Liza hasn't been funny since the first Bush presidency, it's enough to make Victoria's heart sink.

With Rick the betrayal was white-hot, a flashbang she's been setting off since they first started dancing together. Few people get under her skin so effectively or so often. Anna's turn as a traitor just makes Victoria feel sick to her stomach, the sinking realization that her reputation is rooted firmly in the past. If Anna has any sense of ambition, if she has that self-absorbed streak needed to survive, she'll hitch her wagon to Liza instead.

Typical Liza should make her move now, when Victoria is truly inspired for the first time since taking the damn position. Just like with her place in Paris, her one unrealized dream and greatest regret, Liza is there to rise from the ashes of Victoria's chance to make history.

By the time she reaches the car, her knee is complaining with sharp jolts up and down thigh and shin alike, that uncontrollable electrical current of pain. She grunts "home" at the driver and fishes in her purse for her next dose, the one she should have choked down before dinner. If she pops an extra pill, it's not like there's anyone else around to count.

 ⁓⃝⃝⃝

It takes far too long to extricate herself, and Anna is practically vibrating with impatience as she hails a taxi. Victoria hasn't replied to any of the texts carefully tapped out under the table, nor the voice recording Anna had the presence of mind to start on her phone when she realized Liza was a few drinks in and ready to expound on her *vision*.

The town car is parked outside Victoria's building in one of the few parking bays, and as soon as she pays her fare to the chatty cab driver, Anna is darting across the street to rap on the closed window. Sheepishly Victoria's driver rolls down the glass, revealing the meatball sub he's chewing on. Anna doesn't know his name, they change so often, but she's starting to recognize leverage when she sees it.

"Tell me which apartment number is Victoria's and I won't tell her you were eating in the car," she offers, wasting no time beating around the bush. She's bursting with the need to offload her double-agent status, to prove to Victoria that she stayed loyal. Assuming Victoria even cares, but Anna can't forget her stricken expression as she'd stormed away from the table.

"She's in 46C," he offers. "You were out with her earlier, right? You're not some stalker?"

"No, I'm not." Anna's already in motion, nodding at the doorman who doesn't seem inclined to stop someone so clearly on a mission. She calls the elevator, jamming the button over and over again. When she doesn't hear the whirr of machinery, she takes to the stairs. After three floors, she ditches her impractical heels and heads for the top floor.

It's what would be called the penthouse floor in a more modern building, but this apartment block has a pleasingly vintage feel to it. Three apartments share the top floor, and Victoria's is the most remote, alone at the end of a short hallway. Steeling herself, Anna doesn't bother to slip her shoes back on, rapping on the door before she loses her nerve.

Of course there's no answer. Nothing is destined to go right today. Figuring she hasn't much left to lose, Anna bangs her knuckles harder against the door.

A door creaks open, but not the one Anna is staring at. Someone clears their throat and she turns, a sinking dread that she heard the wrong apartment number, or worse that the driver was just screwing with her. Thankfully it's not Victoria waiting at 46B's door, but rather a woman old enough to be her great-grandmother.

"You looking for the dancer?" she demands, and Anna straightens automatically at the authority in that steely English accent. "She'll be upstairs."

"This is the top floor?" Anna's voice raises on the question.

The woman points a bony finger to the other end of the hall. "Roof terrace. Give the door a sharp shove. And tell her not to make any noise when she staggers back down."

Anna nods, because she suspects any other answer will only get her in trouble somehow. She scurries along the dim corridor, shoes still in hand, and shoulder-charges the door. Sure enough, it opens to iron steps and the sparkling neon-tinged darkness of the city. Taking in a deep breath, Anna realizes it's cleaner and cooler up here.

"Come to resign?" Victoria asks, momentarily invisible but sounding dangerously close when Anna reaches the low wall that lines the roof area. "Or are you going to insult me by pretending you left the restaurant when I did?"

"Of course I didn't," Anna counters, her voice wavering in the evening breeze. "Someone had to stay long enough to find out what they were up to. I got the whole plan, I think."

Victoria steps out of the shadows in the corner, bottle of wine in hand. "I'd offer you some, but I didn't bring a second glass. That and I don't share with traitors."

"I'm not the one who betrayed you tonight." Anna's tired. Nothing she does is ever going to be good enough for this woman. "So if you're going to be pissed, I really feel like it shouldn't be at me. I'm trying to help."

"So *helpful*." Victoria says it with a sneer, like it's the worst insult she could hurl at Anna's exhausted feet. "You should put your damn shoes on." She picks up the wine bottle, already halfway empty. "Your feet have been through enough already."

Anna thinks for a moment before responding, "Your roof is easier on them than broken glass." Rubbing her arms as cool turns to something more like cold. "If I was stupid enough, I might think that sounded like you care. But you've already decided I'm helping Liza Wade oust you from your own company."

"Aren't you?" Victoria splashes more wine into her glass before setting the bottle down between them. Somehow, they've moved closer, separated now by not much more than the width of the bottle. The air between them feels lighter than everywhere else, as though they're meeting at great altitude. Anna grabs the wine, intending to drink from the source to show that Victoria can't intimidate her with a bottle of red that probably cost more than Anna's dress.

"From the bottle?" Victoria gasps before Anna can complete her little coup. "Are we savages?" She stills herself, as though not entirely shaken by the night's events. "I wasn't expecting company."

Anna's slow to react when Victoria hands her the glass, but she accepts it as though she expected it all along. She tries not to think about putting her mouth where Victoria's has just been. She tries even harder not to think about Victoria's mouth at all, not when she's pouting over her stolen wine, those lips pillow soft and broad in a way that just invites the tracing of a fingertip.

"I didn't have you pegged for a thief."

"There's a lot you don't know about me?" Anna ventures, confidence buoyed by the rush of red wine through her system. "Like, for example, that I really hate when people go behind each other's backs. There's no way I could ever work for Liza now, not like this."

"I'm sure they'd make an offer that would force you to reconsider," Victoria points out, chased with a sigh. "Or maybe they'll burn you for ever having been associated with me. I suppose I'm sorry for that. You have great promise, Anna."

"Do I?" She has to know. If Anna is going to give her all now the threat is real and has a name, she has to be sure. She has to know that Victoria is sure too. "Because after tonight I'd understand if you can't take a risk on me."

"You're scared?"

"No!" Anna protests. "Well, a little. But one thing I know for sure is that if you still want to go for this? I'm all-in. I'll do whatever it takes, because people like that? They don't deserve to win."

"It's going to be even harder now. Any allowances I might have made, before—"

Anna snorts. She can't help it. "Come on. I think we both know you were never going to do that. I know what I signed up for, but I'm offering you the chance to take it back if you have to."

"Do you want that?" Victoria is curious, sidling closer as they both look out over the city instead of at each other. "I wouldn't throw you out of the company, but you'd accept going back to the corps, just one of the girls making up numbers again?"

With a shake of her head, Anna risks another glance at Victoria before finishing her glass of wine and setting it down in the limited space left between them. "I wouldn't like it, no. But mostly because I wouldn't get to work with you every day the way we do."

"Flattery won't get you anywhere, Gale."

"Still, if you needed that. If it meant you'd still be here next season and we could try again…I'd do it."

Victoria stares back at her, disbelieving. "That won't be necessary." Her words are almost lost in the faint traffic noises floating up from below. She sits on a wooden packing crate that's been left up here.

Anna decides to be bold one more time, sitting down next to her.

"I picked you for a reason, and we'll see it through. I'm going to make demands of you every day. You'll have to work harder and longer than you ever have before, and what you think is your best? That won't be good enough."

"Then what should I be aiming for?"

"What *I* think is your best. I see things you can't, Anna. I see potential in you. We need reviews that blow Rick and Liza out of the water, understood? But if you're having doubts, if you're tempted by something they've offered, then walk away now. Preferably with your shoes on."

"Will you listen?" Anna exhales in frustration and, continuing her streak of uninvited contact, she's grasping at Victoria's wrist.

The touch makes Victoria look down as though her purse has just been snatched, but she makes no move to pull away.

Anna revels in the fragility of the tiny wrist, but it's tempered by the jump of muscle in Victoria's forearm, a reminder that she's every bit as strong. "I'm not siding with anyone but you. You gave me this chance. You did that. How could I go anywhere else?"

"Will you still feel that way on the days where rehearsal starts at seven and you crawl home at midnight? When I'm making you lift and turn the other girls like a workhorse, things that no ballerina ever really trained for?"

"You say that like it's any different to how demanding it is now." Anna almost laughs. "I feel like maybe you could be less mean about it, but fine. I'll be up there, opening night, making you proud, hopefully."

"Let's not get carried away."

It's honest-to-God teasing, and Anna goes weak at the sound of it.

"Whatever did I do to inspire such loyalty in you?" Victoria asks.

"You're just…you, I guess." Anna wishes she had something more eloquent to say, but words have failed her far more than her feet ever could. "And it helps that you're offering me everything I ever wanted."

"There is that." Victoria leans closer, glancing down at Anna's grip on her wrist again but still not moving to break the hold. They're barely inches apart, all alone on the rooftop. "Make sure you bring Bishop or one of the boys to teach you tomorrow. I want lift practice until you're throwing strangers around on the street out of sheer habit."

"Sure, but if I get arrested for inappropriate grabbing, who's going to dance your solos then?" Anna jokes. "You know, we could talk about this indoors. I can play you the whole restaurant conversation back if you have any reservations. Maybe with a second wineglass?"

"If it stops you stealing mine, then by all means." Victoria wriggles free at last, standing and gesturing toward the fire door. "How did you know I was up here? Did the Golden Girl next door rat on me?"

"See, you say that like an insult, but there's no bad way to be a Gold—" Anna stumbles on the doorstep, almost face-planting on the floor. Only Victoria's swift clutching of her elbow keeps Anna upright, better reflexes than expected for someone with the best part of a bottle of wine in them.

"Try not to break both your legs before rehearsal. Honestly, Anna."

"I'm fine!" she protests, a little too embarrassed. Standing up straight just pulls her closer to Victoria. They're both in the doorway, framed by it really, and those thoughts Anna's been trying not to have, about wine-tinted lips and precise fingers, come roaring back until she can barely think at all.

Is she leaning in? No, but Victoria seems to be. Time slows and the inches gradually evaporate, and just as Anna's about to let her eyes flutter closed in anticipation, the peal of her damn ringtone goes off like a siren.

Twice now a phone call has almost ruined her entire life. She has *got* to keep the thing on Vibrate, or better yet completely silent.

Victoria retreats down the corridor just a little.

Anna plucks the phone from her purse and answers with a snappish "What?"

"Anna?" Jess sounds panicked. Two syllables are all it takes for Anna to be sure of that and feel her own heart pound like a kick drum in response. "I need your help. It's Irina."

"Where are you?" Anna asks, shooting an apologetic glance Victoria's way, knowing already that this is one secret she can't share. She acknowledges what Jess tells her and ends the call abruptly. "I have to go," she doesn't quite explain. "Maybe another time on the wine."

"It's not like I actually invited you," Victoria points out, but her heart isn't in it. "What's wrong?"

"Friend drama," Anna says, waving her hand a little too frantically to dismiss the topic. "You know how it is with us millennials."

Victoria's frown says she doesn't believe it, but Anna starts walking away to make it a done deal. "I'll be in rehearsal bright and early," she promises. "This won't affect it."

"Better not!" Victoria calls after her.

Maybe it's desperation, but as Anna makes her way downstairs, she could swear Victoria almost sounded disappointed Anna couldn't stay.

CHAPTER 23

Victoria makes her way through her apartment in the dark, knowing the layout innately by now. Reaching the bedroom window, she pulls the curtain back just far enough to spy on the street below. Sure enough, Anna scurries across, rushing through late evening traffic with barely a glance.

There's no sign of anyone meeting her, and when Anna doesn't reemerge in five minutes, Victoria gives up on her little act of espionage. She has no right to Anna's free time, to know of her every movement outside of her contracted hours to the company. The wine is already making her tongue feel dry; the faint early drums of a headache creeping in at the base of her skull.

Has Victoria really been so reckless? Sharing wine on a rooftop as if they'd sneaked out after curfew? She hadn't done that since her training years at White Lodge, the boarding school that fed dancers into the Royal Ballet like a well-oiled machine.

The legend of Victoria Ford began not on stage, but in the halls of that academy. Even though she'd been a late arrival, barely a year in dorms before being invited to join the company as a professional, she'd made her mark.

She shakes her head at the unexpected bout of nostalgia, the pangs for London fainter these days but no less frequent. How cliché that a near kiss with a beautiful girl should send her into such an indulgent spiral. Setting the almost-empty wine bottle on the table, and the glass beside it, Victoria hesitates a moment.

"Don't be a fool," she chastises herself, heading toward the bedroom. There are wars enough to fight as it is, without embarrassing herself.

ᗤᗝᗝ

"Have I mentioned lately how much I want to kill you?" Anna snaps at her sister as she sees her propping Irina up against the wall outside Anna's apartment. "Doesn't she have a home of her own to go to? Oh wait, she does."

"Just let us in," Jess groans, her eyes glassy. "She was in pain, okay? I just need to keep an eye on her, make sure she didn't take too much. Your place was closer, and you know, just in case..."

Irina swears a brief torrent in Russian before clamping her hand over her mouth like she's going to be sick.

"If she pukes on anything, you're replacing it," Anna warns, ushering them in and rushing to grab the small trash can from the bathroom, handing it to Irina. "Is she drunk, or…?"

"You know what, you don't need details," Jess tells her off, pulling the big-sister card as though Anna can't see her pupils just as well in the bright lights of the hallway.

"Well you two can fight over the couch, because I'm not giving up my bed." Anna makes her way through to the kitchen. "I'm going to make some coffee. Maybe that will help?"

Jess mutters under her breath something like "Maybe it won't," but it's something to do at least. The last thing Anna herself needs is caffeine; even with a drink at dinner and some of Victoria's wine, she's all jittery. It's the work of a minute to fill up the coffeemaker and set it whirring to life, after which Anna watches on in silence as Jess deals with Irina, setting her up on the couch with the exaggerated care of someone who doesn't entirely trust her own movements. From this small distance, in the dimness of the room that's only got one lamp lit, the similarity between Irina and her mother makes Anna's heart ache.

"What the hell happened?" Anna asks when she brings their mugs over. Irina is already passed out, snoring lightly against the cushion. "Didn't you have work?"

"I told you, she just showed up." Jess gulps at her coffee, hissing when it's too hot. She's in her usual stage blacks, no jewelry or anything else that may catch the light while lurking in the wings. "I know this afternoon she had an appointment, but I thought it was just a massage or something. Instead she shows up rambling in what I guess was Ukrainian, because you know, it's like Russian, but the slang… I didn't get all of it."

Anna considers carefully, sitting on the living room floor cross-legged, mirroring Jess. They sip too-hot coffee in tandem, and Anna asks what's bugging her most of all.

"But you didn't come straight here. You got loaded first. I know Irina is doing it for the pain; she's carrying injuries. What's your excuse, Jess?"

"My sister, Nancy Reagan."

"This isn't judging, it's just… Did she say how bad it is? Because we're kind of betting everything on this program. If she can't dance it…"

Irina sits bolt upright, startling them both.

"I will dance," she almost snarls. "One more season, that is all I need."

"What did the doctor say? Was it Kim?" Anna demands, laying a tentative hand on Irina's shoulder.

"No, just another quacking duck," Irina says. "*Blin, gospodi*. You can't tell Vicki. If she cuts me now…"

Anna hesitates. Hasn't she just pledged her every effort to make this season a success? And unless she's going completely crazy, they almost kissed to seal the deal. Is that terrifying, amazing situation really something she can bear to throw away just to let Irina keep pushing through the pain barrier?

"Sick," Irina huffs, leveraging herself off the couch and hobbling toward the bathroom until Jess can catch up and support her the rest of the way. When they get themselves together, she's going to need a full explanation, and an idea of exactly what Irina is trying to overcome with her injuries. The urge to call Victoria and have her come across the street to deal with all this is overwhelming, but Anna holds out.

She can handle it. If this is how the big leagues go? Then Anna has to be ready for it. The thought of keeping this from Victoria makes her feel slightly nauseated, but maybe this kind of loyalty is what they mean by *esprit de corps*.

A phone rings, though Anna doesn't recognize the ringtone. The sounds of Jess cursing are much more familiar. A moment later she emerges, shamefaced but her mouth still pinched in anger.

"Those clowns can't even close up a theater without me. It's all gone to shit. Can you keep an eye on Irina for a few minutes while I talk them through it?"

"Sure," Anna sighs. "Not like I have anything better to do."

"Breakfast is definitely on me," Jess promises, with a quick one-armed hug.

"I have early rehearsal," Anna says. "With your girlfriend in there. Assuming she can walk in the morning."

"She'll be fine," Jess says, already halfway to the door. "Trust me, this is so not the toughest thing she's been through. You two should talk sometime, properly."

Anna sits for a moment alone, waiting for some sound to suggest Irina might emerge soon. When there's no sign of movement, she makes her way into the bathroom with some trepidation and finds Irina sitting on the floor of the shower.

"You'd better not throw up in there," Anna warns. "Come on, let's put you to bed. And by bed I mean sofa. I don't care how great a dancer you are, you're not getting my memory foam."

"You are not a nurse," Irina says with a sigh. "Too rough, little one."

"Don't 'little one' me when I'm dragging you through my apartment," Anna argues back, but she's quietly pleased that even with Irina slumping like so much dead weight, there's not much strain in half carrying her. It bodes well for the lifts she'll have to do tomorrow. Only when she's pulling a blanket over Irina does Anna notice she's humming to herself. The moment she stops, Irina picks up the tune.

She sings in Ukrainian, and it's the first time in over a decade that Anna's heard the lullaby in anything but English. It's one of her greatest regrets that she'd never pestered her mother to teach her more, to learn the little songs and rhymes in the language of a country left behind.

Spaty, spaty, holubyatko, Irina finishes, reaching out vaguely with her eyes closed, fingertips skimming Anna's cheek.

"Sleep, sleep, little dove," Anna translates back to her in a whisper, eyes brimming with tears. There's no denying the similarity now, not with Irina's heavy makeup mostly sweated or wiped off, her face relaxed as she falls into sleep. For a fleeting moment, Anna could swear she has her mother back.

Irina snores to break the moment, a choking little sound that has Anna alert for any signs she's in distress. Confident Irina will sleep it off, Anna turns her into the recovery position and goes to get ready for bed. It's been one hell of a night and, as she settles under the covers, her racing mind says it's not going to get any easier. Anna closes her eyes, but all she sees is her mother's face, faded by memory. The lullaby rings in her ears, and she pulls the pillow over her head.

⟳⟳⟳

She's late.

Barely a handful of hours since all her grand promises, and Anna Gale is late. Victoria scowls into her latte, which isn't even close to hot enough. The studio echoes with the impatient tapping of her right foot, and she checks her watch one more time to make sure the clock hasn't skipped ahead overnight.

Finally, there's a commotion in the hall, and her trio of ballerinas spill into the room, Gabriel in tow behind them. He still has his headphones and sunglasses firmly in place.

Well medicated and fueled with fresh determination to beat Rick and Liza, Victoria prowls the room like a tiger in an enclosure. She snaps, she berates, she straightens a leg here and adjusts an arm there, the fact of only warming up being no excuse for anything less than perfect form. Only with Irina does Victoria know better than to push. She's here, she's upright, and she's dancing. Let that be enough for now, no matter how pale she looks.

Force of habit has her turning in ever-decreasing circles until her entire patrol is the radius around Anna. Distant, consummate professional Anna this morning, who stretches and bends with almost robotic precision. Not a glimmer of eye contact. Victoria might as well be invisible, a feeling she's not used to.

"Vary those *port de bras* for God's sake," she snaps as Anna keeps her arms in second for another set. "Or do you want to tear a bicep before I even show you how to lift?"

Anna only grunts softly in acknowledgment before rearranging her arms.

"*Allongé*," Victoria warns when Delphine skips it from the standard routine they could all do in their sleep by now. Being more focused on Anna doesn't mean the rest get away with anything, though even Irina seems to be applying something like enthusiasm. Perhaps she's finally learned the importance of being properly warmed up.

They spill away from the barre when Victoria releases them from the routines, the usual descent to the floor for one last set of stretches. Anna is rotating her shoulders well, so clearly she's been paying some attention to the boys all these years.

"Gabriel?" Victoria calls out, hiding a frown of disapproval that he still hasn't removed the headphones. Are they really going to have a power struggle when he's supposed to be doing her a favor? "You're the finest male dancer in this company, and I don't need to repeat what reviews have been saying for years about your effortless lifts." A little flattery can't exactly hurt.

"Due respect, Victoria. There's a whole lot of effort behind them."

"I'm well aware. But this season I need a headline, I need a splashy something that might even get the conservative nuts protesting outside. So I need you to walk Anna through the basics of good lifting."

"You finally get a black male principal and you want to sideline me for a white girl?" Gabriel asks, and it's not unreasonable. "I thought jerks like Mike were who I had to watch out for; now you're telling me I gotta what? Get up on *pointe* to stay competitive?"

"Now, you know that's not what I have in mind." Victoria tries to soothe him. Her focus has always been exemplary, but if forced under duress to admit one flaw, it might be her occasional negligence of the bigger picture. "Gabriel, you are our leading man. You're talented, you're gorgeous, and you know I fought for you to be here. I'm taking one minor show and messing with rigorous gender roles. Surely we can all get behind that?"

"You're not touching any of my leads?" he confirms, and Victoria nods. They shake on it, two professionals in agreement once more. "Then let's show this perfectly nice girl how to throw around ballerinas like a man. Delphine, what should we start with?"

"Uh, who's Anna going to be lifting?" Delphine catches up to the number of people in the room.

Irina is already taking up the far corner to work on her solo material. She's the only one to have danced it before, though not with Victoria's spin on the choreography.

"You're the prima, Wade," Victoria points out. "Once Gabriel demonstrates, you can start working with Anna one-on-one."

"You really have lost your mind," Delphine mutters, but everyone hears it. "Victoria, in your entire career, would you have let someone, on their first day, lift and catch you? Come on."

"It's hardly rocket science," Victoria snaps at her. "That's why we're having instruction first. Then it's one *pas de deux* with a handful of lifts. She'll barely have a chance to kill you."

"I'm not doing lifts with someone who doesn't know what they're doing."

"Then you and Irina can go," Victoria answers, keeping her voice low and hopefully close to deadly. "Once Anna has proven herself, you'll dance with her. Or you'll be permanently replaced. It's exactly that simple."

Irina is dissenting from the corner, talking to Anna about something in an urgent murmur that tugs at Victoria's attention. She can't waver. One flicker of emotion now and Delphine gets to win.

"All I'm saying is—"

"Regular class is next door." Victoria gestures toward the door, and Delphine snatches up her bag from the floor, storming out.

Irina follows Delphine. Anna watches them go, her expression wary. Not least because Victoria's irritation at their behavior is now likely to be aimed squarely at her.

"Right, let's start over, shall we?"

♾

They summon a couple of corps girls to work through the lifts. Only one of the girls, the one Victoria elects to keep to run through their hours of lifting and catching, talks to Anna at all. Morgan is just back from injury, Anna knows that much, but it doesn't make her hesitant at all. She runs and spins and does everything that's asked of her, seemingly confident with Gabriel.

"You're lucky," Morgan gasps when they pause to let her catch her breath. "If anyone has good habits to get into, it's Mr. Bishop."

"He's so impressive," Anna agrees, impatient at all the waiting and watching she's had to do. "Have you danced with him before? It sure looks like it."

"I understudied Delphine for two years," Morgan replies. "Before, you know..."

"I heard. That had to hurt like hell."

"At least my titanium hip replacement won't come as a surprise when I'm old," Morgan says with a sigh. "The doctors think it's only a few years away for me. What a treat, right?"

"People still dance after that." Anna hopes it sounds reassuring.

Morgan shrugs it off, reaching for her bag. "I just need to change out this toe stuffing, it's starting to fall apart."

She works quickly, pulling paper towels out of the bag that look suspiciously like the ones from the bathrooms and folding them in a very precise way. Pulling damp ones in a similar shape from her pointe shoes, Morgan frowns as she drops them beside her bag.

"You don't use lamb's wool?" Anna asks. "'Cause I have some with me if you ran out."

"God, no," Morgan says, her pale green eyes oddly captivating. "I don't need the corns. Honestly, try this and your toes will thank you for it."

She hands some of the folded paper to Anna, who yanks off her shoes and copies what she's shown. Sure enough, with ribbons retied, she pops up on her toes to discover that the paper doesn't slip the way the wool sometimes does. Just as she smiles at Morgan in acknowledgment, Victoria comes storming over to interrupt.

"If we're quite finished forming Phi Beta Ballet over here, can we get on with seeing if you were paying attention, Anna? Only you both have studio rehearsal soon, and you're not using me as an excuse to be late for David."

Anna just smiles and takes up position in the center of the floor, as Gabriel departs it with an encouraging fist bump she desperately appreciates.

"Aim for those love handles," he murmurs on the way past.

Anna wants to laugh. If there's one thing not a single woman in the company possesses, it would be those. She's just relieved to be dancing now, to be working out this nervous tension that always builds around Victoria. They're allies now, or supposed to be, yet Victoria seems as irritated by Anna's presence as ever.

"Anna?" Morgan is first to notice she isn't listening. "I trust you and all, but it's easier to throw yourself at someone who's paying attention."

"Sorry!" Anna calls back, and forces her head back into the game.

"Start with a standing lift," Victoria instructs, no music yet. She circles them as they fumble for position like awkward middle schoolers at their first spring formal. "Just take the weight and let your muscles adjust to it."

Morgan frowns at being referred to like a piece of meat, but it's far from unusual.

Oh, it's awkward. For a moment, Anna's convinced she's going to drop this girl she barely knows. She sets her back down and they both dissolve into helpless laughter. It's not quite enough to drown out Victoria's sigh of disapproval.

"Again. Higher."

There's more confidence this time, and Morgan's little hop gives them momentum. Anna wraps her arms around her hips like Gabriel showed her, and it's a long few seconds before she starts to feel a little strained.

Victoria hums in approval, and suddenly there's nothing else in the room for Anna. When did Victoria get so close? She must be inspecting the hold Anna has. Which has to also be why she leans over and squeezes Anna's left shoulder.

"Too tense," Victoria warns, and Anna practically drops Morgan in alarm.

"Careful?" Morgan mutters, and Anna can see she's regretting being the volunteer.

They run through a few more basics with short runs, higher lifts, and Anna is getting a little cocky that she's adapting so well.

"That's enough for today," Victoria decides when they're all thoroughly worked out.

Anna pulls her leotard away from the skin at her back where she's been sweating most and lets the air cool it a little. It's not like she's packing up slower on purpose, but if the others hurry up, she can grab a moment alone with Victoria.

The moment everyone else is gone, Anna pipes up. "Sorry I had to run off last night. And that I was late this morning. I know you noticed. I just couldn't find Gabriel, and there was this whole thing with my sister and—"

"Anna." Victoria holds up a hand. "You don't have to explain yourself unless I demand it. And I am not demanding it. Some aspirin, maybe, but no more of your babbling. Unless it prevents you from dancing, I don't need to hear about it."

"But my lifts were good, right?"

"Not terrible," Victoria concedes, which is as good as a compliment. "I think I'll find someone closer to Delphine's build. It will make the transition more seamless for you."

"Oh, I like Morgan, she's... You know what? Whatever you think," Anna changes tack thanks to Victoria's glare. "Someone new. Will you be sitting in later? For *La B*?"

"*La B*?" Victoria repeats, incredulous. Anna can't help noticing neither of them has taken even a step toward the door, toward leaving and separate activities. "Must we really murder an entire language for the sake of saving two syllables?"

"It's my first stage rehearsal, professionally I mean. Is there anything I need to do differently? I don't want to draw attention now."

Someone kinder might lie and say that Anna could never embarrass them. Victoria's never been renowned for her kindness.

"Just listen. Follow instruction. That show isn't on your shoulders, so enjoy that. You'll be doing it for a paying audience very soon."

"Don't remind me." Anna groans. She doesn't mean to angle for another invitation, but it doesn't look like one is forthcoming.

"Earlier, with Irina?" Victoria speaks after Anna turns away.

She's glad her face is hidden, sure her secrets are flashing across it like a neon news ticker.

"Is everything okay?"

"Oh, we just came in together," Anna says, since that much happens to be true.

Victoria doesn't need to know about the low howls of pain that woke everyone in the apartment before six, or how many pills and God knows what else it took to get Irina out the door, but here they are. "She's…Irina. She likes a willing audience to complain to."

Victoria circles around until they're facing again, and Anna thinks maybe she should have bolted while she had the chance. "That's all? Do I need to worry about these complaints? She's not in league with Rick and Liza, is she?"

"No!" Anna protests. "She really hates Mr. Westin, and Delphine told me earlier that Irina always pretended to think Liza was the coat-check girl or a waitress the few times their paths crossed, so I don't think they're best pals."

"Good. More lifting tomorrow. On *time*."

"Of course." This time Anna really does make a break for it, but it doesn't turn into a run until she's out of Victoria's sight.

⌒◌◌◌⌒

"So this is cool," Anna says when she finds herself on stage next to Delphine.

There's a rumor the first round of costumes will appear today. This entire production is a revamp from top to bottom. David is an oasis of calm amid the chaos on stage, barking out names and positions, shouting orders to stagehands.

"This is hell," Delphine corrects. "But who'd want to go to heaven when you can do this? Oh, and no offense about this morning, by the way."

"None taken. I don't want to be the idiot girl who dropped Delphine Wade, so you were doing us both a favor. And Morgan came to help out instead."

"Really?"

"Is that so weird?" Anna asks.

"Watch that one," Delphine says, retying the wrap cardigan she still has on in the cavernous space of the main stage.

The lights are still warming and no one's moving enough to generate real heat yet. The protective temporary flooring that covers the hallowed board is rough against their slippers and creaks at the slightest movement.

"She's never really done anything I can put my finger on, but Morgan Gresham's mother is a big donor, vice chairperson of the board," Delphine continues. "She's been trying to buy her daughter a principal spot for years, so to the Greshams it's going to look like you just jumped the line."

"She was perfectly nice." Anna bends to touch her toes, limbering up. She looks out at the empty house, the rows of red velvet fading to black after just a few feet. Something tells her Victoria is there, though. Just beyond their line of sight. It's a new sense Anna is developing. "And I need to lift someone if we're going to pull this off."

"Rather her than me," Delphine says. "But if you drop *her*, then Victoria better have a safe house to stash you in."

"Where is my corps de ballet?" David roars over the many conversations bouncing around the stage. It's clearly not the first time he's asked, either.

Anna scurries to join the other girls stage left, leaving Delphine behind with a little wave.

It's time. Her first stage rehearsal for her first full professional production. Anna bites her bottom lip for just a second, all the better to hold back a last-second squeal of glee.

CHAPTER 24

Anna drags herself out of bed with a groan, every muscle aching from yesterday's exertions. The stage rehearsal alone had been brutal, and all the extra standing around meant twice the stretching and trying to stay limber. The different floor, the bright lighting, and the sheer exuberance of dancing on a real stage had drawn Anna into overdoing it, and that, combined with all the new pains from lifting and carrying, makes the walk to the bathroom more of a limp.

When she makes it to work—and she's still not over how living her dream is her actual job, pay stubs and all—it's with a lavender scent still lingering on her skin and a spring in her step. She takes the stairs up to her morning session with Victoria like an Olympic hurdler, barely slowing down until she reaches the studio. Only the new accompanist is there, and she keeps to herself.

Anna gets straight down to business. She's well into her barre exercises when Victoria comes striding in. The door slams behind her, which is strange considering at least a few more people should be joining them. Maybe Anna should have asked for Morgan's number to make sure she'd show up on time.

"As much as I loathe recorded music, we won't be doing anything I need you for," Victoria tells Eve at the piano, not even pausing to remove her oversized sunglasses. "Make yourself useful elsewhere, or get some of the sleep you clearly missed last night. There are pandas with lighter circles under their eyes."

Eve scampers off down the corridor with tears in her eyes, risking a door slam of her own on the way out.

"So," Anna dares to breathe when she's finished her arm work, "do you need me to go find Morgan? Gabriel?"

"Am I so terrifying that you can't bear to be alone with me?" Victoria asks. "Is that what they've all warned you about?"

"I didn't… I wasn't… No," Anna finishes weakly. "I just thought you wanted me to lift, lift, lift."

"And you shall," Victoria tells her. "But to be effective, we need someone much closer to Delphine's frame. Otherwise, you'll bruise her on the first few and she'll refuse to go along with this. We need a smooth transition."

"Most of the corps are much taller," Anna points out. "Delphine is petite, even for ballet. And it's not just that, she has this really narrow frame too. I noticed it yesterday—it's why she and Gabriel make such a great contrast. But the only other person quite that slender is, well, you."

"Sometimes it's as if you've read my mind," Victoria says with a disconcerting smile.

Maybe it's just her good mood, but Anna smiles right back, shrugging off her light jacket and pulling up her favorite leg warmers over her tights. She notices what's different then—Victoria's formal outfits have been replaced by leggings and a simple black tank top.

She looks good. Way too good.

Her hair is clipped back, not long enough for a real bun, and she has on regular ballet slippers without the *pointe* blocks. Their black satin and leather complete the look.

"Well?" Victoria demands when Anna stays propped up against the barre. "Who the hell are you going to lift all the way over there?"

Anna shrugs and crosses the space with long strides. Her blood is fizzing in her veins a little, the aches of the early morning and the panic of the other night receding in the face of pure excitement.

"You're sure?" She can't help asking, because she's always been surrounded by hardheaded types who refuse to accept the limits of the human body at times. "I mean, you know your body, but if I hurt you—"

"What?" Victoria answers with a shuddering laugh, all cracked crystal in a velvet pouch. "I'll never dance again? Bit late for that. Now come on, it would be quicker to get someone over from Covent Garden at this rate."

"Where do we start?" Anna asks, which is not unreasonable.

Victoria steps into her side, grabbing Anna's right arm and pulling it around Victoria's tiny waist. Any idea she might be fragile is dispelled by the flex of her deltoid against Anna's side.

"Just get me off my feet," Victoria instructs, and Anna achieves exactly that with some careful leaning and the power in her arms. "Okay, that was supposed to be easy, so don't get too smug." Right as she sets Victoria down, Anna's stomach rumbles.

They both pretend it didn't happen.

"Now, a little more effort." In two steps, Victoria is free of Anna's loose grip and standing directly in front of her. "Gabriel told you where to hold, yes?"

"Well, that depends…" Anna trails off and puts her hands just above Victoria's hips, fingers splaying across the soft black fabric of her top. To everyone who calls her an ice queen, Anna would argue the warmth she feels radiating beneath her palms right now. "I can take it from here."

"Can you really?" Victoria asks, honey-sweet, but her voice notably lower. The air is charged and it would only take the tiniest spark, but Anna swallows, hard, and concentrates on lifting Victoria easily off the ground, holding her tightly at the waist.

Unlike Morgan, Victoria doesn't stay still in Anna's measured grip. Instead, Victoria plants her hands on Anna's shoulders and leverages herself a few inches higher. Then— oh God, Anna isn't going to survive this—those legs are wrapped around Anna's waist and Victoria's weight shifts.

For a moment Anna thinks she's losing her balance, and she fixes her gaze past tidied blond curls to maintain an upright position. She signed up for lifts, not being Victoria Ford's personal jungle gym. Not that she could stop now. Not for a million dollars. All too soon, Victoria shifts again and releases herself back to standing.

"You really are pretty sturdy." Victoria looks almost impressed for the first time in too long.

It's an instant hit for Anna's newest guilty pleasure, and already she's twitching to do something more, something better. How can she not want to make a day where she's really dancing with Victoria Ford even more memorable?

"But that's not really a lift," Anna points out. "Not the speed and force we'll be moving at. That's just...gymnastics."

Victoria affects a shudder at the word, flashing a brief grin. "Patience. Ever heard sage advice about not running before you can walk? I'm teaching you to be a safe pair of hands, not just muscle. Speaking of which, can you flex for me? I want to see what we're dealing with, if you need to change up your gym routine for a couple of weeks."

Her gym routine is currently not going to the gym other than the occasional steam room session to ease her aches and pains, along with a three-times weekly Pilates class to strengthen her core and vary her workouts.

"Flex like...?" Anna isn't sure what that means.

"Bodybuilders, that kind of thing. Show me what you've got, new kid. I'm not as familiar with you as I am with dancers I've been watching for years. You know my job as ballet mistress isn't just to teach you steps. It's to choose the choreography that looks best on *your* body. You're the canvas, Anna. My dances are the art painted on it."

"That's a little pretentious, don't you think?" Anna wants to die the minute she says it.

Victoria actually laughs.

"Two days of throwing us around and suddenly you're too cool for a metaphor? What happened to 'Yes Ms. Ford, no Ms. Ford, three bags full Ms. Ford'?'" She's moving in close again, and Anna stands her ground.

"You told me to call you Victoria, just like everyone else."

"But you're not like everyone else, are you?" Victoria reaches out to untwist Anna's tank top, right where it rests on her sports-bra strap. The skin beneath is sensitive, and Anna could swear she gets goose bumps. "Ready to take this up a notch? I need Delphine convinced in days, not weeks."

"I'm ready if you are. What's next?"

∽∾∾

Three days of torture, and no end in sight.

Victoria is delirious by the fourth, arriving caffeinated and underdressed and more sleepless than even she's used to being. What possessed her to start this gender-defying idea for a show in the first place? Her entire career at risk, dangling by a single gossamer thread, and here she is working in the closest of quarters with the girl she can't seem to get off her mind.

Any hopes of denying it ended with that pathetic display with the Morgan girl. Clambering all over Anna like a failed audition for the Moulin Rouge. Morgan is a perfectly talented dancer, and she wouldn't be in the company otherwise, no matter who her mother is. Still, Victoria doesn't feel inclined to let any other little showmances develop. Not when they might distract Anna from being on top of her game.

Not when they might distract Anna from Victoria. *Possessive*

Yes, it's ego, and not entirely without precedent. It's hardly the first time a well-defined muscle has caught Victoria's eye, but it's never been coupled with such a sunshine-and-puppies attitude before. Whatever it is, the underlying trait somewhere that caught her attention, it all came to a head with the displays of loyalty. Now the very thought of any of those younger, intact women going after Anna is sickening.

At least she's resolved not to act on it. Teresa had been a mistake, and dipping the pen in company ink rarely works out. The usual excuses apply: that no one who doesn't work the work and live the life can possibly understand the demands, the devotion. Victoria knows, especially now, that she can make it work with a civilian if she tried. The spaces were always there, carved out and set aside. The trouble for workaholics, for the *born to be en pointe* types like her, is that those spaces just become further homes for the obsession.

So nothing is going to happen. If anything, these days of morning rehearsal should be putting Anna off altogether. It's not hard to see her interest, even before the touching incident. Hours of barked commands and exertion and sweating should be making Anna long for someone freshly showered and completely unscarred, yet she still holds on a little longer and a little tighter than is ever strictly necessary.

Trouble is, Victoria's perfectly happy to be held.

They've built up to some fairly impressive lift work considering the start from scratch. Anna is a natural, which goes some way to taking the insecurity and second guessing out of it. The praise spills over now and then, despite Victoria's preferred coaching methods. Anna lights up with every muttered word that passes for a compliment, reinvigorated and ready to go again.

And no, it's still not dancing. It's not the freedom to leap and spin and momentarily feel lighter than air, but damn if it isn't close enough. In Anna's steady embrace, Victoria can close her eyes and almost feel the buzz of an audience again. Lifted high—though not as high as with Rick or with David—Victoria rolls back the years and the injury, reminded only when Anna carefully sets her down again. A reproachful twinge comes from her knee each time, but the injections and lurking behind her desk the rest of each day is mostly offsetting the damage.

In idle moments, Victoria wonders if trying this sooner would have made it easier, would have made her bold again. Was she really just waiting for this girl to come along and shake her from her self-pity? That seems unlike her, but then she's never been easy to change. Perhaps it only happens with exceptional events.

As Anna begs off to fetch more water from her bag, Victoria watches her go, hands on hips. Yes, she thinks as Anna chugs down water, careless enough to splash some on her chin, on her heaving chest. This is certainly exceptional.

ᏅᏅ

"Ready for Tuesday?" Victoria asks as Anna drains her bottle.

It's a change from their mostly silent work on lifting, and she seizes on it. Anna's never been great at keeping quiet. "I think so?" she answers, not wanting to be cocky even though she feels it right now. She can't keep the swagger out of her steps as she makes her way back to the center of the floor that they've made their own. "I can't believe it's coming around so fast."

"It always does." Victoria sounds maybe just a little wistful. "There's nothing much you can do about it."

"Nothing?" This is not the motivational speech she assumed. "How is that supposed to be inspirational?"

"Who said anything about inspiration?" Victoria seems bemused, reaching for a water bottle of her own.

Anna is hypnotized, briefly, watching the lines of Victoria's throat as she swallows.

"Not everything is a lecture to make you a better person, Anna. Sometimes I'm just making conversation. You get the thrill of a live audience next week. Don't take it for granted."

"I won't. Hey, do you think I could bench-press you? Like, if I laid flat and tried lifting you like that?" She's been dreaming about it for two nights now, but that is not an excuse for actually giving voice to thought. The blush is instant and furious; even on already-overheated skin she must be turning almost purple.

Victoria chokes on her last mouthful of water.

"There's only one way to find out, I suppose," she says after a minute of Anna fumbling for a way to take back her inane suggestion. "The bench over there will work. Unless you plan on dragging me down to the gym."

Favoring her injured leg as they move across the room, Victoria tuts under her breath with impatience at it.

Anna doesn't dare ask, but already she's trying to think how she can be more careful in her handling. She lies down on the leather-coated bench, no doubt stolen from the gym, mostly used as an impromptu stretching location for stubborn knots and tightness.

"How do we do this?" Victoria muses. "Should I straddle you and you turn me in the lift?"

Anna almost swallows her tongue. "Well, uh…"

"No, I think if you put your hands up and I lean over, then you just take over once I'm balanced."

"R-right," Anna agrees, raising her hands and hoping she isn't about to make a complete fool of herself.

Then Victoria—with this fearlessness that's emerged in how they work together, the same confidence Anna remembers seeing on stage—bends forward.

Anna's palms are flat and not shaking, which is a start. What she hasn't factored in is where her hands will have to be to keep Victoria balanced. One on the plane of her chest, just below her throat. The other on the lower part of her abdomen. Well. Anna is calling it that. She is not thinking of any other strictly more accurate, pelvic terms for where she's placing her hands.

It works, and Anna giggles at the sensation of it. Victoria keeps perfectly still, rigid as a board, and it's easy to support her this way. After a moment, Anna decides to risk a slow bend of her elbows, and then she really is bench-pressing her boss and director, though it's much harder going than the lifts where she could use her legs to bear the brunt.

"Satisfied?" Victoria asks, and it sounds almost fond.

It's a dangerous question, because Anna doesn't see how she ever can be, carrying around this hopeless crush.

"Sure, let me just put you down." Anna is pleased, but she can feel the strain. No point messing up a pectoral or a bicep on a silly whim.

"Gently," Victoria reminds her, and Anna is as careful as she knows how to be.

That's not good enough for Victoria's knee, unfortunately, and as soon as she needs to stand again, the damn joint crumples underneath her.

Anna is in motion almost before Victoria hits the floor. "Oh God," she gasps over Victoria's short, sharp yelp. "What did I do? Are you okay? I can go get Dr. Sawyer."

"No!" Victoria hisses. "She's already on my ass about doing this extra work with you."

"Then why—"

Victoria cuts her off. "Because I wanted to."

Anna knows she could retreat, run off with another apology and bring someone else to help. Only that's the last thing she wants, because if Victoria is going to need anyone for anything, Anna really would rather it be ~~she~~ her

"I haven't had a chance to move like that since…"

"We can bring Morgan back in," Anna offers.

Victoria's jaw tightens and her eyes flash darker for a split second.

"Or we can not do that. Can you stand, do you need me to…?"

She offers a hand, crouched in front of Victoria. But for the pain etched in the lines of her face, she might be any other dancer, resting on the floor with her legs splayed out to rest them.

Victoria takes Anna's hand, grip firm and sure. "I might just need a moment, okay?"

"No rush." Anna runs her thumb over Victoria's knuckles, neither of them making a move to get up. "I'm so sorry. If I've hurt you, if I've made it worse, I'll never forgive myself."

"Oh, Anna," Victoria sighs.

Instead of Anna pulling her up, there's just the slow-motion fall of Victoria pulling her back down. Whether just reflex or by design, Victoria ends up on her back on the cold, worn floor, and Anna is sprawled on top of her, catching herself in time to prop up on her elbows, breathing harshly at the surprise.

"Did you—"

Victoria silences the question with a kiss. Just the pressing of lips as she leans up, drawing their bodies closer together. Those soft lips Anna's been trying not to fixate on gently drag across her own as the kiss ends, and she's chasing them, turning Victoria's face back toward her for another kiss, then another. Openmouthed, a little desperate, someone whimpers into the fourth or maybe the fifth, and Anna is losing her battle to catalog the details. She wants to remember every second, but conscious thought is giving way to pure sensation, her body lighting up like completed circuits as Victoria's hands start to wander.

One at the base of Anna's neck, ignoring that her hair is wet and her skin is slick. That pulls her farther down, taking the strain off Victoria. Her other hand skims Anna's back, tracing the edge of her leotard and electrifying the bare skin with just the fingertips. If she thought she was overheating before, Anna sees now she had no idea how it feels to be on fire.

The room is suddenly tropical, her hearing is tuned to every half-moan and swallowed gasp from Victoria. Just as Anna thinks she may try shifting position, there are footsteps and voices just outside.

Victoria shoves her away and Anna rolls to the side, the move all but choreographed. The studio door doesn't open, and the gaggle of noise moves on, leaving them sitting silently side by side, the only sound in the room their harsh breathing.

It's easy to tell from that reaction what will happen next. The letdown—harsh or gentle—and the warning never to cross that line again. Anna doesn't need to hear it; she's embarrassed herself enough for one lifetime.

"I should get going," Anna says. "We don't have rehearsal now until Wednesday, right? I think it's *La B* right through the weekend and on Tuesday night. So, uh, do you need a hand? Or I can go get Kim, not a problem."

Pointedly Victoria stands by herself, slowly but without a single wobble. Her expression is back to impenetrable, so clearly Anna made the right call, saving them both the awkwardness.

"Off you go, then." Victoria dismisses her with a flap of her wrist.

Anna does as she's told, lips still tingling and parts of her still clenching with need, despite the shock of interruption. It's absolutely the right thing to do, but she can't help wishing she hadn't been quite so easy to send away.

CHAPTER 25

The first performance does come around too fast. As the afternoon ebbs away, Anna retreats to the rooftop that's become something of a sanctuary. She's joined by Ethan before long.

"Hey, newbie," he says with an easy grin. "Not planning to throw yourself off, are you? 'Cause I'm pretty sure David will make you dance regardless. Can't throw off the symmetry, you know?"

"David's not so scary," Anna says, because she knows the way to his good graces, if not his heart, is to bring coffee every other rehearsal.

"Ah, of course not. Not to the girl who tamed the dragon lady," Ethan says, teasing. "How's all that going, by the way?" He puts a sneaker-clad foot up on the bench and stretches his quads, a little close for comfort give how much his running shorts ride up.

Anna just turns away slightly. "I haven't had solo rehearsal in a few days," she admits. "First live performance took precedence; you know how it is."

"Yeah, you always get that last-minute flurry with the full dress and all. Everything else takes a backseat for a few days. Let the boss lady go do whatever she was up to in San Francisco, anyway, so maybe that will put her in a better mood."

"San Francisco?" Anna repeats, curiosity piqued. She's been so good about not texting or calling Victoria since *The Kiss*, as she's taken to calling it, capital letters very much necessary. "She didn't say."

"I don't think she needs your permission or anything." Ethan ends his stretch on one leg and switches to the other. "Maybe she just wants to throw some rotten fruit at Liza Wade."

"They open this week as well?" Anna asks.

"Yeah, last night. You nervous?"

"Are you?" Anna can't help hoping he is. "I mean, you've done it before…"

"The nerves never go, man. When they do, you don't care enough anymore, and it's time to quit."

"Good point." Anna picks up her phone, wanting to call Victoria and ask what the hell. She decides to get ready instead.

"See you in the wings," Ethan calls after her.

Anna throws up a backward wave in acknowledgment, running through the choreography as she walks.

"You're prowling," David accuses from where he's checking off a list of cues with the fly captain. Victoria ignores him for a moment, knowing it's important they have all heavy pieces of scenery accounted for and sequenced correctly. It's been checked a dozen times already, but no one skimps on safety.

"How was the dress?" Victoria asks, although she already knows the rehearsal went off without incident. "Delphine and Gabriel hitting form?"

"As always." David sends the crew member on his way and joins Victoria in the wings, where they watch the organized chaos all around them. "How was your trip west?"

"You heard about that too?" Victoria is well aware that this company has never kept a secret for five consecutive minutes. "I should really start traveling by private jet, throw you all off my tail. Family business, unavoidable." That was one, mostly factual, way of describing it. No one needed to know the trip home had been sparked by the existential crisis of being lifted or thoroughly kissed by the new principal.

Victoria Ford doesn't *run*. She does, admittedly, make the occasional strategic exit, but seeing her mother and her cronies for lunch had been punishment enough. The very sight of Victoria made them all so desperate to talk about Liza and which tickets they'd secured for her closing run. The best of Victoria's barbs about Liza had gone right over their heads, to add insult to injury.

Absently she bends slightly to massage her knee. It won't be forgiving her anytime soon, but despite more pronounced limping, even her mother had remarked on Victoria looking "perkier." Could it really be some kind of communicable disease, with Anna Gale as patient zero? How irritating.

Even David is looking at her strangely, and he usually knows better than to let himself be caught showing any personal interest at all.

"She'll be fine in with the rest, if that's what you're on edge about," he says quietly. "Her *arabesques* have a certain flavor of you about them, even. Whatever you're doing with her, it's working."

"Well enough to keep the wolf from the door?" Victoria asks. "Do they all know?"

"I tried shooting it down, but the trip to San Francisco was fuel on the fire. Everyone knows Liza was in town, and Rick has been around more."

"Because I wasn't watching my back already?" Victoria sighs. "How many times have I begged Kelly for control over who enters this building? We could all have chips around our necks, like those fancy doggy doors."

"I don't see them going in for collars. Well, some of them…"

"You ever think about giving all this up and going to teach chubby toddlers in Connecticut how to *plié*?" Victoria whines, just a little.

"No." David briefly places a comforting hand on her back. "And neither do you. Now go, have a night off. I'll deliver them all back in the morning."

"Make sure to actually take credit for your hard work tonight, with the donors. I don't want my name even mentioned."

"There's a first time for everything." David smiles. "I know you're only saying that because they'll talk about you regardless."

"The burdens of being a star." Victoria sighs. Now she just has to remember how to feel like one.

⌒♡♡♡

This is exactly what being a ballet dancer should feel like.

Anna is standing in the wings, stage right, watching with the rest of the female corps as Gabriel leads his warriors in their opening celebratory routine. As Solor, Gabriel is an obvious romantic lead, handsome and dashing. The audience is already enthused, breaking into applause at sporadic moments.

With her hair perfectly pinned, thanks to the collective efforts in the corps dressing room, Anna can feel the heavy stage makeup settling on her skin. She still feels a little out of place in a story set in India, but ballet has a long way to go on the accuracy of its casting.

Next to her, Morgan leans across to whisper, "It doesn't get less exciting."

Anna beams at the news. She feels full of energy, enough that it could bubble over.

She smooths out her patterned silk skirt one last time, hearing the music get closer and closer to their cue. The gold brocade is rough to the touch, the contrast enough to ground her.

As soon as she steps out under the lights, Anna is home. She can feel the attention like a warm embrace around her as she steps and twirls in formation with the other women, her sisters for the next two hours. The set design is phenomenal; it's a form of moving art really, and Anna could almost believe she's in a temple thousands of miles away. She tries to share that feeling with the audience with every twist and turn.

She lingers a few seconds in the wings after that, watching Delphine's entrance as Nikiya. Strong and deft in her movements, Delphine seems to have grown at least three inches since Anna saw her just a few hours before. Then Anna has to move. The first costume change is the trickiest, and she plucks her next tutu from the rail.

The break between acts two and three is when she changes her shoes, the box in the left feeling slightly weak on her last turn. Despite her best attempts at confidence, Anna checks carefully inside and out for signs of tampering, even shaking the damn things to be absolutely sure there's no broken glass.

All too soon, the finale is racing toward them, and Anna is as relieved as much as she wants to eke out every last second. There'll never be another first time, not quite like this.

And yet.

Anna watches when Delphine comes to take the final bow, flowers falling at her feet even though that's supposed to be for *closing* night. The pang in her chest takes Anna by surprise, as if some giant has reached in and squeezed her heart for two or three beats. It's not jealousy; she's happy for Delphine and the way the room seems to explode for her. The wall of noise and warmth covers them all. No, it's just a kind of longing that Anna doesn't expect.

A few months ago, just standing here, a season of just doing this kind of role, would have been dream enough to realize. Now Anna knows her head is turned. Victoria has shown her just a glimpse of going all the way, and oh, how Anna wants it. It seems impossible she was ever willing to settle for anything less.

They spill offstage as a company, loud and running on adrenaline. Shouts go up, drowned out by fragments of song, far enough out of tune to explain why they're all dancing and not singing for a living. It's a family, Anna thinks, as she's jostled and congratulated and jokes with everyone around her until they separate into their dressing rooms.

She's quick about her shower, pinning up her wet hair and changing into suitably comfortable sweatpants and a clean T-shirt to go home in. Anna's already fantasizing about how soft her bed will feel and how soundly she's going to sleep after this particular high.

"Come out with us," Morgan asks one more time as Anna makes to leave. She has her kit bag over one shoulder, and both pairs of shoes in her hand, dangling by the ribbons so she can throw them in their designated trash can on the way out. All the girls will be throwing away at least one, and there was chatter that Delphine made it through three. Speaking of their prima, she slips out of stage door as Anna tries to escape the boisterous girls' dressing room.

"Not this time, I'm saving myself for the opening-night party. Have one for me, though."

"Well, don't forget ice and pills before bed. You won't believe how sore tomorrow's gonna be." It's nice of Morgan to look out for her that way, Anna thinks. It's getting harder to see any of these people as competition.

Before Anna can get out of the stage door, there's a tug at her elbow. She turns to see Victoria there, stunning in a fitted cobalt blue dress, hair pinned up in a chignon. Diamonds sparkle at her ears, and Anna is easily led, as though hearing the Pied Piper play, away from the stage door and down toward the fire exit that leads into the alley.

"There's a tradition," Victoria explains, snatching the ribbons from Anna's hand when they're safely outside. "And while you didn't dance as a principal tonight, I don't much feel like tempting fate. Do you?"

Anna shakes her head, biting back an automatic "No, ma'am."

"Don't worry." Victoria nods toward the shoes. "I don't have a fetish. Though I'm told there are people who will pay top dollar if you ever need some extra cash."

"Ew." The subject will hopefully change, fast. "Did you watch?"

Victoria peers into some cans that line the alley. Stopping at the last in the row, she pulls a bottle from her purse and squirts liquid all over the satin shoes.

"Hey!" Anna is getting a little offended. "They're not that bad. I could just throw them with everyone else's."

"No, little one," Irina comes up behind them. "This is tradition. Your foremothers and their mothers before them. It's very Russian."

"It's crackpot superstition," Delphine chimes in, having escaped her adoring fans in record time. The stage door is a lot like running the gauntlet, so it must have been a small group. "Tell me you remembered a light. Nobody did for mine. We had to go bum matches on the street."

"Here." Victoria hands over a silver lighter when the bottle of lighter fluid is safely stashed again. "Try not to set yourself on fire in the process, please."

"Has anyone ever told you people you're kind of dramatic?" Anna says, but she's taking her shoes back greedily, dangling them over the empty trash can. She flips the lighter open, and it almost looks like she knows what the hell she's doing. "Although for true dramatic effect, we could have done this on the roof."

"Fire warden will get us," Irina says, deadly serious. "Come on, before we celebrate your retirement."

There's so much Anna still wants to ask Irina, so many suspicions to confirm, but she doesn't dare. Instead, she sparks a flame at her fingertips and coaxes it toward the now very flammable shoes. They go up fast, and Delphine cackles with a little too much enthusiasm. Anna holds them away from her body, as long as she dares until the flames are licking up the ribbons, getting too close to her fingertips.

She meets Victoria's questioning gaze in the firelight and lets the shoes fall.

⟨σδσ⟩

It takes so long to get rid of everyone, Irina especially, Victoria thinks with a sigh. She and Anna have some back and forth about that Jess woman, drinks, and someone's mother.

Victoria breathes through her nose and waits for Irina and Delphine to finally reach the street. Mercy of mercies, Anna stays put and watches them go. What Victoria glimpsed in the light of the fire, it seems Anna did too. When the other two part ways, they hesitate and talk between themselves, heads bowed close together. Irina looms over Delphine, and Victoria almost risks an impatient step closer to Anna.

At the scrape of Victoria's shoe lifting from the cobbled stone, Anna's fingers twitch.

They don't look directly at each other, not now. The smoke rises from the other side of the alley, acrid and wispy against the evening breeze. The moment they're completely alone, Anna is advancing on her, backing Victoria against the wall of the Metropolitan Center and kissing her senseless over an old, peeling poster for *The Nutcracker*.

"Oh," Victoria moans softly when Anna's hungry kisses leave her mouth and seek out new territory along her jawline and down her neck. "You were good tonight. I wasn't going to stay, but I was curious."

Anna grazes Victoria's collarbone with her teeth before biting down for just a moment. It almost pulls a growl from Victoria's throat. Feisty she wasn't expecting.

"You've got it, haven't you? That high. You want to be front and center, worshipped and adored." Victoria closes her eyes and tries to summon the old feeling. It can't compete with Anna's hands palming her breasts through the material of her dress. Victoria responds by shifting her balance and hooking her leg over Anna's hip to pull her closer.

"I want more," Anna confesses.

For a moment, Victoria is distracted by all the arousing things that could mean. Then she sees the glint in Anna's eye and understands.

"Soon. That stage will be yours, and you can show them what I see. It's going to take a lot more work, Anna."

"I'm not afraid of hard work."

"No, but you are meeting someone for drinks," Victoria reminds her. "And I have places to be. You can't afford distractions, no matter how…pleasant this little interlude is. Understood?" It's cruel to reject her, but safest while Anna can't really register the blow.

"Do you want to come? To drinks? It's my foster mom and my sister—you met her before."

Victoria drops her leg to release Anna, laying a hand on her cheek. "That's not what this is, darling. I don't meet the parents and play nice."

"What about after, should I—"

"I'll see you in the morning," Victoria says firmly. "Time to get Delphine on board. Where's that focus of yours?"

Anna turns her head and kisses Victoria's palm in defiance. Then she visibly gets a grip on her emotions and steps back, leaving Victoria to mourn the closeness. She fixes her dress.

"You're right," Anna admits. "I should go. Walk you out?"

"I'm fine right here for a minute." Victoria sends her off again, and it's supposed to be easy, barely a choice at all. "You go."

Anna does, and Victoria drops her head back against the rough surface of the wall. She's in way more trouble than she realized.

CHAPTER 26

"Fine," Delphine says with a sigh after Anna runs through a demonstration of how easily she can lift Victoria.

The physical part is easy, at least. Not grabbing Victoria by the surprisingly cute crop top she's wearing and kissing her again is much, much harder. Turns out the woman in black is even more appealing in adidas by Stella McCartney, pastel colors and all.

Not that Anna has a problem. Not at all. It's completely, totally, 500 percent fine by her to put her hands on Victoria, with witnesses, and not feel really any feelings about the situation whatsoever.

She has *got* to get better at lying. At least to herself.

It's amazing she actually did sleep last night, albeit tossing, turning, and dreaming about Victoria. Pressed against the alley wall as in reality, and against the studio mirrors straight from fantasy, and frankly there are more fragmented thoughts than Anna has brain power to process. If anything, she's more tired this morning. Only a combination of caffeine and Victoria's presence is making her look anything like alert, and she's back onstage tonight. Her lunch break is going to be a nap, she can already tell.

"Should we start now?" Anna asks, not in any particular hurry to put Victoria down. It's somehow become completely normal to carry her around with her arms wrapped around Victoria's thighs. "Or do you want me to show you some more, Delphine?"

"As much as I enjoy this nostalgic interlude, my calves certainly don't." Victoria practically manhandles Anna on her way back to standing. "Delphine, she's a safe pair of hands."

"Cool." Delphine springs to her feet, the easy grace from last night still evident in her every movement. Clearly the enthusiastic reception has put her in a better mood. "You break it, you pay for it, newbie."

"No pressure," Anna says with a snort, but here she is trading off her idol for one of the best dancers working today. It's not exactly a hardship to endure some studio banter along the way. She flexes a little, more for Victoria's benefit than Delphine's.

It earns Anna a long, dragging look from Victoria, then a water bottle hurled at her to break the spell. Well, Anna is pretty thirsty.

It's much trickier to start putting the lifts into full routines, and when Delphine hurls herself at Anna, there's real momentum behind it. They start on the ground-based choreography when Delphine is satisfied Anna will make a suitable prince, and it's fun in a way that Anna didn't expect.

Delphine has a precision Anna envies, and before long she's mimicking some of her poise and hand gestures, earning a quiet tut from Victoria as she watches on. Eve plays the piano at a jaunty pace, far quicker than they'll dance it on stage, but Delphine insists.

"Do you really want to dance to a dirge over and over again?" Delphine asks when Anna questions it. "Not to mention, if you can do it quicker than necessary, the actual tempo will be a breeze in comparison. It's how you get good, trust me."

Anna looks to Victoria, who half shrugs in something like confirmation.

By the time their session is up, Anna is the pleasant kind of exhausted, endorphins doing somersaults through her veins. David comes to pull Victoria away on some business or other, and she's left to clean herself up and shrug on something warm alongside Delphine.

"Well," Delphine drawls as she tosses her shoes aside. "Haven't you got it bad?"

"Excuse me?"

"I thought it was the curse of the newbies—we talked about that, didn't we?—and you almost had me fooled."

"David wants us in early this afternoon," Anna says, trying to deflect by passing on the morning gossip. She gets her scoops from Kelly, who always has something sugary at her desk to top up Anna's breakfast. "Is that normal, after the night before?"

"Yes, and don't try to play me, Anna. I know exactly what's going on. I didn't think you had it in you, but I'm a little impressed."

"Okay?" There's a lump of panic in her throat, and she can't swallow around it anymore. Her brain rattles like a kaleidoscope through possible accusations, every second thought being *Victoria! Victoria! Victoria!* Even trying to fumble for a story, for a change of topic, leaves Anna feeling like she no longer speaks any language at all. She suspects she isn't the first person to feel like Delphine Wade is something that just happens to them.

"How long? It was totally happening last night, right? I knew we were walking in on something. Irina tried to put money on it, but I could tell it was too late. You just about lit the damn shoes with the heat between you."

"Delphine, please." Anna knows she can't tell. She can neither confirm nor deny. She isn't sure what that would even entail right now other than *if you thought Victoria Ford could dance, then Jesus you should feel her kiss.* Ugh I love Gabriel & Delphine

"Don't get me wrong, I am thrilled there's officially one girl not after my boyfriend."

"It's not official, we're not—"

"I wouldn't be so sure." Delphine zips up her hoodie. "Not just because you look like an actual cartoon princess, but because I know Victoria. I know what her flings look like—everyone kept at arm's length. This is something else. Anna, she hasn't even attempted a lift in twelve years."

Anna's heart pounds against her rib cage. It's the reality she's been trying to deny to herself with each thrilling second. It does feel like more. Not that she can afford to dwell on that.

"Lunch?" Anna asks with a sigh.

"Sushi," Delphine says. "Come on, I know a place."

⟳◎◎⟳

"Jesus!" Anna walks into the changing room after David's picky session correcting all the minor faults from the previous night's performance. She's tired, she's sore, and it's all going to be on stage again tonight, with nowhere to hide. A bunch of girls bundle in behind her, not caring why Anna has stopped short in the doorway. "What are you doing here?"

"I dropped Mom at the airport, and Irina has physio, so I came to see my little sister," Jess says, completely unfazed by sitting in the midst of a dozen stripping dancers. "You've got time to get a drink before the show, right?"

"A soft one, yeah. Let me just have two minutes in the shower and I'll be right out." Two minutes hot, two minutes cold. Washing yet again with the creamy shower stuff that's supposed to have lotion in it, stopping her skin drying out from multiple showers a day.

Anna takes her time, letting the rest of the room clear out, but Jess seems perfectly patient by the time she comes back out to get dressed.

"Tough rehearsal?"

"No tougher than any other day so far. You hungry? I can't eat much this close to curtain, but some fruit maybe."

"I don't know." Jess shrugs beneath her denim shirt. "What goes well with your sister keeping secrets from you?"

"Jess…"

"No, you'd tell me if you could, right? But the fact you can't kinda tells me exactly who we're talking about here."

"I'm not talking about this," Anna snaps. "I'm still waiting for an explanation of whatever the hell was up with Irina. What are you getting into, Jess? I know she's on more than prescription drugs."

"Spiral fracture. She showed me the films. If your doc here finds out, she's done. Her own doctor is giving her enough to get to the end of the season, he swears she can do it if she's careful."

"But if she can't, if she doesn't make it…" It would seriously imbalance the program, wouldn't it? But then injuries can strike anyone, anytime. There has to be some contingency. As loyal as she feels to Irina for no tangible reason, Victoria does deserve to know what she's dealing with.

"And what about you?" Jess asks. "You ready to make the big confession yet?"

"Who says I have anything to confess?" Anna is getting a little exhausted at playing Mata Hari. She's not even getting sex out of all this subterfuge yet. And, oh God, the thought is enough to have her face flushing again. Jess is going to know, and there'll be no denying it.

"Like I said, there's only one reason you wouldn't be able to just tell me. Which means you're hooking up with your boss."

"Shush!" Anna warns, looking around for any lurkers. "Are you trying to ruin my entire life?"

"So dramatic. This isn't high school. Besides, everyone already hates you for your promotion."

"And if there is something happening between me and Victoria, you know that means I have to tell her about Irina, right?" Anna doesn't particularly want to have that conversation, but Jess pulls her into a hug for suggesting it.

"I'm actually surprised you haven't already. I didn't think you were that close to Irina." The hug ends and Jess steps back to lean against the lockers. "Or is there some kind of bro code for ballerinas?"

"No, but nobody wants to be a snitch."

"I just don't want her to get any more hurt. You should hear it when the drugs wear off and she tries to do even basic moves. I don't know how to help her, other than this. She won't let me."

"I'll probably see Victoria tonight," Anna decides.

Jess grins at her.

"Not like that, you perv! We've only... You know what? No details for you."

"Come on, I owe you that soft drink. Let's get it before you have to go put all your stage crap on."

∩δδ∩

"Don't you ever go home?" Victoria asks from the door of her office, pulling her reading glasses off to let her eyes rest.

"I'll go home when you stop giving me enough work for three assistants," Kelly says. "Need something?"

"How's the house?" Victoria asks.

Kelly's frown is as much an answer as the number of seats filled. "Derek came by, said the old-timers were arguing in the foyer about whether they'd seen this exact production last season. Doesn't bode well, does it?"

"No. All the more reason to shake things up post-*Nutcracker*, right?"

"That will keep the lights on, yeah." Kelly gets up from her desk to file something in the archive room. "Full cast went on, by the way."

"On the second night? I should hope so."

"Anna Gale was looking for you, wandered up in full makeup and costume, everything but her shoes on." Kelly's voice is muffled, but Victoria homes in on every word.

She opens her mouth to tell Kelly that of course Anna is an exception to the no-disruptions rule, but both the fact of even thinking such a thing, and the impression it would create, stops Victoria in her tracks.

"Fascinating," Victoria calls back instead, aiming for nonchalance and missing. "When are they off?" she asks, like she doesn't have the show's run time etched in memory from last night, ready to pounce at the perfect moment. Only to be so deliciously pounced on in turn. If she had sense, any kind of self-preservation, Victoria would call her car and head home right now. Or at least to the nearest bar.

"In about ten." Kelly returns with her purse and coat. "You need anything?"

"Leave a note with Stage Door for Anna to come up when she's done?" Because it's just a little less desperate than jumping her in a corridor.

Between the curtain calls, a shower and change, and Anna's own unique way of taking her time, Victoria estimates she has a half hour to make herself presentable—starting with losing the exercise clothing she's been working in all day.

The moment Kelly's footsteps reach the stairs, Victoria yanks a black dress from the rack in her office, freshening up as she changes. The tiniest hint of makeup and pulling her hair down into loose curls seems work-casual enough that Anna won't notice extra effort. A splash of perfume at her wrists, behind her ears. A bigger splash of vodka, neat. Three pills, because recommended doses are for amateurs, and Victoria is ready.

She sits back down at her desk, leafing through some newly printed sheet music, and waits.

CHAPTER 27

If anything, it was a relief earlier when Kelly barred the way to Victoria. Just seeing her outline through the frosted glass had been distracting enough, and Anna needs to be incredibly careful with the subject she's broaching.

Her heart still skips a beat later in that giddy little way when Leonard at Stage Door calls her over to give her a note. Not Victoria's manic scrawl, but something legible from Kelly, just letting her know Victoria is available in her office post-show. Anna's all cleaned up and ready to go, so it's a challenge not to take the stairs three at a time as soon as the invitation is extended.

At least she has a plan. It might not be a foolproof plan, but if Victoria is willing to meet her at least part of the way, they can find a solution where everyone is happy and nobody has to quit.

"Hello?" she calls out, walking into the darkened reception area. A lamp or two is on in Victoria's private office in the back, and Anna is drawn to them as readily as any moth. Thank God she didn't opt for the sweats she wore earlier to hang out with Jess, though suddenly her choice of pale shirt dress and denim jacket feels a little exposing, even though it's only her legs on display.

They certainly seem to be the first thing Victoria notices from behind her desk. She picks up a glass, containing what Anna would bet isn't water, and throws it back. Then there's a long, appraising gaze from ankles to the hem of her short dress. Anna spends her days dancing in what barely counts as underwear, but only now does she feel underdressed, almost bare.

"I was just thinking about you," Victoria tells her, the warmth of the lamplight giving the room the air of a confessional. She gestures vaguely for Anna to sit.

Anna drops her bag at her feet and does as indicated. Only when she's sitting does she slowly cross her legs, in the tamest homage to Sharon Stone ever conceived. Still, it holds Victoria's undivided attention.

"What, um… Can you tell me what you were thinking about?" There's heat in Anna's cheeks, but not as much as she would expect. She's getting used to being around Victoria.

"It's not important." Victoria sets her glass aside and leans forward, bridging her fingers in front of her. All business, but the gleam in her eyes over those dark-framed reading glasses suggest pleasure is the order of the day. "I'm reliably informed that you wanted to see me earlier. Pre-show nerves?"

"No," Anna lies, because she gets the butterflies before every show and is sure she always will. "And no offense, but you don't seem like the 'there, there' type, anyway."

"You have been paying attention." Victoria is mocking, but only gently. Her smile is playful, and Anna finds herself wishing it would never vanish from her face.

"There's something I need to tell you," Anna interrupts, getting a raised eyebrow in return. "It's about *Gala Performance*, and Irina. I know she's struggling with some things, so don't you think we should have a strong understudy, just in case? That way she can have a lighter rehearsal load. I mean, we both know all that Vaganova training lets her pick up anything ten times quicker than everyone else."

Victoria stands, leaning over her desk with her palms suddenly flat. She's far too graceful when she moves, because Anna keeps finding herself mesmerized. "Not content with instant promotion to principal, now you want to be ballet mistress too?"

Anna can't sputter out a correction quickly enough, and Victoria continues.

"Did you have someone in mind? Don't bring me problems, Anna. Bring me solutions."

"Just like that?" Anna leans back in her seat, bouncing her foot a little. She risks a small smile when Victoria glances down again. It's almost too easy, in this post-kiss world, knowing that this heady crush is at least partly reciprocated. "Okay, since you asked… What about Morgan?"

A frown is to be expected, maybe even an eye roll. One thing Anna doesn't expect is a laugh, sudden and melodic.

"That's funny?" she asks, trying not to pout.

"Oh, if you only knew… Of course we'll have understudies, this is a professional company. They're traditionally junior soloists. Morgan's in the corps."

"So was I," Anna counters, and Victoria raises that damn eyebrow again. "I mean, so *am* I. If I can be both, why can't she?"

"She'll understudy more than one part. What if she goes on for you and steals your 'plucked from obscurity' storyline, hmm? It's one thing to replace Delphine or Irina, but you need that media splash."

"That's a risk for me to take. But the only thing that will keep me off that stage is if I can't dance it. If it gets to that point, I've got no business being out there anyway. It wouldn't be right, with what people pay for their tickets."

"Then I'll think about it."

"You will?"

"Yes." Victoria moves away from her desk, fiddling with some brochures on the low counter against the back wall. Framed posters hang above it, some of her best-reviewed triumphs. "Was there anything else?"

Is that an invitation to go over there? To kiss her again? Anna can't be sure. She stalls, remembering that Victoria had asked her to come up. "Did you want to see me for something specific?"

"When I heard you came looking for me," Victoria sighs, "I assumed you wanted to pick up where we left off last night."

Anna's stomach does a backward somersault. "Would that be so bad?"

"No, but it would be distracting. Things get murky when we don't keep it professional. It makes me an easy target for whatever Rick is plotting." Victoria looks hurt even as she says it. She sits at her desk and picks up a book of Tchaikovsky's sheet music without turning a page. Her reading glasses are pointedly pushed back up her nose with one finger. "We have so much to do, and there's everything at stake. This way we stop the...process before anyone gets hurt."

"Victoria, no, this isn't what I want—"

"It's what I want." Victoria has a way of closing down a discussion that Anna usually envies. Tonight it just makes her angry, powerless in the face of Victoria's stubbornness. "You can see yourself out."

"Can we talk about this tomorrow?" Anna pleads, heading to the door with dragging feet.

"No," Victoria answers quite firmly. "There's nothing more to discuss. Morgan will understudy."

⌒○○⌒

Anna slips out of a side door without caring if it'll set off an alarm somewhere. She always walks faster when she's sad or angry, and now she's a perfect mess of both, so it takes hardly any time to get home at all.

She stops at the store four blocks down a side street to pick up something to snack on, settling for an overpriced protein bar and a bottle of water. Only as she's hesitating outside her building does she make the decision to do it.

"Marcia?" She picks up after about ten rings, and it only just occurs to Anna that her foster mother may have been in bed. "I'm sorry, I can call tomorrow."

"Anna, what's wrong?"

"Nothing's wrong, it's just… There's a box in my room at your house. It's all packed and ready to send. I was going to send it ahead when I next came home, but do you think you could mail it to me? You've got my address. Please don't send it to Jess's place."

"Okay, but I'd feel better if you told me why you sound so sad, sweetheart." Marcia is fussing with papers as they talk, no doubt leaving herself a note as a reminder.

"It's just hard sometimes," Anna tells her as she walks. "I think a little extra home comfort will help, and that box has some things I miss."

"Whatever you need. I'll ship it tomorrow, right after lunch."

"You're the best," Anna tells her before hanging up and wiping away a stubborn tear.

∞∞

"Anna's on to you, you know." Victoria is waiting for Irina the next morning. "And I checked with Kim. You've been missing all your appointments except sports massage."

"I don't like her rough little hands," Irina replies, a little too quickly, a little on edge. "And she smells like diesel fuel too."

"She does not. You only say that because you don't like her motorcycle."

"There are many things I don't like." Irina groans, leveraging up from the bench she's lying on. "Don't ask me, Vicki. Your insurance people won't be pleased if you know."

"Let me pay you off. I'll get the money from some incidental budget, Irina. I can put in some calls, get you a job lined up for after surgery. It might have to be Miami or something, but at least you'll get some heat in your bones."

"Won't stop them fracturing."

"Shit."

"You're lucky, just doing the muscle. No illusions there. When it goes, it goes. Bones try to hold together."

Victoria grimaces as she sits on the vacated side of the bench, staring at Irina's hunched back and her wild hair. "*Lucky* isn't really the word I'd go with."

"I hear you were dancing." Irina levels it as an accusation.

"Some lifts, barely a hop, skip, or a jump. Don't believe everything you hear. Or I'd have to start believing the things I hear, and they're not good at all. I want you to take at least two weeks, give it some semblance of healing. I can keep you in the rest of the season that way. If you keep doing what you're doing just to rehearse, you'll never make it."

"Two weeks?" Irina blows out a shaky breath, like it's worse than she thought. "And when I come back?"

"Everything you've already been promised. I need you for *Gala Performance*, Irina. Let me get you there and the send-off you deserve. I haven't forgotten how you stepped in for me, how you kept the press away when I was at my worst."

"I was a star in my own right. But you're welcome."

"That kid is worried about you." Victoria tries for uninterested, tries to make Anna sound so much less than she is.

Irina turns around to give the full benefit of her skeptical expression, sweater slipping to bare her shoulder, pale against the blood red of the fabric.

"Doesn't seem like regular hero worship for you," Victoria adds. "Is it serious, with her sister?"

"Anna is no child. And Jessica is…as good for me as she is bad. She wants me to bow out, but she does everything to keep me in our little game here. What more could I ask?"

"I mean it about the two weeks." Victoria squirms away from the personal chat, knowing what comes next. "If I hear you moved any further than bed to bathroom, I'll fire you."

"I have every faith. Go, tend to your sheep. I'll be back."

"At least time is on our side."

"Even if you're still the only stubborn American who wants to stage *La Bayadère* with a company that's barely large enough to perform it. The big European companies will watch their backs."

"That's supposed to be the point." Victoria picks at a piece of lint on her black silk blouse. "Shaking things up, remember?"

"I always said you were wasted here," Irina grumbles. "See you in two weeks."

⌒⊙⊙⌒

"So where's Irina?" Anna asks the moment the rest of the class is clear of the studio.

Victoria didn't take warm-up, but she slipped in at the end, knowing this confrontation would be forthcoming.

"If you booted her because of what I suggested last night—"

"Which part of 'Morgan can understudy' did you not understand?" It's more snappish than she needs to be, but Victoria is still offended that Anna thinks she's disposable after everything that's been staked on her. "I should go and break the good news. She'll need to call her mommy."

"I'm sorry," Anna blurts, reaching for Victoria, who's too slow to fully pull her arm away. The touch is electric, a test to her resolve. "I didn't mean to push. I can wait."

"I'm not asking you to wait. I'm asking you to be a professional."

"But when the show is up, or in the off-season…" Anna is gathering steam with her suggestions.

Victoria can feel the last shred of stubborn resistance waver. Why push away someone who's going to get her the success she needs? Why push away someone who feels so much better when pulled close? And before she knows it, pulling Anna close is exactly what Victoria does, until their faces are mere inches apart.

Anna's flushed from the warm-up, rosy-pink cheeks and her honey-blond hair darkened by sweat. Victoria reaches out and tucks a loose strand behind her ear.

"Maybe." It's all she can give. It's not just ego, it's the fragile hope of retaining the upper hand with this girl, of retaining the authority and the distance to drive her past the point where lesser dancers would give up. "But it's not just your distraction I'm worried about."

"I distract you?" Anna asks, waggling her eyebrows just a little. She reaches out, touching Victoria's arm so tenderly it's barely contact at all.

"Not if you dance well. Then I can focus on that, and that alone."

Anna considers, before stepping back and letting her grip on Victoria's arm go loose. "Then no distractions." She's so sincere that Victoria aches, just a little. "You want me to tell Morgan to come see you?"

"Please do." Victoria wants to take it back, wants to reconsider all her restraint and sensibility. She takes a seat by the window and waits.

∞∞∞

She isn't disappointed that Anna doesn't return, but Victoria is more than ready for Morgan Gresham when she appears alone, all glossy black hair and nervous smiles that show a little too many teeth for comfort. Honestly, she's not one of the corps members who Victoria knows well—she's missed more than a year with an injury and wasn't Victoria's initial pick from the apprentices. David has a reasonable amount of faith in the girl, but he's always been softhearted.

Anna's suggestion is sound in one regard. Morgan has the physicality and imposing paleness to make for a dramatic Russian.

"Victoria? Anna Gale said you wanted to see me?"

"I do." Victoria turns her attention out of the window, affecting boredom. It doesn't take Morgan long to start squirming.

"Did you need me to get something, or…?"

"You'll understudy all three parts in *Gala Performance*. There'll be other cover, of course. But if you go on, it will be promoted, it'll be a star-plucked-from-the-corps story. Any objections?"

"Wait, what?"

"Do I need to repeat myself?" Victoria unfurls her legs from the windowsill, stalking across the floor toward Morgan. "Of course, if you go on for Anna, that wipes her off the map. That won't be a problem?"

Morgan looks stricken at the thought of it, and Victoria is ready to roll her eyes at the lack of ambition in these millennials. Then with a grin that resembles her mother's, Morgan sees the opportunity for what it is.

"No problem at all. Should I come to rehearsals with the others?"

"Times will be on your board," Victoria confirms. "This won't affect your friendships? Relationships?"

"Well, I don't have much of either," Morgan confesses before biting her lip like she hadn't meant to confess it.

Perhaps Victoria shouldn't invest much in this girl who'll stab Anna in the back for her shot, but it's not a failing, not where Victoria is concerned. She respects a fellow shark at work. It's just Anna who mistakes them all for dolphins.

"I assume word will reach your mother?" Victoria asks, and Morgan almost completely deflates. Oh. "She didn't ask me," she says, correcting where her thoughts have clearly gone. "Anna suggested you, in fact."

"She did?" Morgan smiles a little too brightly. "Oh, okay. Thank you, Victoria. I have to go do the whole rehearsal thing."

"Go on. I'll see you next week."

"Next week." She practically skips out of the room, and Victoria watches her go, tugging at her bottom lip.

CHAPTER 28

It's excruciating. A week of barely seeing Victoria at all. Anna starts to hate David just a little, for the simple fact of him not being the woman she's so enthralled by.

She's sleeping like the dead at least. The combined exhaustion of rehearsing her corps shows, along with preparing for her turn as a prince, and the very early work on *Gala Performance* that's waiting for Irina's return, would be tiring enough. Add a full ballet every night, with the exacting *Kingdom of the Shades* and the exquisite *arabesques*, and Anna has found levels of exhaustion that she can't understand how any human body can endure.

And God, she loves it. It's everything she ever dreamed of and so much more. Even when her legs feel like lead or her back muscles enter brief spasms, she can grit her teeth and bear it. The alternative is not getting to dance like she does, and for Anna that's no alternative at all.

Apart from the emotional bruising around her heart from Victoria's insistence on boundaries, that still *sucks* on a daily basis, and Anna can't find a more mature word for it than that. But Victoria is available to them once again with her new rehearsal plan, and Anna practically skips up the stairs at the thought.

She greets Delphine and Morgan with equal enthusiasm, the brief hugs of people who now work together daily, then nods to Eve as she sets up at the piano with her typical flurry of nerves. It's like the first day of school all over again, and Anna is determined to make nothing less than a perfect impression on her returning director.

When Victoria enters, the first thing Anna notices is that she's leaning heavily on a sleek black cane, almost invisible against the backdrop of her tailored pants that graze the ankle and no more. Her shirt is white, crisp, the collar high and starched, open in that Jane Fonda style that always looks so classy. Anna is drinking in the details as though she'll never be allowed to look again, even as she affects the guise of going through her hamstring stretches at the barre.

"*Mes danseuses,*" she greets them, just the hint of a grin tugging at one corner of her mouth. It's peak fantasy Victoria Ford, the vision who's been haunting Anna's exhausted dreams for weeks, but never more clearly than in the past few weeks. "David tells me you were so very well behaved while I was away. I assume he's covering for you."

Delphine laughs, more used to Victoria than any of them. Morgan has adopted Anna's wide-eyed wonder from the start of the season, and it's something of a relief not to be the least sure person in the room anymore.

Shucking her fitted black track top, Anna unveils the peach-colored leotard that scoops far more daringly than the others. It's what Jess called "as close to naked as you can get without being arrested" and that's statement enough. With tights, tiny white running shorts, and her pointe shoes, it at least looks appropriate for the session.

And yes, Victoria looks. Positively stares for a moment, eyes raking up and down with enough focus that it seems the fabric should shred under her gaze. Anna's almost disappointed when it doesn't, but the jittery excitement of it all just makes her more impatient to dance. Exhausting, repetitive actions are her best hope. There's going to be plenty of those in store.

"Shoes off," Victoria announces with a brisk clap of her hands. "We're going back to the roots today, so throw out your manuals and your muscle memory. It's time we reacquainted you with exactly what these bodies of yours"—a pointed glance at Anna—"are actually capable of. Eve, we'll need something soft, think Philip Glass on Valium."

"Yes, ma'am," Eve says, flipping through her sheets with a faint smile.

Anna sits heavily on the boards and begins untying the ribbons she just pulled taut. Delphine just toes her untied slippers off, and Morgan hasn't thought to change yet.

The three of them gravitate toward each other at this change in routine, nervous glances exchanged.

"Now Irina would only scoff, so it's important we do this work before her Russian training comes to stomp all over my methodology here. Delphine, you did plenty of Bournonville coming up, but we have ourselves some true Balanchine babies in here. What I have in mind is that all three ballerinas have their proud styles, but they have to be talented enough to mockingly dance each other's too. It's going to be a bastard to remember, so there's some unlearning to do first."

Anna raises her hand. First day of school indeed. "Unlearn how, exactly?"

"Oh Anna, just you wait and see."

∞

It's needlessly melodramatic and just what Victoria needs. She hasn't been in retreat, not exactly. Part of her absence has been to fend off Rick, who keeps turning up like a bad penny.

The other is a need for private space. Growing up in the ballet, she's been used to dorms and locker rooms and crowded studios, barely a quiet minute most days. At times, when the demands are pressing and the standards must be exceptional, Victoria recognizes the need for solitude. It's how her best work gets done.

The timing was settled by her knee protesting all the recent exertion in more dramatic fashion. An early morning phone call to Kim after three hours of sweating out incredible pain has resolved the worst of it, but the cane is not optional as long as the sporadic weakness persists.

"You don't have most of the muscle there anymore. It can fake it for a little while, but come on, Victoria," Kim lectured her as she iced and injected and supported.

For once, Victoria hadn't argued.

The choreography is finalized. Victoria may barely have slept—four hours a night is sufficient, really—but she has it now. In her head, in her bones, on the tip of her tongue and the flick of her wrists. If these talented, indefatigable women can do what she believes them capable of, they'll paint her dance on the canvas of the stage, bold brushstrokes and emphatic swirls of color.

They're looking at her like she's lost her mind. Maybe she has.

"Lose some layers, ladies. This isn't your regular warm-up."

"Uh," Morgan interrupts. "How many layers, exactly?"

"Don't worry, your virtue will remain intact. We just need to shake off the staleness. Back to basics, if you will."

Morgan pulls her sweater up over her head, tossing it toward the mirrors. Delphine similarly ditches her fussy additions until, like Anna, they're all in leotards and tights alone. Back to basics. They could be in their first classes, back in whichever church halls and school gymnasiums sparked this fire in them, the incubators that raised three ballerinas of the New York Ballet.

Victoria claps, and Eve starts up with a wistful, caressing little tune that seems oddly familiar. All three dancers nod in acknowledgment of something other than a driving march or lilting waltz. It's going to work, and what's more, they're going to enjoy it.

"I want you to make a full circuit of the studio." Victoria begins her instructions, seeking out the sanctuary of her director's chair, folding into it with only minimal discomfort. She props the cane on the side, still resenting its presence. "Use whatever steps you want. Make your way around the room as elaborately as you can think of. No *pointe*, obviously." She gestures to their bare toes.

"I don't get it," Anna answers. "You don't have instructions?"

"I just gave you them. The rest is up to you."

"Come on, children," Delphine says with a sigh. She might not have been subjected to this particular exercise before, but she's familiar with the concept of Victoria tipping the world on its head. "Just be grateful it's not the one where you can't use your feet."

"Spoilers, Wade!" Victoria calls out, but Delphine is off at a trot, breaking into a jog and then a few experimental spins toward the window wall. The Gresham girl hesitates another moment before closing her eyes and starting a series of small leaps, warming up to full *jetés* by the time she's closing in on the first lap.

Only Anna stands frozen.

This won't do, this won't do at all. Eve's music gets a little livelier as Victoria slips from her seat and approaches her uncooperative principal. Time to lead.

∽∂∞∿

Anna can't seem to make her body do anything at all; she's completely stalled in her own self-consciousness. For years she's taken daily instructions. Even practicing alone, the routines have been drills, repeating what she's been shown in the way she's been shown it. Sure, if someone said, "Show me some ballet," off-the-cuff she might throw a few steps into a routine, but more often than not it would be a prelearned sequence, whichever popped into her head first.

Now Victoria is approaching. God, she looks good. She's been to the hairdresser, the blond brighter and the curls that little bit softer. There's a dull sheen of pearls at her throat. For a second, Anna pictures them between Victoria's teeth and she almost moans.

Why was she pleased to have Victoria back, again?

"Come along," Victoria says, but instead of stopping in front of Anna, she slips around behind her. Hands are on her hips, as though straightening her posture. Anna doesn't dare open her eyes to see if Delphine or Morgan have noticed. All she cares about is the warmth through the taut spandex, the feeling of five fingers pressing almost hard enough to bruise. "You're free, Anna. Have some fun."

"Fun?" Anna opens her eyes and glances back over her shoulder. "Since when?"

Victoria squeezes Anna's hips, and she gasps. With a little shove, Anna is in motion and mourning the contact even as her feet seem to find their way without her direction. She hops and skips and jumps.

By the time she catches up with Morgan, they're competing over who can *jeté* highest and longest, laughing the whole time. Delphine scoffs at them, but then they start spinning wildly, three oscillations that bounce off each other and the walls, the laughs getting louder along with the music as Eve gets in on the fun.

Eventually Victoria summons them all to a halt with one of her trademark bursts of clapping, and Anna sinks to the floor gratefully, still laughing. She feels like a kid in a schoolyard again, lungs bursting and legs burning just a little. Somehow all the throwing themselves around has been more exhausting than performing a whole ballet, but she can't bring herself to mind.

"Much better," Victoria tells them. "Now pick yourselves up and gather round. We're going to keep it fluid today."

Anna executes a perfect kick up from her back to standing, just for the hell of it. She gets a Victoria Ford smile in response, and it's the best idea she's ever had.

⟲⟳⟲

"Hey, Kelly," Anna greets Victoria's righthand woman as she exits the locker room. "Were you looking for Victoria? We left her back in the studio, while we could still walk."

"No, I'm looking for you, Anna Banana," Kelly fires back with a smile. "Package for you, and with all the 'urgent' and 'confidential' stickers on it, I thought I'd better bring it straight to you."

"Oh, you didn't have to do that. But thank you."

"No show tonight at least. You could…well, you could take another shower maybe."

"That bad?" Anna sniffs herself. "Yikes, fair point." She gestures with the package. "This is from my foster mom. She gets a bit carried away when it comes to the postal service."

"Just remember if she sends snacks, you have to share."

"I will," Anna promises, ducking down the side hallway by the changing rooms to sit on an empty bench. She rips apart her own packing skills and unearths the packet of papers she was looking for. The hallways are empty. Distant noise elsewhere in the building says classes and rehearsals are still going on. The packet is in her hands and still she can't quite look directly at them.

When she checks, when she finds out for sure, there'll be no going back. Anna isn't at all sure she's ready for that.

⟲⟳⟲

Victoria leverages herself out of the chair at the foot of Irina's bed. "Your girlfriend, I assume. Doesn't she have a key?"

"Don't be jealous I got myself a Gale sister," Irina teases. "But yes, Jessica has a key."

"It's hardly been five minutes, you walking cliché. Sorry, hobbling cliché."

"Fuck you, Vicki." Irina flips her off as Victoria makes it out of the room.

It's a nice place. Victoria's always thought so. She should have put her insurance money into buying somewhere with this modern style.

"Irina's bellhop service," Victoria says as she opens the door to see…Anna. A tearstained, wild-haired, equally stunned Anna Gale is on Irina's doorstep, and just when the hell did it start raining?

"Is she here?" Anna demands, rubbing her hands on her ripped jeans. The dark T-shirt beneath her jacket is wet through. "Wait, why are you here?"

"I can't check on my injured dancer? What if she's not up to visitors?"

"No." Anna is resolute. "That is not an option. This is too important. Are you going to get out of my way?"

It's a sight to see, all that defiance packed into that pleasing frame with its barely contained muscular definition. Victoria swallows hard, but she steps aside, welcoming the unexpected visitor. In the open-plan hallway, with its high white ceilings, it would be quite easy to keep themselves a respectable distance apart.

Regardless, Anna brushes against her, her rain-spattered leather jacket transferring enough liquid to soak Victoria's shirt. It turns her white shirt almost transparent, and she stares down at it just as surely as Anna does. On the way back up, their gazes meet, and Victoria can't think of a single thing to say.

"Well."

"Sorry. I need to—"

"Through there," Victoria directs, a casual nod toward Irina's bedroom. "Be warned, she's on painkillers and has even fewer filters than usual. Do you need me to come in?"

"Private," Anna says. "Sorry."

Victoria shrugs. What does she care? She can ignore the pang in her chest at being shut out, at not knowing who made Anna cry, what put all the longing and loneliness behind that desperate look.

"I'll be in the kitchen, when you're done."

"Okay."

And Anna's gone, in motion already, bearing down on Irina, who has no idea of the oncoming storm.

∽◌◌◌∾

"*Malenkaya*," Irina greets her, propped up on the pillows. "You remember where I live."

"Did you know?" Anna can barely form the sentence, but she can't chicken out now. "Have you known all this time? My whole life?"

"You're not making any sense," Irina points out, and it's not unreasonable.

"You're not from Russia." Anna sticks to the facts. "You were born in Ukraine. You told me last time I was here."

"Yes, and no. I was born in the Soviet Union. Do we really need to relive history? The wall came down, the gas comes through the pipelines. You can fly on Aeroflot and I can dance in America without defecting. Look how far we've come."

"You knew." Anna knows when she's being deflected. She's so tired of everyone thinking that just because she tries to be nice, she must also somehow be stupid. "You had a sister."

"No." Irina pushes the sheets aside, swings her legs out of the bed.

Anna steps back, unsure how much confrontation this is.

"No, I had no sister," Irina continues. "Not one that I knew."

"But you had one," Anna persists. "Her name was—"

"Inessa. Our parents had great imagination, I see. They got no further than 'I' in the book of names."

"My mother." Anna clears her throat, because this is important and has to be said with the weight due the moment. "Was a Ukrainian immigrant to this country. Her name was Inessa. I could never say her surname quite right, and it made her so sad."

"Ah." Irina's expression is pinched, and she won't look directly at Anna. "There were moments, I wondered. When I first came here, I wanted to pay someone to find her. I never did. *Inessa Sviderskyi*."

"That's her." Anna could swear she feels the fresh crack in her heart from hearing her mother's name correctly spoken after all this time.

"How is it that you and Jess share your name, then?" She leans forward with a hungry look in her eyes that Anna knows must be reflected in her own. "Gale is not a name I think is so very common."

"It's not. My father and Jess's father are distant cousins. A freak coincidence, but it's how Jess and I became friends. I was at their house the night…the night…"

"You said your parents died," Irina completes the thought. "I am sorry for your loss, Anna. But it isn't mine to share."

"No?" Anna thinks she might break if this fragile hope of a connection is shattered. She's lost so much, and to find maybe a little bit of her family in this new place that feels like home would be more than she ever dreamed of. She hands Irina her mother's papers.

Irina reads them with the care and attention they deserve, before clutching them to her chest. She looks strangely normal in her white tank top and running shorts. Not a ballerina, not a star. Twenty years fall from her face with a single tear.

"I never knew my sister."

"I'm sorry," Anna finds herself saying.

"That is not the whole truth. We were separated maybe at the age of four? Not yet five, I think. It's hazy. I went with a family who lived in Moscow. She was supposed to be nearby but something changed. I asked to see her, every day, but for months I got excuses. Eventually I was made to stop asking. The last I heard she had been sent to America."

Irina shudders. Anna steps closer, unsure if her comfort will be welcome. It would be more for herself than Irina, a cheating way to feel something like her mother's hugs one more time. Would it be better or worse if the embrace felt the same? Anna can't think straight; she just draws closer and closer until she's right next to her friend and colleague, her sister's girlfriend.

"Aunt Irina?" she tries, voice high and tight and cracking on the 't'.

"Oh, *malenkaya*," Irina sighs, opening her arms as though they're greeting for the first time. "Come here."

Chapter 29

"You two should probably hydrate at some point," Victoria says pointedly from the doorway. "But I should go. It's late." It's an intrusion, plain and simple, but her curiosity has been pulling her toward the room for the better part of an hour now. Either someone spills the rest of the details, or she's going home.

"Victoria," Anna is the first to speak, her eyes red but her smile returning. "I'm sorry for before. I was so rude on the way in."

"We'll talk later," Victoria promises. "Irina, do you need anything before I go?"

"No, Vicki." Irina's voice is a rasp. "But I think for today I've had enough company. You can take each other home." There's a hint of accusation in her tone, but Victoria lets the fast pitch sail right past, smoothing herself out like she never saw it coming.

"But—" Anna is protesting, because of course she is.

"Tomorrow," Irina says. "Come over anytime. Well, not before nine. I can see you need to be told this."

"She does," Victoria confirms, and when Anna doesn't move from the bed, she's the one to move around and steer Anna by the upper arm. "Good night."

"*Na dobranich*," Irina replies, and it draws fresh tears from Anna as she mumbles back an approximation of the same word.

"Well?" Victoria asks when they're back in the kitchen area. "What fresh soap-opera hell was that?"

Anna shrugs, and somehow looks older than her twentysomething years. "Turns out we're related. I think I knew as soon as I saw her, but denial is a powerful thing."

"You're telling me there's a story now, on top of everything? Our very own Cold War dynasty?" Victoria's blood is racing. "God, even Michelle couldn't mess up an exclusive like that. We'll make sure Irina's going to make it to performance, of course; an understudy isn't going to cut it. The photos could be tricky, we need something—"

"Victoria."

She ignores it. In a minute, the ideas are coming faster than she can process.

"*Victoria.*"

More insistent, but if she can just explain what she needs then…

Anna grabs her by the wrists. "Victoria, stop."

"What?" Some people have no sense of building to a crescendo. Victoria expected better, honestly. No one can touch her with a narrative like this, not Rick or Liza or the crones in the orchestra seats with their dusty checkbooks and jewelry that's the Harry Winston version of Jacob Marley's chains.

"I-I don't want that."

Anna is pleading, and really, is Victoria going to have to drag her to greatness after all? How much more can she do for the girl?

"I won't do it, I mean. I won't."

"Don't be ridiculous. How can you turn down publicity like this? If we play it right, there'll be screenwriters sniffing around. Legacy is such an enduring theme, and throw in the tragic-orphan routine—"

Anna's slap almost connects, but she pulls up short just in time, wrist swiping uselessly at thin air. "I said no. I don't want that," she repeats, lowering her hand. "No one will care, not really, and I don't want to give up this one small part of myself."

"Anna—"

"I swear, on anything you want. You do this, you try to make me do this, and I'll quit the company. You can have Morgan, or whoever the heck—*hell*—you want. But I'll walk before I'll use this for a few pages in a newspaper."

Victoria's seen defiance in her before, but this is breathtaking. Other people get blotchy and puffy when they cry, but Anna is one of the lucky ones whose skin looks polished, whose eyes just get clearer and more hypnotizing to stare into. With anyone else in this moment, Victoria would lay down the law, complete with a diatribe about how lucky she is to be throwing away this chance at all.

But a little part of her, the part that still expects to hear the low rumble of her father's greeting when she goes back to the house in San Francisco, understands what Anna is clinging to here.

"We'll talk tomorrow" is all the compromise she can bring herself to make. "In the meantime, my car is waiting. Don't argue, and I won't mention the story again. Deal?"

"Deal." Anna sighs. She looks like a stiff breeze would knock her over.

There's no resistance as Victoria links their arms and steers her outside, leaning on Anna just a little instead of her cane. The car is idling, and honestly it's barely a distance that requires it, but Victoria has had enough of exhausting her body beyond its limits lately.

They fold into the car, one after the other, a set designed for quick taking apart and reassembly. Their driver doesn't comment on the short journey, or the additional passenger. When he stops on Victoria's side of the road, she can't quite bring herself to walk Anna across through traffic. Instead, she extends her hand from the sidewalk, making it quite clear that Anna can step out on her own or choose the hand that's offered. A moment later, cool fingers clasp around Victoria's own, and she has a guest for the first time in too long.

"Wow." Anna doesn't speak the whole way up until they step inside Victoria's apartment, the moment the door is firmly closed behind them and privacy guaranteed.

"Did you think I lived in a music box? All lace doilies and satin slippers hanging on the walls?" Victoria heads straight for the hard liquor. She pours them both some of her preferred Scotch, and Anna accepts without question, cradling the heavy crystal in both hands as she looks around in wonder.

"It doesn't look like this at all from the outside." It isn't the most obvious thing she could say, at least. "I feel like I'm in a magazine spread. And the color, God…"

After so many years in white-walled or mirror-walled rooms, Victoria's personal taste extends to the bold and splashy. The high ceilings and huge windows of the quasi-penthouse apartment can take the deepest and wildest of tones, something the interior designer seized on like someone in the desert finding water while dying of thirst.

"You need the nickel tour?" Victoria asks. "I don't usually… You just seemed a little lost."

"I think I am," Anna confesses. "Not lost, really. Just…the world is a different shape than I thought it was yesterday. My mom had a sister. I have an aunt. I thought everything about my mother died with her. This is like being given a gift three days after your birthday."

"Mmm." Victoria has no frame of reference for this, because her own losses have been permanent and unyielding. An aunt makes more sense. She'd been wondering about distant cousins. Is it a genetic quality, then, that Victoria has picked out in Anna? Despite the difference in their frames, she does have a flavor of Irina's poise in the way she carries herself. "Do you need another drink?"

"God, yes." Anna comes over, holding out her glass. "I'll take that tour."

"My art collection is limited, so don't bring out your art-school snobbery on me," Victoria warns, looking around the room for a place to start.

"Not even with all the art fairs you go to?"

Victoria sees that she suspects her ruse now. Let her. It's almost refreshing for anyone to be close enough to see through her.

They walk through the living room, glance at the rarely used kitchen, and Anna stares at the framed posters and photos in the hall as though someone might have etched a treasure map on them and she'll only have one chance to memorize it. Victoria answers the peppered questions with minimal fuss, and it's actually pleasant to remember some of her triumphs, some of the wonderful people she worked with.

"My bedroom isn't terribly interesting," Victoria says, trying to gently dissuade her as Anna nudges where the door has been left ajar. "You want the room next door."

"What's in here?" Anna asks, but the door is halfway open and the lights are flipping on before Victoria can formulate her response. "Holy…"

"Still haven't learned to curse?" Victoria leans against the doorjamb, amused.

Anna is slowly turning on the spot, scanning every item as though there's going to be a quiz on exit.

"Welcome to my mausoleum."

The dresses hang from a high rail almost at the ceiling, draped on strings that lower them to head height. The posters interspersed, flat against the wall, are some of the most artistic offerings that Metropolitan's marketing has ever conjured, along with some bold additions from her time in London and San Francisco. Victoria features prominently, and even the abstract shapes and sketches are so clearly her.

"Do you know how many people would *kill* to step inside this room?" Anna is breathless as she asks, already drawn to the display cases with their elaborate headdresses and all the pairs of shoes, some dipped in bronze and others in their ragged post-show state.

"Do I strike you as a killer?" Victoria is moving closer, not entirely of her own volition.

Anna's jacket has dried off, but her hair is still sticking to it in wet strands. It's unusual to see her with her hair down, and from a certain angle she could be another person entirely.

"I thought you were outraged. You almost took a swing at me. Why did you decide to come up here?"

"In case I didn't get another chance." Anna faces her. "This is what heaven should look like, don't you think?"

"No." Victoria's voice is drier than Arizona at the height of summer, but it doesn't dissuade Anna in the slightest.

"Do you think I'll have my own room like this one day?"

"That really depends on your therapist." Victoria shrugs. "Grief needs an outlet, and at times this was mine. But you? Well, maybe a prince's jacket in one corner, Kitri's fan in another. Blow up the magazine spread to cover a wall, until you rack up some more."

She gestures to the far wall, where her own *Vanity Fair* shots as Odette and Odile are separated by a jeweled crown.

"Well, it would have to be the one of us." Anna's voice is lower, a little husky. "Tied up together in satin ribbons."

"A bold choice," Victoria agrees. "Why? Does that one linger in the memory?"

Anna gives a lopsided smile, even closer still.

"I'm not sure I should have asked you up." Victoria feels oddly exposed at the thought of what could happen from here.

"I'm…" Anna yawns, widely, taking herself by surprise. "Sorry, I should go home and get into something dry. Crying really takes it out of me."

"Here." Victoria steers her again, because habits are seemingly hard to break.

Anna sits on the long couch she's directed to without complaint, groaning happily as she sinks into the cushions.

"Wait here."

Luckily for their difference in frames, Victoria has a fondness for oversized pajamas, the crisp cotton kind her father always favored. She plucks a blue pair from the closet, only to find Anna already tipped on her side and fast asleep.

Victoria pulls the throw from the back of the sofa and eases it over Anna, who gives a dreamy smile in her sleep at being cared for. It only takes a moment to prop her head up with a cushion, and Victoria is rewarded by a soft little snore barely a moment later.

"Sweet dreams," Victoria murmurs, watching for a moment to make sure Anna settles.

Sure enough, her body only relaxes more into the softness of the furniture. Victoria's spent many nights on that couch herself, and even her knee hasn't complained about it yet.

Anna shifts slightly. Realizing how creepy it is to watch someone else sleep, Victoria flips off the last lamp and makes her way down the hall toward her bedroom. Should she have offered Anna the bed? That seems excessive. And dangerous, given that simmering heat between them that needs only a breath of oxygen to spark into life.

No. If Anna is invited into Victoria's bed, it won't be for sleeping. And since everything else is off the table…

She throws herself down on the neatly made sheets before pulling a pillow over her head and groaning into it. Yes, this was a terrible idea. Victoria just can't find it in herself to care, so she kicks off her shoes and tries to get comfortable. The rest can wait for morning.

∽∞∾

Anna gets up and it's dark, so dark that nothing is where she thinks it should be. A few bruises on her shins and muttered curses later, leave her at the bathroom sink, the faint light from the window illumination enough to gulp down a few mouthfuls of water.

That's better.

Her eyes are puffy and stinging from the tears cried earlier, so she splashes her face with cool water, reaching for a towel that somehow isn't there. Great. She wipes her face on her shirt and wonders why she hasn't bothered to change into pajamas. Oh well, back to bed. Not the sofa, which is actually way more comfortable than she remembers from propping her injured toes up. She stumbles along the hall and if she can just get in bed before waking up all the way, maybe the alarm won't go off too soon.

Bed is easy to fall into, under the window just like she's getting used to. Anna slips beneath the sheets, and oh, they feel so nice, way nicer than usual. She's going to sleep so well. Just let there be time between now and morning. A blink, one more, and it all fades away.

∽∞∾

The sounds of the street below filter in weakly, meaning Victoria has left a window open overnight. Well, probably better than running the A/C for hours, and the bedroom doesn't feel stuffy at all. She starts to pull the sheets back, wrinkling her nose at having slept in her clothes again, when a strong arm wraps around her torso and pulls her back across the mattress, as though she doesn't weigh an ounce.

If that's a squeak Victoria just allowed to pass her lips, then it's a completely indignant one.

"Listen," she rasps, not exactly unfamiliar with the one-night stand. "I'm sure it was special, but the door's over there." Except why would she be in her clothes? And why does the pillow under her head smell of someone else's coconut shampoo? None of her regular mistakes would wear anything so…

"Morning," her bedmate rumbles into the space between Victoria's shoulder blades. "Are we having a sleepover?"

"Anna?" Victoria hisses and it all comes back in an inglorious technicolor wave of tears and alcohol and exhaustion. "I thought I left you on the couch."

"Wait…Victoria?" Anna sits bolt upright so fast she almost pulls Victoria with her. Only at the last possible second does she release her comforting grip. "How? No, hold on, I was… But Irina. Oh *God*, what?" She's breathing too fast, the words coming out in jerky little fragments.

Victoria may not be a morning person, but she's going to have to summon her leadership skills to salvage this.

"Maybe you got cold," Victoria suggests, extricating herself from the sheets and wincing as she stands. Coffee and some painkillers are necessary, and soon. "Either way, are you over your little family drama?"

Anna just glares from where she's still tangled up in the sheets, hair down and adorably mussed. It's incredibly difficult not to jump back on there and make what they both suspected come true in short order.

"Your little Russian soap opera won't distract you from the work we need to do?"

Anna grabs one of the smaller throw pillows that would usually be tossed from the bed before getting in and clutches it to her chest. There's something to be said for the fact she doesn't bolt, although she's as dressed as Victoria still is, and every bit as rumpled. Then, to Victoria's abject horror, Anna sneezes.

"Sorry." Of course Anna follows it with a shamefaced apology. "I'm sure it's not a cold. It's dusty or something."

"My bedroom is *not* dusty," Victoria retorts, offended at the implication. "Just because I don't bring every fling into my personal domain doesn't mean I'm tucked up in here like Miss Havisham, counting my cobwebs. It may have something to do with sleeping in rain-damp clothes."

"Oh." Anna sniffs, considering her next move. "Well, I should get going. In case, you know, germs."

It's hardly the only reason, but it's one Victoria will cling to all the same. Her horror for getting sick hasn't receded even in these years where there's no performance to miss, no rehearsal to struggle to breathe through. For all her vices, she's regimented in her shots and vitamins each year, banning any dancer with even dubious allergies from ruining one of her classes or rehearsals.

Clearly Anna has heard the rumors, judging by the speedy way she gets out of bed and edges toward the door without ever getting an inch closer to Victoria. From the doorway she offers, "Coffee?"

Victoria folds her arms and bites back the bitchiest response. The tilt of her head is enough to clue Anna in that no, she would not like a germ-laden mug of coffee.

"I'll, uh, see you at the studio," Anna says before darting down the hall to gather her things and stumbling back toward the front door without another word.

There's a single, shining moment when Victoria realizes she can have what she increasingly wants. That she can ask Anna to stay for coffee, offer a veritable alphabet of vitamins, and maybe, just maybe, it would be worth risking health and sanity for just a little more of the comfort of the unexpected *snuggling*, if not the outright thrill of the infrequent kissing.

But Victoria stays quiet, listening to the door not slam, closed with thoughtfulness even in a hurry.

ᘓᕲᕲ

Ducking early morning traffic as she darts across the road, Anna feels hungover although she barely had anything to drink. Crying has a similar effect, and that she definitely did do a lot of.

Irina.

Should she call, should she text? The harsh light of morning has washed away some of the grief that bubbled up, and there's a question of what it means, given that the sisters never really knew one another.

No, it means something. Anna knows her mother would think so, and that Irina already agrees on some level. There's no need for a replacement, not as a grown adult with a life and a career. Still, that possibility for connection is so alluring. That Anna's own love of ballet might somehow be innate, and any talent she has along with it. She often asked her mother why she didn't dance ballet herself, after loving it so much. Her mom had simply hugged her close and shushed her each time. "*Not everyone can be a ballerina, Anna.*"

But maybe the little girl who grew up to be someone who Victoria Ford wants to make into a star isn't the only dancer on her family tree after all. Anna needs to know more. How her mother ended up in America as a child, while Irina ended up in Moscow. Did they harbor *Parent Trap*-style fantasies of reunion? Did they miss each other as surely as Anna missed Jess when they were in separate cities? There's so much to uncover, and not for the first time Anna is crushed by the unfairness of her mother not being there to ask.

Anna tries calling Jess as she barrels into her own apartment, ready to change and head right back out to warm up, where Victoria will hopefully keep her distance. As much as Anna is delighted at the accidental closeness they've shared yet again, she knows her head is too full to even begin to deal with that situation properly. Victoria deserves someone who gives her their whole attention, and it's going to take a massive effort for Anna to turn that on her work first and foremost.

Voice mail again. Dammit. This time Anna leaves an actual message, despite the rants Jess subjects her to about how voice mail is pointless. "Sis, you'd better call me back fast because boy, do I have some news for you."

⦿⦿⦿

"Teresa." Victoria waits at the Starbucks closest to the Metropolitan Center, knowing her pianist is a creature of habit. "You've done well in sticking to other rehearsals. Eve is an acceptable replacement."

Two sentences are enough to send Teresa into a tailspin, almost tipping the venti black coffee over her knockoff Burberry coat.

"Victoria! You're here!"

"I have been known to fetch my own coffee on occasion." Victoria props herself on a high stool at the window, plausible deniability as long as Teresa doesn't join her. She's smart enough not to try.

"So you need something?" The spark of hope that it's something more could be detected from space, and Victoria can't help but pity Teresa for that. All these younger, brilliant women, convinced their worth lies in being desirable, when they should be focused on their talent.

"I need to know what Rick and Liza are up to next. Which I'm sure you can achieve."

"Do I get to ask why? It might help find out the right things." Teresa's instant loyalty, even when so badly tarnished, always leaps right to the fore.

"I have decisions to make." Victoria knows anything more will be blabbed, and she mentally picks through a few red herrings before discarding them as unworthy. "And I need a little insurance in case my season doesn't go as planned."

"Is there a reason to think it won't?"

"Hmm?" Victoria feigns not having heard, but Teresa at least is too seasoned to fall for that one and waits her out. "Oh, no particular reason. But you know how people can be."

"Some people, yes." Teresa preens. Her own obsessive devotion doesn't put her in that bracket. "And if I do this spying for you, does it mean I'm forgiven?"

"You always have to push, don't you?" Victoria's irritation stops her thought process like a record scratch. She sees the wounded expression and decides to make peace, at least for as long as she needs this particular ally. "Although yes, I suppose it would."

"Oh Victoria, thank you!" Teresa squeals, drawing attention from the line of people waiting for coffee. She leans in to kiss Victoria on the cheek, lips still foamy from her drink.

Victoria squirms away, but as she turns her gaze back out of the window, she realizes her timing really has deserted her.

Travel mug in hand, jaw dropped, Anna Gale is starting right back at her, having seen everything that just transpired. Victoria moves to go after her, blocking out Teresa's self-satisfied babble, but Anna takes off at a sprint. With those long legs, Victoria would have struggled to keep up even at peak fitness.

Victoria drops her head toward her chest and sighs. It's going to be a very long day.

CHAPTER 30

Anna only stops when she runs out of sidewalk, perilously close to the front end of a moving crosstown bus. A man behind her yells about watching where she's going, and Anna whirls around to pick a fight. At the sight of her expression, he blanches, and she turns back around in disgust.

Seems nobody stands by a damn thing they say anymore, not even the proverbial man in the street.

Was it really only two hours ago she woke up in Victoria's bed? The same woman who's now hatching plans with her ex? The bitch who tried slicing up Anna's feet? Maybe not even ex judging by the kissing in public places. Clearly Victoria has kept her options open, and Anna's just the latest idiot who let a crush be mistaken for a genuine connection. There's a reason some people add "Ice" in front of that Queen of Ballet title.

Her head of steam gets her to the Metropolitan Center in record time, and she charges up the stairs like the bulls of Pamplona are after her. She ignores Ethan's wave, storms past Morgan, and instead of detouring to the locker rooms, Anna simply strips her outer layer as she walks. She's pissed, and she really doesn't care who knows it at this point.

Every swing of her leg is a kick as she starts to warm up in the half-empty studio. There are curious glances from the others who are milling around for morning class, but the unspoken rule is never to intrude on a bad morning, whether it's a hangover or personal drama. Skipping the *tendus* because she doesn't have to stick to every rigid, stupid idea, Anna starts to regret it as she barrels toward the *jetés*. Her hamstrings are quickly burning and she pulls up, breathing raggedly from the tension she's been carrying in her chest.

She's getting really tired of feeling this damn emotional. First a new family member, now a betrayal. Anna didn't ask for her life to be turned into a network drama, and she has no intention of living out all twenty-two episodes of it. She is going to dance, and trust no one, and who needs to talk to anyone ever again, anyway? It's not like she has time for a social life. In between rehearsal and performance, she has headphones. Problem solved.

Right up until she leaves for first rehearsal, taking the farthest stairs to make for a circuitous route. There's a fragment of a song stuck in Anna's head, some piece of Tchaikovsky she can't immediately place, and it's maddening. She's trying to hum the tune to reach a point she recognizes, and that's why she doesn't see Victoria lurking by the door.

"I said to myself, what's the most dramatic, adolescent-tantrum way of dealing with this?" Victoria drawls, pushing away from the wall and inspecting her manicure. "Short of going straight to bed—and you have too much work ethic for that at least—I hedged my bets on you going for high-school avoidance tactics. Imagine my joy to be proven right yet again."

"Are you done with your monologue?" Anna doesn't have to kiss up to her heroine anymore. Teresa is covering that duty for all of them. "I have places to be."

"My rehearsal? Good luck having it without me." Victoria steps between Anna and the door.

It should be a simple consideration, if Anna wanted to overpower her. Still, something in Victoria's posture says *don't try it* and Anna has had enough of making stupid mistakes for one year.

"Now, about this morning—"

"Kiss anyone you want!"

Victoria steps in closer, gently placing two fingers on Anna's lips to shush her. The touch tingles in a way Anna isn't prepared for, and she loses whatever thread she'd been pulling at in an instant.

"Mmmf?" Anna adds, just for the excuse of moving her lips against Victoria's skin.

"We are not doing this. Soap-opera misunderstandings and needless drama? Not my style. When there's a perfectly rational explanation, you'll do me the courtesy of listening to it. You'll trust that I have our best interests at heart, whatever you see me doing. Have I given you any reason to doubt me?"

Anna shakes her head fervently, dislodging Victoria's hand in the process. "No, but—"

"But what? I need information, and using a snake like Teresa is the most reliable way to procure it. If that means I need some sanitizer for my cheek after seeing her, I'm sure I'll live."

"*Our* interests?" Anna's brain finally catches up to the thundering in her ears.

"I'd say our fates are pretty intertwined at this point, wouldn't you? I need you to keep my job. Is there a better insurance policy than that?"

"Right, but it sounded like you were kind of thinking about us as…a pair?"

"A couple?" Victoria fires back, danger in those three syllables. "Were you not listening to what I told you about distractions?"

"You're the one chasing me down because I got upset about another woman. Were you worried it would affect my hero worship? Because I think we're way past that, don't you?"

"You're not entirely wrong," Victoria concedes with a long-suffering sigh. "Though honestly, I'm not sure what acknowledging any of this actually does."

"I think it does this." Anna closes the tiny distance between them, slipping an arm around Victoria's waist. It's bold, probably far too bold for a semipublic place where anyone could come up or down the stairs. The implicit danger of that makes Anna's heart thud in her chest, or maybe that's more to do with the hungry look Victoria's giving her, gaze settling on Anna's lips. With the slightest move on either side they'll be kissing, but courage seems to fail Anna in that moment.

Usually Victoria can't abide a lack of follow-through, but when the root cause appears to be Anna's overwhelming attraction to her, Victoria's ego decides it's charming. That's reason enough to reward Anna—and herself—with one hell of a kiss, one that banishes all memories of Teresa and anyone Victoria wants her to spy on.

"Don't be jealous," Victoria murmurs when the kiss finally, reluctantly ends. "Now come along. This ballet won't rehearse itself."

Anna looks appropriately punch-drunk, and follows without another word. There's a moment, a brief flicker of insanity really, when on passing the janitor's closet that's halfway along the corridor, Victoria gives serious consideration to whipping out her master key and dragging Anna in there.

No. Focus on the work, not the body. And honestly, stooping to consider closets full of mops makes for a very offended sense of aesthetic. Why lust after someone fresh out of a Gentileschi painting—not Degas nor Manet—only to sully the beauty of it all with the most functional of spaces? Along with the list of other reasons it is resolutely not happening. There's just no telling that to the tug of want that starts somewhere deep in her abdomen and radiates out. It feels tangible, something dark and grasping that wants to reach out and pull Anna close.

It's only in forcing herself not to look at the door that she notices Anna is favoring her left leg slightly. Too rough in warm-up? Or too distracted?

Thank God for a roomful of people, which might well be the first time Victoria's ever held such a sentiment in her adult life. She's especially pleased when Irina limps in with her Moon Boot and a crutch that's more for appearance than real use. She's healing, at last. All she needed was the time and the honesty to get there. It's inspiration enough for Victoria's opening salvo.

"Good morning," she greets them with genuine warmth. These are the people who are going to get her over the line. Gabriel with his athleticism and charm, Delphine with her precision, Irina with her grit, and Anna with her fresh-faced ungodly talent and enthusiasm. Even the latest girl foisted upon Victoria, Morgan, is bringing something to the table. She's willing to understudy any part without complaint, and in the Venn diagram of the three principal women's skills, Morgan is the overlap without much in the way of dramatic extremes. It's exactly what someone in her place needs to be.

"Does *Nutcracker* casting go up today?" Delphine asks. "Because I was really hoping to skip the rotation this time."

"All in good time," Victoria assures them. "And really, you should know to ask Kelly or David by now. In my studio time, we focus on my productions, understood? Even if the *Sugar Plum* snorefest does keep the lights on and the doors open for the rest of the year."

"Oh, I think that's a little harsh," Rick interrupts, strolling into the room in his ripped jeans and overly tight tee. A look he could pull off fifteen years before, but today it's just showing off where he isn't as taut as he once was.

"What an *unexpected* surprise, Rick," Victoria snaps, the briefest flicker of a concerned glance in Anna's direction. "I was beginning to think you'd lost the address for the center."

"I thought I'd take rehearsal today, for shits and giggles."

It takes considerable restraint not to kick someone. Victoria has to literally bite her tongue to keep from lashing out. The rest of the room has stopped pretending they're doing anything other than listening in.

"Your jokes are getting less funny by the day," Victoria drawls as she turns around. "You're welcome to watch, of course. Though next time a little notice would be appreciated."

"I don't mean to pull rank." Rick advances on her like a jaguar having spotted his prey. "But I'm pretty sure it's my name on the checks. I've always reserved the right to check in on my dancers, make sure they're being treated right. So, baby Gresham, why don't you start us off, huh? Show me what you got."

"Uh, show you what exactly? I'm understudying all three for *Gala*," Morgan asks at a loss.

Victoria is relieved Anna hasn't been called on first, even though she knows there's no way she'll avoid being put through her paces.

"Right, right," Rick says, wagging a finger at Morgan like she just told a dirty joke in front of the class. "For making a good point, you dodge the bullet this time. Now let me see… Who can put on a little show, demonstrate Victoria's genius for the room, huh?"

He's walking the whole time as he talks, clearly in love with the sound of his own voice. Anna doesn't see it coming until he slows in front of her, plucking her water bottle from her hand and tossing it toward the trash.

"Uh, that can be recycled—" Anna starts to protest, but he's right up in her face then.

It wouldn't take much for Victoria to pull him away, but she forces herself to hold back.

"I hear you fancy yourself the man about town, Miss Gale," he says. "Not content with displacing the principal ballerinas, you think you can dance a prince as well as… well, me?"

"I *never* said that," Anna says, but Victoria tries to silence her with a shake of her head. "I just do what I'm asked."

"Well, I'm asking for a little preview," Rick says. "Unless you don't think you're up to it? But trust me, I'm a way more patient audience than opening night ever will be."

"If you want a run-through, then speak to Kelly and schedule one," Victoria interrupts, coming to stand between them. "Don't come in here and disrupt my rehearsal. I won't work like this, Rick."

"Hey, if you're offering to lighten the wage bill…"

"Go to hell."

"I can do the scene from—"

"No!" Victoria barks at her, and Anna shrinks back. "Gale, you were favoring your left hamstring. Go see Dr. Sawyer about it."

Anna is stunned. It has been a little tight all morning. How could Victoria possibly have noticed?

"But—"

"Sawyer. Now."

"Fine," Anna mutters. After snatching her bag from the floor, she pulls her phone out of her pocket instead.

Jess rushes over to her at the subway exit, dragging Anna down a side street until they're safely tucked into one of the bars usually half-full of unemployed actors and dancers. Anna tries desperately not to see that as an omen. While her sister orders them a bottle of wine, Anna picks out a booth in back, far from sight of the other patrons who are nursing their drinks or cackling quietly over some script pages. Another lousy audition, probably.

"Thanks for playing hooky with me." Anna takes the opened bottle with her glass, pouring her own out and knocking it back before getting around to filling Jess's. It's barely even lunchtime. "I got sent to PT like it was middle-school detention, so I blew it off."

"Well, you're having a bit of a time. Irina gave me a heads-up about her being your aunt," Jess says, cutting off Anna's complaint about that. "I know, I know, but she was worried, that's all. *I'm* worried. How fucked-up is this?"

A snort is the only response Anna can think of, letting her sister wrap her up in a bear hug that could break ribs, bumping them both against the low table as they gently sway in their seats for a moment.

"So what does this mean?" Jess prompts when Anna stays quiet. "Oh God, does this mean I shouldn't be dating Irina? I swear to God, it better not."

"No... I mean, no. It's a little weird, sure." Anna sees the implication in Jess's vehement denial. "You really like her, don't you?"

"Your aunt? Your hot, talented aunt?" Jess teases. "I'm not really good at talking about this stuff. But...she's amazing. Please don't ask me to stop dating her."

"I was never going to. Besides, if I want to get to know her, I get plenty of opportunity in the studio. If Victoria even wants me back."

"What did the princess of pain do this time? At some point, we really have to talk about your taste in sadists."

"Well, all ballerinas are masochists," Anna reminds her. It takes a lot of effort, but she bites back the automatic defense of Victoria this time. "Apparently when Richard Westin shows up and clicks his fingers for us to dance, she suddenly doesn't think I'm up to the job. No way to treat the dancer who ended up in her bed, right?"

Okay, so maybe Anna had been a little more ambiguous there than strictly necessary. Screw it. Everyone else got to be dramatic and desired, why shouldn't she get in on the action? Even if just by implication.

She gets the luxury of that elongated freak-out because Jess is only just done choking on a mouthful of wine. Red in the face and jaw loose in shock, she stares back at Anna in stunned disbelief. "You had sex with Victoria?"

For a moment, Anna considers the lie. She's never been a particularly good liar, but there's something about spinning the story, about getting to be someone else entirely for a few minutes, that always appeals to her.

"No," she admits a moment later. "I just went over after the Irina thing, and then in the middle of the night I forgot about the sofa and just wandered into the nearest bed. Trust me, she wasn't any more impressed by my sense of geography than she was with my dancing today. But then, if I'm such a disaster that she doesn't want to encourage, how come we were making out earlier, huh?"

Poor Jess had foolishly taken another mouthful of wine. Anna almost ends up wearing this one.

"What the hell is going on at that ballet company?" Jess demands when she's gathered herself.

"I wish I knew. But I'm not going back today to find out. Next bottle's on me, okay?"

"Cheers," Jess answers, raising her empty glass to Anna's, who clinks after draining the last mouthful and starting to refill so they can polish off this first bottle. "Now, go back to the start…"

Chapter 31

Victoria slams the door behind her on the way out of physio, having found no Anna there. Of course it's a swing door, so that completely takes any glimmer of satisfaction from the move. She stalks back to her office, stabbing her cane against the marble floor and wishing the stupid hard rubber tip didn't take the violence out of it.

"Kelly, get Anna Gale in this office immediately. If teleportation still hasn't been invented, then get her on the phone. Failure is not an option, so I hope for your sake you've had her microchipped."

"She's a dancer, Victoria." Kelly has already picked up and is dialing from memory. "You're thinking of poodles again."

"A poodle can be trained," Victoria grouses.

"Sure, but Anna almost never pees on the floor. So she has that going for her. What did she do? Wear neon in your direct sight line again?"

"I sent her to physio, to spare her from Rick trying to humiliate her, and she has the audacity to have skipped out. Does this look like Hickville Junior High? Is she really trying to play *hooky* in the middle of my season?"

"You seem a little worked up." Kelly hangs up and pulls out her cell phone to text instead. "Anything to do with Rick haunting the halls?"

"Don't ever let that happen again." Victoria has almost made it into the sanctuary of her private office, but she turns and marches back out to make her point. "I mean it, Kelly. Not even you are indispensable. Certainly not if you keep letting me get ambushed by that asshole."

"Anna's phone is off now," Kelly reports. "So yeah, microchipping would be handy. And no, I don't have any contacts at the FBI who can track her, before you start."

"Call the theater her sister works at. She's bound to have gone to Jess. Wheedle a likely location out of them, and text me an address."

"Anyone ever tell you that you'd make one hell of a stalker?"

Victoria's glare must be one of her finest, because even the fearless Kelly blanches and starts dialing again, after a glance at her contacts list. Making her way into her office, Victoria can't concentrate for trying to overhear what Kelly is up to. A minute passes, then two. Kelly isn't talking to anyone yet, and the stalker comment is still resonating.

"Kelly?" she calls out. "Forget about it. Just send her the standard *missed a day* email, and warn her that her wages will be docked if this happens again."

Normally Kelly would push back, ask if Victoria is sure. It's a mercy that this one time she doesn't. With the afternoon free unexpectedly, Victoria decides it's time for one more change, to keep Rick out of the loop and hopefully out of her studio. She'll have to get Delphine on board, but it should be a formality at this point.

When her phone bleeps to life with a text, Victoria tells herself her heart doesn't race, and that she isn't disappointed to see Teresa's name on the screen instead of Anna's. If she keeps up this level of denial, she might just start to believe it.

⟋◯◯◯⟍

"I'm dying," Anna groans, picking herself up off the floor she's apparently been asleep on, using her bag as a pillow. Why she would do that with a perfectly comfortable bed only a few feet away is beyond her. At least she gets an answering grunt from Jess, who's similarly sprawled out on the bedroom carpet.

"Jesus." Jess groans as she tries to sit up. "Tell me you have coffee, kiddo."

"You do," Irina says from the doorway. "What a mess you are, Jessica, that you don't even recognize your own apartment."

"Hnnng," Anna grunts in acknowledgment, trying desperately not to hurl. That kind of explains it, then. "I have to get to class."

"Yes, you do." Irina makes her way across the room with her Moon Boot still on, helping Anna to steady herself. "I would say take a very long and hot shower, but you lack the time, little one."

Anna checks her phone, the battery at a precarious 4 percent. She has thirty minutes to make what will be a twenty-five-minute journey minimum at this time in the morning. Unable to hold back on throwing up any longer, she darts toward the bathroom. When she emerges, she's officially running late but feeling a bit fresher.

"Did you shower?" Jess asks from the floor, a location she shows no signs of quitting. "Or just go with a whore's bath?"

"Rude," Anna fires back. "I'll have a proper shower between rehearsals. I'm only going to sweat for most of the day anyway. Don't ever let me go day-drinking again, okay? Regrets, I have so many."

"Get your ass in gear," Jess warns.

As Anna bolts for the door, Irina interrupts her, handing over some bank notes.

"A taxi, or Vicki will have your head. I'll be in after warm-up, but feel free to blame me as needed. She won't pick that fight."

Anna's head swims. Irina, stuff of legend and rumor, barely even a friend in any official sense, but acting like…well, an aunt. It's bizarre, but damn if it doesn't settle Anna's stomach for the first time since she opened her eyes.

"Thank you," she says with a gasp. "I'll pay you back later, I promise."

With that, she's off down the stairs and hurtling out onto the street. Miracle of miracles, the first yellow cab she flags down actually stops, not flipping his light off until she's confirmed her destination.

"You a dancer?" he asks as she collapses into the backseat.

"Mmm" is all Anna can choke out at that point. The motion of pulling out into traffic has made the hangover queasiness come back.

"I thought so, when you said Metropolitan. My kid, she's six years old, and I swear to God she knows ballerinas like I know the roster for the Mets. Obsessed with it. Me, I don't know the first thing, but I know she loves it."

"That's nice," Anna says absently. She decides to brave the calls and message lists on her phone, but the moment she hits the Home button the damn thing up and dies on her. "Ballet's hard," she says with a groan. "Make sure she knows that."

"That's what they say." He catches her eye in the rearview mirror, and Anna returns his easy smile. She's starting to rally a little, and for the sake of her own six-year-old self, she knows she has to do better.

"Henri, right?" she reads from the medallion and ID badge.

"Sure, and Yara, that's my little girl." When they come to a stop at the traffic lights, he taps his phone screen to show a picture of a gorgeous dark-haired little girl, squealing with laughter in her father's arms. They look alike, right down to their broad smiles and light brown skin. Yara's wearing a fluffy pink tutu, the synthetic ones that scratch as they're pulled on, and Anna warms at the memory.

This is where it started. This is why she's doing this. That smile, that tutu that doesn't quite stick out by itself, not like the professional ones. The satin slippers that are gradually replaced by pointe shoes, a rite of passage that can never come soon enough.

"How's her attention span?" Anna asks, fishing around in her purse. "For ballet, I mean? Does she just like the movement, or does she watch it too?"

"Watch it? She's always nagging me to put PBS on, even though they only show ballet once in a blue moon. I've been trying to snag tickets for something at the Metropolitan Center, but you guys know how to charge."

"Does her mom like dance?" Anna finds the notebook she's looking for and scribbles on the page.

"It's just me and Yara." Henri's tight-lipped, watching the traffic too intently for a line that isn't moving much at all. "Her mom split a while back."

"Well, my name is Anna, and this is my first season," Anna explains, folding the piece of paper in half. "And I don't really know anyone in New York, except for my sister and the rest of the ballet corps. I get some tickets as part of my contract. I'd love to set some aside for you and Yara to come see a Metropolitan production."

"Wait, I wasn't—"

"I know you weren't. But I used to go with my mom, before she passed. At Yara's age, I was the only kid I knew who could sit through *Sleeping Beauty* as a ballet and not a cartoon. Maybe she won't want to dance herself in the future, but if she loves it, she should get to see a professional production up close."

"That is… You know what, that's the nicest conversation I've had in five years driving this thing." Henri accepts the piece of paper over his shoulder.

"That's my email. Send me a few dates you can do, and I'll get you tickets for whatever I'm doing that week—it changes a lot, as you've probably seen."

"You're sure?"

"Absolutely." Anna sits back with a lazy grin, watching the Metropolitan Center draw nearer in all its glass-coated glory. What's the point in being a principal if she can't do things like this? "Oh," she adds as they draw to a stop. "If you can make it a bit before the show, I can take her on a mini tour too. Kids love seeing the shoes and the costumes and stuff."

"Oh man, that would blow her mind. You sure you're a ballerina and not some kind of angel?"

"Nah. I just remember what it was like to love ballet that much but be on the outside looking in. This way she'll get the real deal, and hopefully carry that with her, her whole life."

"I'll email tonight. And it's okay if you change your mind, or if you can't—"

"I won't." Anna holds out the cash for her fare, but Henri waves it away. "Thank you, Henri. I didn't realize how much I needed a conversation like this. Email me tonight, I'll be checking."

"You got it! Have a good day, Anna."

She gets out of the cab and jogs across the plaza, finally ready to face the day. They've even made pretty good time, so she won't be late after all.

∩߀߀

Victoria watches the dynamics of the room shift and reshape every year, sometimes from week to week, depending on the company members present. It's gratifying to see that Anna has found her niche, even if Victoria is residually pissed at her for disappearing the day before.

They're almost done with warm-up, a decent sweat worked up and chatter happening back and forth over their repetitions, less breathless than it might be, meaning they're all back in midseason shape at last. Seeing Teresa at the piano hasn't exactly improved Victoria's mood, but she knows better than to approach her right now and draw Anna's attention back to that.

"Is that supposed to be fifth, Ethan?" Victoria snorts on her way past. "How very abstract of you." He quickly shuffles his feet from a lazy approximation to the correct position, practically trembling in his gray tights. She hasn't lost her touch.

It leaves her in prime position to overhear the end of Anna's conversation with Delphine.

"—so sweet, I swear. So I'm gonna get them seats for something good, do the whole dazzle-the-kid thing with a backstage tour."

"Yeah, who wouldn't be dazzled by the smell of sweaty feet and buckets of sand?" Delphine mocks, but it's good-natured.

"Adopting orphans now, Anna?" Victoria can't resist interrupting. "I didn't think I left you enough hours in the day to do that. Although if you're going to set your own schedule—"

She has the good sense to blush, looking down at her feet for a moment.

"Victoria, I'm sorry. I just thought you were saying I wasn't—"

"It's dealt with." It isn't supposed to sound so snippy, but Victoria hasn't entirely forgiven yet. "Clean up after this. You've got a costume fitting with Susan at eleven."

"But—"

"Rearranged. I'll see you in Wardrobe."

If Anna mutters something as Victoria walks away, well, she isn't sure she wants to hear it.

⌢ᘛᘚ

"Susan!" Anna greets her with a happy squeal. "I haven't seen you in so long. You're never here when I come to grab shoes lately."

"Speaking of which." Susan nods toward the rows of shelves, each section marked off with a dancer's name. "Fresh arrivals from London."

Hangover chased away by a long shower and some breakfast, Anna practically skips down the aisle to where *Gale, A.* is written in Sharpie on her cube stuffed full of shoes. Somehow, this is the moment that punches her in the gut. So far she's been grabbing her shoes straight from bags or piles of boxes as they come in, but now she's officially and semipermanently part of the gang, in a way that performances or just showing up every day doesn't quite reach.

Stuffing five new pairs in her bag, Anna is wiping an errant tear as she turns away.

Victoria is waiting at the end of the row, leaning against the shelves.

"What?" Anna asks, composing herself.

"Are we going to talk about yesterday?"

"With Susan just down there?"

"Susan?" Victoria calls. "Kelly has some paperwork for you to sign. And have you left out the Prince costumes for Anna?"

"On the rail," Susan confirms before taking her leave. Clearly she doesn't mind being thrown out of her own domain if Victoria Ford is the one taking over.

Anna shivers at the thought, because she doesn't mind the idea one bit, either. They both listen to the door opening and closing again, leaving them alone.

"So." Anna gathers herself enough to ask, dropping her bag on the floor. "Where do you, um, want me?"

∽∞∼

Of all the loaded questions Victoria has ever been asked, that one is a grenade with the pin long since pulled. She can do what they've been doing—she can bolt and avoid it, and pretend like they aren't going to keep finding themselves in these situations. Or she can lean into it, and actually enjoy the spark that's making them such a formidable pair onstage and off.

"Well, it's not long until you get your chance to play the Prince. Your lifts are coming along well, and Delphine makes a perfect Princess Rose for you."

"If I'm doing so well, how come you wouldn't let me dance for Rick? Are you ashamed of me?"

"What?" Victoria is used to insecurity, predominantly from other people. This business breeds it—from the body image, to the performances, to the critics, there's ample opportunity to stop believing in one's own talent.

"He asked me to dance and you sent me to physio."

"You didn't go."

"My hamstring wasn't that tight." Anna folds her arms over her pale pink sweater. The white leotard beneath it is brand-new, long-sleeved with those darling little loops around the middle finger. It does wonders for the line of the arms. "And I know when I'm being sent away."

"Oh for God's… Will you go try on the costume? We don't have all day, and if Susan guessed your sizing too far out, it's another round of alterations."

"She didn't guess. I was measured for *La Bayadère* fittings."

Victoria starts to prowl down the row, shoes stacked up on either side. "It may be surprising to you, but there are still variations, depending on the cut and fabric. You're just lucky you're tall, and that not all our leading men have been as impressive in physique as Gabriel. There should be options for you."

"Fine," Anna grumbles, stalking off to the rail by the seating area and plucking the hangers labelled *ANNA* from it. Of course, there's no privacy. Defiant, she starts stripping right there, not caring if Victoria gets an eyeful, or who else might walk in. Her gray tights go first, the sweater dropped on top of them.

"This can stay for now," Victoria reaches out to tap the sleeve of Anna's leotard.

She doesn't so much as flinch.

The first costume is ridiculous, and Victoria knows instantly that it's only included because Susan is screwing with her. It's Rick's Romeo from God knows how many years go, and Victoria thought everything from that disaster would have been ceremonially burned. Gray, asymmetrical, sequinned in the strangest of places. She plucks it from Anna's hands and sets it aside.

"Start with this."

The leather pants are baggy in all the wrong places. Such an unforgiving material, it rarely stretches with the body, staying mostly out of shape instead. Victoria has seen some fantastically structured bodices and tutus in leather, but for the kind of androgyny she's going for, it's falling short. The mesh top looks tired, almost sad. At least Anna is a quick changer.

"Not quite." She starts flipping through the selection herself, skirting around Anna. "You know, usually I can trust Susan on the aesthetics, but I suspect I didn't make myself clear. No, wait…I think we have something."

A military uniform, of sorts. Jade green and elegant needlework. With Anna's coloring, it'll be a rich tapestry. With Susan's alterations, it'll be a moving piece of art.

Victoria turns back toward Anna and holds it out with a smile.

Anna just stares at the ensemble in front of her.

"Is everything in this range some kind of fetish wear?" she can't help asking.

"Really?" Victoria tilts her head as though the thought has never crossed her mind. "And what does Miss Vanilla know about fetishes?"

"Who said anything about vanilla?" Anna taps her toe experimentally on the floor, which continues to lack the functionality for swallowing her whole. "Fine, I'll try this on too."

Anna shrugs the velvet jacket on first, running her fingertips over the stiff brass buttons and the elegant brocade. The pants are going to be too big, she can tell that at a glance, but maybe if she rolls the waist down and the ankles up, it could look sort of intentional. Whatever they settle on, her own versions will be brought in or tailored.

When they're pulled up—a better fit than she hoped, but rolled down to skim beneath her hipbones—Anna seeks out the full-length mirror. Well. It's a look. So used to white and pale pastels, she enjoys the contrasts of the darker, heavier materials against her skin.

"Move," Victoria suggests. "Obviously we can tailor something from scratch, but can you dance in something like this?"

"You want me to pirouette barefoot in the wardrobe department?" If Anna sounds dubious, it's because she is.

"A little bending and extending is just fine, thank you." Victoria folds her arms, expectant. Her hair is down again today, a strand falling in her face that she idly blows away.

Anna dips and extends a leg in one direction, then shifts to extend the other. It's comfortable enough, if a little weird.

"A few *tendus*, then," Victoria presses, and Anna complies. "Hmm, it's not really rubbing off those feminine edges like I hoped. You've seen the boys. Where's your swagger, Gale?"

"You want me to get all butch about it?" Anna snorts, but Victoria only folds her arms. "I'm not exactly prepared."

"Why not?" Victoria circles in close.

Anna feels herself slipping straight back into that mode of expecting a touch, a kiss. She thrums with the anticipation of it.

"You won't exactly be packing when you dance on stage, will you?" Victoria asks.

"Will I?" God, can Anna's cheeks actually catch fire? It feels like they might.

Then Victoria, who's worn one of her signature scarves to liven up her black sweater and tapered pants, is tugging at the artful knot in the silk.

A moment later, somehow Anna is pressed up against the mirror where it hangs on the wall, and Victoria's free hand is resting just above Anna's shoulder. In her other hand, Victoria has neatly balled up the silk that comes in a vibrant red and black, white horses drawn across it. Hermès, Anna assumes. That's Victoria's signature accessory, after all.

"Would it help," Victoria asks in a soft voice, mouth barely inches from Anna's ear, "to feel something between your legs?"

Anna gasps in response, nodding once, then twice. With the hand holding the scarf, Victoria traces an idle finger along the waistband of the tights. Just when it seems she won't follow through, she slips that hand inside. The heat of her hand is almost shocking, the silk just decadent as it's pressed between Anna's thighs. She hopes Victoria's hands will linger, but after she's rubbed the scarf into position, and drawn a lascivious little moan from Anna, those wicked fingers are quickly withdrawn.

But then that hand is skimming over velvet and cupping Anna through the tights. If she says something, maybe Victoria will stop. Since Victoria's mouth is now nipping at her collarbone above the open top buttons of the jacket, stopping is the last thing Anna wants.

"How does it feel?" Victoria whispers.

"G-good," Anna admits. Her center of gravity adjusts slightly, the camber of her hips and her stance in general.

"Would you like it to feel even better?"

Victoria's questions have only gotten more risqué, but Anna already knows what her answer will be.

CHAPTER 32

Victoria knows she's way across the line, but they've been struggling to balance on it for far too long. She wants this. She wants Anna. The one who stands up to Rick and Liza, who tries harder than everyone else, who's talented, beautiful, and so unexpectedly kind.

She presses a tender, openmouthed kiss just below Anna's ear. It makes Anna's knees buckle, and Victoria laughs low in her throat at how powerful she feels, holding Anna up by grabbing at the barely appropriate mesh top.

"If we put you on stage like this," Victoria murmurs, "they'll be throwing themselves at you from the aisles. They say ballet can't be hot? We're going to fuck with gender, with convention, and they won't be able to take their eyes off you. You want that, don't you?"

"I want…" Anna swallows as Victoria nips at her earlobe. "I want *you*. This. Now."

Victoria kisses her full on the mouth, swallowing the contented little sigh 'forming on Anna's lips. They kiss almost like it's the first time, enthusiastic but tentative, each taking unscripted turns to lead or retreat slightly. The whole time, Victoria doesn't move her fingers from where they're wrapped around the bulge her scarf is making.

They're interrupted by the department's main door slamming open. Victoria expects to be pushed aside, but Anna just freezes with her hands on Victoria's hips.

"Victoria?" The boy with the cardigans calls out. Ethan. What the hell is he doing here? "Susan said she left you here? We, um, we need you?"

"Christ," Victoria snorts, peeling away from Anna reluctantly. "I'm coming."

Chance would be a fine thing.

She pats Anna one more time. "You can give me my scarf back later, once this annoyance is dealt with. Let it stay put for now, hmm?"

She departs with what she's sure is her most salacious look, and almost punches the air at the wrecked little whimper of Anna's that follows in her wake.

⌒◯◯◯

Anna touches the wall behind her with both palms. It's the only way to convince her legs that she can stay standing.

She peers through the rows of clothes and shoes to watch Victoria talking to Ethan, who looks much more agitated than normal. The speed at which they both depart suggests something's really wrong, and Anna's mind goes immediately to Irina. Has she tried to overdo it? Or maybe Teresa is causing a scene. Either way, Anna can't just stay put. She doesn't bother to change since her casting as the prince is hardly a secret.

The destination turns out to be the auditorium, where the *Coppélia* rehearsals should be in full swing. They open that show in a matter of days, though Anna has enjoyed the luxury of not being in the corps for that one. It might feel like getting off lightly if Victoria didn't work her twice as hard as the extra production would have.

It's chaos.

Anna freezes in the wings as she watches the commotion on stage. Someone—she can't quite see who—is clearly in pain. The noise can only be described as a series of howls, almost animalistic in their rawness. It's like someone trying to scream but they can only open their mouth and let the pain make its own guttural sound.

A glance at the auditorium reveals Irina in the front row, engrossed in her book and only glancing at the swarming crowd of dancers onstage. Just as Anna looks around for Victoria, she hears that imperious voice projecting throughout the space.

"Everyone *not* injured, make your way into the house or the wings. You are not helping. Let David and I handle this."

In a trickle, the sea of women in tutus and men in white tights retreat as instructed. The noise barely dims, the tide of gossip only spreading rather than stopping. It finally reveals the scene to Anna as dancers shove past her into the wings, most of them pausing to give her outfit a derisory stare.

"Jesus Christ!" Morgan gasps from where she's prone on the floor. Tears are streaking down her face, and 'Victoria is leaning over her to check the extent of the injuries. "Oh, it's gone, it's really gone this time." The words are choked out around sobs, and it's awful to watch.

Next to her on the floor lies one of the male soloists who Anna doesn't really know. He's blond and wiry, and she thinks they might have shared the stage for half a moment in *La Bayadère*, and it hits her then how new she still is, how much of an outsider she is compared to the dancers who have been part of this company for years.

David is on the phone, and Kelly dashes in moments later. "Ambulance is out front," she says through gasps, and there are some unpleasant snickers from the girls next to Anna at the fact Kelly is out of breath.

"Can I help?" Anna marches over to ask Kelly. It's an excuse to get a closer look at Victoria, who seems like she might throw up at any moment, kneeling beside Morgan as she tries not to writhe in pain. "Is it her hip?"

"Yes, it's my fucking hip!" Morgan snarls. "Sorry, it's just… Oh God, nobody call my mother. Not yet. Not until there are drugs."

Anna drops to her knees on the other side of Morgan, meeting Victoria's gaze but getting no response. Prioritizing, Anna takes Morgan's hand and squeezes gently.

"They say deep breaths help with the pain. I'm sure the paramedics will give you something to make it better. You're going to be fine, okay?"

"I'm done," Morgan says through gritted teeth, but she follows Anna's example of breathing in deep and then slowly releasing it. "I knew if it went again, after the surgery and all…"

"Hey, hey," Anna soothes. "You don't know that for sure. Doctors can work miracles, and you could be back dancing in no time. It might not even be that bad."

"Oh, stop it," Victoria cuts in, her tone dripping acid. "You don't have the first clue what you're talking about, and the last thing she needs right now is a dose of Pollyanna. Morgan, stick with the breathing. It's the only valuable thing Gale told you, even if she does mean well."

The paramedics arrive then, carrying a stretcher between them. They're brisk and professional despite the warm smiles they offer to everyone. A quick assessment and Morgan is gently strapped to the backboard, an oxygen mask placed carefully over her mouth and nose.

Only then does Irina move from her seat, coming to stand beside Anna onstage as Morgan is readied for a trip to hospital. A careful hand is laid on Anna's shoulder.

"It happens," she says. "This bastard dance we all live and die for, it doesn't care for us so much."

"I thought it was you." Anna's words are strained with worry, but she knows this is very much not about her. "I'm sorry it happened to anyone, but I thought you'd tried to come back before you were ready."

"Well, my understudy is out now," Irina says as they carry Morgan away.

The man she was dancing with is back on his feet, protesting to anyone who'll listen that his lift was perfect, that it was some fluke with the way she landed, and that's on Morgan.

Anna can understand that need to deflect blame, but it makes her not like him very much.

Victoria picks herself up and follows the paramedics without a word. She'll be accompanying Morgan to New York General, then. David ends his call and nods to Irina. "Do we think she meant it about her mother?"

"I would not want to be the person who delayed telling her that her only daughter might have just ended her career today," Irina says.

"As always, you make the bleak but relevant point, comrade," David says.

Irina swears briefly at him in Ukrainian, a curse Anna recognizes but doesn't know the true meaning of. She'll add it to her list, if there's ever time to sit down together and ask the hundreds of questions she has.

"We're taking ten, people. Be back here ready to move," David calls as the dancers reluctantly disperse.

It's probably not so strange that they'll reset and carry on so quickly. Part of Anna expects exactly this. No one died. It just feels like everyone's concern for Morgan left the room when she did, and Anna sees now it was probably the same when she found the glass in her toes, even though that was almost life-changing for her.

"Come, *malenkaya*," Irina instructs. "I am still out of commission with this boot, so it's time for tea."

"The café's closed until the house opens," Anna reminds her.

"Not here," Irina says with a snort. "You should never trust an American to make tea. They give you their strange take on it, which I think is maybe for cleaning floors, only nobody ever wanted to correct them. Street clothes, then meet me in the alley."

"Yes, ma'am." Anna clicks her heels together. "Should I call Jess, or do you want to?"

"Just us today."

Anna's heart skips just a little. They're going to talk, then. "Just us."

⟨༠ზ༠⟩

Victoria's skin is crawling by the time she makes it back to the parking lot. She knows, rationally, it isn't her fault. Who knows better than she how random bad luck is? Some things can be avoided with correct warming up and self-maintenance, by being especially vigilant over the condition of shoes and whether the floor is sprung enough. Others? Well, no one sees those coming.

Why the hell did she insist on tagging along in the ambulance? It's not something she would ever have offered, save for with a close few. Victoria suspects it's Anna's influence, or at least the impulse to get far away after snapping at her. Empathy doesn't come easily to Victoria, and despite having catastrophic injury in common with

Gresham, she hasn't found herself to be any great comfort. She should have let David come as he suggested.

If she keeps being snippy inside her head, if she keeps blasting the anger in a handful of different directions, then Victoria won't have to acknowledge the creeping dread that being back in a hospital has instilled. It's not nausea; that's too faint and polite a sensation for how it affects her. Her legs seem to have replaced their bones with lead, and sweat prickles along her hairline even though the temperature is downright cool. The smell of antiseptic that doesn't quite mask the indignities of what they do here reminds her of the studios. No matter how they're aired out, or how they're cleaned, the bad scents get into the brickwork somehow.

At least Morgan has a private room. The orthopedic surgeon who'd greeted them on arrival had whistled quietly on cursory inspection, and that had only set the girl off wailing again.

No one will speak to Victoria about Morgan's' condition without a family member present, and too tired to wait for her car service, she flags down a taxi. Hours have passed without her entirely realizing, and the evening rush is almost calming, the last flurry of patrons making their way to the Theater District. Texts from David confirm the rest of stage rehearsal went off without incident, so at least they won't end up canceling a performance.

The thought of the bottle of red waiting on her kitchen counter revives Victoria as she enters her building and calls the elevator. She's so preoccupied with unearthing her keys that at first she doesn't see the unexpected visitor waiting on the doorstep of her apartment.

"Oh." She sighs. "It's you."

∽∂∂∽

"Expecting anyone else?" Anna replies, scrambling to her feet. "Morgan's phone is off, so I just wanted to find out how everything went."

"How long have you been sitting out here?"

"Not long. Your neighbor took pity on me and let me use her bathroom after an hour or so. Seriously, how is she?"

"Well, the IV drugs will have kicked in now that she's out of surgery. I didn't get a prognosis, but it's pretty bad."

"Do you know what happened?"

Victoria knows how easy it would be to turn her away at the door. Long day, early start, all the reasons any sane person would accept at face value. The thought of letting Anna walk down the hall is what brings tears to her eyes, so she closes them for a moment and lets Anna ramble.

"The stories in the locker room this afternoon were wild. I had tea with Irina—we went to this Ukrainian café, which was just… Anyway. She wasn't watching what happened, so I'm not sure what went down exactly."

"I wasn't there, either," Victoria reminds her. "But I'm reliably informed she landed awkwardly. It could have been just a dislocation—her hip is weak, after all, but I don't know. Come on, we're not standing out here all night."

"I don't have to come in," Anna says. It's clearly a lie. She looks three seconds away from charging the door.

Victoria unlocks it and nudges it ajar.

"It's just you seemed upset when you left, and I thought it might bring back some crappy memories," Anna continues. "I'm sure loads of other people already checked on you, but I wanted to see for myself."

"Did you?"

"And, uh." Anna reaches into the pocket of her denim jacket as Victoria returns her keys to her purse. "Give you back your scarf."

"You remembered."

Their eyes meet as fingertips brush over the exchange of silk. Truthfully Victoria would have been sorry to see this one go. It's a classic for a reason. With practiced hands, she unfolds it with a flick, whipping it quickly into a long braid of sorts. The spark from earlier reignites, and there isn't water enough in New York to put out the blaze now. Feeling playful, Victoria puts the twisted scarf around Anna's neck and pulls her close.

"Inside," she instructs.

And just as surely as if she'd commanded a sequence of steps in the studio, Anna is unhesitating in doing exactly as she's told.

ⴲⴲⴲ

It's sophomoric, really, to camp out in someone's building. But Anna can't bring herself to feel stupid over it, not now that she has Hermès around her neck and Victoria's mouth on hers.

"Listen, if this is just because you're upset over Morgan getting hurt…" Anna just has to say after kicking the door shut behind them.

"I barely know the girl. It's tragic, especially if her career is over, but why would that affect anything I'm doing tonight? Do I seem unduly distressed to you, Anna?"

"God, I still love it when you say my name right." Anna groans. "I'm just trying to be a good person, okay?"

"Life is short. These careers of ours desperately so. Don't you want to feel alive for a while? Something beyond rehearsal and dead composers and tulle?"

Anna kisses and kisses again, because she can. Only when she charts a course for Victoria's throat does she ask her question. "Is that how I make you feel?"

"Yes," Victoria says, barely a whisper, and Anna has goose bumps from the sultry sound of her voice. "Yes, you do."

She yanks Anna's jacket down her arms, exposing the almost-bare shoulders her camisole straps barely interrupt.

They're making their way slowly down the hall toward the bedrooms; Anna remembers that much from her brief tour. She lets her jacket fall to the floor as Victoria kicks off one shoe and then the other. Their kisses are more frantic now, openmouthed and almost pleading.

Anna presses Victoria back against the wall before they turn the corner, and it gets her a pleasant hiss of surprise in response.

"I imagined this," Anna tells her, hoisting Victoria up, and her legs wrap instinctively around Anna's waist, more tightly with her good leg than the injured one. "Every time I lifted you."

Victoria rakes her fingers through Anna's loose ponytail, letting her hair down.

"Every time you touched me to straighten my leg or elongate my arm." Anna leads them into the master bedroom as Victoria smiles down at her.

"Well, why settle for imagination? I think reality is going to be a lot more fun."

CHAPTER 33

The voice in her head that's been telling Victoria she'll regret this is quiet now.

How could she hear it anyway over the excited rasp of Anna's breathing as she discovers the lace thong beneath Victoria's simple black pants? Or the echo of her own moan against the high ceilings when Anna unhooks Victoria's bra with practiced ease, mouth replacing that lace as though choreographed.

"Oh God," Victoria pants at the first hint of teeth.

Anna isn't quite the ingénue she expected. The faint echo of a growl resounds in Anna's throat, and Victoria realizes she may be getting much more than she bargained for. She expected nice. She expected gentle. She didn't expect all that sinewy strength to have her pinned to her own mattress, but hell, she's not complaining.

Anna's mouth is hot and insistent, peppering Victoria's skin as each new inch is undressed and exposed. The kisses and nips and delicate sucking in different places, all of it is as relentless as the repetitions Anna performs at the barre most days. That curiosity, that burning need to impress, it's all being turned on Victoria's body, and damn if she isn't almost helpless against it.

That is not, however, what they signed up for when this offstage dance between them began. The enthusiasm can be reined in, diverted, almost controlled—something Victoria is more than familiar with. She instructs Anna seamlessly in the studio, so her simple "no" brings everything to an instant, breathless halt. "Not like this," Victoria continues.

Anna scrambles off her, awaiting direction.

"You're still a little overdressed." Victoria leans back on her elbows, right in the center of her bed. If she were staging it, she'd frown at the lighting, but she only managed to fumble for one lamp as Anna carried her in. "But take your time. This isn't the locker room; no need to rush."

What she's trying to say is, *This isn't work, I'm not your boss, and you're free to go,* but that would be ruining a moment they've already let slip too many times. Anna doesn't need to be here right now, and she's choosing it anyway. Victoria's had enough sacrifice for one career, and she's not giving this up.

Her resolve is only strengthened by the way Anna shimmies those skinny jeans down her legs. The camisole takes a bit longer, fussing with the hem and affecting to be shy now, standing at the side of Victoria's bed. Only when Anna looks at her, right before her face disappears behind the silky material for a moment, she's anything but shy.

This is the girl Victoria knew was in there all along. She's *magnificent*.

They're down to lingerie, Victoria's black and matching, Anna's far more cotton and at least in the same general end of the color spectrum. It doesn't matter one bit as Victoria beckons her back down on to the bed, those long, honey-blond curls falling around them like a waterfall as they kiss and kiss, languorous and teasing in turn.

"Now." Victoria leverages with her good knee, flipping them over. Anna's hair spreads out in a halo around her head, but there's nothing angelic about the flush on her cheeks or the redness of her lips as she bites down on her lower one. "You have choices, Anna."

"I do." It's not a question; it's an agreement on the facts.

"You can either watch…" Victoria straddles Anna's hips, slipping one hand beneath the lace of her own underwear and palming her breast with the other. She hisses as she pinches a hard nipple, still faintly damp from Anna's mouth on it moments before. "Or you can let me put you through your paces. What'll it be?"

Yes, it's controlling, but it makes Anna whimper like she's halfway gone, and that gets Victoria even wetter.

"Anything you want," Anna responds, and it's so goddamn reverential that Victoria almost believes herself the queen of her nicknames.

And what better way for a queen to pass the next hour than to discover just what Anna can do under her command? Somewhere between sucking on the perfect lines of Anna's obliques and slipping a third finger inside her, Victoria actually feels dizzy with want. Anna is unrestrained here, thrashing against the sheets when Victoria doesn't let up after the first orgasm, fingers thrusting Anna into a second, stronger one, and halfway to a third before she gasps for mercy.

Not that it takes her long to recover. Anna is careful in how she moves around Victoria, gentle at first in how she tips her back against the pillows and parts her legs like a gift to be savored. Which isn't to say that Anna rushes: in that position she has access to all of Victoria's body, touching her like she's tracing sheet music at first. She's especially careful when skimming her thumb over the white scar tissue on Victoria's knee, and it's the first spot she chooses for her mouth to replace her fingers.

Victoria's never been shy about what she likes and how she likes it, but Anna doesn't need direction in the way others have.

Anna listens and watches and responds, sensitive to how much, and how hard, and more, more, more. She goes down on Victoria like she's just grateful to have been asked, licking Victoria into a fist-biting half scream of a climax, and not letting up until Victoria's crossing her ankles behind Anna's back and riding out the waves until her clit can't bear to be touched.

Anna seems to like it when Victoria pulls on her hair, and that's' how she guides Anna back up for a forceful kiss where she can taste herself on those pouting lips. The relief of weeks and months of longing is better than any drug she's ever been prescribed, so Victoria holds Anna close and pulls the sheets halfway over them while their heartbeats return to normal.

⌒♾️⌒

"Can I stay?" Anna whispers, even though Victoria's head is resting against her shoulder and the arm wrapped around her waist could almost be described as possessive. "I mean, since you actually *invited* me into your bed this time and all."

"I'm comfortable" is all Victoria gives by way of response, and it's enough to have Anna smiling at the ceiling. The sheets are rumpled, heavy over their legs.

Anna's are still trembling faintly, and that only makes her smile wider.

"I can hear you grinning," Victoria accuses.

"Just working my cheek muscles," Anna says, barely holding back a snicker. Her stomach rumbles lightly. "It's still early. I could go get something?"

"They invented phones, didn't they?" Victoria grumbles, halfway to a nap. "I'm sure you have some millennial app for that sort of thing."

Anna wants to pinch herself. She's in Victoria Ford's bed and they're drowsily ordering takeout. Naked. She feels like she could vault the Statue of Liberty, and at the same time could sleep for a week.

"What do you like?" She nudges Victoria gently with her elbow. "Come on, you have to eat too. And don't say something boring like a salad. I think we've decided we're giving in to naughty things tonight, right?"

Victoria sits up. It's practically an invitation for Anna to drag her gaze down those delicate lines again, the very slightest of curves.

As a dancer, Victoria always looked impossibly fragile. Her frame is still tiny in a way that belies her actual height, from the narrow shoulders to her tapered waist, but with those years away from the everyday rigor of dance, she's softer around the edges in a way that makes Anna's mouth water.

"I could murder someone for a cheeseburger," Victoria confesses, clearly amused at how Anna's so thoroughly distracted. "If you can keep your eyes on the phone long enough. I draw the line at eating in bed, though."

"Fine," Anna sighs, putting plenty of drama in it. "I know a place that's gonna blow your mind."

When Victoria rolls her eyes, it seems fond, and that's more than Anna could have hoped for.

Victoria can't quite believe what she's seeing in her own living room, never mind what she's doing. Dressed in nothing more than a short kimono robe that isn't even tied properly, she's somehow been dragged into a picnic on the floor. The tablecloth that was on the perfectly serviceable table by the window is spread out over her Persian rug, and they've demolished cheeseburgers and waffle fries, washed down by more than a bottle of red.

It's bliss, and she has no idea how it happened.

As dinners go, this is a considerable upgrade on the debacle with Rick and Liza. The burgers are insanely good, and Anna is smug at Victoria's obvious enjoyment of them. It's relaxing, in a way Victoria hadn't expected. She's a little boneless from an unexpected series of orgasms. Anna, always so keen to wait for direction in rehearsal, started off the same way in bed.

With a little encouragement, enthusiasm had completely taken over. Victoria knows she'll be walking funny tomorrow, and not just because of her busted knee. Even that isn't really hurting, between her early painkillers and the endorphin surge. More than the stress release, she's actually...happy.

Well, if Big Pharma could bottle this, they'd never go out of business. It's about as elusive as a cure for the common cold, in Victoria's experience. Satisfied, yes. Fulfilled, certainly. That kind of contentment is meant to be temporary, a resting place to push onward and upward to the next achievement. Happiness for its own sake? Victoria is skeptical of it even existing, and yet it appears to be happening to her anyway.

"Do you think if we called the hospital and pretended to be a cousin they'd give us an update on Morgan?" Anna asks, having seemingly been lost in her thoughts and the application of barbecue sauce. "I'm not above a little fraud, in case you didn't know that about me."

God, must she be so charming? "I'm sure we'll hear. I'll check my phone once we're done with this, and then it's back to the real world."

"Or we could not check our phones…"

Victoria smiles, slow and with a flash of teeth that says she's hungry for more than takeout. Anna crawls across the rug toward her, very much the willing prey.

"You do have good ideas occasionally," Victoria muses.

Anna kisses her soundly enough to shut her up for quite some time.

Victoria's finally sated by the time they make it to her little museum-cum-mausoleum. Anna comes against the wall, with Odile's costume at her back, before setting Victoria on the display cabinet and kneeling before her. They have to be much more careful this time—Victoria's tender in ways she didn't expect, but the trembling detail of Anna's touch is exactly what she needs.

Afterward, Victoria makes no protest when Anna scoops her up and carries her back to the master bedroom.

When Victoria emerges from the en suite, freshened up and vaguely ready for bed, she's surprised to see Anna perched on the edge of the bed.

"Are you waiting for something?"

"Oh." Anna shifts her position, uncrossing her legs like she's getting ready to bolt. "No, right, I get it. I'll just, uh, find my clothes."

"I said you can stay," Victoria reminds her. "I don't know where you got the impression I would throw you out before the sheets had settled anyway."

"Could have fooled me," Anna mutters. "But I know you were probably in there trying to work out how to let me down easy, and I get it. I'm not naive, Victoria."

"You're not." It's a statement of fact after the past few hours. "And here you are, beyond the castle walls. I suppose I should tell you I don't generally bring people home, so you're not entirely wrong. I'm careful about who messes with my feng shui." She gives a pointed look to the rumpled mess they've made of the bed, hoping for comic relief.

"I know, and I feel so lucky. That's why I wanted to stay. I mean, if it's a one-time thing, then make as much of it as we can, right?"

Victoria's freezes halfway to the bed, dressed in a scandalous slip of a negligee she wasn't planning on wearing by morning. "One-time?" she repeats, the term sounding foreign on her tongue. The sinking sensation in her chest certainly has nothing to do with her heart, or any kind of genuine feelings. Of course the twentysomething ballerina isn't looking for something permanent. Victoria has had her share of flings over the years. "That saves an awkward conversation in the morning, I suppose."

"Right!"

Anna's enthusiasm seems a little faked, but Victoria is sure she's just projecting. So she's the notch on the bedpost this time. It's refreshing really. And, after all, what really matters is the work. They can only be better for taking this last barrier of intimacy out of the process.

Despite what they've said, the moment the room is dark, Anna seeks her out beneath the sheets and holds Victoria close. There's a kiss pressed into her hair, and it feels like so much more than one night has any right to.

ⲟ⳽ⲟ

Dawn wakes Anna, because in their punch-drunk state neither of them considered the curtains. She fumbles for her jeans without getting out of bed, retrieving her phone with its balefully low battery and a flurry of notifications. Unable to resist, she shoots off a text to Jess.

you'll never guess where I am.

Then she regrets it, because somehow she's talked herself and Victoria out of having anything more than this. If Victoria had put up any protest, or looked even slightly disappointed at Anna's suggestion, she could have recanted.

Seeing her across the pillows now, face free of concentration frowns or faint lines of distaste, Anna almost feels like she's in bed with the Victoria who was still dancing, the years she wears incredibly well falling away. What would someone so sophisticated and accomplished want with her flings nipping at her heels, anyway? No, Anna has stumbled on the perfect adult solution to this necessary development.

Still, if it's absolutely the right thing to do, then why is kissing Victoria again the only thing she can think of doing? Waking her up and saying one more night, and day, and another after that. Would Victoria kiss her back? Or tell her not to let the door hit her on the ass on her way out? It's too big a risk, with everything they have planned for the season.

Anna slips out of bed and dresses quickly in the hall, before slipping into the kitchen. She hopes to make coffee as a parting gift but, to her dismay, Victoria's coffee machine looks like professional-grade equipment, and Anna is no barista. Knowing her resolve will weaken if she returns to the bedroom, she leaves a brief but cheerful note on the elegant cream-colored fridge.

A moment later and Anna is out of the apartment, running right into the nosy neighbor who looks Anna up and down as though they've never met.

"Morning!" Anna says, far more chipper than she feels.

"Hmm" is all the response she gets, so she hurries the rest of the way downstairs.

"If you have company I can make myself scarce," Kim offers, presumably seeing how bedraggled Victoria looks on throwing the front door open.

"No, no, she's gone. Coffee? I sure as hell need some."

"I've got B12 if you want a shot to go with that." Kim drops her bag on the kitchen counter, and Victoria winces at the takeout bag and empty wineglasses. "Oh, you really did have company. Tell me it wasn't that creepy piano chick with the staring. I keep thinking she's going to Carrie the whole studio one of these days."

"No, it wasn't Teresa. And I'd defend her, except she *is* the one who glassed Anna's shoes."

"There is that. I'm glad you're putting regular physical therapy back on the calendar. You ever think about a midweek session? Not to be selfish, but it would save me coming up here."

"I'll think about it. Any word on the Gresham girl?"

"Not good." Kim winces. "Labrum's definitely torn, and the wear on the socket is worse than they realized from last time. The surgeon's giving her less than fifty perfect chance of dancing again with a full replacement."

"Shit."

"I'm going to see her later. I'll see what she's thinking. Done for this season, though, obviously. Haven't I told you about breaking your toys?"

"Just for that I'm pretending I have no creamer for your coffee," Victoria says with a sniff.

"You never do. When did you start getting it? For she-who-sleeps-over?"

"Stop fishing, Sawyer. If you're going to torture me, let me at least splash some water on my face. You *are* fifteen minutes early." Victoria whisks the coffee machine into life with practiced ease, preparing two mugs.

"Force of habit" is all Kim has to say for herself. She moves around Victoria to get the creamer, catching sight of something on the fridge. "Well, at least your guest had a nice time." She offers the piece of paper with a smirk before adopting a dreamy voice. "Is she *A* in your ballet? I think she must be."

"I know you're quoting something sappy at me, but I remain unmoved." Victoria groans, but she can't help smiling at Anna's adorable note. Has she really agreed to one night only? Probably best, considering. That didn't stop the pang of loneliness on waking up to an empty bed. Or the urge to scheme a way around that little agreement, the sooner the better. "I'm going to get that shower."

"Wait, A…Anna? Victoria Ford, are you banging the new girl?"

"No comment," Victoria says as she pours the coffee. She takes hers toward the bathroom as she flees from Kim. "I'll be quick," she calls back.

"Yeah, you'd better be."

∽∞∾

"You did what?" Jess accuses, rifling through a rack of clothes as the thud of music with too much bass plays over their conversation.

Anna just wants to skip the shopping and get to the part where they eat.

"Anna, that's some amateur nonsense."

"I wanted her to contradict me!"

"And tell you that in just one night she'd fallen madly in love with you, go pack your things and move in?" The snort of laughter only makes Anna feel worse. "That U-Haul-on-the-second-date thing is supposed to be a joke, you know?"

"Of course that's not what I thought," Anna says, even as she's picturing them sharing the Sunday *New York Times* at the table with its beautiful linen tablecloth, or taking long showers together in the marble bathroom. "Besides, if she wanted more than to get it out of our systems, she would have said so."

"Or you've just found a way of breaking your own heart when the woman of your dreams had no intention of doing so," Jess says.

"When did you turn into such a romantic? Normally you're telling me there are other fish in the sea before I've even broken things off with someone."

"I just… It's different when it's something real." Jess blushes furiously. "I know I wouldn't be giving Irina an out, not when it would mess me up."

"Well, that sounds super romantic." Anna rolls her eyes and feels how inherently Victoria-like her posture is as she does.

"I do okay." Jess settles on a black shirt that looks a lot like the other many black shirts she owns.

"I need to focus on dancing anyway," Anna says, trying to convince herself. "We go into full-time rehearsal for my turn as a prince this week. Delphine's amazing. I just hope I don't make an idiot of myself."

"Nobody can mess up *Sleeping Beauty*."

"Which would be great if I was dancing that, but it's *The Prince of the Pagodas*. And this choreography was first written for Victoria in London."

"Well, it sounds like you know what you want." Jess wanders over to the counter to pay.

Anna surreptitiously checks her phone, the battery almost wiped. She needs to get home and put her life in order. It isn't disappointing that Victoria hasn't sent a message, of course it isn't.

But when Anna closes her eyes even for a second, all she can see is Victoria on top of her, beside her, then asleep on the impeccably white pillow. *Go back go back go back*, Anna's gut is telling her, but she ignores it in favor of another coffee with her sister.

It's safer that way. No disappointment, nothing getting in the way of her big shot. By the time Jess is done and they're heading for the café, Anna's almost sure of her choice once more.

CHAPTER 34

The more professional Anna is, the harder she throws herself into being the perfect prince to Delphine's Princess Rose, the more Victoria wants her.

It's maddening.

The official costume fitting with Susan is torture. Not because of the tension crackling in the room, but because Anna spends the best part of three hours standing around in her underwear. Even Delphine doing the same cannot distract her from Anna. Delphine is just another body as far as Victoria's brain is concerned, no matter how conventionally attractive. Anna, on the other hand, is distracting with every bend, flex, or reflexive rubbing of her arms because the wardrobe department is always painfully cool.

The final result is worth it: a prince worthy of any production.

"Well." Susan tucks her tools back into the satchel she carries around for alterations. "Even by my standards, that's a damn home run."

"It's your modesty, that's why I brought you in from Miami," Victoria says, but she's impressed.

Anna can't take her eyes off the mirror, and no one could blame her. The jade green, now tailored to her shape in new material, looks as though her thighs were sculpted from actual jade. Those broad shoulders look more than capable of tossing Delphine around now they're crowned with golden epaulettes, and the starched collar only adds to the military bearing.

"I can undo all this and put her in a potato sack, you know," Susan warns.

Anna gasps at the very idea, possessive hands all over her military jacket. "Don't you dare!" And it's the closest she's come to a diva moment of her own.

"Nobody's taking your clothes," Victoria says, but she likes the enthusiasm.

Anna blushes at the mention of removing clothes, and it's a small but predictable victory for Victoria. They've held out for over a week now. This magnetic pull should be fading, but it's only getting stronger.

"I've got some sketches for *Gala*," Susan tells them, rooting around in her satchel. "But we'll make time to go through those before I commit to stitching anything. I'll let you know what labels get back to me."

"I'm still inclined toward a Susan Ramos original." Victoria has been firm on that point. She brought Susan in because she can work miracles with cloth and dye. Her cuts and stitching make the clothes an extension of the dancers, and it's an art form in its own right. "Anna, you can get going. Dr. Sawyer is waiting."

"Right," Anna says, like she'd been about to say something else. "I am so ready for a massage."

Victoria turns away, trying not to think about Anna in just a slip of white towel. It's a *sports* massage, for the love of…

"Have fun," is all she can think to say, not turning back until Anna has made her exit.

∞∞∞

"She gets the preferential treatment?" Irina asks from the doorway. "I see how it is."

"I was here first." When it comes to a massage for her exhausted legs, Anna has decided to be ruthless. "You can have the guy with the knuckles thing, though."

"Girls, girls, don't fight over me," Kim orders. "Irina, take the bed over there. Anna's almost done."

Anna whines in protest.

"Unless you want your hamstrings and Achilles to actually turn into tagliatelle, you're just about done," Kim says. She jiggles Anna's thigh to make her point.

"Fine, but can I lie here for a while?" Anna asks. "I'm too relaxed to move."

"You can keep me company," Irina decides for them both. "We have not spoken much, and Kim here is a vault. She asks no questions, tells no lies."

"I ask plenty of questions," Kim argues. "And it's you dancers who lie to me, all the time. 'I took my shots, Kim. I did my reps, Kim.' I should lock up the painkillers and ban you all from my lovely department."

"You would be so lonely without us," Irina says.

Anna listens to her get ready, the Moon Boot finally off, but her leg still firmly strapped, at least based on warm-up this morning.

"How is the girl?" Irina asks.

"You know I can't discuss Morgan's condition with any of you," Kim warns, pulling a thin sheet over Anna's legs and back to keep her warm. "But since you'll only make up scurrilous rumors if I don't, I suppose I can unofficially tell you that New York General discharged a young woman today. She's going back to stay with her mother, instead of her own place. The second surgery is postponed for now."

Anna sat up, only just remembering to cover her front with a towel. "Seriously? But there's no way she dances again without it."

Kim shrugs. "Some pain isn't worth going through twice. She's considering her options."

"It is not as though she'll lack for options," Irina says. "Still, you know what your beloved Martha said."

"Stewart?" Anna asks, because that would be out of left field.

"Graham," Kim corrects, smacking Anna on the arm for being dense.

"Oh." Anna gets it then. "A dancer dies twice. That's what you mean?"

"Mmm," Irina confirms, already facedown on her massage table. "Once when they stop dancing." Her voice is level as she says it, despite how close she's already come to that reality. "Perhaps Morgan just wants to get it over with. It's the most painful death."

"So…" Anna isn't quite sure where to start, but they managed pretty well over tea the other day.

"You want to tell me about her," Irina asks. "You knew Inessa for longer than I did, after all."

"I mean, what do you want to hear?" Anna asks. "I was a kid and she was my whole world. I don't know if there's anything that will even make that much sense, honestly."

"She brought you to the ballet. You must have been young."

"My lullabies were ballet scores. That and some folk songs I never really got to understand, but her voice was beautiful. A real soprano, you know? My dad always said she should have been a professional singer. Do you…sing?"

Irina groans as Kim attacks her back and shoulders with renewed enthusiasm. "I can carry a tune, yes."

Another detail to file away. Another similarity in a person who's still *here*, still walking around and talking. Sharing DNA with Anna just when she thought there was no one left coded in the same way as she. She's gotten used to knowing that doesn't matter, that it doesn't make a family, but as an orphan far from home, it's amazing how the smallest thing can make her feel that little bit less lonely.

"Tell me about Moscow," Anna says, standing and pulling her shirt and sweatpants back on. "She came to see you dance once, I know. I guess she knew. Did she…?"

"I never had guests," Irina cuts off that fantasy. "If I was asked anytime, I don't remember. I'm sorry for this."

"It's okay," Anna sits on the floor, leaning back against the wall. "The Bolshoi, though," Anna presses. "Is it as hardcore as they say?"

"Oh, do I have some tales for you, *malenkaya*."

Anna opens a bottle of water and settles in for the stories.

∞

The switch to stage rehearsal is a relief. Here, there's a whole company most of the time, and so many fixes and tweaks needed that Victoria rarely has time to dwell on Anna, save for her solos and *pas de deux*. There's a lot of chatter among the girls in the corps about how Anna gets to dance an entire show without pointe shoes, mutters of mild jealousy and curiosity alike. Fairly standard whenever someone gets to color outside the lines. Aside from that, it's almost irritating how quickly the company has taken to her, especially after Victoria's best efforts to keep her isolated and focused. It's that damn sunshine smile, even if half of them are bitching behind her back later.

"Did someone hire a monkey for this production?" Victoria rarely has to raise her voice, but they're a rowdy bunch this afternoon. "Because I fail to see why you'd be playing with those ropes otherwise." Ethan stops turning somersaults between two ropes, having the decency to look embarrassed at being caught.

"Now, if the corps could seat themselves in the house for ten minutes, we might actually get to see our prince and princess dance today. Wouldn't that be something?" Victoria's sarcasm echoes back to her over a sea of bowed heads scurrying to do as they're told for a change. It's hard to tell sometimes if this is a ballet company or a kindergarten.

Delphine and Anna are the only ones left onstage. The lighting design is not finalized, so they're sitting in the glow of a couple of follow spots that won't move yet. That's another meeting—a handful of them, probably—and some agonizing tech rehearsals still to come. Dry tech yesterday hasn't exactly filled Victoria with confidence that her department heads know what's expected of them. These work-light rehearsals have been more tedious than normal, and she's close to losing her temper.

How painful would it be, exactly, to launch Anna in triumph only for her steady and dependable corps to suddenly let her down? For their sake, Victoria had better not find out.

Delphine and Anna leap to attention at the first brisk clap of Victoria's hands, her star performers leading the way with their professionalism.

There's more interest than there would usually be for a work-light run-through, and Victoria spots various technicians and other interested parties who don't need to be there. It's not the first time some gender flipping has gone on, but it is novel for this company. Rick did little to chase off the stuffy, conservative reputation when he first took over, and it's only since hiring Victoria that they've looked much beyond the staples.

"Ladies." Victoria takes up her out-of-place office chair at the front of the stage. "Let's show our colleagues what we've been working on."

∾∞∾

Anna wipes her hands on her tights, glad they're still in their own clothes and not costumed yet. All she has to do is replicate the hard work they've put in at the studio, and it's hardly as though she hasn't danced in front of people before.

She glances at Victoria, and where once that impassive face would have turned Anna's knees to rubber, today it calms and centers her. Her belief in Anna is turning into self-belief on Anna's part.

She's ready.

Eve is back on piano, but Anna has seen Teresa lurking somewhere. Needless to say, her shoes have been checked religiously and she hasn't let her kit bag out of her sight. The music strikes up, and Anna smiles because she likes how jaunty Britten can be compared to other composers. This is his only ballet score, and God, she wishes she had seen Victoria dance this at nineteen, with the rapt crowds in London.

She takes up position, the blocking freshly marked by the stage manager's tape. Anna doesn't know his name yet, and it feels rude to only be asking now. Delphine is fussing with the gauzy fabric tied around her head. This is the blindfold *pas de deux*, and despite Victoria's insistence on being daring, it has to convey the idea of a blindfold while actually letting Delphine see in order to dance safely. If she feels ridiculous with a strip of someone's old tutu over her eyes, Delphine doesn't look it.

Then Anna's cue comes surging out of the piano, and she's taking those first expressive steps. Her ankles pivot the way she wants them to, and her movements are measured as precisely as Victoria insisted they be. She can feel when the dance is right, in much the same way as an experienced contractor can tell if something is straight without a level. Even a fraction off the beat and she'll know, her mood plummeting with it.

The *pas de deux* seems to last an eternity, and apart from a wobbly moment on the second lift, they're confident and smiling into the final few steps, Anna's arms sitting easily around Delphine's waist as they come to a halt.

Applause is not really done for more than cursory acknowledgment in rehearsal, but a wave of enthusiastic clapping and even a few whoops break out from the watching company. Anna wants to punch the air, but instead she trades her habitual curtsey for a deep bow, staying in character.

Victoria doesn't get out of her seat, but Anna can see the sparkle in her eye. She put that there, with Delphine's flawless assistance. "Well, I should make you do it again just for that second lift, but even I'm not that cruel. Well done."

Victoria's guarded compliment roars through Anna's bloodstream far more powerfully than the applauding did. Their gazes meet, earning Anna a wink before Victoria turns to address the rest of her dancers.

"Now, if we could take it from the second act with *that* level of competence, please?" People scramble; nobody's playing anymore.

"You were freaking amazing out there," Anna tells Delphine in the wings, gesturing to untie the blindfold that she's still wearing.

With a nod, Delphine lets her untie it. "You weren't so bad, either, newbie. Victoria reduced to one criticism? That's going in the memoir."

"I thought that was pretty good. It is, right?"

"Still living and dying by her approval, huh?" Delphine teases. "You've got it bad."

Anna could deny it, could even tell Delphine the truth that they were one and done, nothing more to read there. Except that wink doesn't make it feel so done anymore, and Anna can already feel her resolve to be cool and sophisticated slipping away.

Instead, she rolls her eyes, much like Victoria would have, and does some stretches to keep ready for their next call.

♾

The wink is a risk, and Victoria knows it. She does it anyway. Part of her is waiting for Anna to come knocking on her office door—or later, her apartment—and ask who the hell they both think they're kidding.

A better person, one less guided by stubborn pride, might march across the street to Anna's and do the asking. She drinks an extra glass or two, and sleeps poorly. Changing the sheets didn't help, an extra Ambien didn't, either. She wakes up wishing Anna was there in the bed, and there doesn't seem to be a damn thing she does that makes the feeling pass.

They make it to semi-dress—Anna in the costume—and Victoria doesn't think she's going to make it as far as waiting for Anna to come knocking. If there was any way to guarantee privacy in the locker rooms, Victoria's impatience might tip her hand.

She holds out—a pat on the back and a smile for Anna this time, what is she thinking?—and the dress rehearsal is a slow, clunky disaster. Victoria has never bought in to that theater bullshit about a lousy rehearsal meaning a good performance, so she seethes and worries her way through another sleepless night.

Somewhere around three, she gets a text from Anna.

Can you sleep? I can't.

It's the window, it's an invitation, and Victoria is up off the sofa, ready to surrender. Then she catches herself. How selfish it would be to exhaust Anna and fill her head with false hopes before such a big night. No, Victoria will take responsibility for most things, but not for turning Anna's head at the expense of her career.

෨෨෨

Anna stretches her hamstring one more time. The niggling strain hasn't bothered her for a day or two. She's warmed up. She's ready. Tonight's the night.

The ensemble members scurry for places, the heavy damask of the curtain still shielding them from privileged, expectant eyes. Delphine nods at her from the opposite wing, all the acknowledgment they allow themselves before a performance. Her entrance precedes Anna's, and it's a long time to choke back the metallic taste at the back of her throat.

As the orchestra strikes up at last, the conductor wielding the baton, Anna takes her next breath. He'll keep them all in harmony, let their beats ring out loud and true, never faltering. She trusts that as surely as she trusts that the sun will rise over the Metropolitan Performing Arts Center in the morning.

She senses the movement behind her more than she hears it. Her dresser has gone to prepare the first change; no one else enters from stage left until the second act. That leaves one person who would presume to approach at a moment like this.

Anna doesn't turn. She already knows what she'll see. The black Vera Wang was hanging outside the office today, fresh from the dry cleaner. It'll be paired with diamond studs beneath a perfectly sculpted french twist. The impression of lipstick, unwanted but worn anyway, and the slight, immovable frown that has greeted Anna's every effort these past few months.

"Dance," Victoria says, standing close enough for her breath to skim Anna's bare shoulder.

It's an order, a timely reminder, but Anna hears the plea in it too. She kicks her slipper against the ground once in acknowledgment—no block to protect her toes, just the regular slipper. She has faith, stubborn and resolute, despite everything that rides on this one night.

Delphine enters stage right. Anna turns, but Victoria is already gone. She won't sit in her house seat, elbow to elbow with tonight's dignitaries. She might lurk in one of the boxes that wasn't put on sale, counting steps from behind a curtain of her own.

Fourteen bars. Twelve.

Anna listens to the notes that lead to her cue. She takes one more deep, centering breath, and takes the first step.

CHAPTER 35

Anna's first high hits the moment the audience realize the twist, her entrance a dramatic series of leaps from the wings that lead to murmurs and then to a smattering of applause. She's cheeky enough to acknowledge, a sidelong glance to the audience that isn't scripted but feels perfect in the moment. The clapping only increases, and for a moment Anna can't pick out the beats of the orchestra.

They simmer down quickly enough, and Anna pursues Delphine carefully across the sacred space they own for the time being. There's a silky quality to the way Delphine dances, as though she possesses a kind of flexibility mere mortals don't. Beside her, against her, Anna feels stronger than steel, the steadying presence that lets them throw themselves into every turn and extension.

The first time she lifts Delphine—a simple lift by the standards of the piece—the audience erupts once more. Anna squeezes Delphine's hips gently on lowering her, a silent thank-you for being the perfect partner, and gets an unchoreographed touch to her cheek in response. They dance on, in perfect sync.

The curtain calls seem to last half a lifetime, and Anna is almost more exhausted by the alternating bows and curtseys than any of the choreography. Delphine was complaining about a slight backache before their last scene together, but there's no sign of it as they take their rapturous applause.

When the lights dip for a second, she sees Jess and Marcia practically falling over the seats in front of them with how hard they're cheering her on. The whole audience is on their feet, and it sounds like they may just be a hit.

Skipping backstage, Anna picks Delphine up one more time from sheer exuberance. They hug it out until Gabriel comes along to congratulate them. The flowers he brings for Delphine are beautiful, and Anna tries not to miss that part of it. Of course, Gabriel is a gentleman and has a second bouquet behind his back, tied with a blue ribbon to distinguish them.

"I was gonna get you some cigars, but you don't strike me as a smoker," he teases, one arm wrapped casually around Delphine's shoulders. "You done with my girl for the night?"

"Unless you want to join us for dinner and drinks?" Anna asks, already knowing the answer.

"Next time," Delphine assures her.

They head back to their respective dressing rooms, and Anna still can't quite believe she has a principal's space, so close to the stage. No more running up and down flights of stairs between scenes.

The knock comes just minutes after Anna settles in to clean up and change. She throws the door open, revealing Victoria with her hand still raised.

"Did you need something?" Anna asks, but it's friendlier than it might have been.

"You're just out of the shower. I can come back," Victoria suggests, looking right past Anna.

"Nothing you haven't already seen." Anna steps back, gesturing for her to come in. "I won't be long."

Victoria moves straight across to the dressing table, folding her arms over her killer black dress and black coat. Her heels are high enough to make Anna worry, but there's no denying the length and polished perfection of Victoria's bare legs. The hem only just covers her scar, but she glances at the spot anyway.

Mostly dried, Anna starts pulling on her change of clothes. Nothing too fancy, since it's just family drinks again. At the moment, comfort trumps all. As she sprays some perfume and ties her hair up, Victoria holds court.

"We're a hit," Victoria says, and their eyes meet in the large mirror. "We deserve to be too. You didn't put a foot wrong tonight, do you know that? It was textbook. Only more than that, Anna. It was art. You did everything exactly as written but made it look like the steps were just occurring to you that second."

"That's good?"

"That's career-defining. Are your family in from Meadowlark?"

"Dubuque. Yeah, I know that's probably lame, but they get so excited. First time as a principal and all."

"They should be—that's their right as family members." Poking around Anna's personal effects on the dressing table, Victoria hesitates over a picture of Anna with her parents. "She really does look like Irina. I don't know how you ever missed that they were related."

"I've never seen my mom at Irina's age, have I?" Anna asks. "And when you're that young, 'mom' is more of a concept than the person with the face."

"That makes sense."

"The invitation to drinks still stands. Do I need to set fire to anything before I go?" Anna asks.

"You know," Victoria says, lifting Anna's jacket from where it hangs on the back of the door, "I think I might just join you for that drink. If they can make a decent Manhattan."

"Uh, sure." Anna is lying through her teeth. "I can ask Irina too."

"Oh, Irina's out of town. She got a slot with some miracle quack in North…South… One of the Carolinas, anyway. Flew there this morning."

"Right." Anna wishes Irina had maybe thought to mention as much. Just another reminder that family, that caring about someone, doesn't just happen because of names on a piece of paper. "Well, let's go, then."

"Lead the way." Victoria opens the door for them.

Anna snags her leather jacket, but before she can put it on, Victoria is running a fingertip down the thin strap of Anna's pale blue camisole. "This is a lovely color on you. I'll tell Susan to consider it for your next fittings."

"Uh, thank you." Anna swallows hard. They're only a few inches apart. If Jess and Marcia weren't waiting, this would absolutely be a to-hell-with-it moment for a reprisal.

The way Victoria quickly licks her lips suggests she's thinking roughly the same.

"So. Drinks."

"Drinks," Victoria agrees, and they make it all the way to the stage door without touching, which is probably for the best.

☾☾☾

"Are you coming to stay over with Jess too?" Marcia asks as they leave the bar. "I know you're all grown up, but I still worry about you heading home alone."

Victoria emerges last, slipping that perfectly tailored coat back over her shoulders.

"I have my car." Victoria gestures to where the Mercedes idles at the curb. "And Anna lives in the building opposite mine. I'll see her home safely. Can we drop you first? You're somewhere downtown, aren't you, Jessica?"

"We'll get a cab," Jess says. "And I told you, it's just Jess."

"Of course it is, Jessica," Victoria teases.

Anna can't believe she's just spent two hours watching Victoria completely charm her family. If that had been some kind of formal introduction, a meet-the-girlfriend scenario, it would have been the best one in living history, Anna's sure of it. Of course it wasn't, and it's probably never going to be, but she'd been proud to be the person bringing Victoria Ford to the table.

Anna opens her mouth to add to the conversation, but all that escapes is a gigantic yawn.

"To bed with you!" Marcia orders.

Two more rounds of hugs later, Anna's being gently steered into the backseat of the town car. Somehow when they pull out into traffic, Victoria doesn't retreat to her own side. She stays firmly in the middle of the seat, pressed into Anna's side.

"You know," Victoria begins, when the privacy screen is all the way up. "As orders go, 'to bed' isn't bad."

"How do you know if that order works?" Anna asks. "I might just be going home to play video games or sort out my closet."

"Well, let me try. To bed?"

"That sounds nice," Anna says. "I suppose that just leaves the question of which one?"

"Is that so, Ms. One-Time?"

"Okay, in my defense—"

Victoria silences that defense with a kiss. She doesn't play it careful this time, and before Anna knows which way is up, Victoria is straddling her lap and her tongue is flickering playfully against Anna's own.

"To bed," Victoria repeats when the kiss ends, forehead resting against Anna's. "But first—" She thumps her fist on the privacy screen three times. "A little detour."

As soon as the car stops, Victoria slips from her lap and out the door with typical grace.

Anna noticed earlier that the cane has been retired again in recent days, which bodes well. She doesn't even know where they've stopped—somewhere off Fifth Avenue anyway, but for Victoria that could mean anything from a prescription to a new pair of shoes, even at this hour.

Then Victoria is back, coming in via Anna's side again with far less grace.

"Here," she huffs, dropping a newspaper in Anna's lap. "*The Post* has an unfortunate habit of reviewing previews rather than opening night. It's all about getting the jump, about knowing first. I'd shut it down, but we have such limited runs that even one extra day of a good review means maybe a few hundred seats sold."

Anna feels sick. She can't seem to move her hands toward the paper, so she rests them on Victoria's thighs instead, where they rest on either side of Anna's lap.

"I-I can't," she manages to blurt out. "I get, um, carsick if I read in the car."

"We're not moving yet," Victoria points out. "You're nervous, aren't you? Don't even think about ignoring reviews. That's just something people say."

"I just… This is my first," Anna tries to explain. "And if it's bad, or just aggressively mediocre, I don't want that memory. I don't want to picture words that I wish had never been written."

"You're so sure you didn't get a good write-up?" Victoria is incredulous. "After *I* told you that you were magnificent up there?"

"Critics don't know as much as you do?" It's safest to hedge with a compliment. "Could you…?"

"Fine." Victoria huffs, but she looks pleased. Unfortunately she also wriggles off Anna's lap, wincing as she tucks her bad leg under herself as best she can. She thumps the privacy screen again and they're in motion.

"Wait, you didn't read it first to check?" Anna gasps as Victoria searches through the paper. "I thought you were bluffing and knew it was a good review."

"We really have to toughen you up," Victoria says. "Aha, here we are. Oh, a whole section. Remind me to call someone about using the correct promotional shots, would you? No, never mind, that's something to annoy Kelly about." Victoria actually takes out her phone and fires off the message.

Anna is on the brink of combusting from sheer anticipation. She clears her throat, and the smirk Victoria shoots her this time says the delay is entirely on purpose.

What was it Jess called her the other week? Princess of Pain? Yeah, Anna absolutely has a thing for a sadist.

"'In a nod to Matthew Bourne'—ugh, I knew they'd start there," Victoria groans. "'The Metropolitan Ballet has finally begun to deliver the shake-up we were promised when their leading light returned to them just under four years ago.'"

"Leading light," Anna teases. "I'll have to remember that's your title. Maybe Kelly can have a sign made for your door."

"'In choosing a ballerina to dance the traditionally male role of the Salamander Prince'—we changed the… It was a metaphor… Forget it." Victoria frowns.

"It's bad isn't it?" Anna panics. "No, I don't want to hear it. Stop there."

"'Victoria Ford has unearthed a rare gem in the form of Anna Gale (pictured). Her feminine wiles may not be deployed, but she brings a grace and tenderness to the Prince that makes him the perfect choice for the Princess (prima Delphine Wade).'"

No picture of Delphine? Anna can't muster outrage over her bubbling excitement. They think it was a good idea. Not to go full Sally Field at the first hint of success, but they liked her. They really liked her.

"'Of particular interest is the new take on McMillan's blindfolded pas de deux. It was the London performance that launched Ford as a star, but she shares the spotlight perfectly between her stars here. Gale is a revelation with her cutting-edge line and pale complexity. Here is an actor-dancer who will tell the story twice over, once with her movement and again with her expression.'"

Victoria looks giddy as the paper falls into her lap. "Delphine professional, yadda yadda. Get your tickets here. 'Be sure to book if you can, because this first night felt like an *I was there when...* moment, much as the same ballet did in London some twenty years ago for the current artistic director.'"

"That…" Anna licks her lips, fumbling for words. "I mean, that's…"

"A rave," Victoria finishes for her, falling on Anna with a ravishing kiss. Her hands are under the flimsy blue top, and Anna moans low in her throat.

"Your rise, since I promoted you, is already meteoric, Anna," Victoria says when she relinquishes Anna's mouth for a moment.

Not content to wait, Anna's mouth seeks out the base of Victoria's throat when she's back on Anna's lap.

"It's only going to continue that way," Victoria says.

"Thank you?"

"Do you know what turns me on more than success?" Victoria runs her fingers through Anna's hair, stopping short to tug at it with intent.

Their gazes meet, and Anna is openmouthed in her desire to keep touching, to continue being touched. "What?" she rasps. "Tell me."

"*Nothing,*" Victoria confirms, and then her dress is so easy to unzip, slipping down her arms and rucking around her waist.

Anna pushes the high hem up to meet it and Victoria's practically naked on top of her. A cursory skim of Anna's hand between them confirms Victoria is already soaked through her barely-there suggestion of underwear. Apparently fine lace thongs are not an occasional choice.

It doesn't seem like a lot of foreplay is going to be necessary, at least for this early round. Anna is just greedy to be touching again when she thought she'd surrendered the privilege, so when she puts her fingers to work this time, there's firm purpose in the stroking movements.

Victoria drops her head back at first, the touch making her seem electrified as her short nails dig into Anna's bare shoulders, her top barely intact from their initial groping. When they kiss again, Victoria biting down on Anna's lower lip before sucking on it, it's all the incitement Anna needs to slip two fingers inside. Victoria grinds down against them, and Anna flexes her thumb to apply the necessary pressure to Victoria's clit.

There must be traffic on the way uptown. Anna vaguely thinks they may be hitting the post-theater crowds, who tip out of their musicals and plays later than the ballet usually does. She doesn't care much beyond the extra time it gives her to have Victoria rocking steadily up and down on her lap.

Anna surreptitiously moves her other hand to support Victoria's knee, just in case. She drags her fingertips along Victoria's inner thigh as a distraction, knowing how sensitive she is there. Victoria's breathy moans confirm it's a good choice.

They're almost rolling to a stop outside Victoria's building when she comes, muffling the sounds she makes against Anna's shoulder, mouth hot and wet as she nips aimlessly at the skin. Anna is almost out of her skin with need, and, as she shifts to the side, she teases Victoria that as the star of the evening, shouldn't she be the one riding the highs?

"Oh, just you wait, Anna." Victoria sighs. Between them, they zip her dress back to something approaching decent.

Anna just puts her jacket back on and zips it over her half-removed camisole. When they step out onto the sidewalk, they're almost presentable, but they barely make it inside the front door of the building before Victoria is on Anna, kisses fervent and hands determined.

Getting to the actual apartment takes an age, between being too intent on making out to notice the elevator has arrived, and Victoria having her hand inside Anna's jeans when they reach the top floor, meaning they miss that opportunity to step out and bounce around floors for a while. Right up until Victoria, breathless and flushed, announces that they are not *having sex on the damn elevator*, even though they're not very far from proving that wrong.

Anna is so turned on she could cry by the time they finally make their way along the correct hallway, performing an inelegant sort of waltz as they kiss, and fumble for keys, and take turns being pressed against the wall. They attract an audience from the rude neighbor through the peep hole, and Victoria takes extra relish in moaning as Anna kisses her collarbones with exquisite attention.

"Okay." Victoria just about gathers herself long enough to unlock the apartment door. "Come here."

Anna barely has time to close the door behind them, but she manages it before Victoria sinks to the floor, using Anna's jacket to prop up the painful knee. She threads her fingers through Victoria's hair, smiling as her jeans are impatiently tugged down.

There's no way the neighbors can miss the sound of her coming, with more of a scream than a moan, and Anna can't find it in herself to give a damn.

CHAPTER 36

Victoria is standing at the side of the bed the next morning when Anna finally cracks one eye open enough to let light in. More beautiful than the postcoital woman in the robe standing before her are the steaming coffee mugs said woman is holding.

"So I have coffee, but there's a qualifying question."

"The answer is whatever you want it to be, as long as I get the coffee." Anna groans, pulling herself up against the pillows. "You know, I didn't even drink that much. Why do I feel like I've been hit by a train?"

"Adrenaline crash," Victoria says, a little snappish. "Now, to qualify for coffee, answer me this: are you going to have any more genius ideas about one-time things and how that's all I want? Or are you going to be a person who gets to drink their coffee?"

"No more bright ideas," Anna says. "I don't have enough functioning brain cells anyway."

Victoria hands over a delightfully creamy coffee, and a first sip confirms just a hint of sweetener.

It's Anna's go-to order, and much nicer than her usual takeout version.

"So I can come back to bed without you dumping me? Sneaking out when I go for a shower?"

"You're pretty sensitive for someone with a really big ego," Anna says, filters not entirely in place for the day yet. "Uh, I mean—"

But Victoria is smiling, so Anna stops fumbling. They sip their coffees in comfortable silence, Victoria wriggling closer when she's back under the sheets.

"Any chance I can just sleep all day?" Anna asks. "I could live in this bed, for the record."

"It would be remiss of me to let you. But powering through isn't always the answer. You should go easier but keep active. Swim, massage, a couple of light classes today. And before you start worrying, it's what I'd recommend to any dancer not currently naked in my bed too."

"Does that mean you'll join me? If it's so routine?"

"Is that your idea of a date?" Victoria smirks into her mug.

"Are we dating?" Anna drains her own coffee and sets it aside. She has to learn how to work that coffeemaker. "And if we are, I guess I should ask how discreetly?"

"You, the one who likes to assume things, are assuming you're my dirty little secret?" Anna nods. What else could she possibly think?

∞∞∞

This conversation is inevitable, and it's usually the point where Victoria scrambles for the nearest exit. Honestly it's unlike her to even let it get this far, but there goes Anna again being the exception to so many of Victoria's rules.

"Well," she considers out loud. "Fuck that."

"Ex-excuse me?" Thank God Anna has finished her coffee, or it would be all over Victoria's immaculate brushed-linen bedding.

"Oh yes, it's quite the sapphic scandal." Victoria rolls her eyes. "Do you know how many men in my position have fucked their way to greatness? Claiming an exceptional dancer as their muse and riding her talent to fame of their own? Not," she clarifies, "that it's what I intend with you."

"You're already way more renowned," Anna points out.

"Well, of course I am. All I mean is that no one ever judged those men and their muses. Often the fights were more dramatic than the performances, but it never stopped them. Why the hell else are we in the arts, if not to shrug off that pedestrian bullshit?"

"Am I your muse?" Anna teases, leaning in for a coffee-flavored kiss. "Do tell all the ways I inspire you, maestra."

Victoria wrinkles her nose. How cheesy. "You don't need to flip the gender. I'm quite content as a maestro, thank you."

"And this isn't going to be a secret," Anna says, a gleam in her eyes now. "So I can swing by your office any given day and do this." She leans in for a slower, more thorough kiss. "I know, I know, studio time is only for practice, but afterward, I can also do this." She kisses Victoria again, and they're both smiling into it.

"Go get the shower started and I'll ring Kelly about the spa," Victoria orders, already turned on. If she doesn't get them moving, they'll end up wasting the day in bed, and that's an irresponsibility too far.

"You joining me?" Anna hops out of bed. She stretches, the defined muscles of her back pulling Victoria's focus as they flex.

"You know me," Victoria deadpans. "I'm just nuts for water conservation. I'll see you in there."

∞∞∞

Nobody notices at first, and Anna tells herself she's relieved. It's not as though Victoria goes any easier on her in the studio, and the high of performing as a principal each night for more than a week is as exhausting as it is thrilling. She crashes hard each night, more often than not in Victoria's bed, and if that's how habits form, Anna is happy to let them.

With *The Prince of the Pagodas* wrapped, it's time to focus on the holiday program. Anna's big coming out in *Gala Performance* will be in the new year, after some light traveling for the company in January, where the summer touring schedule will also be finalized. She's so busy she almost forgets to be tired, enjoying the relative anonymity of being back in the corps for *The Nutcracker* while the rest of the company is also closing out the regular shows with *Coppélia*.

She's running through a sequence heavy on *développés*, her leg extended vertically, toes pointing to eleven o'clock. There's a second, no more than that, when she thinks it's just someone's elastic snapping.

Then the electric surge of pain that radiates down her leg and up through her hip is like lightning wrapped in barbed wire.

"Son of a—"

She hits the ground hard, because her weight was shifting back to center and her other leg isn't expecting to have to suddenly do all the work. The pain is so sharp that Anna instinctively runs her hand over the back of her thigh, paranoid that Teresa has somehow gotten to her with more glass, or worse a knife this time. It's paranoid and panicky, but it gives Anna something to focus on so she doesn't cry.

There's a crowd around her in seconds, David barking orders as the one in charge of the rehearsal. Two of the boys make a carrying cradle for her and gently transport her down to Kim. As expected, Victoria shows up two minutes later, clearly having rushed right over from her office.

"Are you okay?"

The boys bolt, knowing they'll be sent back to rehearsal anyway if they make eye contact. Kim is still in back dealing with an ankle sprain, so it's just Anna waiting on one of the empty beds.

"It's not so bad," Anna says, promptly bursting into tears.

Victoria scoops her up in a hug that manages not to jostle her at all.

Anna cries harder, into the shoulder of Victoria's gorgeous patterned blouse. She hopes it won't stain, since the little makeup Anna is wearing must be washing off her face about now.

"Hey, hey." Kim joins them, patting Victoria on the shoulder to get her to move away. "What have we got here?"

"Hammy," Anna says through gritted teeth. "Fully extended and then: snap."

"That'll do it," Kim says, and her voice is so calm, so soothing, that Anna bursts into tears all over again. "Hey, get that panic down to a simmer. It's rarely as bad as you think."

"But—"

"Here, here, let me see." Kim rolls Anna over to examine her properly. Victoria watches on, holding Anna's hand the whole time. The new position adds to her discomfort, but Anna grits her teeth. She can't be a baby about this.

Kim is trying to be gentle, but her fingers feel like they're trying to pull muscles out through her skin every time they prod at Anna's thigh. She wants to throw up, always has when she's hurt, going way back to skinning her knees on the playground. But then Victoria's other hand is rubbing between her shoulder blades, soothing circles that make it easier to breathe. Anna closes her eyes and lets Kim work.

"We'll need a scan, but first look says it's relatively minor."

"How long?" Anna grits out, turning back over as carefully as she can. Yet again, Victoria's hands are there, guiding her. "Please don't say months, Doc. Please."

"Not this side of Christmas" is all Kim can offer. "I'll know more when I get an ultrasound. I'll need to get you to move a bit for me, too, check the hip and knee involvement. That's going to hurt like a bitch, Anna, so I'm saying sorry now."

"Great." It comes out as a groan.

"Soon as we have it diagnosed, I'll give you a shot of the good stuff, okay? Just hang in there. I don't think we're looking at a grade three, so thank your lucky stars. You okay, Victoria? You look like you've got an insurance payment riding on this leg."

Victoria dismisses her with a mocking little laugh.

"She's good," Anna announces as Kim wanders off in search of her equipment. "I'm so glad she's our doc."

"Well, she hasn't killed anyone yet," Victoria agrees, kissing Anna's hand that she's holding. "I know you're in pain, but Kim doesn't seem overly worried. When I heard you just dropped, I thought…"

"I'm sorry." Anna reaches for Victoria's face, stroking her cheek with her thumb. "This can't be easy for you. I can call Jess. Don't feel like you have to stay."

"Don't be ridiculous. I'm not leaving you here alone."

"People are going to think you like me, you know."

Victoria kisses Anna's hand again in response. "So let them. What the hell do I care?" It's not quite an admission, but Anna's going to take it anyway.

∞∞∞

The painkillers knock Anna loopy, so it's good to see her sleeping it off. Trapped beneath her on the sofa, at least through choice, Victoria fusses with loose strands of Anna's honeyed hair, half watching some Netflix documentary about somewhere she doesn't recognize.

"Huh?" Anna awakes with a less than dignified snort, lifting her head off Victoria's lap. "What...?"

"You hurt your hamstring," Victoria explains in her most soothing voice. "You're going to miss a few weeks, but it's not too severe. We're back at your apartment, and it turns out you snore."

"No, I don't!" Anna protests, sitting up with some difficulty. She knocks a half-melted ice pack off as she moves.

Eventually, with Victoria's help, Anna is up and on her way to the bathroom. She's awkward with the crutches, but everyone is on the first day or two.

"Hungry?" Victoria asks on her return.

Anna shakes her head. "Can I go to bed? What time is it? Will you stay?"

"I can stay," Victoria agrees. "Let's get you comfortable, then I've got a few things to do before I join you."

"You're so pretty." Anna sighs, as though carrying the knowledge around has been exhausting her. "And you were very nice to me in PT. Kim was making faces about it when you weren't looking, you know."

"Was she now?" Sawyer would pay for that in the morning.

"Victoria?"

"Yes?"

"Am I out of the ballet?"

"What?" Victoria moves closer to her on the sofa, taking Anna by the shoulders. "Why would you think that?"

"Well, I'm pretty busted up." Anna points to her leg. "And Delphine was out sick today. Never mind if Irina will be fit..."

"Delphine is in San Francisco auditioning for her big sister's job. She thinks I don't know this, of course, but it's a poorly kept secret. Irina, you leave her to me. She can dance on hot coals if she puts her mind to it. And you were only in the corps for *Nutcracker*. We have swings to put in for you."

"But what if—"

"You'll be back in plenty of time, and we've already laid the groundwork for *Gala Performance*. In a way, it's almost a good thing. People who've noticed you will look for you in the corps. Now, they won't get a glimpse again until *Gala*. Scarcity, exclusivity. It all sells, in its way."

"That's kinda cynical." Anna accepts Victoria's offered arm, and they hobble through to the bedroom. This apartment and injury seem destined for one another.

"I need to go out for an hour," Victoria says when Anna is in bed. "Do you need anything?"

"Ice cream?" Anna ventures, clearly forgetting there are at least three tubs in the freezer already.

"Sure," Victoria says.

It's all getting a little too domestic, and she wants to flee before her skin starts to itch. All the same, the moment she closes the door behind her, she wants to go back and make sure Anna is okay. Pathetic, really.

The car ride downtown is uneventful, and Victoria steels herself for heading into the damn club again. Must Rick spend his time in such tacky places? Just as before, she's shown to a back room by a hostess who pities Victoria for having passed thirty.

"Rick—" she starts as soon as he enters, but he's in no mood.

"Another one, Victoria? What the hell is going on?"

"You really want to talk to me about injuring my dancers? Tread very fucking carefully, Richard. You could have ended her damn career, long before those great reviews for *Pagodas*."

He doesn't sit this time, doesn't offer her a drink. Rick is pacing, like he actually cares about something for a change. Money really must be tight around the company. Maybe he's finally having to put his hand in his own pocket.

"I've only just convinced Lilith Gresham not to sue, since she doesn't have a leg to stand on. Now your prodigy is out? Are you letting them warm-up properly? Are you working them too hard? Which is it, Victoria?"

"I'm doing everything I'm supposed to. Morgan is a preexisting weakness. Anna was too enthusiastic in her *développé*. It happens, Rick."

"Don't fuck this up for us," he warns, waving that finger again like she's some recalcitrant child. She has a good mind to steal his watch, the only thing in the room heavy enough to knock him out with one swing. "I want to know the minute Sawyer signs her back into the studio, and I *will* be supervising as I see fit. We clear?"

"You'll continue to stay the hell out of my way," Victoria responds with an eye roll. As come-to-Jesus talks go, this isn't her first. "We have a deal. Interfere and I'll walk tomorrow. Can't get Liza while she's still under contract."

"I'm beginning to think you don't even want to stay. Count yourself lucky. If she was available, or Meredith Prince would leave London—"

"Like you could get Meredith." Victoria can't believe the arrogance of him. "Anna will be fit and ready, so will Delphine and Irina. They'll all have understudies, who hopefully won't be needed. That's all I can guarantee right now."

"Fantastic." Rick's voice is dripping with sarcasm. He finally sits, and as he scrubs at his face, Victoria can see he's exhausted. "How the hell did it come to this? Glass in someone's shoe? Plotting with that bitch Liza? I don't want to be that guy, Vicki."

"You stopped trusting me," Victoria says. "I know what I'm doing. And don't ever move against me, or Anna, again. Or I'll make you regret it. Way worse than some broken glass."

"I was wrong to hold back on her. She was really something, as the prince."

"She was."

"Was Delphine as good as you were in London?"

"No, but who could be?" Victoria isn't being immodest. She spent a decade chasing that performance in everything she did. "We're getting divorced, you and I. This is the part where we grin and bear it. For the children. Come the summer, one way or another, we'll be done."

"You don't mean that."

"Try me." Victoria moves toward the door, expecting him to stop her. He lets her walk out, though, and for the first time she really thinks he'll let her walk from the company, too.

◯◯◯

It's late when Victoria comes into the bedroom, smelling like rain and Anna's toothpaste.

"Hey," she murmurs, pulling her head up from the pillow. "You came back."

"I have an apartment of my own. I can always cross the road if you're so mystified by my presence."

Not happy, then. Victoria gets snappish quicker than anyone Anna's ever met. Maybe she should dislike it. Instead, she just wants to kick the person who pissed Victoria off in the first place.

"Sorry," Victoria adds a moment later, sinking back into her own pillow. "How's the pain?"

"Fine," Anna lies. "I've never been out for more than a couple of days before. It's going to be weird."

"You get used to it. Just don't fall into the daytime-television trap. I had nightmares about *Oprah* for months."

"I can't imagine you having nightmares. Nothing scares you."

"Richard is trying his best to," Victoria admits, and she sounds smaller than Anna has ever heard. "He's not happy. Again."

"Because I hurt myself. I'm sorry. You don't need this extra stress."

"I'm fine." It's clearly Victoria's turn to lie, and she's not subtle about it.

In the dim light of the bedroom, Anna can barely make out her face.

"Just focus on getting back. It helps to have a goal. That's what got me through those first weeks."

"You thought you'd go back to dancing?" Anna feels the hidden blocks shifting as things finally shift into place. She's getting the whole story this time. They're both too worn down for anything else. "Even though you knew how bad it was when you landed?"

"My surgeon was an optimist. Despite my mood, I was desperate enough to believe him. The surgeries had gotten so advanced, he thought he could get anyone back on their feet."

"Then why didn't he? Why aren't you back dancing?"

"They were so caught up on the injury, they didn't realize the pain I was talking about was higher in my leg. I was still out of it from the anesthetic, then the painkillers. I couldn't make them understand. It was only a junior doctor looking in the wrong place who stumbled across it. An infarction in the muscle. I was lucky not to lose the leg."

"Wow." Anna sits up. "That's horrible."

"Yes, it was." Victoria glares up at her, that much evident even without Anna seeing clearly. "They caught it just in time, but it ruined the muscle I needed to support my knee while it recovered. It's all water under the bridge, Anna. I don't even know why I'm telling you now."

"Because you know how much I care about you?"

"You're sweet." Victoria pulls her closer. "But I need this win for me. One way or another, I'm going to have to move on at some point. If I don't make a splash I'm going to have to go and teach kids in some backwater."

"Yeah, right." Anna kisses her. "Even if you wanted to, they'd be the luckiest baby bunheads in the world."

"Flattery will get you everywhere." Victoria relaxes for the first time since she got into bed.

"You know, if I wasn't scared to move my leg right now, I'd…"

"I know." Victoria laughs and kisses her on the forehead. "Get some sleep. Kim will want to talk recovery with you tomorrow."

"Great," Anna says with a grumble. "I'm glad you're here, though."

"Anna, I'm not good at this…stuff. I'm apologizing now for all the ways in which I'm going to let you down."

"Don't," Anna says, hushing her. "I don't expect you to play nurse. I've got friends, family. It's not all on you because we slept together a few times."

"Oh." Victoria almost sounds disappointed. "Well, good then. Good night."

"Night." Anna waits until Victoria's breathing slows, and she falls into sleep before reaching for her phone. She hasn't told Jess what happened yet, and that's going to take more than a couple of texts.

CHAPTER 37

"Well, it's the walking dead!" Delphine shouts across the studio floor. "Welcome back, Gale. It's about time you did some damn work around here."

Anna strides in, beaming so hard that the smile hurts her face. It's so good to be back that she feels a little high. Two weeks cooped up at home, another two under Marcia's thumb in Dubuque, and the intense physical therapy have left her desperate to just slip on her pointe shoes and dance.

"You can't keep the audiences happy without me, Delphine?" She feels five pounds lighter just sitting down to sew up a fresh pair of shoes.

Irina enters then, walking as freely as Anna. Instead of her usual position by the far wall, she comes to sit next to Anna's open bag. "*Malenkaya.*"

"Irina."

"You're finally back."

"You know I was actually injured, right?"

"You didn't even break anything," Irina says before dealing with her own shoes. It's only when they're all up and moving that Victoria finally appears.

"Ladies," she greets them, drifting close enough to Anna on the way past to skim her bare shoulder with a finger. "Welcome to crunch time."

"Oh please, at the Bolshoi we mounted *Swan Lake* in four days. Missing a week of rehearsal on this is nothing." Irina waves her hand. "Well, not for Delphine or me."

"Very nice," Anna says. "No sympathy for the newbie."

"We did warn you," Delphine gets in on the teasing. "This is big-girl pants only, this little club. Keep up or get out. We've both got our eye on a corps member to replace you if not."

"Yes, ones more used to the pressure," Irina confirms. "What, you thought you were irreplaceable, little one?"

Victoria brings their fun to an end. "Leave her alone, you witches."

Anna is glad of it. She knows it comes with the territory, but it's been a long, hard slog to get back and get fit. It's tough not to feel a little sensitive, when the thought of watching from the cheap seats instead of performing was a real possibility. "Anna, you've done your modified warm-up already?"

"Yes, Kim kept on my ass about it," Anna says. "Don't worry, I don't actually *want* to be injured again."

"Just be careful." Her smile is fond.

It's the last glimpse of anything kind Anna sees for the next three hours, because Victoria puts them through their paces like ballet boot camp. They've hardly seen each other all month, apart from a very enthusiastic reunion when Anna returned from Dubuque.

Victoria's been slammed getting the rest of the season into shape, and Anna's been trapped in a cycle of intense PT and rest.

Anna had big plans for tonight. By the time Victoria's session comes to an end, Anna's not sure she's going to make it home without curling up and napping on the street.

Irina walks her out, hobbling a little in sympathy.

"It's good for us," Irina assures her. "Like a plunge pool after the sauna."

"Oh God, can someone dunk me in ice water? That sounds amazing."

Victoria follows them out. "You're absolutely right, Anna. I'll have Kim draw up the ice bath. Irina, how does that strike you?"

"Like I'd rather die. I've done my time in the cold, Vicki. You should be careful about giving your girlfriend a cold shower."

"Ice bath," Victoria corrects.

"Oh, that means the girlfriend part is legit?" Delphine joins in. "Took you long enough." She fishes in her bag for a moment. "Can I get an official date? There's a betting pool, and I plan on rigging it so I win."

"Contrary to popular belief, and the graffiti in the third-floor bathrooms, this is not in fact a high school." Victoria shuts them down. "Anna, come with me. Let them speculate."

Anna follows her, taking Victoria's offered hand before shooting a smile back at Delphine and Irina. That's one way to officially break the news. She's on quite the high until she discovers the ice bath is neither a joke nor a euphemism.

Stripped to sports bra and shorts, she shivers before even getting in the damn thing. Kim isn't around today; one of her techs is doing the honors.

"Come on." Victoria sounds encouraging. "The sooner you do it, the sooner I can take you for a late lunch."

Anna hoists herself into the tub, one-third full with cold water from the faucet. It's a shock, but no worse than running a blast of cold in the shower on mornings where she can't wake up fully. Having been so overheated from the strenuous rehearsal, it's almost a comfort after the initial hard slap of cold. Then the tech dumps the first sack of ice in, and Anna hisses through her teeth. He's moving on to a second and a third in short order, the temperature plummeting as Anna sits in it.

"I hate you," she tells Victoria, teeth chattering. "We'd better be going to, like, my favorite restaurant for lunch."

When the tech moves away, after checking the temperature display, Victoria leans in to whisper in Anna's ear. "I'm taking you home for lunch. Any objections?"

The shiver down Anna's spine is far more pleasurable than the ones caused by cold. Victoria presses a gentle kiss to Anna's cheek before going back to her phone.

"Can you read me something?" Anna asks. "No way I can make fifteen minutes without a distraction." She's half tempted to jump out now, but looking weak in front of Victoria is not an option.

"What could I possibly read that's of interest?"

"I don't know, whatever you're reading. Or the politics section of the *Times*. Or the Apple Terms and Conditions. I just…like the sound of your voice."

"I suppose there are decent acoustics in here." Victoria straightens on her stool. "Liza opened *Giselle* last night. Shall we check her reviews?"

Her voice was too high, too light. Victoria must have already read them and found them lacking. Normally Anna would discourage pettiness, but she likes to see Victoria smile.

"Go on, then."

"'In a role she has long since outgrown, Wade brings only the slightest of her star power to the role. Her performance is rote and reluctant, as though only performing as a favor, and for someone she doesn't like all that much.'"

"That's mean," Anna notes. "If that was my review, I would have cried."

"Don't worry, she's probably boiling the critic's bunny as we speak. Liza doesn't take these things lying down. I almost like that about her." Victoria's smile is cruel, but still annoyingly attractive.

"Please tell me it's been fifteen?"

"Not yet." Victoria checks her phone display again. "But not long now."

⌒૦෨⌒

Victoria is absolutely getting soft. Sitting in on an ice bath, reading for comfort. Confirming to her past and present prima that she's seeing Anna. Despite Victoria's bravado about not being cowed into secrecy, she's been somewhat relieved that no one seems to have noticed anything amiss. She has her favorites, of course, and each season requires a certain amount of handholding.

While idle gossip and bitching runs off her like water off a duck's back, Victoria feels preemptively defensive that any of it should be about Anna. That would be unacceptable, especially if they accuse her success of being simple nepotism. It's a worry, one Victoria can't shake, that her selfish desire for the other woman may taint what could be a flourishing career.

Then again, Victoria never was much good at denying herself what she wants. She's so used to going for it after being told no, after being pushed aside or hurt when it matters most, that she doesn't really know if she could stop now.

Getting Anna out of the ice and into warm clothing for a spell adds to the frustration that's building. Victoria didn't object when Anna went home to her foster mother for two weeks, letting her provide the TLC while Anna slowly recovered. Truthfully Victoria should barely have noticed the absence, with the hundred daily annoyances of her role.

It hasn't helped that they've seen so little of each other since Anna returned to the city. Apart from one night that started with Victoria joking about their complementary limps and ended with a broken slat on the headboard, time together has been scarce.

Which is how it has to be. Only it's nowhere close to the end of the working day and Victoria is skipping out with a freshly defrosted Anna for a lunch that's the flimsiest pretext for sex Victoria's ever been party to.

"Oh, I thought I'd never be warm again," Anna says after a long exhale as they step out into the midday sunlight. "Thank you, you know."

"For doing my job?"

"No." Anna leans in to kiss her on the mouth. "You know what for."

And yes, Victoria has to admit she does.

⌢⊙⊙⌢

Stage rehearsal is upon them before Anna knows what's hit her. The work has been relentless, and she's still concerned her own performance is dwarfed by the work Delphine and Irina do in their sections, but Victoria seems pleased even on the days when Anna wants to go again and again out of sheer frustration.

It's also time for the return of Michelle, her camera, and her attitude, since the *Times* is running a spread on this "cultural event of a lifetime." Just seeing that phrase in the press release makes Anna dizzy. How is it possible those words refer to something featuring her?

She's fanning herself with a copy of the release when Irina comes upon her in the wings.

"Trouble? The theater is not hot, not without the lights."

"I know, Irina, it's just…holy shit, you know?"

"Yes, this shit is quite holy," Irina says with a snort, clearly amusing herself. "But hasn't anyone told you how to deal?"

"Uh, I guess? Picture the audience naked?"

"*Blin*, no. Have you seen the regulars?" Irina performs a full-body shudder. "I do not wish to know where the cobwebs are on those relics. Tell me, Inessa picked a ballet school for you young, yes?"

It's a jolt to hear Irina saying Inessa's name correctly, the same emphasis and intonation as Anna's mother herself used. "She did."

"When did you first perform for an audience? Three? Four?"

"Six. Does that matter?"

"No, but it was a small place, this performance? A barn, a school, the ballet school itself?"

"At school, yeah. We did this cute version of *Sleeping Beauty*, but the boys didn't want to kiss any of the girls and…"

Irina's glare silences her. Clearly, there is a point to be made.

"This time on stage, did you cry? Did you freeze? Or did you wave to Mama and laugh with your little friends? Maybe show off a little, ways you had not planned?"

"How did you know?"

"A lucky guess. That's who you take on stage. The precious show-off princess who wants the audience to love her. Leave the millennial who makes bad choices in the dressing room. You go out there as this, nothing can touch you. Not the injuries, not the politics of the Bolshoi, not the old ladies with the cobwebs."

"That's good advice, thank you." Anna decides to go for the hug.

Irina allows it, albeit with a long-suffering sigh. "This last week is long. Save some enthusiasm for each day. Some of us don't have much to go around."

"Of course." Anna reins herself in one more time. "They're just dress rehearsals. I can be chill."

Irina raises an eyebrow, which is all the statement she needs to make about that.

∞∞

The system is working, almost too well. Victoria doesn't trust it. Everyone is fit and on time. Her tech requests have all been achieved. Is it the novelty of the staging? The fact they're relieved there's no behemoth this year, no *Swan Lake* or *Giselle* to accommodate? She jokes around with her crew and has coffee brought in for them to keep everyone sharp.

Susan and her team roll in the rails, with principal costumes on a rack of their own. There's the usual scramble, as though each set isn't labelled for each person to take their turn. Kids desperate to play dress-up, they never lose it.

It's pleasing that Anna knows enough to hang back, making small talk over stretches. There's a dignity in the way she conducts herself sometimes, something faintly regal behind that soft and bumbling exterior. Every time Victoria thinks she has Anna down to the last layer, she develops some new interesting facet.

It's deeply annoying and somehow completely fascinating.

The seamstresses are following dancers around, removing pins they were too impatient to notice. By the time the corps settles down, all three principal ballerinas are being dressed in the wings. Victoria shifts her chair to get a slightly better view. Irina is already zipped into her flame red, ruffling her tutu and cracking some joke about communism that Victoria doesn't hear all the words for, but she smiles at the gist.

Delphine steps away next, resplendent in ivory silk and lace. The cut is magnificent on her, some of Susan's most creative work. It's a tutu, a ballet dress, and a piece of sculpture in one. They'll have to seriously watch her arm placement over the remaining rehearsals.

But they're not the reason Victoria is holding her breath. She weathered every suggestion from Lady Liberty to Ronald McDonald, but her American ballerina will be a more subtle statement, a shift in the paradigm for this reinterpretation. People look at Anna, glance at her really, and assume the same banal things Victoria did at first. They think it's all about that easy smile and big blue eyes. They don't linger to see what simmers beneath.

She expects Anna to slink out onto the main stage, avoiding the interested onlookers. Even having seen the unexpected bursts of confidence, in bed and out of it, Victoria knows that Anna is still learning how to be in the spotlight.

Well, it's one hell of a learning curve, because she struts down the center of the stage like a runway model, drawing gasps and interested murmurs from every side. The look isn't complete without the makeup, of course, but the leather corset over a soft-wave black leather tutu is beyond stunning.

Victoria hadn't been confident Susan could pull it off exactly as described, but it gives milk-and-honey Anna the wild-child look the part so badly needs. She'll have the pointe shoes in black, too, and the fishnet tights if it isn't overkill.

She looks across at Victoria, where she's sitting just in front of the footlights, and hell if Anna doesn't actually smolder.

When Victoria speaks up to call them to order, her mouth is dry.

Everyone's looking at Anna anyway, and she's sure at least some of them are as turned on as Victoria herself. Not that it matters, with hours of blocking and rehearsal ahead of them. They may just be a little late in leaving tonight, because there's no way in hell Victoria can wait for the privacy of an apartment.

"Ladies, gentlemen," she calls more clearly this time. "Let us begin."

CHAPTER 38

They're not in costume for this photoshoot, which Anna is faintly grateful for. She loves the leather, even if the corset takes some outside assistance to lace up. Last night she wasn't lacking for a volunteer to get it undone at least. Victoria seems more than happy with how it turned out, judging by the broken chair and ripped curtain in Anna's dressing room anyway.

"Did we settle on a theme?" Anna asks Delphine as they sip at their coffees, watching the frenetic activity around them. "I still say *Charlie's Angels* would have been hilarious."

"I'm not rocking seventies hair for anyone," Delphine says. "Although you'd just need to let your hair down, right, Irina?"

"This curl is all natural," Irina sasses back. "How was Kevin? You didn't say."

"Does everyone know?" Delphine groans. "God forbid I try and be respectful."

"Victoria knows," Anna supplies helpfully. "But she doesn't seem to mind, so I think you're good."

"Just as well." Delphine applies a little lip balm, although they'll all be getting made up before long. "I got the offer last night. Three years, prima. My own headline tour to China and Europe."

"Delphine!" Anna squeals, pulling her into a hug. For a moment, she feels it, that knife twist of jealousy. Something about this sudden promotion has her hungry for more, even if she knows she's not ready. "That's amazing. Well done!"

"It'll be nice to finally go home," Delphine admits. "I've missed San Francisco way more than I could tell anyone. The only hitch in the plan is Gabriel."

"Kevin won't take him back as principal?" Irina seizes on the problem with a derisive little snort. "Figures."

"It might not be a race thing..." Delphine trails off. "Yeah, I know. We have to talk it out before I accept, but push comes to shove, I'd expect him to go in my position. We never wanted to do the 'settling for any old company just to be together' crap."

"You're still young," Irina says. "There comes a point where having the right person means the right company is negotiable. I think now I would retire rather than try these minor leagues of yours."

"That sounds serious." Anna's bursting with excitement on Jess's behalf. "Is my sister really your right person? Irina, that's huge."

"Somebody tamed Irina?" Delphine gives a low whistle. "What the hell are they putting in the water in Dubuque?"

"Whistling, Delphine? Really?" Victoria looks as impatient as ever.

She left Anna's apartment hours before, for mysterious errands, the details of which she wasn't inclined to share. "Has this circus got a ringmaster, or were you all going to stand in a corner all day?"

"We were waiting for you, Vicki." Irina makes the reasonable point. "And your Michelle won't tell us what it is you signed off on. I don't do pantomime."

"Will you all relax? When have I ever done anything except in the very best of taste? We'll keep it simple—three muses, gold leaves in the hair, gauzy togas, you get the idea."

"Not exactly an original," Delphine says with a huff, but she seems pleased enough. "Still, give the people what they want, right? Where does that leave you, oh wise ballet mistress?"

"On a throne, naturally," Victoria answers, pushing past Delphine to take hold of Anna's wrist. "A word, darling?"

Anna felt as though a big red panic button had been pressed, but she follows Victoria to a quieter spot on the huge floor of the converted warehouse they're working out of.

"Good morning?" Anna ventures, hoping she doesn't sound too nervous. "Is everything okay?"

"Fine, fine." Victoria brushes off the concern with a flicker of her fingers. "Since we're such a poorly kept secret, I thought we might incorporate a few more intimate shots. Michelle sketched out some poses that certainly appealed. Only if you're okay with it. This is your career, Anna. Linking yourself to me can be a great thing. But it can be terrible too."

"Like Delphine and Gabriel," Anna says. "If I got an offer from another company, for example, you'd expect me to take it. To work with other people, learn different things. Victoria, are you breaking up with me?"

"On the contrary," Victoria says with a darting kiss. "I'm trying to take this little liaison of ours seriously, and protect you in the process. It's one thing to be indiscreet around the center, but another entirely with the media. If we come out as a couple, that's going to linger. It'll be mentioned probably for the rest of our careers, whether we stay together or not."

"I might look like an opportunist." Anna is familiar with the argument by now. "Or I might look like someone lucky enough to be chosen by one of the most picky women ever. For dancing and for all the other stuff. Why would I be ashamed of that? Don't you know how proud I am to be with you?"

"Well, I've lost a little of my luster lately. I'd understand if you wanted to insulate yourself."

"You can go back out there and tell Michelle I'll do anything short of nudes," Anna says, summoning all her courage. She even stands straighter, chest puffing out. "Heck, I'll even do those if they're artistic enough."

"Heck, Anna? *Really?*" Victoria kisses her more sincerely this time before shaking her head. "Come on, before you destroy my hard-ass reputation entirely."

Anna risks a playful smack as they walk back. "Seems plenty hard to me."

"I need a penalty system for puns." Victoria sighs, but she doesn't let go of Anna's hand as they rejoin the group.

⌒♾️⌒

It's a different dynamic now, far removed from the intimacy of two of them plus ribbons. The backdrops are bleak and industrial, all the better to offset the diaphanous dresses the dancers are draped in. Paired with stiletto heels, hair coaxed into three different lengths and colors of glossy curls, they're a regular *Midsummer Night's Dream*. A ballet Victoria had grand intentions of reworking next season.

"Can't tempt you into something more risqué, Victoria?" Michelle approaches with her usual predatory skill, pouncing at the last possible second.

Victoria glances at the significant vee of skin exposed by her fitted black tuxedo, the one with nothing under it but some illuminating powder applied by a bored makeup artist. The pants are leather, reminding her pleasantly of Anna's costume. Where the girls have nude heels to not distract from their dresses, Victoria's spiked heels are shiny patent black.

Red lips, red nails—it's a little overdone, but if someone has to play devil to these angels, it may as well be she. This season may be a war to keep her job, keep her place, but it's the most alive she's felt in over a decade.

Which may be more about the laughing blonde swishing her gossamer-thin skirt around than anything else, but Victoria will take it.

The flashbulbs are unbearable as always, and the heat builds up fast under the industrial-grade lighting. Not quite as intense as being back onstage, but the prop throne they have for Victoria is more intimidating than hilarious at least.

Anna bends forward to whisper, "They finally put the queen on a throne, huh?" and Victoria's glad she's already sitting down.

With so many onlookers, Michelle keeps it professional. She has each of the ballerinas in turn pulled aside for some portraits and solo shots that Victoria can already tell will be dazzling. She's glad she made a deal for rights to any unused photos when bartering with the *Times*. They might make for some interesting banners on opening night, strung from the lampposts outside the center's main entrance. She pulls out her phone and fires off a message to Kelly, telling her to arrange as much.

"Okay, muses." Michelle is mocking just a little. "Let's show your director some love, huh? Pretend you can stand her."

They recreate a variety of classic poses, and as the camaraderie builds, hands get to wandering. Anna and Delphine get more daring as the camera keeps clicking.

"Delphine, Irina, we've got a bit to do with you both in those second costumes on your rails for the retrospective. Anna, if you could switch out of yours? It's you and Victoria up next. We good on what we talked about last night?"

"Last night, huh?" Anna asks with a grumble, but she's clearly teasing. She knows exactly where Victoria was for most of last night.

The second set of outfits are up to Michelle, Victoria agreeing as long as she doesn't have to change hers. She sits farther back on the throne, which is probably just an office chair run through a nearby art school, but it's damn comfortable all the same. Her knee is twinging, so she kicks that leg up and over the arm, relieved when nothing appears to crack or fall off.

"Is that an invitation?" Anna breathes the question on her return, barely audible despite the boldness behind it.

Victoria looks at her own position, rather louche all things considered. In response, she quirks an eyebrow at Anna, in a red minidress that's all scooped front and barely any back. The faintest halter straps hold it in place, and the makeup has been changed from angelic to downright sultry.

Victoria can almost hear the tango music playing. The colors, the style, the sizzle and crackle of tension in the air. She hasn't danced a tango in fifteen years, and if not for the way Anna comes to stand between Victoria's parted legs, she'd be on her feet and suggesting it. The moment their orbits coincide, the lights are flashing and the camera shutter is merrily whirring away.

"Help the new girl get across her lap, then," Michelle directs via her intern, who is completely star-struck and hesitates to touch Anna, let alone Victoria.

The concept is simple enough, recreating some classic ballet moves but using the chair for leverage so Victoria can achieve the lift without doing it herself. She doesn't much care, since every variation seems to involve part of Anna pressed against her, the little huffs of sexual frustration from her making Victoria's hands want to wander. Touching as much as she dares, she gets a warning nip of teeth at her collarbone from Anna, who looks like she's seconds away from ignoring the audience they have and grinding herself against Victoria's thigh.

"Control," Victoria murmurs, gripping Anna's hips a little tighter.

They gather themselves, Anna's face drawing close for a dangerous moment, but their lips barely graze as she moves away, changing position. She ends up in the splits, legs balanced on the arms of the throne, putting her profile alongside Victoria's own. The instinctive grip on the back of Anna's neck is possessive. It presses their faces together, side by side, and when they both stare down the barrel of the lens, she suspects they have their cover shot.

"What else do you need?" Anna asks Michelle. "Only, this chair is killing my legs, and I just got my hamstring back in working order."

"We're good." Michelle is already flipping through images on the screen of her Nikon, smirking at her own genius. "Unless Victoria talked you into those nudes."

"Behave, Michelle." Victoria helps Anna back to standing, then looks at her. "Legs okay? You can sit out this afternoon if you're tight."

"I'm fine now," Anna assures her. "I'll go get changed. Think they'll let me keep the dress? Might rock for the opening night party."

"I'll square it with Michelle," Victoria promises.

⌒◠◡◠

Victoria is swept away by Kelly the moment they return, so Anna heads for the roof with an improvised lunch of fruit and nuts, probably more suitable for a woodland creature than a ballerina, but she works with what she's got. The nerves keep building this time, way more than they ever did for *The Prince of the Pagodas*. Playing against type there gave her a certain insurance against messing it up. If she couldn't quite pull it off, the failing would be her gender and not her personal talent.

This production seems so much more about her, and the one thing she can't seem to summon is the confidence to stride out and compete with Irina and Delphine as their supposed equal. Yes, the technical dancing is coming together well, and the costuming is beyond anything she ever dreamed. No matter how hard she tries, though, next to those accomplished women, Anna still feels like the new girl, as though she should be raising her hand before she speaks.

"Thought I'd find you here," Ethan says as he approaches. "Wow, that is one sad lunch. Did you go vegan or something?"

"No, I actually enjoy food. This is just what was nearest." Anna smiles at him. "Heard you're up for principal on the tour, Ethan. Well done."

"It's not for sure yet." He squirms under the attention for a moment. "You all ready for your big moment? I know *Pagodas* was a big deal, but this…"

"Victoria thinks I'm ready." Anna tries to shrug it off. "The weird part is, I think so too? I don't know, it just feels good up there lately. I don't want to jinx it."

"You won't." He fishes a candy bar out of his backpack. "Here. Your lunch is just too depressing."

"Thank you," Anna says, getting up to hug him. "And not just for this. For being my first friend here, and for having my back."

"Just like you've had mine," Ethan replies. "I know you've put in a good word for me, more than once."

"What are friends for, right?" They end the hug at last, and Anna picks up after herself. "Okay, let's go dance."

Chapter 39

Somehow, they fall into the habit of spending every night together at Victoria's. It's only when Anna detours one evening to pick up clean clothes and falls asleep on her own bed that they spend a night apart. Victoria has an early crew meeting, so has to rush in without their now-routine morning coffee together too. It's stupid how much she resents both of those losses.

They meet in the lobby right after warm-up. It's too public, and every sound echoes. That doesn't stop Anna from talking over what Victoria is saying to her at first, before they both pull up and laugh a little at their shared overreaction to a brief separation.

"You first," Victoria insists. "But not here."

"Victoria?" Anna doesn't move, as though her feet are fused with the floor. She looks so anguished, it must be something awful.

It's no lie for Victoria to say that her stomach drops in that moment. Strangely, in this last moment before she knows for sure, all Victoria can think is *I don't want her to be upset.*

"Just hold on a moment, Anna. We'll go sit outside. No one can overhear us with the traffic."

"Okay, but I sort of feel like I might burst, so we should do it now."

"Then tell me." Victoria doesn't want her to, even as she's brisk about walking them outside. As long as the dice is in the air, the currents beneath it can still shift, still affect what number it lands on. She's never been a gambler, but she's willing to start now.

Anna takes a deep breath, closes her eyes, and says it. "I love you." She's barely able to contain her smile. "Oh, there's a *bunch* of other stuff, and we'll get to that. But I do. Head-over-heels, dizzier-than-thirty-two-*fouettés*, totally in love with you. And it's okay if you're not in love with me, but I couldn't wait another minute. I didn't want you not to know."

"Am I dying?" is the only response Victoria can summon for that kind of earnestness. They're gripping each other's forearms, and the first to let go will surely guarantee that the other falls. Outside their building of glass and concrete and wood that's going to feature in any description of both their careers now, Anna has said what Victoria didn't expect.

Or perhaps she did on some level, because when Anna's exasperated little pout forms, Victoria wants to chase it away with the very thing she's been trying not to notice.

"Well, I love you too. I thought that was a given when I let you stay the night."

"Seriously?" Anna clamps a hand over her mouth to stifle a laugh. "Since then? Wow, you are quite the romantic."

"Does the when really matter?" Now it's Victoria's turn to be exasperated, but Anna's sweet kiss melts most of that away in an instant. "Can we please talk affairs of state now? Sands are shifting, Anna, and we are not going down with them."

"One more kiss," Anna insists, and it's not like Victoria wants anything less than that herself.

∽◌◌◌

"Wow, there's no good way out of this, is there?" Anna is asking.

Victoria is listening intently, but her attention is on the traffic coming and going in front of them. Her sunglasses are in place, and to anyone passing they're just two women on a stone bench chatting. "Even if everything goes perfect—truly flawless in every way—it's still going to be crappy for you to work under him."

"I can't work for a boss who hates me." Victoria sounds so tired that Anna's heart breaks a little. "I can't direct if my head is always on the chopping block. Ruins the sightlines. Nobody pushes Victoria Ford around, not like this. I'll coach for the Thanksgiving parades before I'll let him tell me what to do."

She gathers herself, feeling stronger with every word. "I don't know where I'm going to end up, but you'll always have a job with me, Anna. Regardless of whether you stay in love with me or not. We make a great team, in both ways."

"We do. But what if it's Liza put in charge and she does ask me to stay on? Is that betraying you?"

"No. *No*." Victoria is insistent, turning to face Anna. "There are people who've stabbed me in the back, but keeping your career going doesn't make you one of them. I'm probably going to have to leave New York, though."

"We could do long distance," Anna says. "Until there was space for me, maybe."

"I'm not going to ask you for that right now." Victoria pulls off her sunglasses and kisses Anna's cheek. "We know how we feel, but there are other considerations."

"Then we wait for new facts. We were lucky enough to find each other, weren't we? That gives me hope."

"It gives *me* heartburn." Victoria rubs lightly at her chest. "I'm going to have David take rehearsal today. There's a lot I need to put in place. I know I don't have to ask, but—"

"I won't tell a soul. This is our business, nobody else's."

She likes the way Anna says *our*. "I'd like to find the way where we get to stay together."

"Me too." Anna goes for a one-armed hug. "This has been one hell of a season, hasn't it?"

"I should have known the minute I laid eyes on you. Once-in-a-lifetime girls don't show up in a calm season, do they? Now come on. Can't have principals late for rehearsal. What will the corps members think?"

"That I'm off banging the boss somewhere, probably," Anna teases, and it's their first genuine laugh of the afternoon. "I really did mean it, you know."

"Me too," Victoria says, withholding her eye roll. "See you tonight?"

"Wouldn't be anywhere else."

∞

Anna follows in Victoria's wake as she marches from the car to the front of the Metropolitan Center, barely a hint of a limp in Victoria's stride. She doesn't want to speculate, but Anna suspects an extra pill or two may have been popped before coffee this morning.

There's a bike messenger waiting on the stairs, still half-asleep. Victoria hands over the envelope, which Anna knows contains a brief, pointed letter on Victoria's monogrammed stationery. She fishes a twenty-dollar tip from her purse, and that wakes up Bike Boy in a hurry.

"Have this in Richard Westin's hands within half an hour, understood?" Victoria tells him.

Anna wants to smile. There's no time limit on this, but Victoria will have her drama. It's in her choice of heeled boots and sweeping black pashmina in today's ensemble. Anna is very much into it. So into it she almost made them late by trying to thoroughly rumple that flawless look.

"You're really doing this," Anna says, watching the messenger clip a corner in his haste.

She hopes he makes it to Rick's apartment alive. Anna already has the page on her phone to search for company vacancies across the US, not knowing if she'll be a casualty of this internal strife or not.

"Jump before you're pushed. In love, war, and *pas de deux*." Victoria is excited by it, at least. Where most people avoid conflict, Victoria is fueled by it in ways Anna doesn't particularly want to explore. "See you at semi-dress, darling."

The kiss doesn't linger, but Anna's lips tingle all the way to the locker room just the same.

∽∽∽

Anna watches from the stage for Victoria to come in, getting edgy when she doesn't show. Three minutes after rehearsal officially starts, David comes in, clapping his hands for attention.

"You get me today. Let's run it from the top, show me what you've got."

It's a strange ballet, one where the principals do more work in holding the audience than they would usually. The corps are used mostly offstage, or in back of some scenery. Their sense of movement is an ephemeral one, and Victoria has used the physicality of their space so brilliantly in how she's staged it. Somehow a dozen plus dancers feels like a surging stage-door crowd or a baying audience.

Since Anna is on last, the first half hour after her brief introduction is a slow one. She sits in the wings, massaging the balls of her feet. David has some critique for Irina, and he doesn't flinch when she turns to hear it, stony-faced.

Next time, Irina is step-by-step perfect. They're getting close, and something special is definitely building. The atmosphere in the theater alone is crackling, and that's before a live audience.

She's imperious. Even with just basic lighting, nothing like the dramatic color and scope they'll have in the full show, Irina is like lightning as she moves. For such a tall woman, she moves with barely a sound, and Anna swears there's something unnatural that the loudest noise Irina causes is the scuffing of her soles on a landing. When Anna lands from jumps like that, the thud is audible, the sprung floor only absorbing so much kinetic energy.

It's over a few minutes later and Irina stands silent in the opposite wings, shoulders rolled back as she catches her breath. Not bad for something who could only dance on something close to morphine before the holidays. Taking time to heal has given her this extra pocket of time.

Finally, Victoria appears, but she's not alone. She walks down the center aisle with a tall, slender woman. Dark-haired and in a dress coat that's a shade too light for New York's climate this time of year. Momentarily distracted by Delphine's question about the time signature, of all things, Anna looks to see what argument is breaking out with the orchestra conductor. Apparently Delphine doesn't care for his interpretation of 6/8 time.

Only when Anna glances back to Victoria, sitting out in the main house this time instead of among the footlights, does she recognizes her companion.

That's Meredith Prince, one-time prima at Paris Opéra and lately the head of recruitment at the Royal Ballet in London. She's the only dancer Anna tried to save up enough money to go and see in Paris, having to settle for a tour performance in Boston in the end. It was worth the wait.

Not many companies would allow the competition into their rehearsal like this, so Anna can't help wondering if this is some kind of sabotage on Victoria's part. Only there wouldn't be time for Meredith to have flown in from London, not even by private jet.

Delphine has a tough time with her footwork, usually her strong point. It's a relief, because if Anna messes up in front of such a high-pressure viewing pool, it won't be quite so embarrassing. She waits for her cue, for David's attention to be on her instead.

When the moment comes, Anna steps forward, only for something quite unexpected to happen.

As she takes her careful steps, arrogant, domineering, as Victoria called for every day before now, Anna feels her shoulders settling back and her spine straightening. She lifts her chin, regal, just shy of sneering. This is her role. This is her breakout. There's a baton being passed. From Victoria, through Irina, to Anna. So many boys and girls will have seen them and chosen to follow in their satin-clad footsteps. Will Anna be someone mentioned in *Playbill* and programs in years to come? Will some eleven-year-old see her next week and apply to ballet school the very next day?

She thinks of Henri and his little girl, Yara, and makes a mental note to leave him two tickets at the box office for this show, after his enthusiastic email.

Anna is a ballerina. A principal dancer. And for the purposes of this ballet, a star. She stands in fifth position, throws a quick smile in Victoria's direction, and begins.

CHAPTER 40

Victoria knows letting Meredith into the auditorium is probably beyond the pale, but they had a wonderful year in London together, both far from home and adjusting to the British snobbery that seemed to confront them at every turn. Having her show up is just the kind of statement Victoria didn't realize she wanted to make.

So when Meredith admits to being in town on recruitment business, Victoria simply gives a knowing smile and leads her into the meat market. Clearly Meredith thinks she owes her further explanation, but Victoria isn't especially interested. Her two weeks' notice has been silently received by Rick, and now it's just a question of exactly what state she'll leave Metropolitan Ballet in. Whole and hearty, ready to evolve and progress? Or stripped for parts, shuddering to a close in a year or two?

"So—"

Victoria shushes her. It was one thing to keep talking during Delphine, but she won't risk putting Anna off while she's still relatively inexperienced.

But the change in Anna's posture is obvious right away. It's finally clicking. She isn't the misplaced corps dancer anymore. She's a principal, and she's owning it.

Part of Victoria wants to rush the stage and kiss her senseless for it. The professional part wins out, but she leads the assembled group in an uncharacteristic smattering of applause. Having smiled at her before starting, Anna gets bold enough to blow a kiss in lieu of taking a bow. Victoria allows an indulgent smile while everyone else is still too terrified to look in her direction.

"So who is it you're after?" Victoria asks Meredith as the next scene rolls on. "Delphine's got her heart set on San Francisco, and Irina might actually be retiring this time. The boys… Well, only Gabriel is worth the plane fare."

"No, silly." Meredith says with a laugh. She's always been so kind, so easily amused. There are a striking number of similarities between her and Anna, making Victoria idly wonder why she hadn't attempted to date Meredith back when she had the chance. "I'm here for you."

Victoria is incredulous. "There's no way Covent Garden want me to…what? Coach? Even for my favorite place in the world I won't take a demotion." It's a front. There could realistically come a time when that's her best chance, particularly if Rick goes all scorched earth over the resignation.

"If I were here in my actual job capacity, do you really think I'd have walked in, middle of the day? Just hoping you had time?"

"But you were in town already."

"Yes, I had a meeting. With the same people who told Rick they'd buy him out at a profit, just as soon as he got rid of you. I think he put up *some* resistance, but that stunt you pulled with the *Times* put him over the edge, darling."

"I've already resigned," Victoria starts to explain, but Meredith waves her off, flipping her long braid back over her shoulder.

"I'm not here to warn you. I would have been amazed if you weren't already two steps ahead of all this."

"I'm not as omnipotent as I'd like to think, these days. So what *is* this, Mere? A social visit?"

"You have an admirer who's a dear friend of mine. Someone I owe a great deal to. She's thinking of making some changes but can't move in any direction without the right successor in place."

"I'd say I know the feeling, but some of us are too busy jumping out of a building they want to burn down behind me."

"Victoria…Vicki…Queen of Ballet…" Meredith has been mocking that title for years, asking about lines of succession and if the crown is very heavy to wear when dancing. Anyone else would have been instantly blocked. "What would you say if I told you I have an offer for you from Paris?"

"I'd say you'd finally lost your mind. Not that it had far to go."

"Victoria, the moment I heard about trouble here, I put in a call. Olivia wanted you the year you started here, but knew there was no point competing with your history with Rick. You know she's who advocated to make you their first American prima in the first place."

"And instead they got Liza," Victoria recalls all too well. "If this is some kind of pity interview, I'd rather not waste the airfare."

"She's been watching. Heard all about the girl prince. Knows you're staking your season on a new find. The French like that, a touch of…well, the Brits would say brass balls."

"I'm sure they would." Victoria's heart is racing so hard she worries that she never looked up the symptoms of heart attacks in women.

"And it will save a fortune, with no contract to buy out. You just got even more appealing."

"I still don't want to take a step back." Victoria feels something inside her clench at even the thought of turning this down. She can't look at Anna, still on stage and listening intently to David. "But you're sweet to come and ask me in person. I'll shoot Olivia an email, let her down gently."

"Can you please stop being dense?" Meredith sounds tired. "She wants you running the show. Artistic director."

"Of the Paris Opéra Ballet?" Victoria wonders where the hell the punchline is.

"Mm-hmm," Meredith answers quite seriously. "*Qu'est-ce que tu vas dire?*"

What else can Victoria answer, when asked what is she going to say? "*Oui.*"

∞∞∞

"We're going to dinner with Meredith Prince?" Anna pours them both a glass of wine. "When?"

"After you open, don't worry. She's here for a while yet."

"But I don't get why she came to rehearsal? I mean, we don't let people from San Francisco in, so why a headhunter from London?"

"We're old friends." Victoria already sounds thoroughly bored.

Anna's trying desperately not to fixate. "So"—she comes to sit beside Victoria on the armchair, big enough for both of them—"she's not here to poach anyone?"

"Getting ideas above your station there, Gale?" Victoria is joking with her, prodding a slender finger into Anna's ribs. "Some good reviews and you think they're all coming to steal you away? I saw the difference in you today. You hold yourself like that in a few days' time and there will be offers."

"I just don't see that I'm as good as they are. What if the audience laughs?"

"Anna, some of those people haven't laughed since Nixon, and even then it was involuntary."

"There's really nothing to tell?" The voice at the back of Anna's mind says she's missing something, but she's getting tired and there's only so much awake time left to take advantage of. "Well, in that case we'd better have an early night."

∞∞∞

Anna shoots off a quick miss-you message to Victoria. They see each other in rehearsals, but Victoria's been out with all kinds of people most evenings, networking like hell. Anna can't exactly blame her, even if it's meant spending lonelier nights back in her own apartment.

She has a nice brunch Sunday with Jess, who thinks Irina is acting weird.

"Is Pluto in retrograde?" Anna asks, sipping her mimosa.

"You mean Mercury. Pluto isn't a planet."

"Pluto will *always* be a planet. Anyway, maybe it's lead in the water supply, but everyone is super strange this week. Maybe this is how they cope with stress?"

"Or maybe everything's all messed up." Jess sighs. "Irina retiring is good news. I don't want her hurting like she was. But then…where does she go?"

"You know, if where she goes has ballet, they'll have theater too. And stage managing isn't that different on our side of the fence. You know that." Anna squeezes Jess's hand before going back to her eggs. "And with all our chaos, I'm probably back in the corps next year. Unless they find a reason to just get rid of me. I'm starting to think I should have sucked up to Liza more."

"Sounds like not even that can help you. You never know, Richard Westin might see you dance this week and offer you prima for next season."

"Yeah, right." Anna snorts into her orange juice. "Why are you so quick to give up on Pluto, anyway?"

"Let it go, Anna." Jess groans.

ↄ◌◌

It's agony not to tell her, but with all her selfishness of late, Victoria keeps her distance from Anna. The moment there's a concrete offer, when they're on the other side of opening night, of course she'll parse every detail and see what Anna thinks. Somewhere along the way, Victoria has come to see her as a partner, someone whose opinion matters above almost anyone's. Not because she's seen much of the world, but because she considers others as naturally as breathing. If Victoria's ideas pass with Anna, then they can't be all that terrible. As metrics go, it's a workable one.

Dress rehearsal went smoothly at least. It's easier without so many in the cast, and the bulk of the work being done by the three principals. Victoria let them off the reins at last today, in their final match up, directly vying for attention in their respective section of the stage. When Anna—the American—triumphed, it felt correct. Delphine and Irina, perhaps with their priorities elsewhere, have seemed nothing but happy for her.

Which just leaves Victoria's little cameo, one she's refused to do in rehearsal save for the blocking. The part of Stage Manager is little more than a walk-on, but it allows the press to bill it as "Victoria Ford's return!" in a variety of over-promising ways.

Only one preview this time, so they'll have to keep it tight. Victoria is lying on her side, curtains half-drawn this time, watching Anna sleep. She allowed it tonight because Anna showed up looking so wiped. Sure enough, they barely got a chance to talk before she was passed out on her side of the bed. Victoria tugs at her bottom lip. She can't start thinking of things as belonging to Anna—not at this stage.

Settling back in, hoping for a couple of hours' sleep, Victoria presses a tender kiss to Anna's shoulder. Just get the show open, get the raves that are due, and then it's time for truths and decisions.

For now, there's just Anna, warm and soft, so inviting to lie next to. Victoria closes her eyes and hopes this isn't their last night together.

◯◯◯

Anna hangs around after the first preview, but Victoria is mostly occupied with sorting out a fight of some kind between corps members. The early editions are usually put online, but this time every reviewer seems to be waiting for when the show is actually ready. Only one scenery snafu in the preview feels like a good omen, and she gets a healthy amount of applause from the audience. They take their individual bows in the order they perform their solos, before sharing the final bow as a trio. Women are so democratic that way, and Anna loves them for it.

Not in the way she loves Victoria. Who definitely seems to be avoiding her. Is this some prize-fighter mentality of denying sex in the days before the main event? Anna thinks she might be grateful. When she gets in at night, she can barely lift her arms most of the time.

"You came in early on your *ronds*," Victoria announces when she finally appears at Anna's dressing room door. "I have late drinks, sorry. Rest up for tomorrow. No classes apart from PT and the late warm-up session, okay?"

"Okay," Anna agrees, left to head home alone. She's never been so ready to open a show, if it means she and Victoria can go back to some kind of normal.

◯◯◯

Meredith is waiting for Victoria in the bar of the Four Seasons, envelope in hand.

"Contract, plane tickets, including a flexible return for your first trip back—everyone always regrets storing something, or gets the homesickness too soon, you know?"

"When does Olivia want me?"

"Next week."

Victoria takes a sip of the Scotch waiting for her. "Are you…? My God, you're serious."

"Time is of the essence. Some groundwork will be needed, otherwise the French press will savage you before you even pick up a score. Tell me this doesn't change anything? And I could see you all the time, with the trains between London and Paris."

"Oh well, that seals the deal," Victoria says with a hint of mockery. "Do you think there are enough Berlin Wall chunks left for me to blockade myself in Paris? Or at least keep you out of the city?"

"Say yes, Victoria. But for God's sake, tell Anna. You're making yourself ill by not."

"I don't want to give her up," Victoria admits with a hollow laugh. "Pathetic, I know."

"Not pathetic." She flags down a server for the check. "Just love."

ᴄᴏᴏ

Anna doesn't hear Victoria come in, but she's there in the morning for lots of kisses followed by lots of coffee. The day is crammed—radio and television are covering the preparation, which is unusual in itself. Unlike *Pagodas*, this production is getting a lot of hype.

"Who's up first?" Anna asks when she's dressed and ready. "I figure local TV, since they're most likely to try to buy tickets."

"Well, we're almost sold out," Victoria says. "We did better than we thought. Or the marketing tapped into the right thing at the right time, maybe? Either way, I take full credit for my genius."

"You're lucky I love you." Anna fills her travel mug with coffee, then another for Victoria. "Let's go get this show open, huh?"

ᴄᴏᴏ

By a stroke of luck, Anna's cutting around the side of the building where the box office is as Henri is collecting the tickets Anna left at Will Call for them.

"And who's this big girl? This can't be Yara, can it? I thought she was only six. You must be at least twelve, you're so tall."

"I'm six!" Yara protests from behind her dad's legs, but that soon prompts her to come out. They chat politely for a moment, but Anna has to go get into her costume and finish the boldest parts of her stage makeup.

"Yara, next time your daddy brings you, we'll do a tour, okay? You can go onstage and see all the pretty dresses."

"Can I see the drums too?" Yara asks.

"Sure. I bet your dad will just love it if you get into drumming. Enjoy the show, both of you."

಄಄

Victoria will watch the rest of the show from an unoccupied box as usual, but right now she's waiting in the wings for her cue. One scene and flee. Anna waves from the opposite wing, and Victoria gives her a reassuring smile. No last-minute backstage visit tonight. Anna needs total focus, and when Victoria is done with her bit onstage, she'll be handing it over to all three ballerinas.

The applause as she steps out is intoxicating. Dressing all in black is hardly a stretch, but as Victoria mimes her elaborate moments of story, she feels her ankles and knees twitch with the need to dance. Luckily she only has to pull off the simplest of *tendus*, but the audience is old and loyal. They cheer her off as their queen, and Victoria lets herself cry in the corridor for a moment when it's all done.

It won't be so tricky to do that for a few nights. It's just she's a little unsteady, an addict who just got an accidental hit. Oh, far too mild to take the edge off, but enough to remind her what she's missing.

Victoria makes her way to the box, then watches Anna transform before her very eyes. From regular dancer to something superhuman, her precision and heart completely in balance with even her introductory steps. The crowd seems to be holding its breath.

Then Anna is unleashed on them, and the audible gasp as she leaps into her first sequence is everything Victoria hoped for. Part of her wants to close her eyes, to bask in the reactions alone. She's seen Anna dance this time and again, after all. There's something magical about tonight, though, about the tightness in her hair pulled back, and the soft flow of the leather that forms her costume. Somewhere, the same hidden power that lifted Victoria a hundred times and more is carrying Anna through this. She's dancing like a woman possessed, and God, the vindication is sweeter than Victoria could have hoped for.

She aches to touch Anna, even though she's way out of range. There's only one way to fix that.

಄಄

They survive the post-performance red carpet, and the bland corporate catering at the afterparty. Anna chats to every person who seeks her out, making her excuses only when Meredith shows up to talk with Victoria again. The curiosity is palpable, but Victoria still can't find the words to explain it.

The moment comes when Victoria least expects it. Anna turns to her in the middle of the party, twinkling fairy lights and bottles of house wine strewn all over the space.

"Did you get an offer?" Anna asks. She's in the tiny red dress from the shoot, a borrowed silk wrap resting at her elbows. "That's the only thing I can think of, other than you rekindling some old flame with Meredith. I know you've been quiet, and I'm trying not to worry. I love you, and there's nothing you can't tell me. Even if you're moving to London."

"She's just an emissary. I've been offered top job in Paris," Victoria says, and it's plain to see the physical relief when she lets the secret go. "As in *this* job, my dream job. The paperwork is being drawn up right now, so it's decision time."

"Pfft, decision!" Anna flaps her hands. "What can there be to decide? Your dream was Paris. You're getting a second shot, with all the power and skill you have now. This sounds like amazing news."

"Just not for us."

"Well, no, I suppose not. But I'd only be miserable getting in the way of something so perfect for you. I wouldn't be able to live with myself."

"Anna, I know it's soon, but if there's a space, if I can make that demand so early on…"

"I don't know," Anna admits. "My family is here. I have responsibilities. There's always long distance…"

"More like the long goodbye. Darling, can we talk about this tomorrow? I know it's reality and we can't ignore that, but I'd like to put it off for a few more hours."

"Where would you like to spend them?"

"In bed with you, of course."

$$\infty$$

They manage to wait past sunrise for reviews.

With a blanket draped over her shoulders, Victoria flips through her tablet to the usual suspects. Anna fetches the *Times* from the doorstep, flashing plenty of thigh at the nosy neighbor in the process. She looks good in Victoria's robe, relaxed and rumpled despite the tension of waiting for reviews.

Both their phones are off, so they're going in blind. Anna opens the arts section and gasps at the half-page picture of herself, alongside Irina and Delphine. It's so charming, so wide-eyed and wondrous, that Victoria swipes the camera on her tablet and quickly snaps a few candids. They come out exactly as she hopes, Anna fresh-faced and full of life in the early morning sun.

The kind of picture someone frames to remember a person by.

Anna flips to the review itself, oblivious to Victoria's resettling melancholy. Only when she comes to the right part of the page does she push the paper away.

"I can't." She squeezes her eyes shut. "Just like last time. I don't suppose…?"

"If I have to keep reading to you, people are going to assume you didn't pass third grade," Victoria says, but she's already reaching for the pages.

"Okay." Anna takes a deep, steadying breath. Sitting cross-legged on top of the sheets, she seems meditative, downright calm. "Do your worst."

"Let's see… Blah-blah talk about the arts. State of ballet. History of the piece." Victoria reads hastily, eyes darting across the text. "Ah, finally. They've remembered there were people on stage."

Wade is an accomplished prima, a walking advert for the triumph of technique over authenticity.

Victoria sucks in a breath through her teeth. Ouch.

While Irina, for all her presence and power, seems a fading light. The choreography is limited to accommodate her range, and the long history of injuries would seem to have taken its toll. I would be surprised to see her dance for this illustrious company next season.

"Oh God." Anna flops forward, clutching her stomach. "They're going to slaughter me."

"The evening is saved, however, by the company's brand-new star. Sources suggest she is Victoria Ford's personal project—"

"Subtle," Anna groans, hearing only the implication about their relationship.

—now that she has headlined in two of the biggest shows of the season. It's not hard to see why. Star quality is an indefinable thing, but like Ms. Ford, we know it when we see it. As the erstwhile, arrogant American ballerina, Anna Gale steals the show

and the hearts of the audience. For all the frivolity in her section, she dances with her heart so exposed it might well be beating out of her chest. This reviewer almost felt compelled to stand and sing the Stars and Stripes when the foregone winner of their 'contest' was announced.

"Wow." Anna is upright again, clutching her face. "Does it really say that? Are you making this up?"

"I'm rarely this eloquent before coffee," Victoria reminds her.

Making her own brief return to the stage tonight, Ford gave a timely reminder that the city has not had a true prima ballerina of her standing since she retired. If she is to share with us one more gift, it would be the uncovering of a worthy successor.

Anna is crying, and Victoria folds the paper before pulling her in close. "It wasn't so harsh on the girls," Victoria says, trying to reassure her. "Anna, they loved you. It was worth it. The season was a success."

"That's not why I'm crying," Anna says when her sobs are back under control. She tucks her head against Victoria's shoulder, facing away from her as she traces fingertip lines on Victoria's forearm. "As soon as you were done, I wanted to say, *Wow, what if next time...?* before I remembered there probably isn't going to be one."

"I want to say I can turn it down." Victoria is stunned at how much she actually means that. "I want to be that better person who trades in professional success for personal bliss, but God, Anna. I just can't give this up, not after everything."

"I know. I know." Anna moves across the mattress, switching her phone back on. She's clearing notifications, trying to focus on anything that will stem the flow of tears by the looks of it. After a minute, she sits bolt upright.

"What?" Victoria snaps. "Anna, what is it?"

"Rick has sold the company. And the new bosses just appointed Irina as artistic director," Anna says. "There's a press release in five. Irina made it a condition that I can stay on too. So I still have a job. Not in Paris, but a job all the same."

"Then you should stay." Victoria nudges her. "Not to build on this success would be ludicrous. And the touring in the summer will bring you to Europe at least."

Anna's face falls, confronted with the reality that Victoria is going.

"Anna?"

"Yes?"

"If there was ever a time I've come close to not putting this first, my career? It's here, now. This is maybe the hardest thing I've ever done. But we both still have growing to do, don't we?"

The nod is minimal, just a slight jerk of Anna's head.

"I think I have to go. I'm sorry. It's just too hard," she says, barely looking at Victoria. "I wish you everything, Victoria. Every dream you've had to wait for. I'll be cheering you on, even if I can't be there."

"Anna—"

"No, no, I'm sorry." Anna is scooping up her clothes from the chair they were thrown on. "If I don't go now, I won't be able to. And you don't want me crying around your ankles, do you?"

"Even breaking up with me, you're too kind." Victoria slides off the bed, ridiculous in only her cashmere throw. "But please. We still have some time, we could make more of it. And…and… It won't be forever. They could fire me in a month."

"Not if they want you enough to swoop in now. You're too good for that. You know that better than anyone." Anna huffs out a strangled laugh. "I'd tell Irina to go to hell and come be your muse in a Paris apartment for a few months, but we both know you wouldn't be interested in the girl who gives up everything and does that."

Victoria shrugs. There's never been any pretense about that. "I really do love you. How could I not, when you're being noble enough to let me go?"

"I love you too." Dressed now, Anna steps closer, as though the floor might give way beneath them. "I just… One more…" She kisses Victoria with every bit of power and feeling that's crackled between them these past few months. As goodbyes go, it's a classic.

"I'll call," Victoria promises. "I want us still to have that. Please?"

"You don't say please very often," Anna points out, wiping tears. "You must really mean it. Give me a little while? Before you do."

She's walking away, and this is the point in old movies where one witty, heartfelt remark is enough to undo it, to find the magical solution where everyone gets to be happy. Victoria waits for inspiration to strike, but instead there's just a weak "see you tonight" because broken hearts or not, the show must go on. At least for the remaining performances.

Victoria pulls the blanket tighter around herself, the apartment so much colder as the front door closes behind Anna. Picking up the newspaper, she looks at the frozen image of Anna smiling like her heart might burst.

It doesn't have to be forever, she tells herself, crawling back beneath the covers. Because Victoria wants Paris, and she wants Anna, and she loves Anna as much as ballet itself, which may be the first time ever. She'll find a way to make this work, even if not right away.

Anything else would be unacceptable, and Victoria's standards have always been too high for that.

November 10

METROPOLITAN'S STAR ON THE RISE ONCE MORE

By Elaine Greenberg

Though many feared the Metropolitan Ballet might fold in the wake of another star departure, the return to a classical program under its former prima, Irina—the ballerina who needs only one name—has been a steady triumph.

Central to the post-Victoria Ford success is her former protégé, and in Anna Gale the company has a principal to be reckoned with. Dazzling in *Don Quixote*, heartbreaking in *Onegin*, last season's youthful exuberance has been rubbed away on the European tour, and she returns to New York a more complete dancer. The technique improvements come from Irina, but the talent is Ms. Gale's alone.

L'Invasion Américaine: The aftermath

By Lucille Meyer

As the first American to hold the prestigious artistic director role, Victoria Ford has had her share of trials at the Palais Garnier. After firing two soloists in as many months, her shaking up of the repertoire and casting seemed set to cause a mutiny. Far from quitting, the Queen of Ballet has doubled down on her regeneration efforts. Her second thrilling season begins tonight, but the sniping critics and political battles of her first year are consigned to history. As we say here in Paris, vive la reine!

April 6

DANCING DIVAS COUPLING UP?

BY STAR SPOTTING TEAM

Has absence made their hearts grow fonder? Rumor has it that two of the world's best-known female dancers haven't let the Atlantic Ocean keep them apart. A swanky gala in Berlin had the best and brightest of the arts world mingling in close quarters, and these two tore up the dance floor in style more *Dirty Dancing* than classical. We'd love to say more, but we don't want a certain Madame sending us to the guillotine.

EPILOGUE

"You are sure?" Anna's guide asks one more time, and she tells him that she is. They've had quite a journey so far, down diverging staircases, footsteps echoing on marble floors. The gilt-edged trim of everything outside is barely an introduction to the opulence of rich reds and gold that greets her inside the theater.

With a melodramatic sigh, he straightens his tie, fusses with his mustache, and leaves her alone in the auditorium. She runs one hand over the dark wood of a seat frame, contrasting it with the plush red velvet that makes up the rest. Looking around, it's hard to take in the sheer majesty of the place. The low lighting makes the colors seem to bleed—a wet canvas just waiting for Anna to insinuate herself into the scene. She strides down to a seat on the aisle, five rows back, and takes a seat.

"*Êtes-vous perdu?*" comes a voice from the wings. Even to Anna's untrained ear, that's not a native speaker. "Are you lost?"

"No," she calls back. The fact she's been asked in English gets her hopes up even higher. The echoes make it impossible to be sure just yet. "I heard you were looking for a dancer?"

"Auditions are next week."

Footsteps come on the stage. Anna holds her breath.

"Hi" is all she can think to say when Victoria emerges, squinting through the lights at her. Oh, she looks fantastic. The usual dark clothes, of course, but the black pants are cut high on her waist, and barely skimming the ankles. The gauzy blouse is translucent, hinting at dark silk beneath.

"Anna." Not a question. No note of surprise. They haven't talked much in the past week or so, but Anna didn't want to tip her hand before showing up here in Paris.

"Your boss invited me," Anna explains. "Trying to give you options for your new prima. I'm not sure if she knows our history. Please, don't be mad at me."

"Mad at you?" Victoria comes down the orchestra steps and into the parterre where Anna is sitting, gripping the seat in front of her for dear life. As she comes closer, Anna sees the few tears that have been permitted to fall, right before they're brusquely wiped away. "You have no idea how glad I am to see you. And you've had quite a time with Irina."

"She's good. Drives me insane, but we did some amazing things. My sister married her, last month. You didn't RSVP."

"I hate weddings. And we'd just seen each other in Berlin. That was quite a long weekend."

Direct as ever. Anna doesn't answer.

"Did you come to tell me off for not replying?" Victoria looks amused at the thought.

"No, I'm here to dance, if you'll have me," Anna says. "I'm ready, you know I am. I've done my time, two seasons of it. So if you still want me…"

"How could I not?"

Victoria is practically in her lap a minute later, and when they kiss it's electric. Breathless and half-sobbing, Anna takes Victoria's face in her hands. "I'm sorry we had to be apart. There were so many times…"

"Me too," Victoria says. "Every bad day, every sneering review, all I kept asking was why I gave you up for this."

"The reviews have improved," Anna can't help pointing out. "They're calling you a savior now."

"Well, they call me other things, too, but you probably don't have enough French slang for those terms. I do believe we've come to a truce, though. Which means I can choose the best dancer for the job without politics. You always did have perfect timing."

"You certainly yelled at me a lot when it wasn't perfect." Anna nudges Victoria, and they both stand. "Everything I've done, all the blood and sweat and tears, it's been to bring me here. I'm sure of it."

"So you think we might find a new romance in Paris, hmm?" Victoria teases. "It's not every ballet that gets a happy ending, you know."

"True, but we've had our little tragedy already." Anna puts her hands on Victoria's hips, pulling her near once more. "So I think we're owed, don't you?"

Victoria answers her with a tender, lovely kiss.

"I suppose you'll want to see my apartment," Victoria sighs, as though taking Anna there now, and probably straight to bed, is an unthinkable hardship. "Unless you'd like a tour of the city first? We could spend hours—"

"Apartment," Anna interrupts. "Now, preferably."

A gaggle of dancers open a door to the side of the stage, clearly intent on taking a shortcut. One glare and they go back the way they came.

"I can't go getting soft on you, Anna. I have a reputation to uphold."

"You're saying I should get back on a plane? Go be someone else's principal dancer? Someone else's…whatever it is when you reunite with the person you've been in love with for two years? I want more than a stolen weekend between tour stops."

Victoria rolls her eyes. "Of course that's not what I'm saying. There hasn't been anyone else this whole time. I've been waiting for you."

"Then let's not wait any longer, Madame Ford."

"I don't think we're waiting for anything ever again, do you?" Victoria kisses her soundly, then offers Anna her hand.

Paris is ready, a new life for both of them just waiting to be started. Anna takes Victoria by the hand, and together they take their first, unchoreographed step.

ABOUT LOLA KEELEY

Lola Keeley is a writer and coder. After moving to London to pursue her love of theatre, she later wound up living every five-year-old's dream of being a train driver on the London Underground. She has since emerged, blinking into the sunlight, to find herself writing books. She now lives in Edinburgh, Scotland, with her wife and three cats.

CONNECT WITH LOLA

Website: www.lolakeeley.co.uk
Facebook: www.facebook.com/lolakeeley
Twitter: @lolasmish
E-Mail: hello@lolakeeley.co.uk

OTHER BOOKS FROM YLVA PUBLISHING

www.ylva-publishing.com

CHASING STARS

(The Superheroine Collection)

Alex K. Thorne

ISBN: 978-3-95533-992-0

Length: 205 pages (70,000 words)

For superhero Swiftwing, crime fighting isn't her biggest battle. Nor is it having to meet the whims of Hollywood star Gwen Knight as her mild-mannered assistant, Ava. It's doing all that, while tracking a giant alien bug, being asked to fake date her famous boss, and realizing that she might be coming down with a pesky case of feelings.

A fun, sweet, sexy lesbian romance about the masks we wear.

WHO'D HAVE THOUGHT

G Benson

ISBN: 978-3-95533-874-9

Length: 339 pages (122,000 words)

When Hayden Pérez stumbles across an offer to marry Samantha Thomson—a cold, rude, and complicated neurosurgeon—for $200,000, what's a cash-strapped ER nurse to do? Sure, Hayden has to convince everyone around them they're madly in love, but it's only for a year, right? What could possibly go wrong?

The Brutal Truth

Lee Winter

ISBN: 978-3-95533-898-5

Length: 339 pages (108,000 words)

Aussie crime reporter Maddie Grey is out of her depth in New York and secretly drawn to her twice-married, powerful media mogul boss, Elena Bartell, who eats failing newspapers for breakfast. As work takes them to Australia, Maddie is goaded into a brief bet—that they will say only the truth to each other. It backfires catastrophically. A lesbian romance about the lies we tell ourselves.

The Lily and the Crown

Roslyn Sinclair

ISBN: 978-3-95533-942-5

Length: 263 pages (87,000 words)

Young botanist Ari lives an isolated life on a space station, tending a lush garden in her quarters. When an imperious woman is captured from a pirate ship and given to her as a slave, Ari's ordered life shatters. Her slave is watchful, smart, and sexy, and seems to know an awful lot about tactics, star charts, and the dread pirate queen, Mir.

A lesbian romance about daring to risk your heart.

The Music and the Mirror
© 2018 by Lola Keeley

ISBN: 978-3-96324-014-0

Also available as e-book.

Published by Ylva Publishing, legal entity of Ylva Verlag, e.Kfr.

Ylva Verlag, e.Kfr.
Owner: Astrid Ohletz
Am Kirschgarten 2
65830 Kriftel
Germany

www.ylva-publishing.com

First edition: 2018

Credits
Edited by Lee Winter and Amanda Jean
Cover Design by Adam Lloyd
Cover Print Layout by Streetlight Graphics